EROTICON DREAMS

In the secret world of her hotel room the men are happy. The woman is naked. They all are. There are no words, only the sound of flesh upon flesh, of whispers and grunts and the slither of bodies on sheets.

Julia is sandwiched between them. She leans back against Victor, cushioned on his broad chest, his arms around her, hands busy palming the soft weight of her breasts while the young one kneels over her and arranges her legs to his liking. Her skin is creamy white in the half-light — smooth, succulent, unblemished. Luc lowers his mouth to the fork of her body. His tongue is precociously skilful . . .

Eroticon Dreams

Anonymous

Introduced and edited by J-P Spencer

HEADLINE

First published in 1992
by HEADLINE BOOK PUBLISHING PLC

10 9 8 7 6 5 4 3 2 1

ISBN 0 7472 3737 9

Typeset by Medcalf Type Ltd, Bicester, Oxon

Printed and bound by
HarperCollins Manufacturing, Glasgow

HEADLINE BOOK PUBLISHING PLC
Headline House
79 Great Titchfield Street
London W1P 7FN

Contents

Hunger!

'My marriage is a prison. Most of the time I don't care. I'll do what I have to do to keep everyone happy. But sometimes, my darling, I just want to break out and get laid . . .'

So speaks Julia, super-respectable wife, reliable mother, prisoner of convention. She knows that there are times in any woman's life when she has to listen to the voices inside her, when she must prove she's made of flesh and blood – and when she'll put herself on the line to get what she really wants.

That's when, like Julia here, she'll head for a seaport on the Mediterranean, check into Room 13 at the Hotel Racine, squeeze her glorious but neglected flesh into her slinkiest summer dress and take to the streets and bars eager to appease her hunger . . .

The blonde is dining alone in the hot smoky room. Around her the tables are busy, packed with families and tourists and, of course, sailors — for this is a sailors' town. There are six of them at the table just across the room from Julia. They stare greedily at her as she eases bright green stalks of asparagus into her mouth and licks the buttery juice from her fingers. She pays them no attention when they laugh too loudly though she knows the show is for her benefit.

Outside the crowded restaurant the light is fading. People pack the narrow street in search of a Saturday night goodtime, a swing in every step. Many sailors pass by. One looks through the window and hails the table opposite Julia. A loud conversation takes place. Julia cannot follow it all, the patois is so thick and fast, but she is not surprised when the men inside agree to join their friends. A trip to a brothel lies ahead she thinks, or an evening in a cheap cafe on the hunt for some willing skirt.

Four of the matelots rise and leave. The noise of their violent chatter fades as they walk up the street. Two of the boys remain. One has his back to the woman but she can tell from the awkward way he sits and the glimpse of down on the half profile of his jaw that he is very young. Facing her is an older youth, broad and dark, the skin of his face and arms a gleaming teak brown against the starched white of his *blouson*. He has high cheekbones and black liquid eyes which do not waver for a second in their cool appraisal of Julia as she stands to leave.

She is fifty yards from the restaurant before they catch up with her.

'Mademoiselle,' it's the dark one, of course. 'Hey, mademoiselle.'

'Yes.' She keeps on walking and they fall in step beside her, one on either side.

'You want to go dancing?'

No reply.

'You are American?'

She keeps walking.

'English?'

She nods.

'You are very pretty.'

It's still the same boy. He's getting bolder.

'You are the most beautiful woman in this town.'

Julia walks on.

'I think you have marvellous tits.'

Julia can't help smiling. The boy smiles too. He can say anything he likes now.

'I want to put my head up your skirt and suck your pussy.'

Julia holds back her laughter. She wants to know what he will say next.

'I would adore to see your arse shake while you dance on my cock all night . . .'

'And what,' says Julia, 'will your friend be doing all this time?'

Now they are in the bar of the Hotel Racine drinking cognac. The night is still hot. The sailors' white suits are crumpled. Beads of sweat are trickling down Julia's back. Her sky-blue silk blouse clings to her breasts. The boys' eyes glisten like wet pennies and their tongues are loose. The young one cannot speak English but it does not matter to Julia. Victor, the dark one, translates his urgent whispers.

'Luc says you are a famous actress.'

'That's not so.'

'He knows he is not mistaken because he has seen your photographs in some magazines.'

'He is wrong.'

'He is prepared to bet that you are the one. He says he can prove it.'

'How?'

'Because in the photograph he has seen the woman is not wearing any clothes and she has a very special mark on her body. If you have the same mark then you must be the same one.'

'What mark is he talking about?'

'He says this woman has a little butterfly tattooed on her leg.'

'Oh yes.'

'It is very high up on the left leg. On the outside. Just on the *fesse*.'

'Your friend has a lurid imagination.'

'Maybe, but can you prove to us that you do not have a little butterfly tattooed on your bottom?'

Julia does not speak. The two boys are gazing at her intently. Luc is so close to her that she can see the pulse beating in his throat. She drains the thimbleful of brown liquid left in her glass and says, 'Follow me up the stairs.'

The boys are happy now. The woman is naked – they all are. There are no words, only the sound of flesh upon flesh, of whispers and grunts and the slither of bodies on sheets.

She is sandwiched between them. She leans back against Victor, cushioned on his broad chest, his arms around her, hands busy palming the softness of her breasts while the young one kneels over and arranges her legs to his liking. There are no tattoos to be found on her smooth white flesh, but that does not matter to Luc as he buries his face in the thick brown bush between her thighs. His tongue is precociously skilful and she cries out as he finds her most sensitive spot. He looks up in alarm, scared he has hurt her. Such a kind boy. She smiles at him.

'Please fuck me,' she says.

These are words he understands. He kneels up and leans back to display his standing cock. It is an incongruous sight against such a pale and slender frame. The big bulb glows an obscene and meaty red and the instrument thrusts out from his body like another limb. Behind her Victor says something coarse as the boy spits on his hand and oils his big penis.

'Hurry up,' she hears herself saying and Luc laughs.

Then all laughter is forgotten as he slips the head of his organ between the waiting lips of her pussy and slides it sweetly home.

It is thrilling while it lasts. The boy tries to control himself to begin with, slowly working his tool in and out, savouring every tantalising second. But his excitement has been building for a long time, the seemingly unattainable woman beneath him is his to enjoy as he pleases and his mate is lying naked at his side, urging him on. The circumstances are not those in which many lusty youths could contain themselves. For a frenetic twenty seconds he drills into the woman's loins, grunting with animal delight as she wraps her satin smooth legs around him. His balls smack against the underside of her bum cheeks as his hard member roots furiously in and out. Then it's all over as, one, two, three, he squirts his juices deep inside Julia and collapses on top of her.

But there is to be no rest. Victor wants his turn, he has been patient long enough. Julia, too, has yet to be satisfied.

Luc is pushed to one side and Julia turns to Victor. They kiss eagerly, her tongue slyly flicking into his hungry mouth. He pulls her to him, his hands on the curve of her hips, his cock pressed flat against her belly. They explore each other urgently. Her slim fingers on his fat cock, peeling the foreskin down over the glans and swooping down the stubby shaft to cup his balls. He has slipped a hand between her legs to fondle the slippery folds of her pussy, now oiled by the boy's ejaculation and her own excitement.

They connect easily, she rolling beneath his broad brown frame and spreading her legs wide to accommodate his swollen organ. He sets a steady rhythm. This time she is taking no chances and unashamedly slides a finger into the groove of her cunt. As the sailor fucks her she strokes her clitoris, building the fire between her legs, tweaking and teasing her flesh to the brink of the orgasm she has been aching for ever since Victor's liquid gaze alighted on her in the restaurant.

'Oh yes,' she says, 'fuck, fuck, fuck me, you brute.'

Her obscenities spur him on. He slides his hands under her buttocks and lifts her up. He spreads her cheeks and pulls her down on his cock by the flesh of her bum.

The change of angle and the rough power of his lovemaking suddenly overwhelm her. She comes in a rush and cries out as the wave hits her, the shock singing through her body like a jolt of electricity.

Then he too is on the down-slope. The wanton behaviour of this beautiful stranger has intoxicated him. He buries his head between her opulent white breasts, squeezes her arse cheeks in his fists and shoots his semen far into the hot depths of her body.

Now they are in the shower. Julia drinks red wine from a tooth glass while the two boys wash her body with a rough flannel and a cake of soap. They lather every nook and crevice of her, paying special attention to her tits, weighing them in their hands, slapping them playfully so they swing from side to side, rolling the brown pegs of her nipples between their fingers.

'You are mother-fixated,' she tells them.

They don't understand her but who cares about that?

She passes the glass and seizes the soap. Now it is her turn to play with them. She cleans their cocks carefully, stroking and fondling them to stiffness as she does so. They stand up proudly under the foam and she laughs out loud, delighted with their youth and enthusiasm. They echo her laughter, thrilled to be allowed such liberties with this magnificent, whorish woman. Their teeth gleam white in their brown faces and in their eyes she recognises the glint of pressing need.

She drops to her knees, her face on a level with their genitals. She inspects them closely, idly wondering why the smaller man should have the bigger implement. When she is sure all the suds have been rinsed from their flesh, she takes a cock in each hand and begins to suck them in turn. First Luc, then Victor, then Luc again, swallowing the swollen helmet of each organ, rubbing the sensitive flesh against the roof of her mouth, jerking her hands on their shafts with the time-honoured skill of the experienced masturbator.

It would be nice, she thinks, to take both of them in her mouth at once. She presses the two shafts together, wanking them in a double-handed grip, but the two-headed monster won't fit. Never mind, to lick and suck and hold them like this is fun. She's never done this before. Not exactly, that is.

Still working the two cocks in harness, she lifts her head. The boys are leaning against each other for support, all laughter gone from their faces. Victor's smile is set in a rictus of desire. His hand descends on the top of her head and roughly pushes her back to her task.

Julia had not intended to be so unselfish but she is as happy to give as to take. It must be my Catholic upbringing, she thinks.

Now she begins to suck and squeeze with a steady rhythm, switching from one stalk to the other, trying to gauge the relative levels of excitement, excited herself at what she proposes to do.

It is Luc who finishes first, his big cock spraying spunk into her face like water from a garden hose.

Then, with both hands on Victor's weapon, Julia cleverly sucks his sperm into her mouth.

She leans back on her haunches and raises her face to her two sated lovers. She grins up at them, happy in her generosity. As she does so their juices mingle with the shower stream and swirl down her body over her big white breasts.

It is late afternoon. The sun is still hot on the bleached shutters of the Hotel Racine.

In Room 13 nothing stirs. The occupant of the rumpled bed sleeps on in the half dark until the buzz of a motorbike in the street below finally penetrates her dreams. The sleeper turns onto her back, pushing the sweat-damp blonde hair from her face. She opens her eyes and gazes without seeing at the chaos of the room.

An empty wine bottle stands on the dressing table. Clothes litter the floor. The wastepaper basket has rolled on its side beneath the desk in the far corner, a trail of orange peel and stained tissues in its wake.

The blonde woman fumbles on her bedside table for her watch. It is an expensive make. A Cartier. As her fingers close on its silver she thinks she is damned lucky that she still has it. The two boys last night must have been more honest than they looked.

She holds the watch close to the face to read the time. Aperitif time. If she can make it.

Now she is perched on a stool in the bar across the street from the hotel. It is an uncomfortable position because she still aches a little from last night. The sailors were so eager. The energy of youth! She has been a bit excessive of late she knows. And lucky too. Not just with the watch and things like that but in not attracting too much attention. She has learnt to be discreet but sometimes it's not easy. Somehow adventures just lie in wait for her.

Like now. That man at the table on the street is staring at her legs. She's not surprised, of course. Most men do.

Pleasure-Bound
Afloat

An Edwardian sex romp that doubtless found a devoted clandestine readership in the days before the First World War, *Pleasure-Bound Afloat* is the middle book of a trilogy. It follows *Maudie*, an account of gross indecency in the Home Counties which culminates in naked flapper races at the home of the eponymous heroine. Alas for the participants, the scandal breaks in the Press and Maudie and her party flee England on the yacht which she, far-sighted woman that she is, has kept 'in full commission' for just this eventuality. The continuing story of their amorous adventures on the high seas forms the content of *Pleasure-Bound Afloat*. Maudie and her pals turn pirate on the good ship *New Decameron*, captained by a virile and nameless nobleman similarly exiled from the Mother Country and bound for a South Sea paradise where anything goes – in particular, sexual frolicking on a scale equal to the capacities of heros and heroines such as these. And that, needless to add, comprises the content of the third volume, *Pleasure-Bound Ashore*.

In this excerpt we are in the company of the noble pirate leader and some of his new and far from unwilling captives, including the adorable young Honoria Tittle, Hony for short – '"Hony soit qui maule ses pants," as a rude young man once said as he was feeling her in the dark. She was sixteen, deliciously pretty and her figure, though in the flapper mould, gave men to think a good deal . . .'

The days slipped quickly by. Aided by perfect weather the *New Decameron* put the knots behind her at an astonishing rate. The weather became very hot and the very lightest of costumes prevailed. The Sisters Lovett initiated the custom of appearing on deck in open-work chemises and nothing else, and the pirates all worked stripped to the waist. Of the lady pirates, Maudie invariably came on deck naked in the mornings to be douched with the hose, an example soon followed by Hony and Carrie.

The pirates showed themselves splendid seamen, and if debauchery was allowed a free hand in the evening, it was hard work during the day. The *New Decameron* was as spick and span as the hand of man could make her, and necessary fire and boat drills were never omitted.

The love affairs of the pirates and their guests soon settled down into recognized grooves. The Sisters Lovett frankly professed themselves harlots and were openly raffled for every night. Carrie developed a sentimental affection for several of the young men, and let them share her. Little Hony stuck religiously to the 'young man.' It had gone much further than mere lust with her now, and she was genuinely in love.

Miss Jepps, too, considered the matter from a purely financial point, but she threw herself heart and soul into the game, and the various pirates got full value for their money. Her one sorrow − that she had left nearly all her frocks behind on the *Mesopotamia* − was solaced by loans from the lady pirates, who had some exquisite toilettes on board.

A word as to these lady pirates: though none so exquisite as Maudie, the 'divinely tall and most divinely fair,' yet in their various styles they were very, very tempting. Connie was a brunette, apparently quite young, petite, with a perfectly moulded, supple little figure. She had laughing, hazel eyes, and a most delicious foot and ankle, which she took every opportunity of showing; in fact, when she sat down and crossed her legs she generally showed well above the knee, so that the pretty tan-coloured flesh showed a tempting bare streak between her stockings and drawers. She fell to the lot of Mr Silverwood. Mamie was American, widow of an English nobleman, who had done something really shady on the Stock Exchange and shot himself. She had been implicated but had escaped in time. She was very svelte and *Gibson girlie*, and she suited Mr Moss Hell down to the ground. Lucy, the last, was an older woman, probably thirty, very dark and Spanish, with a figure almost corpulent. Hannibal McGregor devoted his rough and ready Scotch method of love-making to her.

And what of the remaining two male captives? Herr Kunst was far too busy concocting novel schemes of piracy, with which he bored the 'young man' to extinction, to think of bodily pleasures, and as for Lord Reggie, he 'let go the painter,' frankly dated himself back, and stuck to Cyril.

Lady Tittle was rapidly assuming command of the ship. The 'young man,' infatuated with Hony, allowed her mother to do pretty well what she liked, and she *was* enjoying herself. She more than suspected her little daughter's liaison, but she winked. Her own *flagrants delits* with the bosun were so obvious that she hardly dared comment on her daughter's. She felt practically certain now that the young man *was* the Duke of St Eden, but still pried for proof. Lord Reggie, of course, knew, but his lips were sealed. Two days after the putting-in-irons episode the young man sent for him.

'You know who I am, of course,' he said.

'Of course, I do, Archie.'

'Now — now — not even here. Well, no one else does, though the old woman has her doubts, and has set the kid on to pump me. Now, I want your word that you won't give me away. One of these days you'll know the whole story.'

Lord Reggie promised, and the two shook hands and split a pint on it.

On about the seventh day out, the young man was sitting in his cabin, reading. Little Hony was curled up between his legs, her head resting on — well, where it shouldn't have been, and there was a something pressing against the girl's ear which she knew wasn't his hand. One arm was round her head, and her hand gently caressed it. As she felt the throbbing of the young man's member she gently stroked it with her soft head, and his thoughts came down to earth with a crash. He had been thinking out a wireless telegraphy problem, but now all the wireless telegraphy had descended from his brain into the top part of his trousers. He bent down and kissed her.

Hony twisted herself round between his legs, and let her fingers slide gently over the palpitating member in his trousers. Slowly her little fingers undid his fly buttons, till his cock sprang out and slapped her on the cheek. Her fingers played with it, tickling it gently with rosy, deftly manicured nails. She breathed her warm, sweet breath softly and sweetly on the delicate membrane of his penis, and then her tongue just touched the orifice of that 'root of all evil.'

Her hair − Hony could sit on her hair easily − fell forward over her face as she bent quickly down. Her soft tresses swam over the young man's penis, and he twisted a lock round it. 'By Jove,' he murmured *sotto voce*, 'this is Danaë's shower the other way round; gold, gold, gold, but she shall be paid for it in *white* − the *whitest* diamonds that ever left the Rand. "*Corpo di Baccho* − what Elysian drink have the gods sent me!"'

'*What* a shower of gold from the mount of the gods,' he said aloud.

Hony hadn't the slightest idea of what he was talking about, but she thought it sounded nice and she made no objection at all when the young man collected all her hair he could lay his hands on round that which he sometimes regretted he had ever had.

The young man knew music above a bit, and he remembered the 'Habanera' from *Carmen*.

'Listen, little darling,' he said, 'while I sing this, and keep the movements of your head in time.'

He sang, in his rich, baritone voice, that fatal song — patting little Hony's head to keep her to the right beats. He gave himself absolutely away to music and lust, and the lust won by a short head. At the last:

'And if I *love* thee, then beware'

the young man forgot *all* about the song of Bizet, and would have blinded little Hony, but she — *knowing* before her time — knew from the kiss on her head what was coming.

It came, *not* on her hair, but in her mouth: she was just in time to twist her little lips round his penis, and to drink — well — what ought to have made another pirate.

Hony wiped her lips on her delicate little lace-bordered handkerchief. The young man raised the little figure kneeling in front of him, and pulled her gently onto his knees.

He poured her out a glass of champagne, and she drank it. He took a glass himself, and sank back into the luxurious armchair with the delightful exhaustion of satisfied desire.

Hony lay in his arms, her head resting on his shoulder. With one hand he clasped her tightly to him, with the other he softly caressed her luxuriant, silky tresses.

Dreamily he closed his eyes: pictured to himself the beautiful girl as he had seen her on that first evening in the embraces of her dark-skinned lover, divested of everything, the perfect white flesh, the delicately moulded, miniature figure, the silky curls only just beginning to show between the dainty thighs.

As he recalled the vision, all his vigour returned to him, and Hony felt something between those little thighs that Leighton would have loved to paint (the thighs − not the something − though that something might have appealed to a famous Cornish artist). She was glad, for she had not been satisfied herself, and her first taste of a male organ in her mouth had made her long to feel it again in the spot which nature had designed for it.

She was consumed with desire, and her thighs twitched together as she sat on his lap − but she was not to be so easily satisfied.

The young man's hand stole over her legs, and under her light skirts. He softly smoothed the velvety skin and played with her firm little bottom, while his fingers wandered and gently tickled the tiny orifice.

It was too much for Hony. Raising her head, she slipped her arms round the young man's neck, gripping him tightly, and pressing her lips to his. Her tongue shot out, right down his throat. She writhed with lascivious passion.

The young man's fingers still further wandered and entered the cleft valley, which he had but so recently opened. It was already moist from the overflowing of her lust.

Hony withdrew her lips from his, and the young man whispered, 'Hony, darling, you remember our *first* evening when I came in and saw you with Carrie?'

Hony did not reply. She blushed and hid her face on his shoulder, and he continued. 'Hony, I want to see you like that again.' She raised her head and gazed at him.

'When?'

'Now,' he said, and Hony slipped off his knees. She commenced unfastening her dress, but he stopped her. 'No, darling, let me do that.' And bit by bit he himself gradually removed her clothes.

He stopped every now and then to kiss and admire her; he raised her arms to kiss the down beneath them, and inhale the perfume.

At last Hony was reduced to silken chemise, almost transparent. He stepped away, and watched her with intense admiration as she stood half ashamed and half pleased.

Then he said, 'Hony, let it fall to your feet and step out of it.'

Timidly, she complied. It was not mock modesty, but her nervousness was because she really loved him.

He posed her in nearly every way he could think of, watching for the effect. Each time he came back and kissed her.

At last he lifted her up, as he would a child, naked as she was, and laid her gently on his bed.

He kissed each little breast, toying with them with his tongue, and sometimes savagely sucking them as if he would bite off the rose-coloured nipples. His kisses went lower and lower; his tongue travelled over her honey-sweet skin; he came to the soft downy mount, and kissed it, opened her legs, and buried his face between them, his tongue working furiously — he almost hurt her. He felt at that moment he would like to devour her, then his kisses went still further down each exquisitely formed leg to the tiny foot. He loved the delicate feet, so perfect of shape, and so pink and white. He kissed them long and fervently.

Gently he turned her over, kissing her neck, her back, and the two beautiful rounded curves of her bottom, and one long fervent kiss between them.

He could stand it no longer, and roughly he turned her over.

Hony had almost fainted with the ecstasy of her sensual passions, such as she had never felt before, but as she felt him turn her over, instinctively she opened her thighs.

Without hesitation, the young man was on top of her, and in a few, all too brief, seconds, it was over. Hony fell asleep in his arms.

As the weather gradually grew warmer, the deck again became the favourite haunt, and the voyage perfectly enjoyable.

Hony had got accustomed to go into the young man's cabin whenever she liked, though of course she usually knocked, but one morning, rising earlier than usual, she stole out, and cautiously made her way there. She was feeling hot and excited, she felt she wanted to be cuddled and kissed, she meant to wake him gently with a kiss, then creep into his bed beside him, and she felt sure he would be pleased to see her, and *it* would happen again.

When she got to the door she quietly tried the handle, and it turned; she stepped in quickly and closed it before looking at the bed. As she did so she gave a little gasp of surprise.

The young man lay there quite naked, and on him sat Maudie with a leg on each side of his body. They had stopped all movement as the door opened.

Also on the bed was Jim; he had an arm round Maudie, and was kissing and sucking one of her breasts, his other hand was between the young man's legs under Maudie's buttocks; she could see he was playing with the young man's balls.

At first she was seized with the pangs of jealousy.

The young man noticed it, and said, 'Come here, Hony, and kiss me, you must not be jealous *here*, you know; we are all good friends, darling.'

She came over with a shade of reluctance, and kissed him, but the kiss he gave her in return drove all else from her head. He kept her mouth glued to his as she bent over him, and to her it felt as if he was sucking out her life's blood; his hand wandered under her delicately shaded, simple dressing gown, and under the soft, light fabric of her night dress it came in contact with the cool, firm flesh of her legs. An intense thrill passed over them both, and he pressed her lips even more tightly to his. His body quivered, and his buttocks rose and fell with a quick spasmodic motion. Maudie helped him, first relieving him of her weight, then letting it press down on him as much as she could, engulfing his rigid member to the uttermost fraction. Jim's hand slipped down from the young man's testicles, and he gently thrust a finger, moistened by the juice of life that had already escaped from Maudie, into that aperture which was not designed by nature to receive.

The young man's thrusts grew faster and more fierce; he roughly thrust his hand between Hony's legs, and two fingers up her now quite humid sheath. With one final convulsion he spent, and for a few seconds his body became quite rigid — then the intoxicating spasm was over.

He lay quite still, keeping Hony's lips pressed to his, and not letting Maudie get off, as she had tried to.

Notwithstanding the intensity of his feelings, and the profuseness of his discharge, he continued to feel unsatisfied.

No mere physical relief could drown the craving of lust which then possessed him.

After a slight pause he at last released Hony's lips, and drew her onto the bed.

He asked her to kiss Maudie, which she did passionately, their tongues darting in and out between each other's lips. As she turned her back to him the young man took advantage, and raising her, placed her astride his face, her beautifully rounded little bottom just above it. When her position dawned on her she softly sank back on him, almost smothering him, but he loved it, and the movements of his body recommenced.

One hand gently caressed Hony, the other he laid on the youth's stiff prick; Hony's hand also stole to it, while she still continued to kiss Maudie, and the sensation of their two hands meeting and touching on it was exquisite to those two. One of Maudie's hands crept round and toyed with the girl's dainty bottom and pink opening just above the young man's eyes.

The movements grew fast and furious, sighs escaping them all, and this time all four of them simultaneously paid their tribute to the deity of love and passion.

Hony scrambled off the young man, and lay down, exhausted and satisfied by his side. Maudie and Jim crept softly from the room.

The young man told Hony about his island, of his palace, of the natives, *and* of the perfect climate.

He told her also of the sports and amusements by which they whiled away their time, and kept themselves in good condition. He was lord and master there, his word was law, as much as on his ship. They had no *socialists* or *suffragettes* among *his* community.

Hony could not resist the temptation to ask him if he did not at times long for the Old Country, and regret that, now a pirate, he would never be able to return. He only smiled, and then he told her, what even those nearest to him of his subordinates had not dreamt of — his plan to reinstate himself and all those under his command. He was positive of his success when the proper time came, and under the most solemn pledge of secrecy, he gave her a glimpse of what it was.

It bewildered her.

These confidences led to more endearments, and this time it was Hony's turn. They did not hurry — the delightful contact of their naked flesh, and Hony's rapture that the vacuum she had been sensible of was now filled and stretched to its utmost capacity, was too heavenly to be put an end to before Nature compelled it, but at last Nature triumphed — and the commingling of their *bodies* seemed to be but part of the commingling of their *souls*.

The Cousins

The origin of the uninhibited orgy that follows is the publication in the 1880s of a novel in French entitled *Les Cousines de la Colonelle*. This delicately wrought account of two sisters who suffer the inadequacies of the male sex in a variety of relationships has frequently been used as the starting point for rather more direct literary offerings. Such is the nature of this excerpt from *The Cousins*, which is definitely from the 'ooh-aah' school of erotic writing. In this instance the names have not been changed to protect the innocent; just about the only points of resemblance between *The Cousins* and *Les Cousines* are the names of the two sisters, Julia and Florentine. However, it must be added that they have rather a better time in this version than in the original!

Not long after Dorothy had surprised her mistress and Madame Vaudrez in the latter's bedroom where she had screwed her mistress with a dildo, Madame Lucy gave one of her famous, intimate soirees. Julia and Florentine were lucky enough to be invited; they both went under assumed names: Pomegranate Flower and Miss Evergreen. Although it was against the rules of Madame Lucy's establishment, Dorothy had explained to her former employer that both ladies had plans for the future where these names might become very important. They would only visit Madame Lucy's establishment once, because in matters of sex both ladies were very inexperienced. Madame Lucy was flattered, and allowed the house rules to be broken, just this once.

Her small, select parties to which only a lucky few – mainly the very rich, the very important and the titled – are admitted, enjoyed among the highest circles a remarkable, or rather extremely curious, reputation. The secrecy which surrounded these gatherings had made them notorious throughout Paris, and everyone who was anyone desperately tried to get an invitation.

Dorothy, of course, belonged to the small groups of friends of this hospitable lady, and she had really kept her word to wrangle an invitation out of Madame Lucy. She did not hide the fact from her mistress and Madame Vaudrez that getting the invitation had been exceedingly difficult. She also had some misgivings.

'My dearest ladies,' the devoted maid said, 'you may have to count on the possibility that as newcomers you may become highly involved, and I am almost afraid . . . what I mean is, once you are in Madame Lucy's salon, anything goes, and it is impossible to refuse anything. Won't you reconsider while there is still time?'

'Ah, rubbish, my dear Dorothy,' Julia said. 'I am not such a prude when I happen to be in the proper company, and neither is my sister. And besides, now you have really aroused our curiosity!'

Julia was not just curious but truly eager for an introduction to the home of Madame Lucy. When she was still the mistress of Count Saski she had picked up enough allusions to this famous establishment, and under no circumstances did she want to pass up the chance to see for herself what was going on. She knew full well that the happenings in Madame Lucy's house were incredibly licentious, and ladies from the finest families in Paris fought for the honor to be admitted to the odd entertainment of the intimate little groups that gathered there.

Two very important rules had to be followed strictly, exactly as laid down by the Madam of the house. In the first place, utter discretion was a must, and in the second place, everyone – without exception – had to accept the rules of whatever games were played at the particular party. If one could agree to these two stipulations, an evening of incredible delights was held out as a proper reward.

And Dorothy had told the sisters what Julia already had guessed, that whatever happened at the home of Madame Lucy was not exactly commonplace.

Madame Lucy was a widow of about forty years old, although she looked no more than thirty. She had a sister, Laura, who lived with her, and who appeared to be a few years younger. Laura was about to divorce her husband and, as far as the sisters could gather, this man lived in the colonies and made only very infrequent, short visits to Paris. Rumour had it that he lived with a negress in Africa. Anyhow, he was very rich, and his charming wife had a considerable income.

When the two sisters, together with Dorothy, entered the salon of the beautiful Madame Lucy, they met a small gathering of about ten persons.

There was the old Count de Paliseul, a very interesting gentleman 'in between the two ages,' with graying temples and a tendency to become corpulent; an officer of the General Staff, Baron Maxim de Berny, tall, blond and muscular and – as one could expect – the spoiled lover of all the courtesans and respectable women in Paris. Then there was Dorothy, well dressed and very ladylike, blonde and stately, with an enormous bosom and wide hips. Miss Elinor D. MacPherson was from the United States. She was a redhead, a real Irish devil with sea-green eyes, a wicked mouth with an incredible amount of lipstick and very beautiful pointed breasts. It was impossible to overlook this detail, if detail is the correct word. These huge things were truly remarkable, especially since the gown of this lady had the lowest plunging neckline Paris had ever seen. There was a banker, Monsieur de Lyncent, and a very pale, fragile-looking woman from Andalusia. She was Senora Padilla, who was at the party with her husband, a small, lean gentleman with pitch-black hair that seemed to be pasted down on his skull. He was the Consul from Spain. Finally there were John and Molly Teeler, brother and sister, abrim with youthful innocence, so much so that the sisters were beginning to doubt whether the soiree would take the course they had expected.

But then they were told that the latter two were performers; he an accomplished musician and she a so-called 'plastic dancer' – one of those girls who sprinkle themselves with bronze powder and then portray all the females inhabiting Mount Olympus. They were then satisfied that the evening would fulfil their expectations.

Besides, a small speech of the gracious hostess enlightened everyone completely, and there was no doubt left in anyone's mind as to what was about to take place during the course of the coming evening.

'Ladies and gentlemen,' Madame Lucy said in a low tone of voice – shortly before her little speech all the lights in the house had been doused, except for a few hidden ones which spread a discreet glow – 'you want, as far as I understand from your own words or those

of your friends who were kind enough to introduce
you to me, to taste with me the delights which are so
frequently denied to us. You and I have now gathered
in this small group. All have the same thoughts about
this particular subject, and it is therefore that we shall
be able to enjoy our desires without undesirable results
and, above all, without restraint. I have seen to it that
my servants, as usual, have the night off. There will
be absolutely no unwanted witnesses to the
proceedings. I fervently hope they will soon start, and
I beg you to use your unbridled imaginations, and to
throw off all your inhibitions. After all, we have
gathered here with a delightful idea in mind and I beg
you not to forget this, no matter in what situation you
might find yourself.'

A softly murmured 'Bravo' interrupted the smiling
Madame Lucy.

'Now, please allow me to repeat the few most
important rules of our little get together. There are
actually only three. Number one: shame is a plebian
attitude. Number two: everyone is for everyone.
Number three: the ratio is three to one which means
that the ladies are allowed to reach a certain delight
three times. I presume that I do not have to go into
detail. The gentleman can enjoy the same ecstasy only
once. For further proceedings the ratio may become
six to two, and so on . . . let your imaginations work,
give them free rein. It is a ratio at which I arrived after
many delicious experiences, and I hope that the
gentlemen can be trusted upon their word of honor.'

The last reminder, obviously, was only meant for

the men present. It seemed that the official part of the little soiree was over, and Dorothy whispered a few little explanations, telling Julia and Florentine that everyone was expected to follow the instructions of the hostess, and moreover that the rules of the game were of the greatest benefit to the ladies.

They were gathered in a rather large living room. There was no lack of a place to sit – or rather, to lie down. The rug in the middle of the room was free of any furniture, though grouped around it were four large, oversized couches. There were several sofas in the corners of the room, and many love seats and over-stuffed easy chairs. Several small tables throughout the room were loaded with bottles and plates, filled with all sorts of delicious snacks. Various exits led into smaller rooms which were discreetly lit and tastefully decorated.

The guests walked around, inspecting the various rooms, getting acquainted with one another, and slowly pairing off in small groups. If it had not been for the words of the hostess, no one would ever have thought they were amidst a rather special gathering of people.

But then came the voice of Madame Lucy again. 'Gentlemen, would you care to dance? Mr Teeler, please start the music.'

And the next moment, soft music filled the room and soon several couples danced to the exotic music. Maxim de Berny walked over to Florentine and invited her to dance with him. She accepted, and his strong arms embraced her passionately. He was a very good dancer.

Julia was asked by Senator Junoy. After a few dances they remained standing together and then sank down upon one of the couches.

'Did you get a little bit warm, my dears?' Again it was the voice of Lucy, clear but husky. 'I believe the gentlemen should be allowed to take off their coats. And I also think that the ladies should be permitted to unbutton their partner's flies . . .'

The two sisters were speechless. That is what one might call speeding up the proceedings! Hastily, the gentlemen, led by the Senator, that wicked creature, took off their coats.

'Well, Monsieur de Berny? And what about your tunic. That uniform must be extremely uncomfortable. And please, Madame,' Lucy said to Florentine, 'you will have to struggle with that hermetically sealed uniform fly!'

Florentine noticed that her partner's face reddened. 'How funny,' she thought, 'and this is only the beginning!' But at the same time she looked around for Julia. There was her sister, sitting on the next couch, together with the little Spaniard. Madame Lucy was standing next to them, obviously repeating her invitation. It seemed that the couple needed some urging, but finally her sister stretched her hand toward the pants of Senor Padilla.

Florentine had already put her hands between the legs of her escort, and what she found there exceeded her greatest expectations.

One great sigh seemed to drift through the room. All the couples were now standing, or sitting, in a big circle. The gentlemen's behaviour was still correct, though all of them were now dressed in their shirt sleeves. The ladies had their right hands extended and encircling the hardening members of their partners of that moment.

But Madame Lucy was watching carefully, and she was in full control of the entire affair.

'Well, my darlings,' she said pleasantly but firmly, 'I believe that the first introductions are over and done with, and I assume that you don't need my instructions any longer. I am very sure that all the gentlemen are now more than ready to pay slight compliments to their ladies. Please, gentlemen, don't hesitate. We women would love to get thoroughly acquainted with that which interests us most. Come to think of it, I would assume it to be very entertaining if the gentlemen would now take a firm hold of whatever is of greatest interest to them. Now, please, let's do it all at the same time. Grab firmly whatever charm it was that attracted you first to your female partner.'

What followed was positively hilarious.

Madame Lucy's suggestions were followed to the letter. Though the women had obeyed Madame Lucy's instructions rather hesitantly and shyly, the gentlemen were rather more direct and firm.

Florentine looked over at Julia and Senor Padilla. And, indeed, the little Spaniard had already taken a firm hold of those charms of her sister which had undoubtedly intrigued him most, namely her perfect, delicious breasts. His brown, strong hands fingered around in Julia's low-cut gown, and he quickly succeeded in freeing one of Julia's full, well-formed breasts.

Somewhat further on were the banker, de Lyncent, and the wife of the Spanish consul. Florentine could not exactly see where he had his hands, but it was easy to see that he was kissing the languishing Andalusian upon the mouth, trying to wriggle his tongue between her teeth.

'Our friend de Lyncent is a saint,' a gentleman remarked. He looked like one of Ruben's fauns, with his little, twinkling eyes, his reddish face, and his full white beard. 'A chaste little kiss satisfies him completely.'

This remark surely did not describe the gentleman's own desires, because he had just taken a firm hold of the charms of the silver-blonde Molly Teeler who looked, with her tousled hair and big blue eyes, like an appetizing little doll. One hand was energetically kept busy with her well-formed, obviously firm and hard bosom, and the other hand had crawled under the pretty young girl's dress. The gentleman did not even take the trouble, once he had reached his goal, to rearrange his partner's skirt, so that her marble-white upper thighs were completely uncovered. He had put his faun-like head slightly down, and was nuzzling under her armpits. It seemed to tickle her, and she burst out in a loud giggle.

'Ooh, I can't stand that . . . please . . . please . . . Oh, sir, you're tickling me too much . . . no, please, no . . . aaaah.'

The slightly tortured-sounding giggle had stopped,

because Count de Paliseul had let go of his partner's armpit and had begun to nibble upon her strawberry nipples which were smiling at him from her half-opened gown.

Without a doubt, one of the gentlemen, Monsieur de Laigle, knew his manners, because he was entertaining both ladies of the house. Each one was sitting on one side of him. Laura, who had opened his fly, was softly playing with his stiffening scepter, and he was tenderly stroking her full behind. At the same time his legs encircled the thighs of Madame Lucy, and it was obvious that his hand had already reached that spot which is covered with a tuft of hair.

The talented young Johnny Teeler — he could not have been more than nineteen or twenty years old — did not interrupt his soft musical playing. Nevertheless his hands no longer played waltzes, but they magically performed known and unknown singing melodies which increased the enchanted mood that now permeated the room.

And when Julia looked carefully at the dimly lit corner where he was playing, she noticed that he executed his paraphrases and melodies with only one hand. True, it was done with such virtuosity that nobody seemed to notice this. The only one who knew for sure was the American Miss Elinor because his left hand had taken a firm hold of one of her incredibly pointed breasts. She had taken it out of her dress and offered it to the piano player, holding it in both hands which made this pointed pear appear even larger. It was enchanting to behold this fascinating woman. Her well-filled yet slim figure rested upon a pair of firm, long-stemmed, gorgeous legs for which the American women are so justly famous. She had an unusual piquant face which was framed by fire red — one could almost call it indecent red — hair which contrasted strangely with her nymph-green, incredibly large eyes. It was not surprising at all that the young musician, whose fly was open like those of all the other gentlemen, displayed an enormous hard-on.

Maxim de Berny, too, had taken the charming cue of the hostess without any hesitation. He had become an entirely different person ever since Florentine had liberated his enormous manhood out of its uncomfortable position. Florentine loved to caress this gigantic, swollen, stiff prick. She was dreaming about how it would fit into a certain pink-coloured sheath.

His military reserve had made way for a zealous kindness. And, when the gentlemen had been asked to take possession of the charms that attracted them to their ladies, he had come more than just zealous and kind. He immediately grabbed a very firm hold of Florentine's legs.

'My dear and precious lady,' his hot breath whispered into her ears, 'I . . . I . . . have only seen you tonight for the first time. Oh, I am sure that you did not even notice me . . . there were so many other interesting people present . . . but ever since I saw you tonight, I have been haunted by a wild desire . . . I have dreamed passionate dreams . . . and I hope fervently that they will come true. My thoughts have been possessed by only one desire . . . to touch your legs . . . those beautiful, gorgeous, long legs. They seem to be sculptured out of marble . . .'

His strong hands firmly underscored his words, confirming that he meant what he said. But he seemed not only interested in Florentine's legs, since his hands were also very busy with her thighs and the tuft of hair in between. He paid homage to her fleece that left no doubt as to his intentions. However, it did not disturb Florentine in the least. After all, that was what she was here for, and she fully intended to make up for her years of widowhood and her years with an impotent husband. She felt terribly passionate and could not have cared less if the blond giant had taken immediate possession of her. In fact, she would have welcomed it. But he was still playing with her legs, her thighs, her breasts and her slowly moistening hole. When enjoyed in the proper manner, erotic delights can be continued endlessly. The passion, after all, is always there. It is only a matter of the right place and plenty of time and a willing partner. Of course, Florentine knew that a brutal, quick embrace can have its own particular charm. One can even do it standing on a front porch, while the husband is occupied with opening the door, or in a men's room of a station when one's lover is about to depart for a prolonged time and hastily requires a last parting favour. It can even be done, she knew, in a public park, where one is protected by the impenetrable branches of the bushes.

.The large room in which the thirteen people were gathered was now filled with the most unusual sounds. One could hear a peculiar soft smacking, the rustling of the silken gowns of the ladies and the starched shirts of the gentlemen. There were the loving grunts and groans of the men, and the giggling and soft moans of the women. Breathless moaning, and the panting and gasping which left no doubt as to what was going on. Added to this was the typical, very exciting creaking of the furniture caused by the movements of the bodies that occupied them.

But the soft, enchanting music of John Teeler had stopped. In its place an occasional note was heard whenever Miss Elinor's elbows hit a key of the piano against which she was leaning while she straddled with widespread legs the lap of the young, blond piano player. In this strange position she went with him through all the motions that people usually perform when they are firmly pinned down on a mattress.

And they were not the only couple busily engaged in this particular delight. The skinny Spaniard had succeeded in inducing Dorothy to stretch out on the couch, and he was kneeling between her powerful legs. He was working a little bit too fast for Dorothy's taste, pushing his lance with such enervating speed against the girl's belly that she finally took his prick in her hands, forcing him to slow down. Her full breasts served as supports for the nervous Spaniard's outstretched arms and his skinny brown fingers voluptuously kneaded these enormous snow-white balls.

Monsieur de Laigle had put Lucy's sister in front of him. She offered her full, white buttocks up to his throbbing spear and he took possession of her behind with a certain nonchalance. Even while he penetrated her from behind, dog fashion, he refused to take his cigar out of his mouth. It was a curious sight. He fucked her, puffing his cigar, giving her enormous jolts. Laura kept very still, but breathed passionately and deeply every time the huge shaft of her partner disappeared up to the hilt into her wide-open cleft.

The hostess had not yet actively joined one of the many couples. She wandered from one little group to another, now cheering them on with a witty remark, then removing a piece of clothing which might be in the way, occasionally fondling a buttock, a breast or a pair of balls, whenever such a part was uncovered.

'Well, Monsieur de Berny, I am sure that Miss Evergreen is ready for you. Don't you want to honour the lady with your, as I can observe, more-than-ready sword?'

At that particular moment the couple did not need these doubtlessly well-meant encouragements, because without any further ado the strong, muscular officer had pushed Florentine down upon the couch and . . .

The girl did not think that she had ever experienced such powerful thrusts ever before in her life. The blond officer had mounted her as if he were a wild stallion, and he worked her over with tremendous force while he raised her legs high. He raved madly against Florentine's belly, his balls slamming hard against her buttocks. In a very short time she felt pains as she had never before endured. But strangely enough, the pain became pleasant, and her hips started wildly gyrating, her cleft wide open, as if she was about to swallow the whole man.

His breathing was rattling, but strangely enough, though it seemed that he could hardly get enough air, he kept exclaiming exciting words. Their monotony was, at first, strange and frightening, but ultimately Florentine became as hot and passionate as she had ever been.

'Aaaaah . . . finally, finally . . . now can I fuck between those legs . . . between those legs . . . I am fucking between those beautiful legs . . . between the legs of a most beautiful woman . . . aah . . . and what have you got between those sweet, beautiful legs? A cunt . . . a cunt . . . aah . . . how I have longed for that little hairy honey-pot of yours . . . right between your legs . . . ooh! Your legs, your legs . . . and I am fucking your right between those gorgeous legs! Ooh . . . aah . . . let me die fucking between those legs . . . the legs of an angel . . . I will never take my prick out of this cunt again . . . I want to stay between your legs . . . my hard prick in your hairy cunt . . . aah . . . how delicious to fuck that cunt between your legs . . .'

It was by now quite obvious to Florentine that her partner was particularly fascinated by her legs. It was also possible that their perfect line and form exceeded his wildest secret dreams. Anyhow, the muscular lover became wilder and wilder.

'Sweet . . . oh, how sweet . . . the way you raise those legs and spread your thighs . . . those legs . . . so that I can fuck between them . . . can you feel my balls slam against your ass? Ooh, I am fucking between the most divine legs . . . legs that seem to be praying for a harder and wilder fuck . . . I will give it to you, my love . . . I fuck that cunt . . . between your marvellous legs . . . and now you are spreading them so wide that I can put my prick in all the way . . . Ooh, don't you like it, this big dong between your divine legs? Ooh, feel how it rubs . . . ooh, my prick is at home at last . . . I am fucking you between your legs . . . I never want to stop . . . I want to fuck between your legs forever and ever . . . ooh, divine one, I am fucking you . . . between your legs . . . ooh, please, allow me to die between your legs . . .'

Florentine had to admit that it was a rather novel experience to have her legs honoured in such a peculiar way, while she, as a person, did not seem particularly attracted to the officer. But, she told herself, she did not come to find eternal love; sex was enough. And as far as that was concerned, their coupling was extremely satisfactory, and they rammed their bellies voluptuously together.

The behaviour of her partner reminded Florentine of a famous composer, a friend of her late husband, who had enticed his mistress — a divinely talented singer — to submit to him while she was singing a well-known, very difficult aria. And ever since that day he was unable to listen to her singing without being overpowered by the wild desire to possess her while the beautiful tones ran from her lips. To make this technically possible, the couple had agreed that he would rest on his back and have his mistress with the golden throat settle down upon him so that she would be able to sing her beautiful aria while he was pushing wildly under her, listening to her enchanting voice. Occasionally he would reach a certain height which would cause in her a sour note. But, on the whole, the arrangement worked perfectly for both people.

Julia, too, was literally drowning in passion. She had come twice already, though she had masterfully succeeded in hiding this. She wanted to enjoy the precisely measured, powerful jolts of Senor Padilla to the utmost. He worked without letting up, and his powerfully swollen muscle of love penetrated deeper and deeper into her longing body with every ramrod jolt.

Dorothy kept her partner working on her incessantly while she was crying out, 'Oh God, I am coming . . . I am . . . coming . . . oh, my God . . . how I . . . am coming . . . again . . . again . . . oh, God . . . I am . . . coming . . . you screw so marvelously . . . I . . . am . . . coming . . . again . . . ooh, it's fantastic . . . I am so . . . horny . . . you fuck like . . . a bull . . . aah . . . I am . . . coming all over . . . again . . . aah . . . aaaah!'

It was really very enjoyable to watch all these happy people. The big, blonde woman had turned slightly sideways. One of her extremely strong and powerful long legs, covered with a blue silk stocking, was held high up in the air by her partner, who held on to it as if it were a main mast of a sailboat, tossing in the wild seas. His lower body pushed rapidly with speedy thrusts against the widely opened cleft of his partner. He almost squatted between her full thighs, straddling the one under him with his skinny legs as if he were riding a wild pony.

Dorothy was resting upon her mighty hips, showing a full view of her large and imposing behind. The gigantic cheeks shimmered milk white in the subdued light of the room. They jerked and palpitated continuously, pushing violently backwards against the belly of her partner, who kept pushing against her with short, very rapid little strokes. His peter must have sealed off her twat almost hermetically, and Julia decided to try out this obviously very satisfying position as soon as she had the opportunity.

The wife of the thus busily engaged Spaniard was about to enjoy special delights herself. She had been selected by the hot-blooded Count de Paliseul. It appeared that he was more attracted to her than to the silver-blonde Molly, and maybe he had reached his goal quicker than expected. He was now about to experience new delights.

He was zealously bearing down upon the tender, completely disappearing wife of the fiery Senor Padilla. The speed of the good gentleman was surely much slower than she was used to, but the force of his thrusts must have been incredibly more powerful than those of the skinny Spaniard. The Senora was whimpering quietly, but it could have been because of incredible delight which was forcing this soft meowing out of her throat.

'Aah, Monsieur, aah, so good you are doing it to me . . . ' she almost sobbed. 'It is so good . . . aah . . . aah . . . more, more . . . please . . . please . . .

aah . . . ooh . . . you satisfy me much . . . you are so much better than my husband . . . oh, how delicious . . . no, please, don't stop . . . it feels so good . . . more, more . . . aah . . .'

Her partner was as red as a boiled lobster. It was obvious that he was driving his shaft into her with his last remaining force, but it was equally as obvious that this task was not an unpleasant one for him. In fact, he was enjoying himself tremendously. This pale Andalusian woman, with her exotic beauty, had beautiful, graceful, finely chiseled legs and incredibly gorgeous, slender thighs. The panting, gasping fawn had put both legs across his shoulders and his heavy, fleshy hands gripped her small but muscular buttocks firmly, pressing them with a slow but regular rhythm against his own belly. This small woman was incredibly voluptuous, because every muscle in her small body shook and vibrated. She pushed herself against the huge man on top of her with such fervor and passion that it seemed as if her frail body consisted of one heavily tensed muscle.

The blonde beauty, the sister of the pianist, was now possessed by the horny banker. But it was not the normal position in which all the other couples were engaged. Either because of weakness, or because of perversity, the banker was busily engaged in an entirely different way. His gray-haired head disappeared almost completely between the widely opened white thighs of Molly, who languidly stretched out on one of the sofas.

One could almost say that the young girl was an

extraordinary beauty. Most interesting was the radiance of her appearance. Everything on her contributed to making her look like an angel. Her hair had the color of finely spun gold. The skin of her body and face was almost translucent. It was impossible to make out whether the snow of her bosom or the lilies of her thighs were whiter.

The form-fitting black silken gown, which did not hide anything on her perfect figure, was pushed up high above her waist by the horny old goat who was about to shove his facial duster into her small mother-of-pearl boudoir. It gave everyone present a peculiar feeling of tension to watch the balding gray head of the banker mix with the shimmering pubic hairs of this beautiful, innocent young girl. The zealous money lender had also pushed the gown of his willing beauty down her shoulders, thus exposing both of her full, pointed, yet very innocent-looking breasts. He took this opportunity to grab them both with lustful hands, playing around with them as if they were rubber balls. From time to time he rubbed both divinely red strawberries between thumb and forefinger — the same way a lieutenant of the guards twirls his moustache — eliciting excited groans from his beautiful partner.

The beautifully formed legs of this gorgeous creature rested upon the shoulders of the old man who was kneeling before her. It was incredibly obscene and shameless. Her legs were held up high and bent backwards. The high heels of her black lacquered shoes pierced deeply into the back of the totally absorbed man, slowly pushing him closer toward her. There was actually no need for her to do so, because the head of the insatiable banker had almost completely disappeared into her widely opened cleft, and he looked for all the world like an animal trainer, sticking his head into the hungry jaws of a lion.

Truly, the night afforded so much variety, and it was so exciting, that the sisters could not, with the best will in the world, recall every single detail. They also had no recollection how, after a certain time, the four enormous couches that formed a circle around the rug in the middle of the room were suddenly transformed into a gigantic resting place. Upon this enormous area, the couples sought and found one another. The watchful hostess saw to it that her guests' activities did not degenerate into selfish single acts, which would have robbed the people present of their sense of belonging, and which would have prevented the mutual orgy which now followed.

The bodies of the participants at this sensational soiree soon formed an incredible whole. They all formed one huge body with an enormous amount of arms, thighs, legs; a great, living thing − breathing, panting, moaning, groaning and sighing out of its many lungs. It offered breasts in all shapes − huge ones, pendulous ones, pear-shaped and melon-shaped, dark-skinned and milk-white globes, with an equal variety of nipples − from tiny strawberry-red ones to big, jutting firm ones, begging to be sucked and bitten. Buttocks, cunts, mouths, pricks, and balls in delightful opulence invited the many groping hands and eager mouths. The people who had become this huge thing moving on the enormous bed seemed to consist entirely of semen-filled cunts and mouths, throbbing pricks and slamming bellies. Now rule number two achieved its end. 'Everyone for everyone' took on its true meaning.

It would have been impossible not to follow this rule, once caught up in this indescribably wonderful mass of naked and almost naked bodies. It was impossible for any of the participants to avoid the embrace of the nearest neighbor, or to escape from a throbbing prick, a yawning cunt, or the voluptuously grabbing hands of another.

But then, nobody had the slightest intention of doing such a thing. They did everything in their power to pull as much flesh as they possibly could, to hold as many hands as was bearable and to kiss eagerly the many hungry mouths and tongues. The smell of sweat and semen worked like a powerful aphrodisiac. The groans and cries of the others seemed to spur flagging powers to even greater deeds. The two sisters found themselves now on top and then under many bodies. Sometimes they were pressed against one another and, then again, against another partner. They were in one continual hot embrace, completely entangled. It was a mystery how the various couples, or rather groups, always succeeded in getting loose from each other only to form new connections, new couplings with new partners, trying new and different techniques. They did things, and enjoyed them, which they had hitherto never thought possible.

The most incredible combinations were formed by all these steaming hot bodies! The permeating smells of come, perfume, body odors from armpits, cunts and pricks were unbearably exciting.

Everything was mixed, from the most primitive wild grabs to the most refined techniques. And each deed caused ripples of delight, running the complete gamut from voluptuous desire to gasping climax . . . over and over again. The hot spark would fly from body to body, jumping through the entire group, using the nerves of these people as if they were one single medium.

Whenever on one end of the enormous bed a female body jerked in the spasms of an incredible climax, shuddering as if tortured with unbearable pains, the next moment a body on the other side would groan and jerk, coming equally as ecstatically, as if an electric jolt had passed through the entire mass of bodies in the short span of a single second.

Florentine was no longer pinned down and fucked by the massive, muscular body of Maxim de Berny, and Julia had long since lost Senor Padilla who had had his delights both with her and Dorothy. It seemed that all the male participants of this peculiar soiree at one time or another had deposited their seed in the more than willing laps of Florentine and Julia. The two sisters, who had so far lived a chaste life, were reluctant to ever get off their backs.

In the wild group which the guests of Madame Lucy now formed, it was next to impossible to recognize even the most intimate partner of the moment, though the girls tried to identify some of them. But how should they know whose mighty member was pushing and jolting from the back against their sopping cunts? They were thrown across the heaving belly of another, like helpless booty slung across the back of a wild stallion, while at the same time they were trying to swallow someone's throbbing manhood that was trying to impale their open mouths. Julia thought that it must have been young Teeler who was stretched out next to the officer, but her hands were caught, left and right, between their wildly banging bodies, so she could hardly be sure.

And who was working her over with such vehemence? Judging by the technique, and the words he muttered, it must have been Maxim de Berny, who had spent the earlier part of that evening ripping her sister Florentine apart. On the other hand, she suspected that it could be Dorothy who had strapped on her dildo.

There . . . oooh . . . just now . . . Julia had just started to climax and already the jolting prick had squirted into her and was about to pull out of her hot and hungry quim. She was just beginning to feel sorry for herself when suddenly two powerful arms pulled her thighs even wider apart and another throbbing prick penetrated her hospitably moistened grotto . . . how delicious! Her new lover, with renewed vigor, continued the task of replacement, jolting and jarring her shivering insides. She was drowning, floating in voluptuous delights she had never known before. Her wild desire temporarily quieted down with the regular thrusts. Suddenly she felt a pair of hot lips take possession of her tickler, and the head below her formed an exciting buffer for another partner who was giving it to her from behind.

Florentine, on the other side of the bed, stretched out one hand which was just released by one of her partners. There! Wasn't that the heavy club of our insatiable faun? Yes, indeed! And before she fully realized what was happening, it had already pushed itself halfway between her lips. Then, suddenly, Florentine began to bob her head, trying to swallow it all, wanting to have this gorgeous throbbing member deep in her throat. She sucked some precious drops from it and then someone else pushed her greedy mouth aside.

The heavy cylinder, which for a short moment lay there like an orphan upon his belly, disappeared into a very moist opening, barely needing the help of someone's guiding hand. And now, in the place of the soft mouth of Florentine, another, even softer pair of lips encircled the throbbing flesh pole of the elderly gentleman, speeding up and down without stopping.

Florentine was fascinated to be allowed to witness this variation of coupling, and she tried to give both the heavy prick as well as the encircling lips as much pleasure as she could.

It is impossible to describe the heady atmosphere that ruled the orgy room. The air seemed to boil satanically. Continuous, almost frightening gasps, shrill screams, and tortured sighs filled the air. The silence which now and then fell was even more sinister.

And then, suddenly, a thumping rhythm would set in whenever several couples started to hump and fuck each other again. Accompanied by the creaking of the furniture, one could hear fanatical hands slap naked flesh, the rubbing of nude bodies slamming together, and the slurping of voluptuous lips. Now and then could be heard the characteristic sound of a softening penis slipping out of a vagina, or someone's hardened nipples slipping out of puckering lips.

Most characteristic, and also most exciting, were the spontaneous exclamations. Sometimes they were involuntary, while others were said with the specific purpose of giving vent to the wild urge of having everybody take part in the enjoyment of a particular act. Even the rather reticent wife of the Spaniard called out her feelings without shame. While she was busily engaged upon this jolting and shuddering altar of lust and passion, she chanced to come upon her husband. He was just about to attack Laura, the sister of the hostess who herself was engaged in a battle to take on the enormous prick of the blond officer.

The Senora called out in wild ecstasy, 'Miguel . . . he screws me delightfully . . . I tell you, his prick is as heavy as the spear of Saint Isidore . . . aah . . . aah, darling Miguel, I love it soo much . . . aaaah . . . aaaah . . . you, Miguel . . . Miguel . . . I have to . . . please, quick . . . quick! Tell me, darling, are you getting fucked as heavenly as I? Quick . . . quick . . . it . . . is . . . so . . .' Since she started to come at that moment the rest of her confessions stuck in her gurgling throat.

Some of them were less lyrical with their expressions. The redheaded Elinor was positively obscene. Her true character showed itself when she tried to spur her partner, or rather partners, to even greater efforts.

'Why don't you fuck me harder? Come on, let me feel that you have a Goddam hard-on in my cunt! I said harder, you dirty son-of-a-bitch! Come on, I want to be screwed . . . put it in deeper, harder . . . ball me as if your worthless life depends on it . . . stick it in deeper . . . is it in? Jesus, I can't even feel your balls slam against my ass . . . faster . . . deeper and quicker/ Come on, who can give me a real good fuck? I want to be raped as if you were a bunch of horny Cossacks who haven't seen a cunt in years! I don't want you to shove it in like a gentleman . . . ram it up my cunt like a cowboy . . .'

She veritably screamed, foaming at the mouth, 'I am horny, so Goddamned horny! Isn't there a prick among this damned bunch that knows how to fuck well? Come here with it . . . I'll stick it into my cunt myself. . . quick . . . quicker! Can't you hurry it, come on, fuck me . . . my cunt is burning up . . . Give me that hot dong . . . screw me to pieces . . . shove it up my cunt harder . . . deeper!'

And the raving redhead snatched furiously at the dripping prick of the Spaniard who had just pulled it out of Laura.

'Ha . . . here's one that just came . . . boy, did that one come! That's how I want to be screwed . . . come on, you bastards . . . I'm horny and I want to get fucked . . . by all of you! One prick after the other

. . . stick in your dong . . . dammit . . . yeah, that's it . . . one after the other . . . I want to be laid by every Goddamned prick in the house . . . deep . . . hard . . . and quick! Hurry, hurry . . . that's it . . . work it in deeper . . . a little bit faster . . . deeper . . . aah, that feels good. Finally I'm beginning to feel good . . . this one fucks me even better . . . come on . . . I . . . want . . . to . . . harder, dammit, deeper . . . a little more . . . aah . . . aah . . . ooh! Eeeeek!'

Her voice suddenly gave out, but not because this horny creature had reached a climax, or even found some satisfaction. One of the gentlemen had suddenly put his swollen penis into her opened mouth, penetrating deeply into her throat. The cork effectively stopped this wellspring of Anglo-Saxon lechery.

There was one more special climax to this evening worth mentioning. It was not that the mood of excitement had abated, but the participants were becoming slightly tired. Yet, it was obvious that all had a desire for stronger excitement. In short, the following proposition was eagerly applauded by all, even before it had been completely uttered. Young Johnny Teeler was going to fuck his own sister! Strangely enough, this had not yet happened, and it must have been by pure chance. It could never have been because brother and sister avoided each other on purpose. This would have been simply impossible in the ingenious mixing machine upon which everybody had been romping around. But now they had to make up for their omission.

'Oh, Johnny,' Molly suddenly blushed, 'should we really do . . . this?'

Like all the others, Julia and Florentine were very curious to see how the handsome Englishman would react to the proposition.

'Come on, you simply have to do it. It really makes no difference. Everyone here has fucked everyone else. Even the married couples have seen their partners screwed by others. And that does not happen too often, either!' This argument was brought forth by Miss MacPherson, who had finally caught her breath. She was still busy gagging the juices of her last partner, which dribbled out of the corners of her mouth.

'Molly, don't forget our cardinal rule, "Everyone for everyone!" After all, we can't help that you two happen to be brother and sister. After all, Laura and I are sisters. That never prevented us from showing affection for one another. And, as I understand, the ladies Pomegranate Flower and Miss Evergreen, who are sisters, have a nice thing going together, too! Think of all the famous lovers in history and mythology who were brother and sister. Why, even the Pharaohs of Egypt and the Incas in Peru couldn't get married *unless* they were brother and sister. Now, come on . . . don't be so ridiculously bashful! And don't tell me that the two of you have never slept in one bed together when you were kids. Even without touching each other!'

'Yes . . . that is true. We also used to play around a little . . . I mean, with our . . . with our . . . But what you order us to do, we have never done,' Molly stuttered excitedly.

'Well then,' Madame Lucy resumed, 'you two will just have to catch up and rectify that mistake. Oh, come on, Johnny, don't be a party pooper. Here is Molly . . . she is gorgeous . . . who cares that she is your sister. Throw her on her back and get it over with!'

The resolute Madame Lucy, with Laura's help, had already pressed the blonde girl down upon the huge bed, holding her nude body firmly upon the pillows.

'Here, Laura, help me. Take a hold of her legs and pull them a little apart. No, not roughly, just hold her lightly. It will only take a few seconds of good banging and she will lap it up.'

'Oh, please, dear Madame Lucy! Don't you know that it is a deadly sin? We have never done a thing like that! Johnny . . . don't . . . no . . . don't! You are my own brother! No . . . don't . . . no, no, no . . . how can you dare to force me . . . no . . . don't . . . no . . . no . . . ooh . . . I . . . aah . . . Johnny . . . no . . . ooh, Johnny, Johnny!'

During her last exclamation, her brother pierced his heavily swollen prick deeply into her belly. It was a beautiful performance. Her brother, one could easily see, had no difficulties whatsoever. It could have been possible that he had been waiting for a long time for an opportunity like this one. He possibly had lusted after his own sister for years, eagerly wanting to enjoy her charms. Anyhow, his zeal and his powerful thrusts were proof enough that as far as he was concerned, passion was more powerful than prudish conventions.

The guests formed a circle around the balling

couple. Everybody was curious and wanted to see everything. It was no longer necessary to hold the girl down. She was panting wildly with every thrust and her thighs opened wider and wider. The two formed a nice, charming couple. It gave everyone great satisfaction to know that Molly, who was getting the hang of it, would from now on allow her brother to screw her more often.

'Ooh, Johnny, how good . . . how good . . . how beautiful it feels to do it with you . . . Please, please, go deeper my sweet, sweet Johnny! Do you remember . . . how we . . . used to . . . play . . . husband and wife? But this is really much better . . . it is . . . really good . . . only . . . this . . . way . . . please, Johnny . . . go on, deeper . . . push deeper . . . only . . . a few more . . . I have to . . . come! Aah . . . aah! Oh, Johnny . . . lover . . . I am . . . coming . . . ooh, Johnny . . . don't stop now . . . go deeper, quicker . . . please, please . . . Johnny, screw me some more . . . fuck me, dear . . . I want to come again . . . fuck . . . fuck me . . . aaah . . . you . . . have . . . to . . . fuck me . . . often . . . and hard! Always, always . . . I want you . . . to fuck me . . . always . . . tell me, Johnny dear . . . promise that you will . . . always screw me like this . . . aah . . . aaaaah . . . you . . . you . . . you!'

And the charming little sister of Johnny Teeler reached her climax.

With Open Mouth

For aficionados of the erotic novel of the 1950s and 60s the books of Marcus Van Heller have long been held in high esteem. Though this pseudonym came to be used somewhat indiscriminately by the Olympia Press in both its French and American guises, the excerpt which follows is from the 'real' Van Heller canon. First published in Paris in the mid-fifties as part of the Traveller's Companion series, *With Open Mouth* is one of the first and best of the Marcus Van Heller novels.

The spoilt and aristocratic Janice has tired of the debauched life she lives in Barcelona and is recuperating out of the city. An unsophisticated peasant boy, Avelino, watches her sunbathe naked by the sea, finally managing to strike up an acquaintance. There on the deserted beach Avelino makes love for the first time. Intoxicated by her beauty and flagrant sexuality, he finds himself falling hopelessly in love . . .

They lay together for some time with her stroking his neck gently. He noticed that the sun had withdrawn farther to sea and he felt a slight return of his previous embarrassment. He was not sure how to move off her, although he felt he must be heavy upon her. Inside him, apart from the embarrassment was a feeling of wonder and achievement at what had happened. But he could not bring himself to look at her.

'Look at me.'

It was as if she had read his thoughts.

'How does it feel to be no longer a virgin?'

Avelino stared at her searchingly for a moment. There was a warmth in her eyes which melted his embarrassment and in answer he kissed her gently on the cheek.

She laughed quietly, clasped him fiercely against her and then whispered:

'We'd better have a quick swim before we go.'

They swam naked out to the sun and afterwards he collected his clothes and they climbed the wall of hills which enclosed the town, to the little café with its open-air terrace overlooking the bay.

Later Avelino went home, having arranged to meet

the woman, whose name, she told him, was Janice Harvey, at the isthmus on the following day.

Once out of her presence, Avelino was beset by all sorts of mixed emotions. He felt, now, much more a man and yet still contained within himself a sense of shame. He was not sure how he felt about the woman, Janice. Fascinated by her, he was nonetheless annoyed at the ease with which she had been able to have intercourse with him. He was also very aware of her maturity in face of his own boyishness. He wondered how many men had enjoyed her and he felt, even now, a twinge of regret that there had been others.

All the Spanish girls he knew clung, by reputation, tenaciously to their virtue. It was only married women who, according to report, occasionally fell from grace. Of course, she might be married. The thought struck him like a wave but he cast it immediately out of his mind. She didn't seem married. He refused to think of it.

Avelino lived with his mother, father and two younger brothers in an old, white-washed house with blue shutters whose front door opened straight into one of the cobbled narrow streets of the town. The streets were not streets in the modern sense but narrow pavementless spaces ribboning between the houses, sandcovered, their uneven cobbles jutting at all angles.

It was to this house that he went, feeling that his secret of new life was written on his face. He felt it would be difficult for them not to see that he had changed during the afternoon.

Avelino ate his evening meal separately from the rest

of the family as he had to play and sing with the band early in the evenings. Tonight he was very thankful for the absence of his brothers and the interminable chatter of conversation that went with their presence. His father had not yet come in from the fishing and his mother was preoccupied with the neighbours' laundry which she did to supplement the family income.

The sun was still shining in a yellow half-circle above the hilltops when Avelino took his place on the orchestra dais at one side of the open-air dance floor.

The western hills were a dark, dusty green with the sun behind them and their summits were clothed in a fiery aura of red and yellow which cast a rose glow over the town. The white houses were tinted rose, and the white hulls of yachts swaying gently at anchor in the bay. The colour of faces was heightened and there was an atmosphere of the soft evening waiting for her lover, night, to come.

Avelino took his clarinet and the orchestra plunged into the well-known tunes of the sardanas. The brassy notes swept out in the still air, travelling up the narrow winding streets, pervading the houses and the little shops hidden amongst them. The tune soared out to sea, its warmth surrounding the little boats of the fishermen coming into the bay. And suddenly, it seemed, both inside and outside the dance enclosure, people were joining hands, forming circles to dance.

Letting his eyes stray from his music which he knew so well, anyway, Avelino wondered if the woman, Janice, knew how to dance the sardanas. There had been a time, which all seemed misty and lost to him when the sardanas had been forbidden in Catalonia. That had been just after the days of the civil war which had wracked this part of the country and left scars which still remained.

But gradually, the ban on the sardanas, which were typically and peculiarly Catalonian, had been lifted and now, wherever the music started, immediately little circles of people sprang up to perform the daily shuffling dance which reminded them always that Catalonia was Catalonia.

As the sunlight faded into a streak of lighter blue and rose on the hills and the lights of the town popped on merrily around the coastal path, the people were still dancing. By the time the sardanas had come to an end it was dark, the sea was calm and the sea-shore bars were ablaze with light and humming with the noise of tourists.

The concrete dance floor was thronged, now, with people of many nationalities. The light from the orchestra dais and the lamps on the tables which surrounded the floor, lit up the animated faces and movement as the rhythm of a rhumba danced on the air.

It seemed to Avelino, eagerly watching the entrance gate, that the whole of the town had taken on a new glow of interest. For months he had played the same tunes, sung the same tunes without inspiration. Since the afternoon the world seemed to have changed.

When, at last, she arrived at the gate, his heart beat a little faster, his playing almost wavered. Watching her cross the floor to the table which was always reserved for her, Avelino was suddenly overcome with a feeling of disbelief in the reality of the afternoon's events. Janice — and it almost seemed an over-familiarity to use her first name — seemed quite out of his world. In the touristic sophistication of the dance, in the glamour of the string of coloured lights which stretched like a vine around the enclosure, she appeared more beautiful and poised than ever.

As she passed the orchestra, she glanced up at Avelino with a quick smile and the exciting reality flooded back in him. At the same time however, he felt a twinge of embarrassment. He knew all about the sort of gossip that swept from door to door through the town. It was a gossip which would certainly not approve of his relationship with a woman so much older than himself — although there might be certain sections of the community who might be rather proud of it in their old age and others envious in their young. However, he had been sufficiently imbued with the spirit of the small town to feel some awe at its mass opinion.

Nonetheless she had smiled at him. It had happened. He glanced from the corner of his eyes at the rest of the orchestra. Nobody seemed to have noticed. Why should they? Any beautiful tourist might smile at the band.

By the time Avelino rose to sing into the microphone, Janice was dancing with someone who looked like a Frenchman. Her eyes, over his shoulder sparked, sometimes, in Avelino's direction, and he felt a surge of excitement and power from the secret intimacy he had with this woman.

The song he was singing was a soulful one of his being all alone, and his dark brown eyes as he sang swept the jostling throng of dancers, resting finally in a glimpse of fierce recognition on Janice. Each time she responded to his look, half-closing her eyes at him, or smiling slightly.

At the end of the dance she followed her usual habit of refusing to join the Frenchman's table. Nor did she, throughout the evening, in spite of repeated requests, which Avelino, his neck hot from the sight, witnessed, accept any of a number of similar requests.

She was still being asked to dance, however, when the night came to a close with the final quick waltz, from which couples retired continuously to their table in a flood of laughter at the mad whirl.

Unable to keep his eyes from her, and uncertain yet of the power of their relationship, Avelino watched with a growing feeling of jealousy against her partner who was a handsome young Spanish tourist he had seen strolling around the town.

But, once again, at the end of the dance, there was a little clinging to the hand by the Spaniard, a polite and smiling shaking of the head from the woman, and once more she had brushed her way back to her table to finish the drink she had poured for herself from the miniature bottle of benedictine she had ordered.

Many people sat quietly chatting, recovering from the dance, after the orchestra had stopped for the last time that evening.

The coloured lights around the enclosing trellis lit up the animation of the faces. Far out over the sea, a crescent moon shone amongst the stars, lighting up, in turn, the calm sea. It shone in great puddles of light on the water, silver against the surrounding black.

From a nearby bar, packed with people in its turn, the music of a radio floated faintly to the dance-floor and one or two couples got up to dance to the ghost music while the orchestra packed away its instruments and the dismantling of the microphone wire to the amplifiers was begun.

Janice sat, cross-legged and lovely, watching the orchestra as it disbanded.

Avelino took his time about packing his clarinet into its case. He tried to appear casual, but eventually was unable to avoid raising his eyes towards the spot where Janice was sitting.

Immediately he looked in her direction, she made a little motion towards him with her hand and her eyes invited him to join her.

He waved back, almost surreptitiously, and hesitated, a hesitation due in part to his youthful embarrassment in being seen associating with this rich, sophisticated-looking woman and in part to his knowledge of the explosion of curiosity and speculation it would give rise to in the village. But against these arose a feeling of sheer pride that he should be the only man she had any desire to ask to her table — and that all those sitting in the enclosure would see it.

Pride triumphed and with a casual farewell to his

colleagues, he strolled with studied unconcern towards her table.

He was aware of the eyes which turned and followed him as he reached her table, aware of the murmuring voices which accompanied them. He looked only at the table and at her.

Janice's eyes were laughing as she invited him to order himself a drink.

'You sang beautifully,' she said. 'I can't understand why everyone in Spain thinks Frank Sinatra's so wonderful.'

'They're used to voices like mine, but everything about the faraway world of North America seems wonderful,' he explained.

'Then you should go where you'd be more appreciated – back to Barcelona with me, for example,' she retorted.

Avelino glanced at her, startled, and she laughed merrily and he laughed and the drinks arrived.

Around them seated parties were still speculating on the event of the past few minutes and the old fishermen and young yokels, who formed a permanent leaning border on the townside rail of the enclosure, stared openly and avidly. Soon the news would have spread throughout the town in spite of the late hour. And in the morning the many who knew would be delighted to pass on this titbit of gossip to the few who didn't.

'Do you go straight home after the dances?' Janice asked, after they had been talking for some time.

'Generally I do, but it doesn't matter if I'm late,' Avelino replied.

'Good. If you'd care to walk home with me, I'll make coffee and we can have another drink.'

Avelino had agreed from the sheer unexpectedness of her blunt invitation, before, once again, doubts assailed him in a tempest. What would they think when they saw him leaving the dance with her? Where did she live? Did she live alone? What would they think if they saw him going into her house at this time of night? What excuse could he give to his parents when, as was inevitable, they heard about it?

He had answered none of these questions before he found himself, feeling completely unequal to what was taking place, strolling out of the enclosure with Janice, bidding casual goodnights to the townsfolk clustered around the entrance.

They wandered away from the still crowded enclosure and were soon beyond the streams of light flung out from its centre.

On the dusty coast road, cut off from the sea in places by a low wall against which the surf dashed, in others by sudden, expansive beaches specked with still, shadowy fishing boats, they walked.

Here and there a young couple were sitting on the sea-side parapet, or the quiet animation of old men's voices and the smell of strong tobacco would drift from a patch of shadow. The moon was a thin crescent.

As if Avelino's doubts had been spoken aloud, Janice made no motion to move in close to him or to hold his hand as he had thought she might. He was relieved, but, at the same time, the fact that she made no move in that direction, filled him with an overwhelming longing to do so.

He could see her charming, clear-cut profile as they strolled and the black stole she wore gave a pale, moonlit beauty to her skin.

As the sound and the glitter of the bars in the main plaza began to dwindle and appear only occasionally — and each time more distant as the road curved out around promontories which jutted deeply into the sea — Janice dispelled one of his unspoken doubts.

'I've rented a house here,' she explained. 'It's about the last one we come to before the wilds.'

He knew the house now. It had one Moorish turret at the eastern end, was set back from the coast road and surrounded by a small, sparse plantation of olive trees. It was doubtful whether anyone would see them go in. Already the road was deserted, although there was the cliff restaurant further on which sent a late-night wave of tourists along the road, singing and buffooning.

Beyond the house, the coast road began to cut through the hills as the coast itself became high, rocky cliffs. It wended a lonely way through scrub-covered hills to the next town some miles distant. During the day little bands of people wandered along it looking for a comfortable place to picnic. At night its only occupants were the carabinieros, patrolling in couples in the green uniforms which looked so like the scrub, in their interminable watch for smuggling.

'Here we are,' Janice said quietly, as they reached

the iron gate which opened from the road onto the dusty barren grounds of the house.

Away from the possibility of spectators, Avelino felt the dawning of nervous excitement. His worries concerning the outer world disappeared and he became doubly aware of the woman walking gracefully beside him, and their solitariness. When their hands brushed in walking, his heart pounded and suddenly they were hand in hand and she was close to him, her shoulder pressed against her chest, her hip brushing his, bodies inturned as they walked.

He inclined his head and kissed her gently on the forehead. Her fingers squeezed his and he felt suddenly overcome with a gush of feeling for her. He drew her round to him and she raised her head, pressing her body tightly against him. Their lips brushed gently and then locked in a fierce devouring.

They drew apart and then together again and then she whispered:

'Quickly, it is so comfortable inside.'

They walked on, slowly and entwined towards the great, brooding shadow of the house. It was a still phantom, solitary and eerie as they moved into the stone patio with its shadowy entrance arches. Around them in the grounds were the thin shadows of the olive trees, above them the dark blankness of the hills, behind them the moon glittering on the sea.

'Aren't you afraid to live here alone?' Avelino whispered.

'No. I like it,' she whispered back, gently mocking his awe. 'I get so tired of the city with interminable people, cars, complications all around me. I love the simplicity of all this — the sea, the hills, all the elemental things and sweet uncomplicated people.'

Avelino was silent for a moment, considering what she had said, while she unlocked the heavy, wooden, blue-painted door.

'Have you had a *very* unhappy life?' he asked eventually.

He followed her into the dark vestibule, listened to her fumbling for the switch.

'It's been all my own doing,' she replied, answering several questions ahead. 'A question of reading, studying, idealising, searching, reforming, trying to find a solution for the happiness of society and making oneself miserable into the bargain.'

She shut up suddenly as if aware of the fact that he would not be understanding her. But Avelino had read a few books, mainly about fallen men and women and he felt some inkling of her problem.

'Are you happy now — at this moment?' he asked.

He felt her move away from the switch in the darkness. He felt her hands on his chest, her lips against his with the soft, warm touch of the sun.

'Yes, at the moment I am happy,' she breathed.

She whisked away before he had time to hold her and the light went on, that soft, inadequate light of the low-wattage bulbs which were necessary when the influx of tourists made the demand on the power too great.

Avelino followed her from the vestibule into a long, blue room with modern furniture of varnished olive and a high ceiling with dark beams. She pulled back the heavy blue curtains which covered the French windows, opened the windows and then the heavy shutters which led out onto the verandah. Moonlight streamed into the room as she turned off the light.

She came close to him again and he felt stifled with emotion as she laid her blonde head gently on his shoulder in a gesture which seemed to demand his protection.

'It's quite romantic,' she said softly in a tone which hinted that she was trying to laugh at herself, but couldn't.

'It's very beautiful,' Avelino whispered, looking out over the glistening sea as if he were seeing it for the first time.

'How long can you stay?' she asked.

'An hour or two.'

'Let's go to bed.'

Avelino's heart began to pummel in him at her words. He tried to hide a fresh fit of quivering.

As if, with some incredible thought, she were afraid he was going to refuse, she caught his hand and drew him gaily towards the door.

'The bedroom is pink,' she laughed. 'I'm very traditional really.'

Avelino allowed himself to be pulled after her, passion and longing fighting with images of his mother looking at the clock in their strict austere home.

'I mustn't stay too long,' he said.

She looked round at him with a happy smile of triumph.

'Go now if you're afraid,' she mocked.

In answer he pulled her to him with a swift jerk and they seemed to sweep fluidly into each other in a fury of desperate passion. Avelino felt lost – completely lost. He was no longer master of himself. He was in a great deep pit whose bottom he could not see. All the longing of his adolescence had turned against him, weakening his mind so that in this first, sympathetic, beautiful contact he found a reason for living.

'I love you,' he whispered as if he were in agony. 'I love you.'

She drew her head away from him so that he could see her hazel eyes vaguely glinting in the moonlight, the shadows hollowing her face, tracing the clear lines of the bones. Her eyes were searching him as if she, now, was afraid, and then her lips had closed with his in an engulfing pressure.

The bedroom led from a short white corridor and was furnished in similar style to the first room they had entered. Janice turned on shaded wall-lights on each side of the bed and the room was suffused with the pink of the walls, carpets and draperies. The bed was enormous and low. It might have passed for a divan but for its size. Avelino was still trembling with anticipation as he looked at it, shadowy and inviting in the dim light.

It seemed too wonderful, too incredible to be true that in a short time he would again be holding this woman, naked, in his arms, this time in the warmth and comfort of a bed.

'Do you like the room?' she asked him gaily. He

had the impression that she, too, was trembling.

'It's delightful,' he said, contrasting it mentally with his own adequate but bleak bedroom which he shared with his brothers at home.

He wandered across the room to look at a set of red, leather bound books in a varnished bookcase and when he turned back Janice had already removed her dress.

She stood looking at him, almost coyly, a vague and graceful sylph. Her breasts were hardly covered in the provocative bulging by the small black brassiere – and the flimsy black briefs with their frilly edge creased tightly in the triangle of her abdomen. He could see the brown tautness of the flesh of her ribs, taut enough to accentuate enormously the proud thrust of her breasts.

She moved towards him and the flesh of her thighs rippled in sinuous hollows.

Avelino stood rooted to the spot, gazing at her. He was unable to move, could only wait for her to come. Forming a great jut under his thin trousers, his penis was hot and pulsing. He felt helpless against its pulsing and its jutting. He was aware only of her, a movement of firm, beautiful flesh towards him and the enormous, scorching tingle at the lower tip of his loins.

She reached him and as she clasped him the tenderness and love he now felt for her made his longing even stronger.

Her hands clasped his neck and pulled his face down against hers so that their cheeks caressed. At the other intimate end of her she pressed and jiggled against him, rubbing up and down against the hard protuberance of his erection.

With a feeling of despair that they were two people rather than one, Avelino buried his lips in her neck and moved his hands quiveringly down the smooth, flawless skin of her back. As his exploring fingers reached the start of the outward bulge of her hips, he strained her against him. And then his hands moved on down her body until they were cupping her buttocks in a sensual ecstasy of their own. He forced her hips in at his, crushing her against his penis until it hurt him, torturing himself.

Her buttocks were smooth and hard as she strained into him and then she relaxed and her buttocks relaxed and expanded fully into his hands.

She kissed his throat and began, at the same time, to unbutton his shirt. His whole body was trembling slightly now as his shirt came open all the way down and she eased it gently out from his trousers and helped him to pull it off his arms.

She kissed his chest tenderly and her own hands seemed to indulge in a tremoring delirium as she stroked his back, his sides and then moved down to his fly buttons.

Avelino was panting. He found it impossible to keep still as she jerked the top button open. His stomach hollowed and expanded, his hips writhed gently as if a great outside force were making them do it.

Her hands had nearly completed their work. He waited tensely for the first touch of her deftly moving fingers on the thin tissue of his pants. As he felt it he jerked his hips away and she ripped undone the last few buttons.

His trousers fell to the floor, a ridiculous pile around his ankles and he stepped out of them, revelling in the sensual freedom of the cool air on his limbs.

Janice slipped away from him and went towards the bed, stripping off her brassiere and her briefs. He watched her buttocks swaying as she walked.

At the bed she turned towards him and there once again, but more charged with sex than during the afternoon, were the heavy breasts and the naked slimness with the broad roundness of the hips. She was lovely. She looked fragile, but a fragility which he longed to take and massage in his hands, to all but break.

'Take your pants off,' she said softly.

Avelino reached down and untied his espadrilles. Where the tapes had been around his bare ankles they had left shallow red weals and he massaged the flesh for a moment, feeling slightly embarrassed, hoping she might get into bed. But she stayed where she was, looking at his strong, graceful body appraisingly.

After a moment's hesitation he slipped his pants from his hips, his strong penis flipping into view as he bent pushing the garment down his legs. His penis felt hot and clammy. he had a blind, helpless feeling like a bat brought suddenly into light.

When he had kicked his pants away and looked up, Janice's eyes were fastened on his organ and her mouth was slightly open. She moved her gaze up his body until their eyes met. Her breasts were heaving and there was a shade of anguish in her eyes.

For a moment they gazed at each other. Avelino

gulped. He had no control over the tremoring of his body. Janice moved her hands up to her breasts as if she would try to still their rise and fall and she breathed, almost as if to herself the one word: 'Come.'

Avelino stepped swiftly towards her, crushing the rug under his bare feet. He felt his testicles sway and brush against his thighs as he moved.

She waited for him to reach her hand as the impact came, her mouth opened wide and her arms swept around him . . . Their naked flesh seemed to fuse, their bodies to suck at each other, flesh against flesh in gentle pressure and oozing.

She bit at his lips as he kissed her and then her tongue was worming silkily into his mouth and she was drawing him back to the bed. The covers were drawn back and she allowed herself to fall backwards onto the soft sheets, pulling Avelino down with her.

His organ was pressing hotly against the soft, cool flesh of her thighs and the weight of a great animal instinct raged in his loins.

Janice moved one arm away from his shoulders and whipped the covers over them so that he felt the soft caress of a sheet on his back. The feeling of the covers gave him a sensation of comfort and exclusiveness as if they were in a little home of their own from which they need never go out.

For a while they lay together, he warm on top of the soft, flesh cushion of her breasts and hips. There seemed no hurry. Avelino suddenly didn't care. The whole night was ahead of them.

They kissed over and over again and from the

pink warmth of the bed, he heard her voice whisper:

'Why don't you come back to Barcelona with me?'

'To Barcelona!'

'Yes. It would be wonderful.'

Her fingers caressed his hair and his ears.

'Oh, it would be impossible. I am too poor and my mother would think I was mad.'

Her lips brushed against his cheek and came to rest close to his ear.

'You would live with me and I would give you money. I have far too much.'

'I could not take money from you in that way.' Avelino's pride was piqued. The thought of living on a woman was too much for him.

'Why not?'

'It would not be fair to you. It is the man's job to earn the money.'

She laughed softly and kissed him passionately on the lips.

'It would be more than fair to me,' she said. 'My money has done nothing but make me miserable up to now. If I choose to give you some to make myself happy, you should be pleased at the way it shows I love you.'

The words came as a shock to Avelino. Greater than the shock he had experienced when he had been chosen to sing with the local orchestra. *I love you.* They filled him with a warm, wonderful feeling which brought tears to his eyes. They made everything sure and the world evolved from a half phantom to reality.

'You love me?' he whispered.

Her arms moved around his neck in reply and the pressure was so great that when she kissed him his lips were crushed back on his teeth and he could hardly breathe.

'I love you,' she answered softly.

Under him her thighs wriggled apart and caught his penis between them, squeezing it gently between the walls of now warm flesh. His genitals seemed to break out in a sweat.

Gently Janice levered him off her and he allowed himself to fall away to her side, willing to be instructed, obedient to her greater knowledge. He subsided on his back with her warmth pressing along his side as she rolled over towards him.

With a quick movement she threw back the covers and his rampant penis, thick and veined, its broad, sensitive tip almost purple from the sensual friction with her thighs, shot into view.

He lay quiet, stroking her breasts with one hand while her eyes wandered down the length of his organ. She reached over and brushed the thick mop of hair away from its protruding rigidity and at her touch his penis gave an involuntary jolt, moving sharply towards his belly and then receding again to the perpendicular. Her eyes moved away over his testicles and her fingers moved away too to stroke them.

Avelino tensed his buttocks, giving himself over to the incredible continuation of the unbelievable set of events which had brought him to this particular place at this time. He closed his eyes and, as he tensed, his penis seemed to elongate a little more and offer itself to Janice like a rigidly rearing snake.

As if the slight movement of tension had been an offering to her lips, she suddenly flopped her head down to his loins and sucked the knob of his organ into her mouth.

At the soft, painful, startling pressure, Avelino opened his eyes. With his entrails contorted in the pain of a new sensation, he saw her, blonde head bent, eyes narrowed in passion, concentration on the gentle sucking. He watched her cheeks hollowing, her lips moving as she sucked and the urgency of his passion seemed to become unbearable.

His hips began to writhe, his sweating buttocks clamping together with each upthrust. He felt her tongue licking at his point of passion as she sucked voraciously. As he began to grunt and his lips breathed her name, she suddenly pulled her head away from his loins, drew her lips from the labour of love.

Sharply she turned on her side, extending her smooth, rounded buttocks toward him. She reached behind her, caught his hips and pulled him over so that he was lying along her back. She pulled one of his hands across the soft flesh of her hip, round to the front of her, across the softly protruding flesh of her abdomen, through the silky hair of her muff and left it at the portals of her moist vagina.

As Avelino began the gentle insertion of his finger, she gasped and undulated her buttocks against his loins so that the firm smoothness of them imprinted itself against him.

Exploring, Avelino found the hard little clitoris

which he had read about in sex books and he massaged it gently while Janice groaned and writhed her buttocks furiously at his loins.

'That's wonderful,' she breathed, almost indistinctly, and she pressed his hand hard against her orifice.

With her writhings, Avelino's penis had ridden up so that it lay along the lips of her vagina, its base lying in the groove of her buttocks. Her thighs were extended in front of her and she drew them up even higher as her hand reached behind her, searching for his penis. She found it, grasped it, squeezed it for a moment and then guided it at her welcoming aperture.

Still caressing her clitoris with his hand, Avelino drove into her vagina from behind. He entered her forcefully with a sensation of hot relief mingled with a passion which drew his lips apart in a gasp.

As he thrust he felt the tautness of her buttocks against his loins. He pushed his other hand under her body and caressed the globes of her breasts.

Already excited from the caress of her lips, Avelino felt his loins to be a tangle of tortured nerve ends. Janice, too, was already gasping and moaning with a great gush of feeling.

Brokenly, between her gasps, she whispered words to him and Avelino moved his face against hers to hear as his penis slipped in and in with a soft slippery facility.

'I'll kneel,' she was trying to say. 'That way you go deeper. It is better for both of us.'

'All right.'

She knelt up, moving onto her hands and her knees and he got to his knees with her, leaving his penis vibrating inside her as they moved.

She lay her head on the pillow and her back sloped up towards him, broadening into the buttocks between which his penis seemed to disappear. She spread her legs, moving her knees wide apart, and, ranged in a kneeling position behind her, Avelino shuffled his knees towards her between her opened thighs.

Now he could see his penis and the pink folds of flesh into which it was searing. He could also see the little ruffle of flesh, pink and hairless which was the slit between her stretched buttocks. It was the first time he had had this view of a woman and it filled him with a lust which was quite apart from his feeling of tender passion for Janice.

Moving his hands over her buttocks, he rammed into her with growing ferocity. He could see the thick stub of his flesh withdrawing in wet rapidity and then plunging into her intimate passage again until his hips cannoned into the soft buffer of her rump.

Clasping her hips tightly so that his fingers dug red marks into her brown flesh, he surged into her, swivelling his hips for greater pressure. Her passage contracted around him, sucking him in in a tight embrace. She moved her hands helplessly on the sheets and then lifted her arms behind her, reaching back to clasp his hips and pull him at her with greater force.

Feeling her fingers on his hips, virtually asking for even more, Avelino pushed her knees wider apart with his own and leaned heavily with his hands on her back, forcing her bottom up towards him. He thrust in and then left his penis in her to its full extent while he moved his abdomen against the soft flesh of her behind, from side to side so that he felt fresh stabs of exquisite agony from their flesh brushing lightly together – and then he began the punishing piston movement again, slowly, powerfully.

Gasping, groaning in a complement to her gasping, groaning, he felt her hands release his hips and brush down under her own thighs to gently grasp and caress his testicles. She fondled each separately, writhing her bottom on the end of his raging penis and he felt a fresh injection of passion from the cool touch of her fingers on the heat of his hairy lobes.

Janice began to cough out sounds from her throat until he was not sure whether he was hurting her or whether it was some choking passion. With a great effort he slowed his stabs of penetration, but immediately she forced her widespread crotch against him.

'No, no! Don't stop!' she pleaded. And her hands moved back to his hips, trying to reach right round to his buttocks to pull him more forcefully at her offered opening.

With that encouragement, Avelino bored into her again with such strong strokes that his abdomen felt bruised against her buttocks. Each thrust flattened the light brown globes of flesh as he gave a last upward flick of his organ.

'Now, now! It's coming, it's coming,' she breathed in broken, staccato tones.

With the sweat glistening lightly on his upper lip and his forehead, Avelino slowed his strokes to thickening, grinding penetrations behind which his whole body flexed and surged. His lips curled away from his teeth in the sheer barbarous sight of the woman prostrate at the mercy of his loins. He swooped his head swiftly and kissed her back and inside him there was the hot, burning sensation of hot liquid simmering.

It grew and grew into a great crushing at his penis, a sucking as if his inside was being siphoned through the tube towards the open channel. He felt powerless. Nothing could have interfered with the movement now. Had it meant he was to die if he shot into her, he couldn't have stopped himself.

She was pleading with him to hurry, seeming to hold herself back, waiting for him to reach his climax.

He felt the overwhelming weight of an undefinable sensation gathering from the root of his being, seeking for an outlet. He was panting furiously, his belly heaving. He began to breathe her name with every thrust and as he felt the weight too much to bear, sensed with gritted teeth the inevitable breaking, he in turn shouted: 'Now, now!'

Another thrust and another and Janice uttered a sudden long, low whine and her channel seemed to open to three times its size and at the same moment, the hot liquid rushed, seeming to whirl inside him and then burst, in an agony of contorting buffets and cries, from him. Each release, like a spurt from a machine gun, gave him a gorgeous relief. Throughout his emptying into her he uttered one long, low moan and her flushed face, swung in agony from side to side on the pillow.

With the last weakening thrust, he flopped forward around her, kissing her neck and after a moment she collapsed on her face so that he lay along her back, his penis deflating and slipping out of her to nestle in its shrivelled state against the join of her buttocks.

They lay there for some seconds, breathing heavily, and then he rolled from her and buried his face in her breasts, overcome with emotion.

'I love you. I love you,' he almost sobbed into the tight, brown flesh of her soothing mounds. Gently she stroked his head. There was a glint of happiness in her eyes.

'Frank' and I

A spanker's tale with a breeches part, this confession of a Victorian gent has much to offer the connoisseur. When an orphaned boy, 'Frank', is offered a home by the philanthropic Squire Charles it is indeed an honest gesture and proffered with no ulterior motive. But, as is usually the way with philanthropic gentlemen in tales of this nature, chance now throws in the way of our hero a means of gratifying those lustful urges which inevitably dictate his conduct. For Charley is a 'lover of the rod' and makes no bones about the pleasure he takes from applying a cane, a slipper, a birch branch — any damn thing at all — to the naked and wriggling posterior of a youthful miscreant. Inevitably, young 'Frank' commits a crime, his sentence is sure and then, what luck for the philanthropic Charley —

'I tucked his shirt up and began to apply the rod and, as I was angry with him, I laid on the cuts smartly all over the surface of his white bottom. He wriggled, writhed and cried as the stinging strokes fell with a swishing sound on his plump, firm flesh . . . He drew up his legs one after the other and then kicked them out again, he jerked his hips from side to side, half turning over on to his side for a moment, so that I saw the front part of his naked body. And what I saw paralyzed me with astonishment, causing my uplifted arm to drop to my side, and the rod to slip from my grasp. In that momentary glimpse, I had caught sight of a little pink-lipped cunt, shaded at the upper part with a slight growth of curly, golden down.

'"*Frank*" *was a girl!*'

From now on, of course, Charley has it made. Here is the scene in which 'Frank' finally comes clean and Charley takes full advantage.

I was detained in London longer than I had expected; but I received a letter nearly every day from 'Frank,' and I could see from the way she wrote, that she was pining for me, and longing for my return. I also wished to go back to her; I often thought of her, and I did not go near Maud, but lived in chambers close to my club.

At last the day came when I was able to leave London, and I felt quite glad to find myself in the train on my way to Winchester.

When I arrived at the station, my dog-cart was waiting for me and in a short time I reached Oakhurst, where I found 'Frank' on the terrace, waiting to receive me. She welcomed me warmly, her face beaming, and her eyes glistening; but as we were under the observation of the servants, she had to suppress all outward show of emotion, but I saw that she was much moved.

As it was rather late, I proceeded at once to my room and changed my clothes, then I went down to the dining-room, and we took our seats at the table. During dinner, 'Frank' did not talk much; she appeared to be quietly happy, there was a soft light in her eyes, she did not bother me with questions, and she seemed perfectly content to sit and look at me. When dinner was over, and I had smoked a cigar, we went into the drawing-room. It was a beautiful evening; the sun had been set for some time, and it was beginning to get dark; the long windows were open, and a gentle breeze wafted into the room the sweet scent of the roses which grew in profusion in the garden. On a tree, not far off, a nightingale was just commencing to sing, giving forth every now and then a few mellow notes; all else was still. It was an ideal night for love-making.

I was sitting in a low easy-chair, and 'Frank' was sitting on a stool beside me. We were both silent; the light faded, and the room grew darker. She put her hand on my arm, and nestling close up to me said, 'Oh, I am so glad you are back! I have missed you dreadfully.'

There was such a loving tone in the girl's voice that it made me think she was about to tell me her long concealed secret: so I put my arm round her waist in lover-like fashion, for the first time, and whispered in her ear:

'Why did you miss me?'

I could feel her tremble as I pressed her waist; she made no answer, but she rested her head on my breast and heaved a long, tremulous sigh.

'Why do you sigh? What is the matter with you, *Frank*?' I said, emphasizing the name.

Still she kept silent. The nightingale burst into full song, its liquid trills filling the air with melody; I pressed her closer to me, and bending over her, said coaxingly, 'Tell me, *Frank*.'

Then she suddenly threw her arms round my neck, murmuring in a voice choked with emotion: 'Oh, don't call me Frank! My name is Frances, I am a woman, and I love you! I love you!'

My heart bounded with a feeling of joy and gratification. The confession had come at last! My patience was rewarded!

I lifted her off the stool on to my lap, and folding her in my arms, I kissed her passionately, on her eyes, her forehead, her cheeks, and her warm mouth. It was too dark to see her face, but as my lips pressed her soft cheeks, I could feel that they were hot with blushes; and she lay like a little child in my arms, her bosom rising and falling quickly.

After a moment or two, I said: 'I knew you were a girl, Frances!' She started, and uttering a little cry of intense astonishment, asked: 'How long have you known it? How did you find it out?'

'I have know it for a long time. I found it out by seeing something you accidently showed me on the day I birched you so severely.'

'Oh! Good gracious!' she exclaimed in a horrified tone. I laughed, and stopped her mouth with a kiss, saying: 'What does it matter when or how I found it out. You have said that you love me, and I love you.'

'Oh, do you really? I am so, *so* glad. I was afraid you would be angry with me. I have been wishing for a long time, to tell you I was a girl, but I never had the courage to speak,' she said in a low voice, clinging close to me. Then, after a pause, she asked timidly: 'Why did you not tell me that you had found out I was a girl?'

'Because it would have caused bother, and altered all my arrangements; besides I preferred to wait until you told me yourself. I felt sure you would tell me some day; and I am glad the day has come at last. You are now my sweetheart, you dear girl,' I said, kissing her.

'Oh! how patient and good you have been to me all these years; and how happy I feel at being your sweetheart,' she said, in a voice vibrating with emotion. Then she got off my lap, and sitting down on the stool, put her little hand on mine and pressed it warmly.

'Now,' I said, 'tell me when you first began to love me.'

'Oh, I began to love you the day you took me into your house, when I was homeless and friendless, and ever since that time, my love for you has been growing greater and greater.'

'Did you never feel angry with me when I whipped you?'

'No, never. Of course I did not like getting a whipping, as it was painful; − the rod was dreadful − but somehow or other, I seemed to love you more after you had given me a spanking.' Then, after a pause, she added rather bashfully: 'And I will confess to you, that at one time, I used to be naughty on purpose that you might spank me; for I liked to lie across your knees, and feel your hand stroking my bare skin; although I dreaded the pain that was to follow; for you always made me smart a great deal.'

I laughed at this queer confession, but was pleased to hear it, for it showed that the girl had a rather voluptuous disposition. Then I said: 'So it gave you pleasure to lie across my knees, and feel my hand stroking your bare skin? Well, I shall be delighted to let you have that pleasure now, if you like.'

She made no answer, but gave my hand a squeeze, which I took as a sign of assent; so I at once lifted her up, placed her in position, and took down her trousers; which I had not let down for upwards of six months.

It was too dark for me to see her bottom, but nevertheless I had great sensual pleasure in passing my hand over the swelling hemispheres of plump, firm flesh, which I stroked, squeezed, and played with in all sorts of ways, for a minute or two.

'Did you like that, Frances?' I asked, when I had done paddling with her bottom. 'Oh, yes!' she replied, still lying face downwards on my lap. 'It was very nice. It gave me a most pleasant sensation.'

I smiled; and to give her another sensation, I put my hand under her belly, and gently touched, for the first time, her virgin cunt. She started, and a tremor passed over her: then I took away my hand from the 'spot,' as I did not wish to frighten her by going too fast. I intended, however, to take her maidenhead that night – and I did not think she would object – but I meant to do the job comfortably in my own bed later on; so I put her on her feet, kissed her, and told her to button up. Then I rang for lights, as it had become pitch dark in the room. In a few moments, one of the servants came, and after lighting all the lamps, went away again. Then I looked at Frances, who was sitting demurely on a chair at some distance from me; and, as soon as she caught my eye, she blushed, but instantly came to me, and perching herself on my knees, laid her cheek against mine, with a low sigh of perfect contentment; saying: 'Oh, how nice it is not to have any secret between us!'

'Yes; it is very pleasant. We are lovers now; so you must give me a nice kiss.' She laughed softly and at once pressed her cherry lips to mine, kissing me warmly, and repeatedly. She had never kissed a man before, and no man but myself had ever kissed, or touched her in any way. It was most delicious to feel her virgin lips pressed against mine, and to inhale her fragrant breath: and it was also extremely pleasant to feel her soft bottom pressing against my upright prick, as she sat on my lap. I wondered if she could feel the peg underneath her!

I thought it was now time to speak plainly to my sweetheart. She loved me, and she was a clever girl, who had read a great deal; therefore she, no doubt, had a very clear idea of what generally happens when a man and a woman love each other. I said: 'Frances, I have something to say to you. We love each other, and tonight we will set the seal on our mutual love. You understand what I mean?'

She blushed rosy red, and hid her face in my breast; then, after a moment's hesitation, said in a low, but firm voice: 'Yes. I understand. I love you, and will do anything you wish.'

I raised her head, and kissed her on the lips, saying affectionately: 'I love you too. You are a darling girl.'

She slipped off my knees, and seated herself in a chair, looking at me timidly, and I saw that she was rather frightened at the thought of what was before her. And I must say, that under the circumstances, her timidity was only what one would have expected. Her 'courtship' had been short; my 'proposal' had been sudden, and the 'marriage' was to be consummated that night. No wonder the girl was a little startled!

I did not bother her with talk, but I rang the bell, and ordered the servant to bring up a bottle of champagne, and some cake. In a short time, the cake and wine were placed on the table; then I told Frances to cut her 'wedding cake,' which she did, smiling a little, and we both ate a piece. Filling her glass with champagne, I made her drink it, and at the same time I drank her health as the 'bride,' making a joking little speech which amused her, and the wine exhilarated her, so her face soon lost its timid look; she again became the loving girl, and she seated herself beside me; not talking much, but holding my hand in hers, and occasionally looking up at me, with a soft, lovelight shining in her pretty blue eyes, and a slight smile dimpling the corners of her ripe, red lips.

I do not know whether the 'blushing bride' felt impatient, or not, but to me, the 'ardent bridegroom,' the time seemed to pass very slowly; and when the big ormolu clock on the mantelpiece chimed eleven, I rose from my seat, and tucking Frances' hand under my arm, said: 'Come along dear; it is time to go to bed.' Then I led her out of the drawing-room, and upstairs into the long corridor, off which both our bedrooms opened. To get to my room we had to pass her 'virgin bower,' but she never faltered as we went by the door, and in another moment we were in my room, where we were sure to be undisturbed, as all the servants slept in another wing of the old house.

My chamber was large, and was handsomely furnished as a bed-sitting-room, with tables, cabinets, sofa, and easy chairs: there were some good pictures on the walls, and the polished oak floor was partially covered with fine, old Eastern rugs. The bedstead was a big, brass one, with ample room in it for two persons. I turned up the flame of a tall, pedestal lamp, and I also lighted all the wax candles in two Dresden china candelabra, which were on the mantelpiece, as I wanted the room to be brilliantly illuminated, so that I might have a good view of my 'bride's' charms.

But the fact of my 'bride' being at that moment dressed as a man, made me feel rather inclined to laugh. However, the masculine attire would soon be off, and then the feminine figure would be revealed in all its naked beauty.

Kissing her as she stood bashfully in the middle of the room; I said: 'Now, Frances, I want you to undress yourself, as I am longing to see the whole of your figure quite naked. You know I have often seen half of it bare.' A little blush marked her cheeks, but she smiled, saying: 'Very well. I will do as you wish.' Then she quietly took off her coat and waistcoat, collar and tie; and sitting down for a moment, pulled off her shoes and socks; next she unfastened her braces, unbuttoned her trousers, and let them slip down her legs on to the floor; finally, after a moment's pause, she drew off her shirt and undershirt, and throwing them on the floor, stood before me, perfectly naked. She trembled a little, and her sense of modesty made her instinctively assume the attitude of the Venus de Medici: one arm stretched downwards, the hand hiding the secret spot, the other arm raised and held across her bosom; her head was turned aside, her eyes were cast down, and she was blushing scarlet from her brow to the upper part of her breast – even her ears were red.

I gazed with admiration, and also with a strong feeling of lust, at the pretty, naked, virgin girl. Her skin was smooth and white as alabaster; she was as plump as a partridge, and her figure was beautifully proportioned in every way; her small, well-shaped head was gracefully poised on her slim neck; her arms were well-formed; her bubbies were fully developed, round as apples, and firm looking, standing well out from her bosom, and tipped with small, erect, rosebud-like nipples; her belly was broad, and smooth; and her little cunt, which she was trying to screen with her hand, was shaded with soft, silky, golden hair.

When I had sufficiently feasted my eyes on the front part of her charming figure, I turned her round, and looked with increased admiration at the hinder part of her body – for to me the back view of a naked woman is more pleasing than the front view. Her shape, as seen from behind, was perfect. It presented the true line of beauty and grace, as depicted by Hogarth: the gently sloping shoulders, the smooth, white back, curving slightly in to the fine loins; then the rounded contours of her broad, plump bottom, swelling out in grand curves, and sweeping down to her splendid, round, white thighs, which tapered to her beautifully shaped legs. Her ankles were small, and she had tiny feet without blemish, the toes tipped with little pink nails.

I did not touch her, and she let me inspect her, standing quite still; like a beautiful statue; only instead of the lovely figure being cold marble, it was warm flesh and blood.

Putting my arms round her, I lifted her up, carried her to the bed, and stretched her upon it at full length; then, after I had undressed myself, I put out the lamp and most of the candles, but I left several burning, so that the room was still well lighted.

The girl never moved, but lay just as I had put her, flat upon her back, on the outside of the bed; she had covered her blushing face with both her hands, and I noticed that every now and then a slight tremor passed over her whole body.

However, before making the grand assault, there was a final preparation to be made; and that was to spread something on the bed to prevent it being stained by her blood; so I got a couple of large bath towels, and put them doubled, underneath her loins, bottom and thighs.

The victim was on the altar, ready for the sacrifice!

Burning with a fierce desire, I got on the bed, clasped her lithe, yielding body in my arms, and pressed my hand in all directions over her deliciously smooth, satin-like, white skin. I toyed with her beautiful, round, firm bubbies, squeezing the elastic flesh, and gently pinching the tiny, pink nipples which seemed to stiffen slightly at the touch of my fingers. I stroked her soft belly; ran my hand up and down her thighs; and felt the calves of her legs. Then turning her over on to her face, I played with her magnificent bottom in all sorts of ways; I smoothed it, I pinched it gently, and I spanked it slightly; I put my hand in the division between the cheeks and separating them a little, I looked at the little violet spot in the middle; then grasping with both hands the plump firm flesh, I pressed it with my fingers till the blood came and went. She never made a movement, but I could feel her body quiver every now and then. I turned her over on to her back again, and burying my face in the warm valley between her titties, I kissed them all over; and taking in my mouth one of her little nipples, I nibbled it, at the same time inhaling with pleasure, the sweet, subtle, feminine odour which always emanates from the body of a clean, healthy young woman. I then looked at her small, virgin cunt, kissed it, and laying my hand upon it, gently put my forefinger between its lips, making the girl shrink convulsively, and utter a startled little cry; and at the same time, she instinctively pulled my hand away from the 'spot.'

I prepared for action. 'Frances,' I said, 'the moment

has come. What I am going to do to you, will give you a little pain at first; but afterwards, you will experience nothing but pleasure when I do it to you. Do you feel much frightened?'

'No,' she whispered; but nevertheless she looked a little alarmed, as she lay before me, naked and palpitating, waiting for the stroke.

I stretched out her legs as widely as possible, then, after placing myself in position to make the assault, I separated with my fingers the tightly closed lips of her little cunt and inserted the tip of my prick; the girl, as she felt the stiff member entering her body, shrunk away from me slightly, and uttered a little cry. I pressed my lips upon her mouth, and laid my breast upon her naked, heaving bosom; then putting my hands under her, and taking hold of the cheeks of her bottom, I began to fuck her with long, slow strokes, each thrust forcing my prick a little deeper into her tight cunt which clipped my member closely in a warm embrace. The sensation was delightful! With a few vigorous movements of my loins, I gradually drove the weapon further and further into the sheath; the pain making the girl wince and groan; but she could not help moving her bottom briskly up and down to meet my thrusts. I worked away, till at last the tip of my tool touched the maidenhead which barred the passage. And now, the increased pain she felt as I battered away at the tough membrane, caused her to utter little squeaks, but she did all she could to help me; wriggling, arching her loins, heaving up her bottom, and pressing me to her bosom. I poked away as hard as I could, and she bounded under me, groaning, and squeaking. I thought the membrane would never yield. I paused for a moment to recover my breath; then taking a fresh hold of her bottom, I recommenced fucking her with increased vigour, making her quiver all over; but she managed to gasp out between her squeaks and groans: 'Oh! Oh! You – are – hurting – me – dreadfully!'

At last I felt the thing beginning to yield, and after a few more powerful thrusts, her maidenhead gave way; she uttered a sharp cry of pain, and my prick buried itself to the roots in her cunt. Then, a few short digs finished the affair; the supreme moment arrived, the delicious spasm seized me, and I spent profusely, pouring out a torrent of boiling sperm, while she gasped, squirmed, and wriggled her bottom furiously, uttering little squeaks of mingled pleasure and pain as the hot stuff spurted in gushes up her lacerated cunt. And when all was over, she lay trembling in my arms, her breath coming and going quickly, her bosom heaving tumultuously, and the flesh of her bottom twitching nervously; her cheeks were scarlet, and there was a languorous look in her moist eyes.

As Frances was 'small,' and as I was 'great,' she had suffered a good deal of pain; – much more than a larger made woman would have suffered, – there had been a considerably effusion of blood, and the proof of her virginity was plentifully displayed on the hair of the 'spot,' on her thighs, and on the towels under her bottom. And as soon as she had fairly recovered herself, she noticed the sanguinary stains. 'Oh-h!' she exclaimed in a horrified tone, beginning to cry. 'I am bleeding!'

I kissed her, and soothed her, calling her all sorts of endearing names; telling her that it was nothing, and that every woman bled more or less, the first time she was embraced by a man. She soon grew calm, and smiled at me faintly; then I got a basin of water and a sponge, with which I carefully removed all the traces of my 'bloody' work from her person, and dried her with a soft towel, while she lay, with outstretched legs, and blushing cheeks, looking up at me; finally I got one of my nightshirts, put it on her and made her get between the sheets. I then washed my 'gory weapon,' and got into bed beside her, where she at once cuddled up to me, saying with a deep sigh: 'I am glad it is over. It was very painful, and it did not give me the least pleasure.'

I laughed, saying: 'I suppose it was rather painful. Never mind. You will find that it will give you great pleasure in future.'

She looked rather incredulous, and made a little face, as she laid her head on the pillow. She appeared to be quite worn out; her eyes closed, and in a few moments, she fell fast asleep. Then I got up, extinguished the candles, and crept quietly into bed again, without disturbing the sleeping girl; and soon after I fell asleep myself.

I woke two or three times during the night, each time experiencing a feeling of pleasure, and getting a cockstand at the contact of the girl's plump, warm flesh, but as she still continued to sleep soundly, I did not disturb her. I woke again when it was broad daylight, and on glancing at the clock on the mantelpiece I saw that it was six o'clock. Then, sitting up in the bed, I gazed at Frances, who was lying on her back, sleeping like a child, and looking exquisitely pretty. Her short, curly, golden hair was ruffled over her broad, white forehead; her blue-veined eyelids were closely shut; the long, curved eyelashes resting on her smooth cheeks, which were flushed with a delicate pink tinge like the petals of a rose; her red lips were slightly separated, showing her small, pearl-white teeth; and as the collar of the nightshirt was a little open, I could see the upper part of her titties, which looked like tiny mounds of snow. Bending over her, I pressed my lips upon her rosebud mouth in a long, hot kiss, and she woke up with a little start, looking rather bewildered, as if she could not quite make out where she was; and she gazed at me for a moment, with her big blue eyes wide open, her cheeks at the same time growing very red; then a bright smile lit up her pretty face, and, throwing her arms round my neck, she kissed me, saying: 'Oh, how funny it seems for me to be in bed with you!'

'I think it is very nice,' said I, feeling her bubbies with one hand, and stroking her bottom with the other. 'How did you sleep?'

'Very soundly. I never opened my eyes from the time I went to sleep until you woke me. I was very tired after what happened last night,' she added, glancing at me slyly.

'And sore too, I daresay,' said I, smiling and

pinching her thigh. 'Now let me have a look at the tender spot.' She laughed, and at once laid herself flat down upon her back; then I turned down the bedclothes, and pulled her nightgown up to her chin, so that the whole front part of her lovely body was naked; her delicate skin looking even more beautifully white by daylight, than it had by candlelight.

After I had sufficiently admired the charming spectacle presented by the girl as she lay naked before me, I made her stretch out her legs, and then with my two forefingers, I separated as widely as possible the outer lips of her cunt, and examined the inside of it; finding that it was rather inflamed; the inner lips being a bright pink colour, and also a little swollen; and, on looking up the vagina, I could plainly see the lacerated edges of the ruptured maidenhead. 'Carunculæ myrtiformes,' they are called by surgeons.

'The "spot" looks rather sore,' I said.

'It smarts a little, and I have a feeling as if something was still sticking in it, and stretching it.'

Taking her hand, I placed it on my rampant prick. 'There, Frances,' I said. 'Feel and examine the thing that did all the damage.'

She sat up in the bed, clasped her little white hand round my tool, and gazed at it with eyes round with astonishment, exclaiming: 'Oh! what an enormous thing it is! No wonder it hurt me!'

Then, with her fingers, she measured its length, and pulling back the foreskin, exposed the ruby tip; the appearance of which seemed to amuse her, for she laughed softly. 'Oh, what a funny-looking thing it is,

with its big red knob! I never should have believed that
such a great thing as that could have got into my little'
— she stopped and looked comically at me. She really
did not know what to call her thing.

'Do you know what the things are called?' I asked
her.

'No, I don't. I wish you would tell me,' she replied
eagerly.

I laughed, and told her the names of the various
parts of man and woman, and also all the terms in the
vocabulary of love; and in addition, I explained to her
the different positions in which a man may embrace
a woman. She listened with rapt attention, her cheeks
flushing, and her eyes sparkling at my graphic
descriptions; and during the whole time I was
speaking, she kept hold of my tool, occasionally
squeezing it, and making me feel intensely randy. So
I said: 'That is a very different 'thing' to the one you
felt between little Tom's legs when you spanked him.'

She let go her hold, blushing very red, and gazing
at me in speechless astonishment, and looking so
utterly mystified, that I burst out laughing and told
her how I had seen her spanking the boy, and also
putting her hand under his belly.

'Oh, dear me! Did you see me do that?' she said,
looking a little shamefaced for a moment; then she
added, with a gleam of merriment in her eyes:

'It was such a funny little morsel. It felt just like
a worm. But you must have been surprised to see me
do such a thing?'

'No, I was not,' I replied laughing. 'You had the

boy lying across your knees with his trousers down, and it was quite natural that you should have wished to feel what he had between his legs. You were a big girl at the time, and all big girls like to touch boys' things.' And, I added, 'all big boys like to touch girls's things.'

She looked at me for a moment, with a demure expression on her face, but with a twinkle in her eyes; then she remarked: 'Do they really?'

I rolled her over, pulled her nightgown up, and played with her; paddling with her bubbies, pinching the cheeks of her bottom in turn; pulling the soft, silky hair which covered the 'mon veneris,' and tickling the 'spot,' till she got very excited. Her bosom heaved, a sensuous look came into her eyes, her cheeks flushed, and she stretched out her legs; evidently wishing me to poke her. I was quite ready for the job, so, clasping her in my arms, I got into her; this time without much difficulty, as there was nothing to bar the passage, though it was very tight.

She winced, uttering a low cry as my prick against stretched her sore little cunt, but she braced herself up, clenching her teeth, and holding her breath for a moment. I began to fuck her vigorously, but as slowly as I could, for I wanted to make the pleasure last as long as possible.

My lips were on hers, my breast was on her bosom, my hands gripped the cheeks of her bottom, and at each thrust I drove my prick into her, as far as it would go; then, drawing it out again through the clinging folds of her cunt, till only the tip of the weapon remained in the sheath, I again forced it in up to the hilt, with powerful movements of my loins; making Frances bound and wriggle in voluptuous pain.

It was delicious! She worked her loins vigorously, heaving up her bottom to meet my downthrusts, groaning a little, but embracing me tightly, and evidently enjoying the poke. In a very short time I was obliged to come to the short digs; she wriggled, and squeaked; the spasm seized us both at the same moment, and as I discharged, she came, uttering a long, shuddering sigh, squirming under me, and wriggling her bottom in a most lively fashion; — hugging me tightly, and actually biting my shoulder in her delicious ecstasy, till she had taken in every drop of moisture from my still stiff prick, round which the lips of her cunt clung tightly, as if loath to let go.

It had been a most delightful poke. I do not think I had ever enjoyed a woman more. I held her in my arms till she had done panting and sighing; then giving her a kiss, I asked her how she had liked her second lesson in the 'art of love.' 'Oh,' she replied, 'it was rather painful at first, but after a few seconds, I had no sense of pain, my only feeling being one of pleasure; and at the last, the sensation was quite delightful, when I felt a peculiar thrill pass over me, and the hot stuff gushed out of you. It seemed to go right up me in a burning stream, and I could not help twisting myself about. Oh! It was nice!'

I did not poke her again, but we had a little amorous dalliance, which she entered into with spirit, thoroughly enjoying the fun, and showing that she had a decidedly voluptuous disposition.

At last I told her to go to her room, and rumple her bed, so that it should look as if it had been slept in as usual.

She laughed, and jumping out of bed, huddled on her clothes; then she picked up the bloodstained towels, saying: 'I will take these away, and when I am having my bath I will wash them, and leave them in the bathroom.' Then she added, looking with a meaning smile at me: 'I have had to wash many a towel before now.'

'By Jove! Frances,' I exclaimed. 'It is lucky you thought of the towels. I should have forgotten all about them, and left them lying on the floor. Now give me a kiss, and run away.'

She came to the bedside, and bending over me, pressed her soft lips on mine in a long kiss; then she left the room, and I turned over on to my side, and went to sleep; not waking until my man brought in my bath.

Two Flappers
in Paris

Sometimes it seems that there is only one hero in Victorian and Edwardian erotic literature. He is an English gentleman of the upper classes, usually in his early middle-age but of a virile and passionate nature. This confirmed bachelor is nevertheless a ladies man, whose wide sexual experience renders him particularly attractive to the nubile adolescent females who fall eagerly under his spell in order to rectify their ignorance in matters of sex. These girls invariably call him 'Uncle' . . .

Such a man is 'Uncle' Jack, a diplomat who picks up a pretty Parisian schoolgirl during a rough Channel crossing and offers her a day out to complete her education. Naturally the curious Evelyn jumps at the chance. There's just one snag – her friend Nora must come along too. What a hardship for Uncle Jack! Now he has two delicious young ladies to escort on a guided tour of 'the most famous of all Parisian bordels' – there to show them 'interesting cinema films' and other exotic delights. Jack's motives are, of course, the finest and his concern for the girls' wellbeing irreproachable. 'I was certain,' he says, 'that nothing would be done to shock my two flappers.' Unsurprisingly, as it turns out, these particular flappers are unflappable.

Without in any way disclosing my personality — which indeed, would be of my special interest to the reader — I may say that I occupy a somewhat important position in our Diplomatic Service, and it was in this capacity that I had to visit Paris in the month of October 19 . . .

I have often had occasion to visit Paris and it is always with the greatest pleasure that I return to this delightful city where every man can satisfy his tastes and desires whatever they may be. But on this occasion, more than ever before, chance, that great disposer of events, was to be on my side and had in store for me an adventure of the most delightful description.

I had had a pleasant run down to Folkestone and had gone on board one of those excellent boats which cross to Boulogne in something under two hours. It was blowing decidedly hard and the boat was rolling heavily but I did not mind this for I am a good sailor and I thought to myself that I should be able to enjoy in comparative solitude that delightful poetic feeling which results from a contemplation of the immensity of the ocean and of our own littleness as well as the wild beauty of a troubled sea.

And, as a matter of fact, the deck soon became deserted and I was left alone, but for the presence of a young girl who was standing by the side of the boat not far from me. From time to time my looks wandered from the white-crested waves and rested upon the charming figure that was before me, and finally I abandoned all contemplation of the infinite and all poetical and philosophical meditation and became wholly absorbed in my pretty travelling companion. For she was indeed lovely and the mobile and intellectual features of her charming face seemed to denote a very decided 'character'.

For a long time I admired her from a distance, but at last, by no means satisfied with this, I decided to try to make her acquaintance, and for this purpose I gradually approached her. At first she did not seem to notice me. Wearing, over her dress, a light waterproof which the strong wind wrapped closely round her body, she was leaning on her elbows on the rail, one hand placed under her chin and the other held the brim of her hat which otherwise would have stood a good chance of being carried away into the sea. She seemed to me to be about seventeen years old, but at the same time she was remarkably well made for a girl of that age. My eyes devoured the small and supple outline of her waist and the fine development of her behind which, placed as she was, she seemed to be offering to some bold caress, unless perchance it might be to a still more delightful punishment . . .

On her feet she wore a charming pair of high-heeled

brown shoes which set off to the best advantage the smallness and daintiness of her extremities.

I came close up to her without her making the slightest movement or even looking in my direction, and I stood for a few moments without saying a word, taking a subtle and intimate pleasure in examining every detail of her beauty; her splendid thick pigtail of dark silky hair, the fine arch of her ears, the whiteness of her neck, the near delicacy of her eyebrows, and what I could see of her splendid dark eyes, the aristocratic smallness of her nose and its mobile nostrils, the softness of her rosy little mouth and the animation of her healthy complexion.

Then suddenly I made up my mind.

'We are in for a rough crossing!' I said. She turned slowly towards me her little head and for a moment examined me in silence. And now, seen full face, I found her even more beautiful and more attractive than she had seemed before when I had only been able to obtain a side view of her.

Apparently her examination of me was favourable, for a slight smile disclosed the prettiest little teeth that it was possible to imagine and she answered.

'Do you think so? I don't mind if we are!' this paradoxical answer was quite in keeping with her appearance.

'I congratulate you.' I said, 'I see that you are a true English girl, and that a rough sea has no terrors for you!'

'Oh,' said she quickly, 'I'm not afraid of anything; and as for the sea, I love it. Of all amusements I like yachting best.' I could not help laughing a little. Evidently of all the amusements that she was acquainted with yachting might be her favourite one, but a day would come, and perhaps was not far off, when she would know others: and then, yachting . . .

However, I considered that it was impossible to continue the conversation without having gained her confidence, and to effect this my best plan was to introduce myself.

'You must excuse me,' I said, 'for having taken the liberty of speaking to you, but our presence on the deck here, when everybody else has taken refuge below, seems to indicate that we are intended to know one another . . . and, I hope, to appreciate one another. My name is Jack W—, and that I am attached to our Foreign Office.'

She gave me a charming little bow, and, at once, by the smile in her eyes I could see that I had attained my object.

'And my name,' said she, 'is Evelyn H . . . and I am on my way to school. I am travelling alone as far as Boulogne but there a French governess will meet me and take me on to Paris.'

Let me here state that I cannot mention her surname nor that of any of the other characters who will appear in this story, which is an absolutely true one in every particular, for some of the characters are well known in society and might be known to some of my readers.

'Oh really?' I exclaimed. 'You are on your way to Paris? I'm going there too. What bad luck that we can't travel all the way together. But at any rate we can keep one another company till we reach Boulogne. Shall we sit down together in that shelter: we shall be fairly out of the wind there?'

There was a convenient seat close by which we proceeded to occupy. My blood was already beginning to course more freely through my veins.

'Where are you going to in Paris?'

'To Mme X . . . at Neuilly. That's where I am at school.'

'I know the school well,' said I. 'It is certainly the most fashionable one in all Paris. I suppose there are a large number of girls there?'

'No, not more than sixty.'

'You are one of the elder girls?'

'No, not yet!' said she, uttering a sigh. 'I wish I were, but I shall have to wait till next year for that.'

'And why are you so anxious to be one of the elder girls?'

She gave me a rapid glance and smiled.

'Because,' said she, 'the elder girls know things that we don't know . . .'

'Oh, all sorts of things. And they are very proud of their superior knowledge let me tell you. They say that we are too young to join their society.'

'And what is this society?'

'It's a secret society. They call it, I don't know why, the Lesbian Society. But after all what does it matter: our time will come!'

I was more and more delighted with Evelyn's candour and with the decidedly interesting turn which our conversation had taken.

'Oh, yes. I have a special friend there who is more than a sister to me. We have no secrets from one another. Her name is Nora A . . . and I love the walks we have together.'

'You go into Paris sometimes, I suppose?'

'Yes, but of course there is always some one with us to chaperone us.'

'Have you ever been to the Louvre?'

'Oh, yes! What beautiful pictures, and other things too, that are there.'

'The statues for instance; you have seen them? Now tell me, were you not rather surprised when you saw the statues of the men without any fig leaves as they are always represented with in our galleries?'

Evelyn blushed slightly and smiled. I saw her eyes sparkle but she covered them with her long lashes.

'At first I was,' said she. 'And of course I noticed the difference that there is between . . .'

She stopped and nervously began to tap her knees.

'Between what?' I said. 'Between a man and a woman?'

'Yes . . .'

'The statues,' I continued, 'do not give you a very exact idea of the difference. I have often said to myself, when I have watched a bevy of our charming schoolgirls in the statue room examining the statues, that this difference would be much more pronounced and obvious if the statues of the men were real men, and if these men knew that they were the objects of admiration of a number of pretty girls!'

Evelyn raised her eyes to mine filled with a kind of mute interrogation.

'I don't understand what you mean,' said she after a short pause.

I hesitated for a moment but only for a moment. Already I was plunging headlong into this delightful adventure the memory of which, in its minutest details, will never leave me.

'You don't understand?' I resumed, moving a little closer to her so that now our forms were actually in contact, and taking her little hand which she abandoned to me with a slight tremble of emotion. 'I will explain it to you. It's quite simple and these are things that a girl must know some time or other; and, upon my word, in my opinion the sooner they know them the better.' Her little hand seemed fairly to burn mine and her lovely eyes, full of curiosity gazed into mine and I felt that already a powerful tie existed between us. How completely I had forgotten the magnificent surroundings of sky and sea!

'You must have noticed that the statues of the men,' I observed, 'are not like those of the women?'

'Oh, yes, of course,' said she and her colour deepened. 'The forms are different.'

'Yes, the breasts of women are much more developed, their waists are smaller, their hips broader and fuller, the seat is much longer and plumper, and the thighs are bigger and rounder. But there is something else too − ! You know what I mean.'

'Yes,' she murmured.

A troubled look seemed to fill her eyes.

'And this something else,' I continued, 'did you notice how it was made?'

'I . . . yes . . . I think I noticed it . . .'

'It's like a great fruit, as large as a peach, with a double kernel, isn't it? And hanging down over is a kind of appendage: it is like a rolled up loaf of flesh which seems to wish to hide the fruit . . .'

'Oh, yes, it's just like that!'

'That is the way that sculptors represent what is called "the male sex." But as a matter of fact it is not really made like that, at least not the appendage. This object which you have seen hanging down and lifeless is, in reality, the most sensitive, the most lively, and the most changeable thing that it is possible to imagine. It is the most wonderful thing that exists and also the most precious, for it is capable of giving life and the most delightful pleasure.'

Evelyn was evidently much excited but her eyes avoided mine as she murmured.

'I think I understand . . . It is with that . . . that babies are made.'

'Exactly!'

'Then,' she continued almost in a whisper, 'each time that . . . that a man makes use of that thing is . . . is a baby made?'

The laugh with which this innocent question provoked in me completed Evelyn's confusion. She hid her lovely face, now blushing crimson, in her hands. I whispered in her ear.

'Forgive me for laughing, but your innocence is perfectly charming. But how is it that you know so little about such things? Have your companions at school never told you about anything?'

'No,' said she. 'I am only seventeen and a half, and I shall not be able to join the Society which I have mentioned to you till I am eighteen.'

'Tell me more about this Society.'

'The elder girls call it the "Lesbian Society." I just long to be a member of it, as, indeed, do all the girls who are not yet eighteen. Oh, what jokes they must have together and what things they must do! If only, before joining the Society, I could know as much as the "seniors." What a score it would be, and how delighted I should be!'

'Oh,' said I, 'there's no difficulty about that. You need only have complete confidence in me, and to let me act as your instructor. It would be a great pleasure to me and a real advantage to yourself. And, in the first place, let me tell you that you have nothing to fear from me, nor from anyone else while I am looking after you. Now, tell me, have you ever seen any naughty photos or cinema films?'

She shook her pretty head.

'No,' said she, 'but how I should love to see some.'

'Well, that could easily be managed, and you would see then how one can make use of what we were talking about just now without there being the slightest fear of a baby resulting! And this information I consider not only useful but absolutely necessary for a well-brought-up young lady.'

I must confess that so much candour, combined with such charming grace, excited me strangely. I took her soft delicate hand which she abandoned to me readily and continued.

'As we are both going to Paris, and as Paris above all other places lends itself to obtaining instruction in all matters in which you are so interested, we must arrange some plan which will, I think, be as simple as it will be certain . . .'

'Oh, do go on!' said Evelyn.

'Well, this is my idea. When we are settled, you at your school, and I at the British Embassy, I will write to you, pretending to be your uncle, and will offer to take you out for the afternoon. My letter, written on the official Embassy notepaper, will, I feel sure, have the desired effect and will readily induce your headmistress to let you come out with me. What do you think of my scheme?'

'It's splendid! But there's one thing I must tell you. Madame has a rule that no girl is ever allowed to go out alone with a gentleman, even if he is a near relation . . .'

'What on earth is to be done then?'

'Wait a moment! If, however, the gentleman invites another girl to accompany his relation, then Madame never raises any objection.'

'Ah, really!' I said, feeling somewhat disappointed, for I did not care for this idea of a second girl, which might upset my plans.

'So, if you would invite Nora,' continued Evelyn calmly, 'the matter would go swimmingly, I'm certain.'

'Nora, and who may she be?'

'My friend, the girl I was telling you about. Oh, she's perfectly charming and would be so delighted to know about . . . about things!'

'Right you are then; by all means let Nora come too. You are sure we can trust her?'

'Absolutely certain.'

'She is a real friend? She has your tastes? She thoroughly understands you?'

'Nora is more than a sister to me. She seems to guess my thoughts almost before I have formed them: and then, if I am seedy, nobody knows how to comfort me as she does. Oh, her kisses are delightful; and sometimes she bathes me in her beautiful golden hair which is much finer than mine, and mine is generally considered rather nice. But the chief charm about her is sweet manners, sometimes serious but more often roguish. Oh, you have no idea what a little darling she is!'

'Little?'

'Oh, that's only a way of speaking. She is about as tall as I am and rather bigger, and so chic and has such a beautiful figure, and she dresses delightfully, almost like a "Parisienne". But you will see! Oh, what splendid fun we three will have together; you see if we don't . . . uncle!'

'Your uncle, Evelyn — you must let me call you by your Christian name — is delighted to have discovered a niece at once so fresh, so beautiful, so sensible, and so eager for information. He undertakes to make you easily surpass in knowledge all the young ladies in the Lesbian Society, so that, when your age permits you to join the secret circles of this mysterious club, you will astonish your fellow members by your remarkable knowledge of matters which are always of the greatest interest to girls!'

And so we chatted on till the boat was about to enter the harbour of Boulogne where we parted with much mutual regret, lest the governess who had come to meet Evelyn should see us together. Short as had been our acquaintance we had indeed become good friends.

It was a lovely day, such as one often has in Paris in the month of October. The terrace of the Café American was crowded with people but we managed to find three seats and at once I could not fail to notice that the beauty, the grace, the youth, and the charming get-up of my two companions attracted the eyes of all who were present.

And this admiration was indeed well deserved. I have already given a description of Evelyn. I have noted her beautiful dark eyes and hair, the delicacy of her features, ease and elegance of her carriage, and the aristocratic smallness of her hands and feet.

She was wearing a charming *crêpe-de-Chine* frock of light pink colour, with a broad crimson sash round her waist, and a pretty bow of the same material at the end of her splendid pigtail. The blouse, which had a small sailor collar, and the fronts and pocket of which were ornamented with hemstitching, was decidedly open in front thus allowing a glimpse to be obtained of her lovely breasts. A sailor hat, in silk beaver, with folded crown, and finished with silk

Petersham set off the beauty of her hair and eyes to perfection. The skirt was just pleasantly short, thus allowing one to see the beginning of a beautifully shaped pair of legs which were encased in open-work black silk stockings, the feet being shod in a dainty pair of high-heeled French shoes.

Nora, as I have said, was fair: of that delightful fairness which one so often comes across in the North of Ireland. Her eyes were a lovely deep blue, her nose small, her nostrils palpitating and sensual, while a rosy-lipped little mouth permitted one to see two perfect rows of pearly white teeth. Such were the chief features of Nora's really lovely face. Do not, however, let it be supposed for a moment that she was in the least doll-like! Far from it! She was remarkably lively and gay, and had a most winning and attractive smile, and as I think of her I recall to myself the opening words of the old song of Tralee:

'She was lovely and fair like the roses in midsummer, yet 'twas not her beauty all alone that won me!'

She was wearing a pretty dress of light blue cotton voile, with a blue sash to match and a blue ribbon at the end of her pigtail, which I noticed was even longer and thicker than Evelyn's, as the latter had told me. Light blue stockings, a pair of high-heeled brown shoes, and a becoming straw hat completed a most charming costume such as you may see so often on 'Children's Day' at Ranelagh, or at Lords on the day of the Eton and Harrow match.

We did not stay long on the terrace but mounted

to the restaurant on the first floor, the girls being much amused at the number of mirrors that decorated the staircase. There we enjoyed a most excellent lunch and consumed between us a bottle and a half of champagne.

Evelyn and Nora had become quite merry and their colour had risen, so I thought that the time had now come to speak of what, no doubt, was in the minds of us all.

'Now, tell me, Evelyn,' I said, 'does your friend know about our conversation on the boat?'

'Oh,' said Evelyn laughing a little nervously, 'if she didn't she wouldn't be here!'

Nora blushed deeply but began to laugh too.

'Capital!' said I. 'Now tell me frankly. Are you both prepared to pass a decidedly . . . unconventional afternoon?'

The two girls were now equally red and they were none the less charming for that.

'We are prepared for anything!' said Evelyn.

'Is that correct, Nora?'

'Quite correct!' said Nora after a moment's hesitation.

'And the more . . . "unconventional" the better,' said Evelyn, hiding her face behind one of the little fans which I had just handed to her.

'That's right,' said I. 'Now we must come to certain arrangements. Nora, like you, must call me "Uncle Jack". You are my two nieces, do you understand?'

'O, yes, yes!'

'And next, you must not be surprised at anything, but must have complete confidence in me. I can promise you one thing: that you will come through all the experiences that we are about to encounter as intact, physically I mean, as you are at the present moment. You understand what I mean?'

Both of them seemed to tremble a little, but after a quick glance at one another Evelyn answered:

'Yes, we understand, and that's just what we should have wished.'

'Capital!'

'There's only one thing that we are anxious about,' said Nora, who was becoming more and more at her ease with me; 'and that is to know more than the girls of the Lesbian Society, and to be able to . . . to . . . what do the French say? a funny word . . .'

'To *épater* them?' I asked.

'Yes, that's it! To *épater* them.'

'Very well, my dear nieces! I will guarantee that you shall be able to fairly *épater* them if you relate faithfully to them all you are going to see and learn this afternoon. And now we ought to be on the move.'

I settled the bill and sending for a taxi, very pleased with ourselves, we set off for the rue Ch—.

As had been arranged we were received by Madame R who showed us into her private sitting-room. There was nothing to give a hint to my 'nieces' as to the occupation of the lady of the house, and accordingly they were very curious as to who and what she might be. Madame R having left us alone for a few moments to attend to the details of the arrangements. Evelyn and Nora began eagerly to question me.

'Where are we? Who is the lady? Dear Uncle Jack, do tell us: oh, please do!'

The champagne assisting, they became so pressing that I felt my own feelings beginning to rise. The contact with this young and charming pair, the idea of their absolute virginity in which wholly unknown sensations were so soon to be aroused, their eager and warm looks, the pressure of their hot and soft little hands, all this seemed to endow me with all my youthful vigour, and I felt standing up inside my trousers the delicate and sensitive instrument of flesh, by which man measures in himself the degree of his sensual pleasure, as hard and stiff as it would have been had I knocked off fifteen of my thirty-five years.

'My dear young ladies,' said I, 'restrain yourselves. I am here only to instruct and, I hope, amuse you. The house belongs to a lady friend of mine. She is the manageress of a Temple to which one can come to adore, in return for a liberal remuneration, the Goddess of Pleasure!'

'Oh, Uncle Jack, how you do tease!' said Evelyn with a delightful little pout. 'Do put things more plainly!'

'Very well then! There are certain houses where men, by paying liberally, can enjoy all the pleasures of the senses. In these houses . . .'

'Then,' broke in Nora eagerly, 'it is this lady who provides these pleasures?'

I began to laugh.

'Not exactly the lady herself,' I said. 'She has some assistants, charming girls and young women, who have not taken a vow of chastity, who are no longer virgins, and who make themselves agreeable to gentlemen who are nice to them and pay them well.'

'Oh, I never! . . .' broke in Evelyn with astonishment. 'How can they? For my part I shall love one man . . . perhaps two, but not a whole lot!'

'That's right,' I said. 'You are very sensible, Evelyn; but these girls are sensible and practical too. They know what you are ignorant of at present but have come here to learn. Thanks to their instructions you will presently be more learned, not only than all your companions of the Lesbian Society, but also than most ladies even if they have been married for twenty years and to a husband who lets himself go in his marital relations!'

Evelyn clapped her hands with pleasure, but Nora, who had got up from her chair, and was making an inspection of the room, called out to us and beckoned us to approach.

She was examining a fine eighteenth century engraving which bore this delightful title 'The Whipping of Cupid'.

The artist had represented the chubby, well-developed lad half-lying across the divine knees of his mother, Venus, who, with a bunch of roses instead of a rod, was applying to his bottom the charming punishment.

The two girls examined the picture, blushing scarlet.

'This is symbolical,' I said. 'Love is often whipped!'

'Oh,' said Evelyn, 'but why?'

'Well, you will know later on! The birch, nicely applied by a skilful hand, is the most delightful caress, don't forget that! But I hear steps, let us sit down again.'

Scarcely had we resumed our seats when the door opened and Madame R appeared.

'If you will be so good as to follow me,' she said, 'I will show you the cinema room, I have arranged a little entertainment for you.'

We got up and followed her.

The room was small but comfortably furnished. Facing the stage, or rather the sheet, were five boxes the partitions of which nearly reached to the ceiling. In the one that we entered were three chairs and behind them, a small sofa. We took our places on the chairs, I of course sitting in the centre, and Madame left us, saying as she retired:

'If you require me touch the bell, and I will be with you in a moment.'

Then we were left alone.

Suddenly words appeared on the sheet and we read.

> Before the representation of
> 'The Devil in Hell'
> We present a slight sketch:
> 'Miss Barbara, school-mistress'

And at once this first film, which I had not been expecting, was set in motion.

The picture represented a class-room fitted up in the

usual way with a teacher's desk, blackboard, maps and pupil's desks, etc. One of these desks was occupied by a nice looking, well-made young man. At first he was writing but suddenly he rose from his place and made for the teacher's desk where he immediately proceeded to upset the ink-stand; he then went to the blackboard and, with a piece of chalk, drew a ludicrous head of a woman with a huge chignon and large goggle eye-glasses. Having done this he resumed his seat and a moment later the door opened and Miss Barbara, school-mistress, sailed into the room. She was a fine young woman of about thirty with a learned and severe expression. She soon discovered the condition of her desk and the drawing on the blackboard. Examining the lad's fingers she found direct evidence that he was the culprit.

An inscription appeared on the sheet.

'So you have been up to your tricks again, Billy. Very well, sir. I shall have to give you another whipping. Prepare yourself!'

She came up to Billy and took him by the hand; then she drew him towards the open part of the room, that is to say towards the spectators, and having removed his coat proceeded to unbutton and let down his trousers. Having slipped them down to his knees, she tucked his shirt in under his waistcoat both behind and in front thus completely exposing the lad from the waist to the knees. She then, with her left arm, bent him over and with her right hand began to smack his bottom soundly. It was a most amusing sight to see the youth wriggle and dance under the smarting whipping that he was receiving but what raised the emotion of my two friends to the highest point was the sight of Billy's tool in a full state of erection which could be plainly seen when, in his struggles, he was turned towards us.

Both of the girls had seized one of my hands and were squeezing it hard. I could feel that they were highly excited and all their nerves were on the stretch, and Evelyn whispered to me:

'It's not a bit like it is on the statues now! . . .'

Miss Barbara paused in her whipping and seemed to become aware, with a well-feigned indignation, of Billy's disgracefully indecent condition.

First she pointed with apparent horror at the offending instrument, then she took it in her hand and began to move the soft skin up and down, and then the film, changing suddenly, showed only the hand, very much enlarged, working the skin up and down, and covering and uncovering the well-defined head.

Evelyn and Nora, as the picture changed, uttered a little cry and gripped my hands still more tightly, and Nora asked me softly:

'Is she punishing him in doing that, Uncle Jack?'

'It is a punishment which is really a caress,' I said, 'and it acts through the feeling of shame, and the effect which it has on Billy's modesty.'

'Oh!' sighed Evelyn. 'How I should love to punish a naughty lad like that!'

Her looks were bathed in voluptuousness and Nora was in the same condition.

'Yes,' said I, 'but you would have to spank him first.'

'So much the better! I should like to do that too!'

Then the film returned to its normal size and Miss Barbara began to smack her young pupil again, at the same time passing her left hand well round his waist and taking a firm hold of his well-developed young prick. At last the punishment was over, Billy received his pardon with a warm kiss from his mistress, they left the room together, the film was cut off, and the light turned on in the room . . . My two 'nieces' at the same moment heaved a great sigh of satisfaction.

'Well,' said I, 'did that interest you?'

'Oh, yes!' said Evelyn, and Nora agreed. 'I had never seen this . . . this thing in that condition. I had no idea that it was made like that. Was Miss Barbara hurting Billy when she rubbed his thing like that?'

'Certainly not,' I answered, 'quite the contrary! And I am quite certain that he would gladly have received another spanking on condition of being treated in the same way after it.' Nora, blushing delightfully murmured:

'Uncle Jack, shall we be able to see this . . . thing . . . really? A real live one, I mean?'

'If you are very good girls perhaps I shall be able to let you see a real live one! This thing as you call it is called a "prick" but you must never pronounce this word in public. You must not even speak of the thing. It is enough to know about it and to think about it. And now, you darlings, let me tell you that this thing is capable of giving girls the greatest pleasure that it is possible for them to experience.'

'Oh! I can quite believe that!' said Evelyn. 'How delightful it must be to touch it, to stroke it, and to fondle it as Miss Barbara was doing!'

'Quite right, Evelyn, but the pleasure which you would feel in doing that is not to be compared with the other, the true, the supreme pleasure, which results from the introduction and movements of the prick in . . . in . . .'

'In what, Uncle Jack?' asked Nora tenderly.

'In what corresponds in you girls to what we men have; you know what I mean! . . . Come now, don't you?'

'Oh,' sighed Evelyn, looking sweetly confused; 'do you mean in . . . in the little crack . . .'

'Just so, Evelyn. This little crack is the entrance to the sheath which nature has provided in woman to receive the "prick" of man.'

'Really?' sighed Nora. 'And is that how babies are made?'

'Yes, indeed it is, Nora. But one can enjoy pleasure, in fact the complete pleasure, without having children. One can even enjoy this supreme pleasure without being obliged to introduce the "prick" into the rosy little nest which you girls have ready for it, and you will know presently how this can be done. But I wanted you first of all to know the natural destination of this living sceptre which man always carries about with him, for you will understand better the film which is to follow and which is called "The Devil in Hell." The

Devil is the "prick". The hell is the hot little nest towards which destiny urges him . . .'

'Oh!'

They uttered this 'oh!' both together. Their minds were being opened; they were now for the first time catching a glimpse of new worlds filled with strange and voluptuous marvels. I was intensely excited as can easily be imagined, and it was with difficulty that I restrained myself from at once proceeding to caress the two charming girls and from teaching them how to caress me. But I have always been a man of method, and having fixed on a plan I was determined to carry it out in every particular.

Discreet taps were heard at the door and in reply to my call to come in Madame entered the room.

'And how did you like "Miss Barbara"?' she asked me.

'It was quite interesting,' I replied, 'but the end seemed rather tame.'

Madame laughed.

'The end is really quite different,' she said. 'The sketch was only intended as an introduction with the object of preparing the young ladies for the picture which will follow . . . I thought that you would explain it to them sufficiently and I did not wish in any way to detract from the effect of "The Devil in Hell" in which the incidents are much more exciting and given with much greater detail than in "Miss Barbara".'

'What then is the real ending of the film which we have just seen?'

'You saw Miss Barbara lead Billy away. She

conducts him to her own room where she gives him a very complete lesson in the way in which a man should behave to a lady. And now I think you are ready for "The Devil in Hell", but would you not be more comfortable on this little sofa, see, there is just room for the three of you.'

I at once appreciated the excellence of Madame's advice, and moving the chairs and putting the sofa in their place we took our seat upon it; Madame then left us and the light was again turned off.

Instinctively Evelyn and Nora moved closed up on each side of me. I took advantage of this to place my arm round their waist and then, gently and with infinite care, my hands slipped down and I began to stroke and fondle the outside of their thighs and of their soft young bottoms. It was most interesting to notice that neither of the girls raised the slightest objection to this little attention, but on the contrary each slightly raised the cheek that I was squeezing as though inviting my hand to pass more completely underneath!

Meanwhile the film began to be displayed.

I must describe it as shortly as possible, although for my own satisfaction and for that of my readers I should much like to dwell in detail on the voluptuous scenes which took place between the charming and naive little Alibech and the cunning hermit, Father Rustique.

In the first scene, which might have been a landscape from the 'Arabian Nights' we saw a lovely girl of about seventeen dressed in oriental costume, approach an old man. Headlines informed us that Alibech, a young girl of Caspia, was anxious to lead a religious life and was asking the old sage how this could be done.

'You must abandon pomps and vanities of this wicked world and live as the Christians do in the deserts of Thebais,' said the old man. Next we saw Alibech setting out for these famous deserts. She was very lightly clad, for the weather was very hot, and the glimpse which from time to time I caught of her lovely forms made me think that I would gladly play with her the part which was to be taken by the hermit.

Presently Alibech reached the hut of a lonely saint and explained to him her mission.

Astonished, but fearing at the sight of her beauty that the devil might tempt him, he praised her zeal but would not keep her; he however directed her to a holy man, who, as he said, was much more fitted to instruct her than himself.

She therefore goes on her way and soon arrives at the abode of Father Rustique, for such is the name of the saint in question. Like his good brother he questions her and, relying on his moral strength, decides to keep her with him.

Father Rustique is a handsome young man in the prime of life and we soon see by his burning looks, his gestures and his attitudes that he is a prey to the demon of the flesh. He succumbs. But in order that the sin may be his alone he makes use of a stratagem to accomplish his ends.

He explains to the innocent girl that the great enemy of mankind is the devil and that the most meritorious act that a Christian can do is to put him as often as possible into the hell for which he is destined!

Alibech asks him how that is to be done.

'I will show you directly,' says Rustique, 'you have only to do as you see me do . . .' Then he begins to undress and the girl does the same. When they are completely naked he kneels down and placing the beautiful woman before him his eyes wander over the lovely charms which are now fully exposed to his enraptured gaze.

The girl looks timidly at the Father and suddenly her eyes are filled with astonishment and pointing to a great thing which is standing out from the holy man's belly she asks:

'What is that, which is quite unlike any thing that I have?'

'It is the devil,' says Rustique, 'which I have been telling you about. See how it torments me and how fierce and proud it is!'

'Ah, how thankful I ought to be that I have not such a devil, since it is so troublesome to you!'

'Yes,' says Rustique, 'but you have something else instead!'

'And what is that?'

'The hell!'

At this Alibech shows the greatest fear, and the Father goes on:

'And I think that you must have been sent here expressly for the salvation of my soul, for if the devil continues to torment me and if you will permit me to put him into your hell we shall be doing the most meritorious action that it is possible to do.'

Alibech states that she is quite willing to do whatever the holy Father may deem right.

He immediately takes the naked girl in his arms and, carrying her into the hut, places her on her back on the little couch, and opens her thighs as wide as possible. Then he kneels between them and for a few moments examines with gleaming eyes the lovely body exposed before him. Then stretching himself along the docile little virgin, and taking a firm hold on her, he whispers to her to take hold of the devil and guide him into hell. The obedient young woman obeys and the head of the devil is placed in the very jaws of hell. With a downward thrust of his powerful bottom the Father begins his attack and the head of the devil enters the outskirts of his domains. A look of surprise comes over Alibech's face, and as, with another powerful thrust, the devil is driven halfway home, and the obstacle which stood in his way is pierced, a little cry is drawn from her lips and is followed by another as, with another steady lunge, the devil is driven up to the hilt into his burning home. For a few moments the hermit lay enjoying the completeness of his victory. Then his bottom was set in motion and the devil was driven in and out . . . in and out . . . in and out, slowly at first and then quicker and quicker, till a spasm seemed to shake the whole of his body, and the convulsive jerks of his bottom showed that the devil was pouring out into hell the very vials of his wrath.

One bout however was not sufficient to humble the pride of satan and it was not till he had been plunged into hell on three separate occasions that his head finally drooped, when the hermit rested and allowed his little partner to repose also.

All this time I had been pressing Evelyn and Nora closely to me and from time to time I had taken a stealthy glance at them.

They had watched the development of the story panting with pleasure, their lips slightly open as though inviting my kisses, their eyelids drooping, and their cheeks suffused with blushes. I could feel them quiver with the depth of emotion of young virgins before whom the mysteries of life are being unfolded.

Each time that Father Rustique buried his devil in hell, one could see, thanks to the excellent way in which the picture was presented, the great red head penetrate the fresh young lips, as pouting and soft as the mouth of a baby, and then work its way in and out, till the final spasm shook the lucky hermit. And all this time I could feel the two girls trembling with emotion, their bodies stiffened and contracted with the intensity of a desire hitherto wholly unknown to them.

And now the film was set in motion again, and we could see, on the next day, the holy Father recommence with his charming pupil his pious exercises. And now it was evident by her lascivious motions that Alibech was beginning to find these religious observances exceedingly pleasant, so that she was plainly urging the good hermit to be as zealous as possible in the prosecution of his good works; and as her imagination developed in the joy experienced in thus doing her pleasant duty she invented new positions and fresh ways of inserting the Father's devil into her hot little hell.

Thus it was that we saw her kneel on the edge of the bed and present her lovely soft bottom as if she had been inviting her companion to chastise her. But he knowing that this was not her intention, and excited by this delightful situation, opened the thighs of the little angel and plunged his weapon into her from behind. And here too every detail of the operation was most admirably represented. And so the picture went on and on and Alibech became more and more expert in varying the method of putting the devil into hell. Sometimes, so as not to fatigue her instructor, she would place him on a chair and then getting astride of him, so turning her back to us, she would, a thoughtful girl, take all the hard work on herself, and here too we could see that she made as excellent a rider as she had proved herself a docile mount.

Nora, who had very quickly become perfectly at her ease with me, while this little scene was in progress, pressed my hand which was squeezing her trembling bottom, and resting her sweet head against my shoulder, whispered in my ear:

'Oh! Uncle Jack, Uncle Jack!'

'You would like to be in Thebais, Nora, dear?' She only answered by an eloquent look, in which already the voluptuous and lovable woman which she was to become later on was revealed to me.

Evelyn said nothing but I was aware that she was just as excited as Nora. She did not miss a single point of the interesting entertainment which I had provided for her, and I felt sure that she was registering every detail in her faithful memory in order, later on, to be able to overwhelm with her science the 'seniors' of the Lesbian Society.

I will leave the reader to imagine the condition in which I was myself during all this time. I do not wish to dwell on this more than I can help, my object being, as far as possible, to write of these things *objectively* to use the expression of a certain modern school.

Then, as the picture went on, we saw the repeated punishment of the devil beginning to have its inevitable effect on the worthy hermit, whose food consisted for the most part only of fruit and water. Little Alibech became distressed at his want of zeal and found it necessary to rouse the devil into action, till at last, evidently much to her disappointment, Father Rustique had to inform her that his devil was now thoroughly humbled and would not trouble him for some little time.

The light having been turned on in the room, my two companions awoke from the voluptuous dream which they had been living through and sighed deeply.

'Oh!' said Evelyn, arching her delightfully supple and small waist. 'I should have liked it to go on forever!'

'Really?' said I. 'So it interested you very much?'

'Oh yes! And you too, Nora, didn't it?'

'I should think it did,' said Nora. 'I can't imagine anything more delightful and exciting!'

'But what I can't understand,' said Evelyn excitedly,

'is how the devil which is so big can get into the hell which is so small? . . .'

'The entrance to hell has this peculiarity, it is extremely elastic,' I explained. 'Without any trouble, and with very little pain, it can admit the most voluminous demon provided that he does not set about his work roughly . . . It is only the first time that it hurts a little, and the intense pleasure soon makes up for the slight pain! . . . And now you know how, in order to be perfectly happy, a man and a girl behave together. You are, I expect, already much more learned in these matters than the most learned of your companions but this is only the beginning! For besides putting the devil into hell there are many other caresses by which the supreme pleasure, which Father Rustique and Alibech enjoyed so often, may be obtained by the excitement of the senses, and in these ways I hope to instruct you too, my darlings; you are not tired?'

From their sweet little mouths issued a double 'oh!' of protest which made it quite unnecessary for me to pursue that point further . . .

Bare Necessities

It is another beautiful day in California. A leggy blonde housewife mooches around her perfect home, restless, bored out of her mind – and horny as hell. This is small-town America in 1970, a world far removed from the peace, love and pass-the-joint atmosphere of the big cities and university campuses. In *Bare Necessities* there is no free love for Carol Kimberly and her brutish husband, Bart – here every roll in the hay (and there are plenty) has its price. For Bart is ambitious, he is attempting to use his newly established motor-repair business as a stepping stone to prosperity and local influence. Which is where Carol comes in. More than a provider of meals, a cleaner of overalls and a convenient lay, Bart's beautiful wife is a business asset. One he can use to win over Link Arthur, the town's Mr Big, and also his entrance fee to the local wife-swapping club.

Unfortunately for Bart, Carol is not just a body. Though she can't help responding to every sexual manoeuvre in Bart's game plan, she resents each trade-off and soon begins plotting a few moves of her own . . .

It was a beautiful morning, the sun burning down out of a brilliant blue sky. Carol was alone in the house. Alone, bored and, she hated to admit it, horny. What was wrong with her these days? She'd been getting more than she'd ever had, with a whole slew of people, and here she was still not satisfied.

She stood at the kitchen sink, one hand up beneath her T-shirt toying with her bra-less breasts, rolling her nipples between her fingers. She could feel the skin puckering into hard points as she plucked and squeezed. She imagined Bart — no — some other man, suckling at her bosom, sliding a hand up her short skirt to play with her pussy. Gently slipping a finger between the crisp blonde curls to tickle her clit. Like she was doing now.

Thrilled with her own wantonness, she pulled up her skirt and shucked off her panties. Then, standing on tiptoe, the muscles in her long brown legs straining, she leaned her pelvis against the kitchen cabinet. There, just at the right height to snuggle into her crotch, was a small, rounded drawer-knob. She'd done this before, occasionally — well, quite a lot recently, since they'd started going to that damned club — and she knew just the right height to stand and the way to rub herself on the smooth wooden knob so that it built the pleasure and scratched the itch that was already raging in her loins.

She tried to settle her thoughts on a man she desired, a man untainted by recent events, a fantasy man. She'd like a really big guy, broad-shouldered, barrel-chested, all muscle but with a neat, tight ass. *How about a football player?* One of those hunks running around in skin-tight tunics, all strength and power allied to speed and skill . . . *And blond maybe, a big blond quarterback with a little blond moustache which matches the hairs on my pussy as he pushes his tongue between my cunt lips and licks up my juices. A guy who'll pick me up like a doll and sit me on a cock that fills me so full I won't be able to walk for days after. A guy I've never seen before and who I'll never see again. A guy who'll just fuck me silly.*

Maybe a guy who looks a bit like the driver of the truck parked just over the way. Yeah, just like him. Look at those tight jeans and long legs and broad shoulders. Hope he can't see me through the net curtains. It's okay, buster, there's broads all over California this morning so horny they'll fuck the kitchen cabinets . . .

The sound of the doorbell was so unexpected she took no notice. Then it came again, puncturing her excitement and deflating her instantly.

'Oh shit,' she said to herself, now frozen rigid. The bell sounded again and she knew she couldn't ignore it.

She was still flustered when she opened the door. Even more so as she looked up at the blond truckdriver standing on the doorstep. She could feel a pearl of juice rolling very slowly down the inside of her left thigh.

Up close he was huge, nearly a foot taller than her and twice as broad. He had an open, honest face — *but no moustache, dammit* — which was currently shrouded in gloom. At the sight of her his depression seemed to deepen. This was not a happy man.

'Is Bart Kimberley at home?' he asked.

'Oh no. He's at work. At the garage.'

'No, ma'am. I've been up there and they sent me here.'

Carol suddenly remembered, Bart had said he had to meet up with Link Arthur.

'Well, if it's a job he'll be back at the garage later.'

'Are you Mrs Kimberley?'

'Yes.'

'Well, it ain't a job. It's something personal. Something *Goddamn* personal and you an' me are both in it.'

His face creased further with pain and he looked as though he were about to burst into tears. It occurred to Carol he was probably younger than that college kid, Stan.

'In that case you'd better come in, Mr — '

He looked relieved and followed her down the hall into the living room. 'Call me Charlie, please.'

'I'm Carol. Please sit down.' She suddenly felt much better. She was in charge and somehow the man of her recent sex fantasy was sitting right across from her staring at her legs. How weird!

'The thing is, er, Rita, my wife, her car broke down on the freeway and . . . she knows your husband.'

'Yes?'

'Well, she was with my sister and I believe they invited him and a friend to a party . . .'

'So?' Carol sounded nonchalant but she had a funny feeling that she knew where this was leading.

'And then . . . what I mean is – oh shit! I'm sorry, ma'am – Carol – but you'd better take a look at these.'

As he leaned forward and pushed an envelope into her hand, Carol's stomach turned over.

She looked at the photos as coolly as she could. Appraising each one carefully, taking her time.

'I presume,' she said in the awkward silence, 'that this lady is Rita?'

'Yeah, that little slut is my fucking wife.'

An apt description, thought Carol as she took in the details of a brunette with big tits sprawling half out of her clothes across the lap of her husband. This doubtless was the nature of one of darling Bart's 'out of town' deals. She couldn't understand it – didn't he get enough at home and at the club? And there was Bob Adams, his tongue buried in the tramp's snatch – what would Shirley say? The thought occurred that Shirley would simply induct Rita and Charlie into the club . . .

'Oh God,' she said. 'I'm sorry but I've got to have a drink.' And she stumbled into the kitchen and grabbed the vodka bottle.

Charlie sat like stone, his boyish face crumpled in pain. He accepted a glass without a murmur and sank an inch of spirit in one hit.

'So, Charlie, what was the purpose of your visit? Simply to make a lonely housewife unhappy?'

'I was going to kill Bart − Mr Kimberley, that is. But first I was going to make him tell me where I could find that other guy. Then I was going to kill him too.'

Unbidden, he held out his glass for a refill.

'Well, I've got to say your idea has some merits. What about your wife?'

'Oh yeah. Rita. I put her over my knee and gave her a real good whipping.'

'If you don't mind me saying so, she looks like she might enjoy it.'

'Ah well.' His expression changed, for a moment agony was replaced by the recall of ecstasy. 'She took it like a real good gal. Afterwards she was very sweet to me. It wasn't really her fault at all.'

'So you've forgiven her?'

'Well, yeah. She swore to me she would never see those guys again.'

'Suppose I forgive Bart, too? I'll make him swear never to see Rita either − then we'll be quits, right?'

'Huh?'

'I mean why go to all the trouble of killing Bart now you and Rita have made up? You'll spend the next ten, fifteen years of your life in jail just thinking about what Rita may be doing on her own. Is she the kind of woman who could stay faithful for that long?'

Confusion now ruled Charlie's features. Carol took

the opportunity to top up his glass. She noticed that his eyes had drifted once more to focus on the expanse of thigh revealed beneath the abbreviated hem of her skirt. Then she remembered that her panties were scrunched up in a ball on the kitchen floor.

The alcohol was racing through her veins. Right now she couldn't care less if this big dummy broke Bart into matchsticks. But there *were* other, pleasanter ways for a girl to take revenge. She crossed her legs.

'Look here, Carol.' Charlie had reshuffled his emotions — now he was aggrieved. 'I bin done wrong,' he said with emphasis. 'Your husband took something that was *mine* and he ain't gonna get away with it!'

'That makes sense. I agree with you.'

'You do?'

'Sure. He took something of yours, now you've got to even the score. Take something of his.'

There was silence. Carol imagined she could hear the gears change in Charlie's head. She realized she was still sopping wet between the legs.

'Like what?'

Oh God, he was forcing her to spell it out —

'Like me, you big dufus. He took your wife, you take his . . . it's obvious.'

'But — '

'What's the matter, Charlie? Don't you like blondes with long legs? Or do you only go for short dark girls with melons on their chests?'

Carol could have bitten her tongue off after that last crack. Vodka and frustration were getting to her.

Fortunately Charlie was still digesting the significance of her earlier remarks.

It was time for action. She rose from her seat and stood over him, her feet between the angle of his great sprawling legs, her crotch two feet in front of his face.

'Come on, Charlie, be a man and even the score. At least – do it for my sake.'

And she took hold of her skirt at the sides and began to pull the material upward. His astonished eyes were glued to the hem as it rose, centimeter by centimeter, up the length of her smooth golden thighs.

'I suppose I ought to tell you,' she said as she reached the point of no return, 'that I'm not wearing any panties.'

'I know,' he replied, sliding two spade-like hands up the back of her thighs to cup the bare cheeks beneath the flimsy cotton of her skirt, 'I bin looking up your twat ever since you sat down. Boy, was I embarrassed. And, boy, have I got a hard-on now.'

'Oh Charlie.' The skirt was up around her waist and she held his curly blond locks in her fist as she pressed his great boyish face into the wet folds of her pussy.

For a dummy he ate her out pretty good, she thought. But then doubtless Rita had him well trained in that department. She ground her crotch into his face, shamelessly rubbing herself to the relief she had been cheated of by his unexpected arrival.

'Oh God, Charlie,' she wailed as the first shockwave hit her, rippling through her belly and buckling her knees. Then she tore herself from his grasp and pulled him to his feet.

Part of her was amazed at her own manic behaviour as she began to rip at his shirt and claw at the belt of his jeans. She wanted him nude. She wanted this great blond hunk stripped naked for her pleasure and she wanted it *now*!

'Hey, honey, go easy. Hey, Carol!' he cried as his shirt buttons flew across the room and her long nails tore into his belly. But he stood there placidly as, on her knees now, she yanked down his jeans and shorts in one violent tug. Then she stopped.

'Oh Christ,' said Carol.

He looked down at her smugly. Charlie knew that girls found this part of his anatomy — impressive.

'It's beautiful,' said Carol as she placed both hands on the stiff distended limb. It was almost hairless, the skin of the trunk-like shaft a snowy white in contrast to the brilliant puce of the ruby red helmet. A golden fuzz of hair shaded the pink plums that dangled beneath. Carol gripped the base of the root with one hand, then measured upward, hand over hand three times. 'Like a horse,' she said to herself, 'three hands high.'

'Satisfied?' he asked.

'That depends on where you put this thing. It sure as hell won't go in my mouth.' It was true, she was gagging on the glans now, trying without success to fit it inside.

Charlie laughed. He felt good. Especially to have this classy blonde so hot for him. Sometimes girls changed their minds when they saw the size of him. This chick wasn't running anywhere.

'Lick it,' he commanded. 'Make it nice and wet. You know how.'

She did, of course. Knew how to make herself wet, too, slipping a hand between her legs to make herself ready to take the biggest cock she'd ever seen.

He slipped his hands beneath her armpits and lifted her upwards.

'Hang on to my neck,' he said and slid his hands beneath her ass, cupping a buttock in each palm as she twined herself round him, hooking her legs over his hips and linking her ankles behind the small of his back.

'I call this the Five Easy Pieces,' he whispered into her ear as the little fingers of his hands delved into her split and delicately spread open the flaps of her cunt. Carol could feel the air between her splayed lips. She felt incredibly helpless. And incredibly excited.

'What do you mean?' Where was it, that great thing. She knew he was going to stick it in her at any moment.

'Five Easy Pieces. The new Jack Nicholson movie about this guy and all these broads and he has a big row with a waitress in a diner.'

What was he on about? And where was his great cock? She wanted it, needed it right now, up her to the hilt.

'Oh, Charlie, put it in me please. Please, Charlie. Please fuck me!'

'Well, in one scene, old Jack is dorking this girl —'

There it was! She could feel the head of it wedged between her thighs, right at the junction of her legs, solid and broad and, oh God, big, searching for the keyhole like a midnight drunk on the doorstep.

'She's daffy little babe with blonde curly hair and these really cute tits — '

Carol jinked her ass, trying to position the hungry mouth between her legs, he, too, cleverly jockeying her as he bent his knees and then — thrust up . . .

It was in her now, a column of solid flesh invading her insides. A living rod pushing higher and deeper and 'Oh, oh, oh!' — she was sitting full on it as it still pushed in, threatening to split her in two, to fill her up with pain but miraculously spreading a sweet golden glow through her veins like honey . . .

' — and Jack is walking up and down while he fucks her!'

He was still talking as she came the first time, sinking her teeth into his neck, clinging to his torso like a gibbering monkey up a tree.

Then he began to walk her around the room, jogging her up and down on the solid arm of his dick as she did so. 'Oh God, oh God,' she cried, 'don't drop me please!' But there was no chance of that, not before he had finished his party piece. Now he began to walk into the hall.

'No, Charlie! Don't go by the window!'

But he had turned and begun to walk upstairs, still holding her firmly beneath the ass, his great dick spearing in and out of her as they mounted the stairs. By the time they had reached the top landing and he had pushed the bedroom door open with her back, she had run out of protests.

He stopped in front of the full-length mirror which hung on the open door of the wardrobe.

'Aha,' he said in triumph, 'now we can see what we're doing!'

And so they could. Looking over her shoulder Carol took in the bizarre sight of her body wound round the giant's torso and the obscene out-thrust of her ass bulging over his huge sausage-like fingers. The pink eye of her anus winked out at her above the rear view of her slick pussy-mouth gorging on the thick rod of his cock. He jiggled her up and down, making the creamy ovals of her ass shiver, the hairy sack of his balls joggling oddly beneath her spread cheeks.

Then things got just little hectic. Either the erotic vision in the mirror was too much for Charlie, or else his strength finally gave out, for he suddenly pitched forward onto the bed, Carol pinned beneath him helplessly, and began to shaft in and out of her like an unleashed jack rabbit.

'Oh Charlie, of Charlie, oh Charlie – ' she found herself crying, either in pleasure, or pain, as he crashed into her with all his strength.

When it was all over, and it didn't last long, she was amazed to discover that she felt great. Satisfied, sexy and – amply revenged. What's more, she could now think straight again.

'Charlie,' she said, 'will you be up to any more vengeance today?'

'Uh?'

'I mean, the other guy in the pictures, you ought to straighten yourself out with him.'

'Right.'

Carol reached for the phone by the bed and began to dial.

Shirley answered after one ring.

'What are you doing right now?' said Carol.

'Is this an invitation?'

'You bet. I want you over here to meet a friend of mine. He's a film buff. And he's got a surprise for you.'

'What kind?'

'The kind you like best, Shirley. A very big one.'

The Three Chums

Like *The Pearl*, the scurrilous Victorian magazine *The Boudoir* — 'A Magazine of Scandal, Facetiae, Etc.' — was the *Penthouse* or *Men Only* of its day, providing saucy entertainment for a (presumably) male readership. *The Boudoir* only survived for six issues but nevertheless its contents are still of interest, being comprised principally of naughty verses, off-colour jokes and lewd stories bearing titillating titles such as 'How Maria Got a New Pair of Garters' and 'What I Saw in a Garret'.

The mainstays of the magazine, however, were the longer stories which ran as serials. Such a tale is *The Three Chums*, reproduced here in its entirety, an account of a young rake's randy frolics in the great metropolis. As can be guessed from its title, the writing is strictly of the 'jolly japes' variety and naturally young Charlie Warner's sexual prowess exceeds the merely mortal. This is a world of pure erotic make-believe — although it does raise the question of exactly what the young students of the day did get up to when celebrating Queen Victoria's birthday. One thing is certain, if it even approached the antics of The Three Chums, the old lady would not have been amused at all . . .

I

Charles Warner, the son of a wealthy squire who owned a large estate in the Midlands, had just arrived in town, and taken up his apartments in Gower Street, for the purpose of becoming a medical student, as of course being only a younger son, and the freehold property all entailed, his jolly parent could think of nothing better in which his sharpest boy, as he called Charlie, would be so likely to make his way in the world.

'Be a good lad, Charlie; stick to your profession, and I'll set you up with ten thousand when you marry a girl with some tin; that's the only thing a younger son can do. Should I die before that it's left you in my will. Your allowance is three hundred pounds a year, to be five hundred years when you come of age; but mind, if you disgrace me or get into debt, I will turn you adrift without a penny, or pay your passage to Australia to get rid of you. My boy,' he finally added, a tear in his eye and a slight quiver of the lip, as he said tremulously, 'you have always been a favourite; your old dad reckons on you to keep away from the girls and bad companions.'

He was thinking over these last parting words of his father as he sat by the fireside after tea awaiting the call of his two cousins, Harry and Frank Mortimer, who had written to say they would call to take him out, and see how he liked the rooms they had found for him.

He presently rang the bell to have the table cleared, and a remarkably pretty maidservant answered his summons.

'And what is your name? As I am going to live in the house and should like to know how to call you. I'm so glad Mrs Letsam has a pretty girl to attend on the lodgers.'

'Fanny, sir,' replied the girl, blushing up to her eyes. 'I have to wait on all the gentlemen, and a hard time I have of it running up and down stairs all day long.'

'Well,' said Charlie, 'I shan't ring for you more than I can help, although it is not at all strange if some of them trouble you so often, if only for the pleasure of seeing a pretty face. I suppose it isn't proper here in London to kiss the servants, although I often did at home; the girls were older than me, and had been used to it for a long time.'

'La, no sir, you mustn't, indeed you mustn't, if Mrs Letsam knew it she would turn me out of the house in a moment,' exclaimed Fanny, in a subdued tone, as if afraid of being heard, as she turned her face away from his unexpected salute.

'You mean to say you mind a kiss from a boy like me? What harm is there?'

'I — I don't know; I can't say,' stammered Fanny. 'But it's so different from those old fellows downstairs, who always give me half a crown after, not to tell.' Here she blushed tremendously. 'I — I didn't mean, sir, that I want to be paid, but that you are so different than them; they're old and ugly, and you — '

She could not say any more, for Charlie pressed his lips to her rosy mouth, saying, 'Well then, give me a kiss for forgiveness. If you only keep good friends, and look after my small wants, I shall buy you ribbons and little things of that sort, so that you can think of me when you wear them.'

His only answer was a very curious look as she returned his kiss; then slipping away took up her tray and was gone.

'I'm in luck,' soliloquised Charlie. 'Dad may lecture me to keep away from the girls. Polly and Sukey at home didn't kiss me for nothing; the sight of this pretty Fanny and the thoughts of last night when they had me between them for the last time, makes me feel quite so-so. In fact that girl has given me the Irish toothache; it was all very well for dear old dad to caution me, but they say like breeds like, and I know he got a girl with twins before he was eighteen, and had to be sent away from home to get out of the scrape.'

Here there was a tap at the door of his room.

'Come in, my boys; I know who it must be,' shouted Charlie, expecting his cousins, but to his surprise Mlle. Fanny re-enters.

'If you please, sir, there's two young gentlemen for Mr Warner, they have sent up their card.'

'Where is it, Fanny?' asked Charlie, holding out his hand for the bit of pasteboard.

'Well, I am pleased they've come early,' he said, catching her by the wrist, 'and especially as it gives me the chance of another kiss!'

'For shame, sir; you'll keep them waiting in the hall,' as she struggled to get away from his encircling arm.

'Just a moment, Fanny, I want to say to you they are my cousins, who will often come here, and are much better looking than me, so don't you make me jealous by taking any notice of either of them. Now, ask them up, quick, please; then run for a bottle of fizz, and keep the change for yourself,' he said, handing her a sovereign. 'We must wet the apartments the first time they call.'

It is not necessary to refer to all the greetings and enquiries of the cousins when they first met; but presently, when the champagne was opened, Harry and Frank asked if Charlie was too tired to go out for the evening, saying, 'You need not come back here to sleep, but turn in with us, as you know the governor will be so pleased to see you at breakfast in the morning. We know three jolly sisters — little milliners — who work in Oxford Street, such spooney girls, and as three to two is sometimes awkward you will just make the party complete; they live in Store Street, close by, and if we call about nine o'clock they will be expecting us, and glad to see you; it is awfully jolly, and not too expensive, we only have to stand supper. The girls think too much of themselves to take money, although nothing else comes amiss from jewellery to dresses. Nothing coarse, no bad language, and they only permit liberties when the gas is turned out.'

'I'm with you,' replied their cousin, 'and what do you think of the little servant here?'

'Charlie, you ought to be in luck there,' answered Harry, 'it's so convenient to have a nice little servant to sleep with sometimes, or now and then to let off the steam with her on the sofa, it keeps you from going out too much. My advice, Charlie, is not to live too fast, save your money for a good spree — say every ten days or so. Your racketty ones don't get on half so well with their governors, who are always grumbling. Now our dad thinks us quite good, never out after half-past eleven or so; but we make up for it with the servants at home, and keep the housekeeper square, by taking turns to poke her on the sly. She once caught us both in the girls' bedroom, but we went into hers to beg her not to tell, and what with kissing and telling her what a fine figure she was (she was half undressed when she came to see after the servants) that we took first one liberty then another, till seeing she was on the job I ran out and left Frank to roll her on the bed, which he must have done to some purpose, for she kept him all the night.'

'Ah, Charlie, I never thought a woman of fifty could be so good at the game; how she threw her legs over my buttocks, and heaved up to meet every push of John Thomas; she was a perfect sea of lubricity, and drained me dry enough by morning,' added Frank, in corroboration of his brother's assertion. 'You must try her for yourself, a fair lad will be a treat to her after us two dark fellows, and there's no fear of having to pay for kids with her, as she is past the time of life, but I believe all really warm-constitutioned women get hotter the older they are. We use French letters for safety with the slaveys, or we should soon do their business, they want so much of it when we get in their room, or they slip into ours for a drop of brandy and a "bit of that", as they call it; there's nothing like good brandy to put you up to the work, but never drink gin, my boy, or your affair won't stand for some hours, it has such a lowering effect.'

A couple of hours of similar conversation soon slipped away, and then going round to Store Street Charlie was introduced to the sirens his cousins had spoken of.

II

'My cousin, Charlie Warner, just from the country to become a medical student. Miss Bessie, Annie, and Rosa Robinson, three as pretty and lovely little milliners as you ever saw or will see again,' said Harry, making the introduction as they entered.

The brothers kissed all three girls, and as it seemed the correct thing Charlie was not slow to follow their example, beginning with Rosa, the youngest, a fair, golden-haired, little beauty of seventeen; then Annie, with her light brown hair and hazel eyes, and finishing with Miss Bessie, a twenty-year-old darling, with dark auburn hair, and such a pair of glancing eyes as would almost ravish the soul of any soft-hearted youth who had not a stronger mind than our young hero, who looked on all girls as playthings rather than as being worthy of serious love.

'What a pretty supper the confectioners have sent in for you — fowls, tongue, and champagne — it made us rather expect something unusual, and we are so pleased to see Mr Warner; besides you know there is no jealousy here, and his fair face is a delightful contrast to you two rather dark gentlemen,' said Annie, adding, 'and you, Frank, are my partner for the evening, as Harry was my cavalier last time; and I'm glad there's Mr Warner for Rosa, although Bessie and I shall feel rather jealous about it, we can wait for our turns another day.'

'This is the jolliest place I know of,' said Harry, handing Bessie to her seat at the table; 'everything ready to hand, and nothing cleared away till we are gone; no flunkeys or parlourmaids to wait on us or listen to every word, and we can do as we like.'

'Not exactly, sir,' put in Annie, 'even when the light is out you must behave yourselves.'

'We have a little longer this evening for our dark séance,' said Frank; 'we are taking Charlie to the theatre, and to Scott's for supper, so they don't expect us till half past twelve or so, and the housekeeper will sit up for her reward, won't she, Harry?'

'What's that,' pouted Rosa, giving a sly look; 'oh, those two boys are dreadful, just as if they would want any more of "that" when they get home.'

'Oh, she never tells tales, so we kiss her,' answered Frank.

'Tell that to your grandmother. As if you could kiss without taking other liberties, sir,' said Annie.

This kind of badinage lasted all supper time, but Charlie pledged the sisters one after the other so as not to show any marked preference, still at the same time in a quiet sort of way he tried all he could to make himself particularly agreeable to Rosa, who evidently was rather taken with him.

'It's so nice to have you to myself,' she said archly, as the supper had come to an end, 'but mind you are not too naughty when they turn out the gas.'

Something in her deep blue eyes and look so fired his feelings that taking her unresisting hand under the table he placed it on his thigh, just over the most sensitive member of the male organisation, and was at once rewarded by the gentle pressures of her fingers, which assured him she quite understood the delicate attention. The others were too absorbed in some similar manipulation to notice Charlie and Rosa, as he adroitly unfastened about three buttons of his trousers, and directing her hand to the place, and presently felt she had quite grasped the naked truth, which fluttered under the delicious fingering in such a way that very few motions of her delicate hand brought on such an ecstatic flood of bliss as quite to astonish Miss Rosa, and necessitate the sly application of a mouchoir to her slimy fingers, as at the same time she crimsoned to the roots of her hair, and looked quite confused, whilst he could feel that a perceptible tremor shot through her whole frame. Fortunately just at that moment Bessie turned off the gas, and instinctively the lips of Charlie and Rosa met in a long impassioned kiss. Tongue to tongue they revelled in a blissful osculation.

He could hear a slight shuffling, and one or two deep-drawn sighs, as if the ladies felt rather agitated.

There was a convenient sofa in a recess just behind Charlie's chair, and Rosa seemed to understand him so well that he effected a strategic movement to the more commodious seat under cover of darkness. There he had the delightful girl close to his side, with his right arm round her waist, whilst his left hand found no resistance in its voyage of discovery under her clothes. What mossy treasures his fingers searched out, whilst for her part one arm was round his neck, and the warm touches of her right hand amply repaid his Cytherian investigations in the regions of bliss. His fiery kisses roved from her lips all over her face and neck, till by a little manoeuvring he managed to take possession of the heaving globes of her bosom. How she shuddered with ecstasy as his lips drew in one of her nipples, and gently sucked the delicious morsel; a very few moments of this exciting dalliance was too much for her. She sank back on the couch, so that he naturally took his proper position, and in almost less time than it takes to write it, the last act of love was an accomplished fact.

Then followed delicious kissings and toyings; no part of her person was neglected, and when, as a finale, she surrendered the moist, dewy lips of the grotto of love itself to his warm tonguings, the excess of voluptuous emotion so overcame her that she almost screamed with delight, when the crisis came again and again in that rapid succession only possible with girls of that age.

They had been too well occupied to hear or notice anything about Bessie and Annie with their partners, but now an almost perfect silence prevailed in the apartment, till presently Harry spoke out, saying, 'I think the spirits have had long enough to amuse themselves; what do you say to a light?'

This was agreed to, and they spent another half hour with the ladies before taking leave of them for the night. It was as curious a feast of love as Charlie could possibly have imagined, and he was quite puzzled to make out what manner of girls these three sisters could be who bashfully objected to a light on their actions, and yet were as free with their partners as any of the mercenary members of the demi-monde could have been.

'What a darling you are!' whispered Rosa to Charlie as he took a parting kiss, 'but I shan't have you next time unless there is an undress romp in the dark.'

Bessie pressed them to come to an early tea on Sunday, and have a long evening, when they would arrange some pretty game to amuse them. This was agreed to with many sweet kisses and *au revoir*, &c.

III

It was nearly one a.m. when the boys got home to the Mortimer mansion in Bloomsbury Square.

'How late you are,' said Mrs Lovejoy, the house-keeper, opening the door to them, 'and you have brought Master Charlie with you. I'm so glad to see him; your father has gone to bed hours ago, and I thought you would like a second course after your oyster supper at Scott's, so there's a little spread in my own room upstairs, only we mustn't keep it up too late.'

'You're a brick,' said Harry, 'we'll go upstairs so quietly past dad's door, and kiss you when we see what you have got for us.'

Mr Mortimer père being a rather stout gentleman, who objected to many stairs, had his bedroom on the first floor; Harry and Frank's room was on the next flight, where their sisters also had their rooms when at home from school; the two servants and Mrs Lovejoy located above them.

'There's my kiss,' said Frank, as on entering Mrs Lovejoy's cosy room he saw a game pie and bottle of Burgundy set out for their refreshment.

Harry and Charlie also in turn embraced the amorous housekeeper, who fairly shivered with emotion as she met the luscious kiss of the latter.

'He's only going to stay this one night, so it's no good taking a fancy to my cousin; besides, can't you be content with Frank and myself?' whispered Harry to her.

'But you are such unfaithful boys, and prefer Mary Anne or Maria to me at any time,' she replied, pettishly.

'Yes, and Charlie is no better; he hasn't been in London one whole day yet without making up to the pretty Fanny at his lodgings; oh, she's a regular little fizzer, Mrs Lovejoy.'

The second supper was soon discussed, and Mrs Lovejoy had placed hot water and spirits on the table just for them to take a night-cap as she called it, when there was a gentle tap at the room door, and a suppressed titter outside.

Harry, guessing who it was, called out 'come in', when the two servant girls with broad grins on their faces walked into the room, only half dressed – in petticoats, stockings, and slippers, with necks and bosoms bare.

On perceiving Charlie they blushed scarlet, but Mary Anne, a regular bouncing brunette, immediately recovered her presence of mind, and said, 'We beg your pardon, Mrs Lovejoy, but we thought only Master Harry and his brother were here, and felt so thirsty we couldn't sleep, so ventured to beg a little something to cool our throats.'

'We'll make a party of it now,' said Frank; 'this is only our cousin Charlie, so don't be bashful but come in and shut the door.'

'Gentlemen don't generally admit ladies, especially when only half dressed, as we are,' said Maria, a very pretty and finely developed young woman, with light brown hair, rosy cheeks, and such a pair of deep blue eyes, full of mischief, as they looked one through.

'No, but ladies admit gentlemen,' put in Charlie, 'don't mind me,' getting up from his chair and drawing the last speaker onto his lap. 'I guess we're in for some fun now.'

The housekeeper looked awfully annoyed at this intrusion, but Harry laughingly kissed her, and whispered something which seemed to have a soothing effect, as she at once offered the two girls some lemonade and brandy. Hers was a very comfortable apartment, being furnished the same as a bachelor's bed and sitting room combined; the bed was in a recess, and there were two easy chairs besides a sofa, table, &c., in the room.

Harry secured the sofa, where he sat with Mrs Lovejoy on his lap, and one of his hands inside the bosom of her dressing gown, whilst her hands, at least one of them, were God knows where, and very evidently gave him considerable pleasure, to judge by the sparkle of his eyes, and the way he caressed her, as well as the frequent kisses they inter-changed.

Charlie was admiring and playing with the bosom of Maria, who kissed him warmly every now and then, giving the most unequivocal signs of her rising desires for closer acquaintance.

'We shall never be fit to get up in the morning if you keep us out of bed; let the girls go now,' said Mrs Lovejoy.

Each said 'good night', and Harry, having something to say to the housekeeper, stayed behind. Frank and Mary Anne quickly vanished in the gloom of the outside corridor, and Charlie, at a loss where he was to sleep, asked Maria to show him to his room.

'You'll sleep with me, dear, if you can, and I won't keep you awake,' she whispered, giving him a most luscious kiss; then taking his hand she led him into a very clean but plainly furnished bedroom.

'Mary Anne won't be back tonight, so you shall be my bedfellow. I guess by this time Master Frank is being let into all her secrets,' saying which she extinguished the candle, which had been left burning, and jumped into bed, Charlie following as quickly as he could get his things off.

'I've got a syringe, so I'm not afraid, although Harry and Frank will always put on those French letters. Do you think they're nice?' asked Maria, as she threw her arms around him, and drew him close to her palpitating bosom.

'Never used such a thing in my life,' replied Charlie, 'for my part anything of that sort spoils all the fun.'

'Do you know,' continued Maria, 'Mary Anne and I lay thinking, talking, and cuddling one another, in fact we were so excited she proposed a game of what girls call flat c——, when we heard Mrs Lovejoy take you to her room, and we made up our minds she should not have both Harry and Frank to herself, never thinking there was anyone else; and to think I've got such a darling as you!'

The girl fairly quivered with emotion as she lay on her side kissing and cuddling close to his body, but his previous encounters during the preceding twenty-four hours rendered him rather less impulsive, in fact he liked to enjoy the situation, which was such as none but those who have lain by the side of a loving expectant young wanton can thoroughly appreciate. Her hands roved everywhere, and she conducted one of his to that most sacred spot of all, which he found glowing like a furnace, and so sensitive to his touch, that she sighed, 'Oh! Oh!' and almost jumped when she felt his tickling fingers, as they revelled in the luxuriant growth of silky hair, which almost barred the approach to the entrance of her bower of love. Charlie never had such a sleepless night in his life for, impatient of his long delay in making a commencement, she threw a leg over his hip as a challenge, and, having his wand in her hand as fit as busy fingers could make it, she directed Mr Warner so straight that he found not the least difficulty in exploring the very inmost recesses of her humid furbelow, which to judge from its overflowing state was a veritable fountain of butterine. How he rode the lively steed, till, exhausted by the rapidity of the pace, he fell off, only to find Maria had reversed positions, and there was no rest for him till seven o'clock in the morning, and at breakfast his looks only too plainly told the tale of the night's orgy, as Mr Mortimer railed at all three fellows of having had a rakish time of it, remarking that he hoped they would be more moderate in future, but it might be excusable for a first night in town.

IV

Our hero was glad to stay in his own rooms and rest the next evening, and felt rather too used up to indulge in much more than a mild joke and a kiss with the pretty Fanny, who had a rather pouting expression on her face as she bid him goodnight after what she considered to be a decidedly languid kind of kiss.

'He isn't so fresh as when he arrived, but perhaps he will be more lively at breakfast time,' she mused, going downstairs to the lower regions of the house. 'I hope Mrs Letsam won't get at him, that's all!'

Charlie was so done up that he went to bed by ten o'clock, and slept so soundly that he awoke quite early, feeling as frisky as a lark, and with the peculiar elevation of spirits which most healthy young fellows are subject to when they first open their eyes in the morning.

'J.T. is quite himself again,' exclaimed Charlie, as he threw off the bedclothes to survey the grand proportions of that part of his anatomy sacred to the service of the fair sex. Then looking at his watch by the aid of the lamp which he had left burning, 'By jove, how early; only half-past four. I'll look outside in the corridor in search of adventure, there is just a chance I might find Fanny's room, as this is the top storey; she can't go higher up, and isn't likely to be lower down.'

Quick as the idea flashed across his mind he stepped out of bed, and taking the little lamp in his hand opened his door very gently and stepped into the corridor, which was a long passage with three or four doors of rooms besides those of his own apartments. He listened at the first one, but hearing nothing passed on to the next, which was slightly ajar; hesitating for a moment he heard the loud stentorian breathing of a heavy sleeper, so shading the lamp with his hand he pushed the door gently open, when what should he see but his fat landlady, Mrs Letsam, lying on her back in bed with her knees up and mouth open. Although so bulky Mrs L was what some would term a truly splendid woman, not more than forty, very pleasing of face, and rich brown hair; whilst her open night dress displayed all the splendours of her mature bosom's magnificent orbs, as white as snow and ornamented by the most seductive strawberry nipples. In reality it was only a chemise, not a proper nightdress, she was sleeping in, so that, as well as the bosom, a large but finely moulded arm was exposed to his searching gaze, and gave him such curious ideas as to the development of other unseen charms, that he resolved to satisfy his curiosity by a manual exploration under the bedclothes. Turning down his lamp he put it outside the door in the corridor, then in the darkness knelt down by the bedside, and slowly insinuating his hand till he touched her thigh, rested till it got warm, then trembling all over with emotion he continued his investigations. His touches seemed marvellously to agitate the sleeper, for after one or two slight involuntary kind of starts, she stiffened her body out quite straight as she turned on her side with something very much like a deep sigh, and Charlie withdrew his impudent fingers, just as he felt the flow of bliss consequent on his exciting touches.

'She'll think it was a dream; most likely the old girl doesn't often feel like that,' laughed Charlie to himself as he sneaked out of the room, little guessing that Mrs Letsam had been thoroughly awakened, and stepped out of bed the moment he was gone, peeping out into the corridor to see who it was.

'Ha, Mr Warner, it's you, is it? It won't take me long to be even with you for this lark!' she said to herself as she got into bed again. 'I wish the dear boy had got into bed though; his touches gave me the most exquisite pleasure.'

Meanwhile Charlie had got to a door at the furthest end of the corridor, which opened at once as he turned the handle, and sure enough it was Fanny's room, for there lay the object of his desires in a broken restless sleep, with nearly all the bedclothes tossed off. What a sight for an impressionable youth! There she lay almost uncovered as it were, her right hand on the spot which so many men who scandalise the fair sex say they always protect instinctively with their hand whilst asleep for fear of being ravished unawares.

However that may be, Fanny's hand was there, and Charlie conjectured that it was not so much for protection as digitation, judging from the girl's agitated restless dreams; for she was softly murmuring,

'Don't! Pray, don't. You tease me so. Oh! Oh!'

He could see everything as he shaded his little lamp so as not to let the light fall on her eyes − her lovely thighs and heaving mount of love, shaded by the softest golden-coloured down, whilst one finger was fairly hidden within the fair lips of the pinkest possible slit below the dewy moisture which glistened in the light.

'By heavens! What a chance!' said Charlie to himself. 'Perhaps I can give her an agreeable surprise.'

Quick as thought he extinguished his lamp, which he placed on a table, then in the dark groped towards the bed where the pretty Fanny lay quite unconscious of his presence.

The sleeper having tossed off most of the bedcovering, it was quite easy for him to lay himself by her side. He kissed the inviting globes of her firm plump bosom but without awakening her. She simply moaned soft, endearing words as if she felt herself caressed by someone she loved so much. His right hand pushed hers aside and took possession of the tender cleft it had been guarding and pressing at the same time; then he gently placed one leg over hers, pressing his naked person close to her body. What thrills of delighted expectation shot through his whole frame! He quivered from head to foot. The temptation and the intensity of his feelings would stand no further delay. So, he glued his lips to hers in a long luscious kiss, whilst one arm held her firmly embraced, and the other was deliciously occupied in manual preliminaries for the attack on her virgin fortress below.

'Fanny,' he whispered, as she unconsciously responded to his kissing. 'It's me, darling, let me love you now?'

At first he thought she was going to scream, but he sealed her lips by the renewal of his fiery kisses, which seemed fairly to stop her breath. She did not speak but appeared awfully discomposed; deep, long drawn sighs came from her as her bosom heaved with excitement, and her hands feebly tried to push away his intrusive fingers. But desire evidently overcame modesty; her return of his willing kisses became more ardent, and her legs gradually gave way to his efforts to get between them, and instead of repulsing his advances her arms were entwined round his body.

'By Jove!' thought Charlie. 'I'm not the first; she's too easy!' but to his delight he did not find the citadel of her chastity had been stormed before; the battering ram of love had to be vigorously applied before a breach was made sufficient to effect a lodgement. What sighs! What murmurs of love and endearment were mixed with her moans of pain.

'My pet, you are a woman now,' he whispered, lovingly, at the conclusion of the first act, kissing her again and again.

'Oh, Charlie, what a darling; you have been so gentle with me. How I love you now; you will always love me, won't you, dearest? But you can't, you can't marry me, I know.' Here she sobbed hysterically as that thought broke upon her mind. Our hero did all he could to comfort her, but found nothing so conducive to that end as drawing up the curtain for a second scene in the drama of love.

'I don't know what upset me so in my sleep but, dear, I went off thinking of you, and suppose I must have wanted you. Your kissing has made me feel so uneasy and all-overish since you came to the house. No one ever upset me like that before,' she confessed to him in her simplicity, as they lay toying and kissing till daylight. She advised Charlie to take leave of his new love, and retreat to his own room for fear of discovery.

Charlie was so enamoured of Fanny that when she brought up his breakfast he urged upon her a repetition of the pleasures of the night.

'How dare you, sir, talk to me like that by daylight?' she answered, repulsing his bold advances. 'What I may do in the dark is no excuse for this. Mrs Letsam is always watching me like a cat, to see I don't stop in the lodgers' rooms a moment too long.'

It was very reluctantly he let her go. After breakfast having nothing particular to do, and feeling rather sleepy, he tried to take a nap on the sofa, when just as he was dozing off there was a light tap at the door, and in answer to his 'Come in,' who should it be but the landlady with his night lamp in her hand.

There was quite a grin upon her full, round, good-looking face, showing a beautiful set of pearly teeth.

'Mr Warner,' she said, seating herself quite familiarly by his side on the sofa. 'I didn't think you were such a young rake as to ravish my maidservant only a couple of days after coming here. Don't say a word; I know all about it, and have seen the stains in the girl's bed, as well as found your lamp in her room; a pretty scrape you'll be in if the girl falls in the family way!'

Her eyes sparkled, and she looked so curiously towards a certain part of his person, that Charlie saw at once he would have to square the fat, fair, and forty lady to prevent unpleasantness.

'My dear Mrs Letsam, how can you accuse me of such things? Now if it had been you—' he said, laughing.

'That's exactly it, Mr Warner, you despised my more mature charms for a chit like Fanny. Pray what were you doing in my room last night? As if I could sleep and not be woken up by the rude hand you pushed under my bedclothes. I ought to call a policeman and give you in charge for an indecent assault.'

Her soft hand had been placed on his thigh, right over Adam's needle, which fairly throbbed under the pressure.

'And this is the thing to run away from a lady? I shall now take as great liberties with you, young sir,' she said, proceeding to take possession of his manly jewel as it now sprang forth in all its grandeur when she opened the front of his dressing gown.

'The love! Now it's mine! What a beauty!' she exclaimed, leaning over him, and imprinting hot, wanton kisses on the head of the rampant prisoner. Charlie fairly sighed and heaved with excitement under such osculation, he had never felt such an ecstatic thrill before, it was almost a new sensation to him; a simple kiss or two by an enraptured girl, who had just experienced the delights such a darling could give, he understood as a token of extraordinary desire, but the tonguing and pressures of the sucking lips of this wanton woman opened up such a new source of delight, that he almost fainted under her caresses.

'There,' she said, 'you darling, that is my style of love, and beats all the vulgar, straightforward ways of enjoyment. You may have Fanny as much as you like, but let me suck a little of your honey now and then or I will get rid of her; I don't care for a many any other way; besides, I'm not so old but I ought to be careful.'

Charlie kissed her pretty mouth, and told her how delighted he was to have got into such a nice house, adding, 'I never felt such pleasure before, so you may be sure the least touch or kiss will put me in a state to meet and rise to your requirements in a moment,' as he stood kissing her when she rose to go. 'No one ever excited me as you have done. Were you ever struck by lightning? I have heard that such people have an electric touch.'

'No, dear,' she replied, smiling, and showing her lovely teeth, which fascinated him so. 'Although I'm stout, I'm only three-and-thirty and have the misfortune to come of a particularly warm family. Goodbye, now.'

V

The reader can easily guess that Charlie felt considerably enervated after the departure of the lecherous Mrs Letsam. He spent the day reading, and also wrote a letter to his father, telling him how kind the Mortimers had been, and how he liked his rooms, which they had taken for him. Retiring early he was awakened from a sound slumber by warm moist impassioned kisses on his lips, and felt a soft lithe form nestling close to his body, as he heard the whispered words — 'Mr Warner, Charlie dear; I've come to return the visit you paid me last night. It was so nice, I couldn't sleep by myself knowing you were all alone.'

It was impossible not to respond to such a loving invitation.

'It's jolly of you, Fanny, coming into my bed like this, as it proves you do care for me a little but; I feel rather tired after our fun of last night, so I mean to make you be the gentleman this time; straddle over me and help yourself to the tit-bit I know all the girls always long for; then I can lay on my back and take it easy.'

'I rather like your saying I made you tired,' she laughed in reply; 'but you didn't know I saw her knock at your door this morning, and listened and heard all your game together. But I am not jealous, especially as I heard her say you might have me as much as you liked, if you only pleased her in a certain way. What was it, dear, I couldn't quite make out what you did with her; do tell me, there's a very nice darling?'

'It's a very curious taste, but nice to me; she doesn't care for a man to have her in the ordinary way, she prefers to suck his affair, and swallow every drop of the love juice when it comes. How would you like that, Fan? It felt awfully nice to me.'

'Ugh! That must be nasty! What do you think? I once had a girl sleep with me who would kiss and lick my crack, and it made me feel so funny, but I wouldn't do it to her.'

After this they got to business in earnest, Fanny, mounting as directed, soon rode Charlie's rampant steed till she had drawn the essence of life three times from his palpitating loins, their mingled juices making quite a little flood round the root of King Priapus. At length falling asleep in each other's arms, they slept till daylight, and Fanny had to go away about her domestic duties.

Having heard from his cousins what larks went on in the parks at night, Charlie made up his mind to see it for himself, and, having no particular engagement on Friday evening, took a stroll as far as the Marble Arch, and turned into the park, taking the path across towards Knightsbridge, arriving at the drive which leads to the Serpentine, he walked along the path observing the couples sitting on the seats kissing and groping each other.

Presently near the gate he met a couple of young, good-looking girls, who as coolly as possible took him by the arm on each side. 'Come along with us, dear, and feel our soft little fannys,' said one.

Charlie made very little objection, and was soon sitting on a rustic seat under the dark shadow of a big elm tree.

'How much are you going to give us, dear? My little sister is too bashful to speak for herself; you know it's always money first in the park, we are so often bilked by mean fellows, who can't afford a proper bit of kyfer.'

Charlie gave each girl a shilling, with the promise of another if they pleased him.

They were really young and pretty girls, such as the park lecher seldom is lucky enough to pick up, the dark paths and seats being mostly haunted by worn-out hags who cannot stand the illuminating ordeal of the gaslight of the streets.

It scarcely required the groping of a soft little hand inside his unbuttoned trousers to raise all his usual fiery ardour. Each girl (they were not more than eighteen and seventeen respectively) put their arms round his neck and kissed him, the eldest whispering – 'You are a darling young fellow, so different from the dirty old men we generally pick up here, I should so like you to have me properly; my little sister doesn't know what it is yet; she is only up to the tossing off business, but I like the real thing you know, when I can get a proper young bit like you. We can only get out Tuesdays and Fridays. Will you meet us on Tuesday, and go into the Green Park; there you will see lots of fun, and can get out at any time; in Hyde Park we get shut in, and have to climb over the gate.'

He could feel her give a shudder of desire as she said this, whilst one of her hands began to play with his appendages, at the same time as her sister was delightfully manipulating the shaft above. They had slits in their dresses, so that both of his hands found employment, exploring and groping on the one side the soft incipient moss of the elder one's grot, as well as the hairless slit of her sister. The situation was altogether too piquante to last many moments. The ecstatic crisis came almost instantly, and he could also feel them both bedew his fingers with their female tribute to the touches of love, which his roving fingers made them feel so exquisitely.

Our hero was so pleased that he gave each one half-a-crown as he kissed and took leave of them, promising to keep the Tuesday's appointment at the same time.

'You are a darling,' said the youngest, Betsy. 'Won't we keep ourselves for him, Sarah; we don't want much money, do we?'

'No, that we will. I hate the nasty old men; we only do it because mother can't keep the home over us unless we bring in five or six shillings a week somehow,' was the rejoinder.

The girls left him, as they said, to go straight home, refusing his offer to treat them to a drink outside the park.

Sunday came, and with it the tea party at the pretty Misses Robinson's in Store Street. His cousins called to take him with them, and the loving greeting of the young milliners was if anything even warmer than before. Bessie, the eldest, the dark auburn beauty, seemed fairly to quiver with emotion as she kissed him rapturously, whispering as she did so – 'You are my partner this evening, Mr Warner.'

'Nothing will please me better, Bessie, dear; for luscious as I found pretty Rosa, your riper charms must be superior to those of your little sister.'

'I hear what you say, Mr Charlie; just wait till I have

a chance to pay you for your broken promises of constancy to me,' laughed Rosa.

It is needless to say much about the conversation, etc, during tea time, except that Charlie induced Bessie to feel his manly instrument under the table as they sat side by side over their orange pekoe.

After a little time spent in music and singing, the usual turning down of the gas took place, and our hero soon found himself and partner seated very cosily on a sofa in one of the alcoves.

'How I have longed to caress you, Mr Warner,' sighed Bessie, 'for Rosa has done nothing but talk of her darling Charlie ever since the last evening you were here, how delightfully you pleased her, and what a splendid affair you were favoured with; she seems to think of nothing but you, as if you really belonged exclusively to her; but indeed, Charlie, it has made me long to feel in person those thrilling love strokes she must have enjoyed so much, what did you do to please her so?'

'I can't remember just now what we did,' Charlie replied, 'but no doubt as your mind is made up for a little love sport we shall play very much the same game.'

His lips met hers in a long luscious kiss, so exciting that his Aaron's rod was as stiff as possible, whilst her bosom rose and fell in palpitating heaves, and her arms pressed him to her bosom.

Presently he slipped down on his knees, and his hands were exploring the mysteries of her underclothing; her thighs opened readily at the slight pressure of his hand, and he was soon in full possession of the centre of attraction, which he found all glowing and humid from the effects of suppressed desire.

'I must kiss this jewel of love,' exclaimed Charlie, in a quick sort of suppressed whisper; 'my tongue will soon make you feel all that Rosa much enjoyed the other evening.'

She inclined her body backwards, and gave up her person entirely to his tonguing caresses, both her hands lovingly pressing the top of his head, as he ravenously sucked the very essence of her life, which she constantly distilled in thick ambrosial drops under the voluptuous evolutions of his busy tongue.

Deep-drawn sighs, too, well told of the intensity of her feelings; she threw her legs over his shoulders, and squeezed his dear face between her quivering thighs, till at length, giving one long-drawn respiration of delight, he heard her say softly – 'Now, now, Charlie, love, let me have him now; you have excited me so I can't wait another moment for the supreme joys of the strokes of rapture I know you are so well qualified to give.'

No charger ever responded to the trumpet call quicker than did our hero, his trenchant weapon was brought to the present in less time than it takes to say so, and the head, slowly entering between the well-lubricated quivering lips of her pouting love grot, was soon revelling in all the sweets she so plentifully spent from her womb. What heaves and sighs of excessive rapture followed this conjunction; each seemed to dissolve in ecstasy over and over again, till exhausted nature at last compelled them to call a halt.

They sat kissing and caressing each other in mutual satisfied delight for some little time, till Frank was heard to call out — 'Don't you think it is time for a romp without clothes?'

Harry and Charlie assenting at once, each youth slipped off his garments, and assisted his partner to do the same, till presently there was an indiscriminate groping and slapping of bottoms, as an incentive to renewed exertions by the young gentlemen, who were a little limp after their first exertions of love. Rosa somehow instinctively found Charlie.

'Now, sir,' she whispered in his ear, 'you have to do penance for saying the more mature charms of my sister must be superior to mine.'

She was holding his throbbing priapus, which she had caught him by, and the touch of her hand seemed at once to renew all its usual *élan*, he was ready for the charge in a moment, and would have pushed her down upon a convenient sofa.

'No, no, not that way; I want to suck the last drop of its fragrant essence, whilst you treat me to the same pleasure. I don't care to enjoy you the same way you have just had my sister.'

Side by side on the sofa, with heads reversed, they sucked each other's parts like two bees, till the last drop of the honey of love had been extracted.

'Now you can go and try Annie, if you can find her in the dark,' said Rosa, 'but I don't think you've much left for her.'

'Let's go together to find her,' whispered our hero, as he took her round the waist, and they searched about till in another recess they found all four of their companions, almost equally exhausted (not the ladies, for they were handling and laughing at the futile endeavours of their champions to respond to their amorous challenge). At length it was time to dress, but some mischievous one had so mixed all the apparel, they were compelled to invoke the aid of the gas before any of them could resume their attire.

This luscious tableaux of nude figures completed the evening's amusements, and the young gentlemen took their leave with promises of a renewed love feast in a day or two.

VI

Tuesday at the appointed time, Charlie went alone to meet the two sirens of Hyde Park, and found Betsy and Sarah true to their appointment.

After sitting down on a quiet sofa for a few minutes, where they enjoyed some kissing and groping, the two girls suggested a remove across into the other park, and the trio were soon seated on a bench by the walk close to the railings which divided the park from Constitution Hill.

'Now,' said Betsy, 'I want a proper one, my dear. Sarah will look out, so no one can surprise us, and if anyone sees us through the railings it doesn't matter.'

This was a matter sooner said than achieved, for Charlie found the amorous Betsy so difficult to enter on account of the narrowness of the passage, that she had to bite her lips in suppressed agony from the pain of his attempt. But courage effects everything, she was so determined to have it that at last he found himself most deliciously fixed in the tightest sheath he had ever before entered. It was simply most voluptuous, the pressures of the girl's sheath on his delighted instrument made him come in a moment or two. Then, the lubricant being applied, things went easier and a most luscious combat ensued. Betsy was perfectly beside herself with erotic passion, whilst the elder Sarah, instead of standing on guard as she ought to have done, handled his shaft and appendages in her soft hand till the excitement was more than he could bear, making him actually scream with pleasure without interruption, and Sarah would have him place the head of Mr Peaslin just between the lips of her pussy, but would not allow more at present. After spending an hour or two in this delicious al fresco amusement, they took him round the park to see the unblushing games that were going on. Soldiers rogering servant girls, old fellows fumbling young girls, and no end of the most unblushing indecency on every side; the fact being that if people, or couples rather got into the Green Park before the gates closed at ten p.m. they might stop there all night, or could at any time go out by the turnstile at the end of Constitution Hill into Grosvenor Place. The one or two bobbies who patrolled the park seemed to take no notice, or were easily squared by the girls who used the place for business.

In fact, Charlie, saw one stalwart guardian of the

peace doing a glorious grind on the grass till a Lifeguardsman came up and, slapping his naked rump as hard as he could, told him he ought to set a better example. This caused great fun to several who were looking on, especially when the soldier challenged the policeman for half-a-crown to exhibit his prick against his for that amount, the girl he was poking to be the judge.

At this moment a regular old swell came upon the scene, and offered half a sov as a prize, in addition to the wager.

'I won't show for less than a quid,' said the policeman, going on leisurely with his grinding, as he had evidently passed the crisis at the moment his arse was slapped by the soldier.

'Lend me your bull's-eye then, and I will give the quid just for a spree; but I'm damned if I don't have a good sight. I'd give five hundred pounds for a genuine cock-stand for once, it's so long since I had one. A fine prick just drawn from a swimming cunt is the most glorious sight in the world.'

The bobby handed up his lantern to the old swell, who at once turned its glare full on the policeman's arse, standing rather behind as he did so, and even stooping a little, to throw it well underneath, and enjoy the luscious sight, as they still went on with their fucking.

'Here, my boy, lend me your cane, and I'll make him feel nice,' said the old swell, tipping the guardsman a bit of gold.

'Right, your honour!' replied the soldier, taking out

a penknife and splitting the end of the cane up so as to divide it into a lot of thin ends.

Quite seven or eight persons were now round the fucking pair, as the gent commenced to lay on the bobby's brawny rump.

We could hear the stinging cuts and see big weals rise at each impact, which made the plucky fellow bound, and almost groan in pain but, in two or three minutes, it might have been less, he grew intensely excited, ramming into his girl (who evidently enjoyed it) with long, lunging strokes, as she clasped him convulsively, returning a heave of her buttocks for every home thrust.

The red weals looked as fiery as possible, for a network of lines had sprung up all over the blushing surface, when they both seemed to again come together in a perfect frenzy of excitement.

'Now, bobby, show up, before you lose that fine stiffness, see, the guardsman has got himself ready!' exclaimed the old swell, suddenly turning the bull's-eye on the soldier, who had been masturbating himself as he enjoyed the sight, but he was nowhere in the show by the side of the tremendous truncheon which the policeman exposed as he withdrew it with a plop, all glistening with luscious moisture from the girl's yet clinging and longing crack.

The bobby had his quid, and the old fellow walked off, as we supposed, to grope the soldier, who went with him.

Betsy and Sarah drew our hero to a quiet seat, where all three spent quite another hour in fucking, groping, and kissing, till at last Charlie was milked as dry as a stick, and reluctantly bade them good night, with promises of another rendezvous in a day or two.

VII

It would be too tedious to relate all the luscious little incidents that occurred to Charlie with Fanny or Mrs Letsam, or even to describe more of his frequent visits with his cousins to the three pretty milliners of Store Street.

Things went quietly for a time, as the three chums were agreed to save their coin for one grand spree, when père Mortimer would be out of town, and never know if they stayed out all night. This was to be a grand winding-up orgy, preparatory to serious study, when their term began, as all three really wished to prepare themselves to get on in after life in some good profession.

When the day arrived Charlie was to meet his cousins, or rather call for them in Bloomsbury Square, at about ten p.m.

'There's some mischief on tonight, I guess,' said Fanny, who had helped him to put on his overcoat. 'Mind where you go to, Charlie, dear; those cousins will take you to see girls, and God only knows what you may catch!' as she threw her arms round his neck, and almost sobbed with vexation. 'Why can't you come back and have the poor little pussy you pretend to be so fond of, instead of sleeping out as you say you are going to do?'

But he released himself as kindly as possible from the loving embrace, for fear his rising prick should lead him to give way to her endearments, and spoil him for the spree on hand.

'You'll get tipsy, and perhaps be locked up,' she said with a pout, as he skipped downstairs.

He found Harry and Frank quite ready to start, and all three walked off in the highest possible animal spirits. They walked along Oxford Street just as the theatres and music halls had dispersed their audiences to swell the usually crowded thoroughfare. A bevy of students were creating a disturbance, and hustling everyone off the pavement, bonneting the policeman, and behaving very roughly, even to delicate girls who might get in their way.

'Oh, do protect me, and see me safe through the crowd!' said a sweet, pretty well but modestly dressed girl of about seventeen, 'those students always frighten me so!'

'There's three of us, and we'll see you safe. Where do you want to go?'

'My brougham is waiting by Swan and Edgar's, in Regent Street; if you will see me so far, I shall be so obliged.'

'And no further?' enquired Charlie.

'Well I didn't like to be so forward; besides, you would not like to leave your friends,' she said, quietly.

'Take us, too,' said Harry; 'have you no lady friends you could ask to join the party? You must know a couple of pretty girls, for we want to make a night of it.'

'Quick, then; or we may lose them. If not engaged I promised to call before twelve at Blanchard's for two young friends and drive them home; you will be delighted if we find them; and I am pleased enough with my partner,' she said, pressing Charlie's arm, and looking archly in his face, with an expression which spoke a whole volume of voluptuousness.

The brougham was quickly found and ordered to pick them up at Blanchard's. As they walked the short distance to the corner of New Burlington Street, Charlie inquired of his charming companion if she was prepared with supper at home, and finding her resources at that late hour not quite adequate to a party of six, they secured a large game pie, bottle of champagne, brandy, &c., at the restaurant, as soon as they had made sure the young ladies were there; then calling for two bottles of fizz, they wetted the acquaintance before starting off in the brougham for Circus Road, St John's Wood.

Three more exquisitely charming girls could not have fallen to their lot than Clara Seymour, and her companions, Alice Morris and Lena Horwright, the latter an especially voluptuous creature, as will be seen in the sequel.

At length it was closing time for the restaurant, and they embarked on the voyage to the north-west, it being as much as they could all do to squeeze into a brougham only intended for four.

Jehu was in a hurry to get home, so that the clock striking one saw them at their destination, but short as the journey had been the girls managed to rack off a spend from their gentlemen, who enjoyed a delicious grope in the dark, as they jolted along.

Miss Seymour lived by herself in a neat little cottage residence, which had a coach-house and stable attached, Lord Cursitor, her chief patron, allowing her £150 a year to keep a man, horse, and carriage. A rather demure-looking middle-aged servant ushered the party into the house, and showed them into a good-sized elegantly furnished front parlour, which opened by folding doors into Clara's own bedroom, to which the ladies at once retired, leaving the three young gentlemen to themselves for a minute or two.

They were evidently high-spirited girls, to guess from the laughing and joking which seemed going on between them in the bedroom, and presently a succession of gurgling rills could be distinctly heard when they used the *pot-de-chambre* to relieve their bladders.

Charlie rapped at the folding doors, saying, 'I wish you ladies would lend us your spare chamber, we're simply bursting for relief.'

'Are you, my dears?' said Lena, opening the door, pot in hand. 'It's something thicker than water you want to get rid of, I expect.'

Charlie produced such an erection that he rushed to place his prick in Clara's hand, asking her to ease him at once. Nothing loth she drew him to the side of her bed, and raising her clothes exposed the lovely cleft to his amorous gaze.

'My fanny always expects a little kiss first,' she whispered to him, as her face slightly flushed, which added very considerably to her beauty.

Charlie was on his knees in a moment, paying his devotions to that divinely delicate-looking, pink slit, just shaded as it was by reddish golden hair, as soft as the finest silk. His tongue divided its juicy lips, searching out her pretty clitoris, which at once stiffened under the lascivious osculation. It was more like a rabbit's prick than anything, and his fingers could just uncover its rosy head as he gently frigged it, sucking at the same time.

A perfect shudder of emotion thrilled through her body.

'Oh, oh! Fuck me, quick; your kisses have set me on fire!'

Suiting the action to the words, she threw herself backwards across the bed, and Charlie rose to the charge in a moment, throwing himself over her, gluing his lips to hers, as his distended weapon forced its way between the moist but yielding lips of her tight little quim.

A quiver of delight thrilled through her frame as he gained complete insertion, her lovely legs encased in delicate knickerbocker drawers, fringed with lace, and set off by rose-coloured silk stockings and high-heeled Parisian boots were thrown amorously over his fine manly buttocks, whilst his hands were clasped round her lovely rump as it rose in agitated heaves in response to his vigorous thrusts.

Harry took Alice, as Frank was Lena's cavalier, and the three couples came to a crisis in a chorus of amorous ejaculations, as the floodgates of love gave down copious streams of mingled spunk.

Presently, when the first bout was over, they sat down to supper, the gentlemen in their shirt sleeves, and the three young ladies, who had dispensed with their dresses, were in the most charming dishabille.

As soon as the game pie was demolished, each took a girl on his lap, alternately pledging each other, glass in hand, or groping and playing all sorts of larks with each other's pricks and cunts.

Charles was anxious to elicit from each fair one the story of her first seduction, but was met with the usual reticence in such cases, till presently Lena, standing up, said she could recite them some poetry, which exactly tallied with her first experience of the forbidden fruit.

'Bravo, Lena! Go on,' they all exclaimed.

'Yes, but only on one condition, and that these three gentlemen shall have me all together, while you girls give their bums a touch of the twigs. Do you agree?'

'Yes, yes. Bravo, Lena! Go on.'

'Well then, here goes, The Maiden's Dream. But I must recline upon the sofa, with nothing on but my chemise.'

Then, suiting the action to the word, threw off her dressing gown, laid down in a luxurious position, with her eyes closed, feigning a tumultuously excited dream, one leg bent up, the other hanging over the sofa, her chemise turned up, exposing all the thighs and quim, one hand frigging gently, she lay squirming in ecstasy, as she recited:

One night, extended on my downy bed,
Melting in am'rous dreams, although a maid,

My active thoughts presented to my view,
A youth, undrest, whose charming face I knew.
His wishful eyes express'd his eager love,
And twinkl'd like the brightest stars above.
'Bless me,' said I, 'Philander, what d'ye mean?
'How come you hither? — Pray, who let you in?
'Undrest! — 'Tis rudeness to approach my bed:
'Consider, dearest youth, that I'm a maid.'
With that between the sheets one leg he thrust,
Mix'd it with mine, and sighing said, 'I must!'
Then clasp'd me in his arms: I strove to squeak,
But found I had no power to stir or speak;
My blood confus'dly in its channels ran,
My body was all pulse, my breath near gone;
My cheeks inflam'd, distorted were mine eyes,
My breast swell'd out with passion and surprise.
And still in vain I strove to make a noise,
Something, methought, I felt that stopp'd my voice,
And did at last such tides of joy impart,
That glided through each vein, and fill'd my heart,
Recall'd my dying senses back again,
And with a flood of pleasure drown'd my pain.
Thus, for a time, I lay dissolved in bliss,
As if translated into Paradise;

Alas! one prick's a farce, 'tis not enough for me.
Come on, my boys, I'm game to take all three!

All now stripped to the buff, except the slippers and
the silk stockings, which added to the natural beauty
of the ladies' legs and feet.

'Ah! I had a delicious spend!' exclaimed Lena, springing on the bed, 'but not to be compared with what I expect now, for I shall ride a St George on Charlie, take Harry in my bottom, and Frank in my mouth.'

She was raging with voluptuous desire, and straddling over our hero, as he lay on his back, impaled herself on his pego, which previous efforts to please the ladies had now brought to a chronic state of enormously stiff erection, it seemed to fill her luscious quim to its utmost capacity, to judge from the stretched appearance of the vermilion lips, as they amorously clung around the staff of life, they so delighted to suck in and out.

Harry was at, or rather in his post of duty as quickly as it can be written; then Frank, kneeling over Charlie's face, presented his prick as a bonne bouche for Lena to gamahuche, her bottom and head now moved in slow and graceful undulations, as she commenced this three-fold bout of enjoyment.

Alice and Clara, each provided with light birches, of about three long sprigs, gently touched up the exposed bottoms, till they fairly reddened under the smarting cuts, and quickened the love canter into an impetuous gallop, so that, when the emitting crisis came, the three young fellows fairly howled and shouted with excess of delighted emotion, whilst Lena, going into a fit of hysteria, laughed, cried, and stiffened herself over Charlie, almost throwing Harry out of her bottom, whilst her teeth closed so convulsively on Frank's prick that his delight was considerably mixed with pain.

When they had a little recovered themselves, 'After all,' said Clara, 'if you have ever read the "Education of Laura," there is a scene there that beats you, Lena, for Rose finishes off five young fellows at once, by frigging one in each hand, as well as three, like you just had our friends.'

'I could very soon do that,' retorted Lena, 'But I don't want to be selfish. Now, which of you girls will volunteer to let me birch you, to excite their three cocks to another grand fuck.'

Alice was agreeable, if someone would horse her on his back and hold her firmly by the wrists. 'I'm such a coward, the first cut will make me wince, yet I know how nice and delightful the finish is,' she exclaimed.

Frank engaged to be the horse, as he felt rather spiteful and wished someone to feel real pain, saying he should much prefer to hold Lena on his back, and know her bottom was being well skinned for biting his poor John Thomas.

'I am very much obliged to you for your kind wishes, but Alice's tender rump will give you just as much satisfaction, poor boy, when I once begin to apply some of Mrs Martinet's scientific touches to it.'

'This is a serious business,' she continued, 'so I shall just take a double-sized switch of twigs, from the cupboard. Those thin ticklers are only useful just to touch up a man in the act of fucking. Alice's whipping must be much more severe in order to stimulate the now languid tools of our friends, and rouse them again to a state of lustful fury by the sight of the red flesh and dripping drops of the ruby, as it is distilled from the abraded skin.'

'Oh, pray don't be so bad as that, Lena,' said Alice, apprehensively, as she slightly resisted Harry and Charlie trying to mount her on Frank's back.

'No, Miss Pert, no nonsense, no drawing back, or I really will make it worse for your bum!' exclaimed Lena, standing up and looking fiercely at her helpless victim, now firmly held over Frank's manly back, whilst Harry and Charlie knelt down on either side to hold her legs, whilst the pretty Clara promised to play with each of the gentlemen's cocks in turn, so as gradually to work them up to a state of glorious stiffness.

'Oh, it stings so! Ah, not quite so hard, Lena, dear,' sighed Alice, as the first two or three light touches made her buttocks tingle under the smart.

'Is that better, you rude girl? Didn't I catch you frigging yourself in bed this morning?' asked Lena, with a spiteful smile on her face.

'Ah, ah, oh, no! My God, how you cut me! I shall die. I never frigged myself. I should be ashamed to do such a thing,' she sobbed, the tears trickling down her blushing face.

'Just listen to the hardened thing. It's as bad as saying I'm a liar!' retorted Lena, with two vicious cuts, which made poor Alice scream in agony, and drew the blood up under the skin of her rump.

'Ah, you bad girl, I'll whip the frigging fancy out of you. Wouldn't it be nice to be frigged just now your fanny is rubbing against Frank's back?'

'Oh! Oh!! Oh!!! I didn't!' screamed Alice.

The cuts fell in rapid succession on the devoted bum. The victim still struggled and writhed under Lena's scathing cuts, but her head fell forward on Frank's shoulder, her face suffused with crimson flushes, and eyes closed in a kind of voluptuous languor.

Charlie had acted on the frigging suggestion, and, by his light touches on her excited clitoris, had made her almost faint under the combination of excitements, as she spent so profusely that her thick, creamy emission trickled over his busy fingers and down Frank's back.

'Lay her on the bed and fuck her,' exclaimed Lena, flinging down the rod. 'Who'll have me on the horsehair sofa? Will you, Harry?'

'I'm randy enough for anything, my love!' exclaimed Harry, flashing his pego. 'Charles and Clara are not thinking of us; see, he is into her on the hearthrug; look, how she heaves her arse! It's just how Adam and Eve must have shagged on the grass in Eden.'

'Oh, it does prick the flesh so,' exclaimed Lena, as she plumped her bottom on the horse-hair, 'but it's the finest thing to stimulate a woman you can think of, the little prickly ends of the stiff hair are like pins, and make your arse bound under every single stroke, it's simply delicious; no one but those who try it can appreciate the delights of a horse-hair sofa fuck.'

How she bounded and writhed as Harry fairly and furiously pounded his prick into her swimming cunt, which seemed to be perfectly insatiable; she was spending again and again every two or three minutes, till at last, with a perfect howl of delight, she drew down his pent-up emission, which shot up into her vitals like a stream of liquid fire.

Kissing and billing they lay entranced in each other's arms for a few minutes, till someone remarked that it would be soon time for breakfast, if they didn't have a little rest.

Thus ended an ever-to-be-remembered night of Charlie Warner's student life, and after breakfast a few hours later they left the three ladies with many expressions of gratification, and promises to renew the pleasures of the past night at an early opportunity.

VIII

Four o'clock, a.m., of a glorious sunny morning, as Charlie Warner opened his eyes to find himself lying in Fanny's arms, almost naked on his bed, the covering having evidently slipped off onto the floor during the amorous play of the preceding night; they were fast embraced, or rather locked together, his prick as stiff as possible, throbbing against the soft ivory skin of his companion's person, the curly hair of their organs of love mingling together in the close conjunction of their bodies.

Fanny's lips were slightly open, displaying a lovely set of small pearly teeth whilst her arms ever and anon clasped his form with a light nervous tremor, as if she was still dreaming of the delights of the past night.

'She fucked me as dry as a stick, last night,'

soliloquised Charlie, 'yet I feel brimming over with spunk again, and ready to spend over her naval.'

'Wake up, Fanny, my love!' he softly whispered, putting two of his fingers into her still damp slit, and rubbing gently on her excited clitoris. 'Wake up, sleeping beauty, I must have one quick. See how stiff he is. Look at your darling. Don't you know that is the Queen's birthday, 24th May, 18 — and, in honour of her Majesty, I mean to fuck as many girls as I can today, at least between now and tomorrow morning, and I mean to begin with you.'

'You randy fellow, do you think I will oblige you after such a speech as that?' laughed Fanny, as she woke with a start. 'I can't help myself this minute, because I've been dreaming of you all night. You seemed always in me, spending and spending till I seemed actually dissolving in love, and then you wake me up with a reference to having other girls during the day. Still I can't refuse this delicious morsel just now, but it will be different when you come home tonight, after your day's whoring. I shall look at you with disgust then.

'Oh, put it into me quick!' she ejaculated with a sigh, opening her legs, to receive the object of her desire.

It was a short hot affair, as most first fucks in the morning are, when the blood is heated from wine, champagne, &c., imbibed over night.

He stroked her twice, to Fanny's infinite satisfaction, before he withdrew from the tight folds of her deliciously warm cunt.

Then they slept till nearly six o'clock, when Fanny had to get up for her daily work.

Our friend Charlie indulged in another two hours' snooze, till he was awakened by the sensation of feeling his prick sucked by a delightfully warm mouth, and found Mrs Letsam, his landlady, indulging in one of her erotic suckings, which usually gave him so much pleasure and, on this occasion, the thought that she was cleaning his pego of all the dried-up spendings that Fanny had left on it so excited his fancy that he came in a perfect frenzy of emission, till the spunk fairly frothed in her mouth and oozed from its corners as she ravenously tried to swallow every drop.

After breakfast, Charlie again racked off Fanny's juice on the sofa, and then started to call upon Clara, in her little house at St John's Wood.

Only Lena was at home with Clara, but they were overjoyed to see him so brimful of spirits, and his prick, as soon as he got into their company, was as rampant as ever.

The two girls were having a light breakfast as they sat in their dressing gowns, fresh from the matutinal cold bath, their cheeks rosy with youthful health, stimulated by the cold douche which, with the hard rubbing they had given each other, had roused all the warmth of their blood, till they were in that state of voluptuous readiness, so fit for the reception of a fine young fellow like Charlie.

Each pretty girl tipped him the velvet end of her tongue, as he kissed their cherry lips, Lena saying: 'How nice of you to call so early, Mr Warner; it is

just in time to give each of us "one of them", before
we go out for a drive round Regent's Park. Don't you
know a fuck is truly delicious to a girl in the morning,
just after she has had her cold bath, when she is all
aglow, and the blood tingles through her veins from
head to foot?'

'A cup of coffee, and then — ' said Clara, pouring
out one for their visitor.

'Without milk or sugar, if you please,' replied
Charlie. 'I shall get all that as I gamahuche you both,
and suck up your spendings.'

Impatient for another go in, he soon led them into
the bedroom, where there was a delicious and soft cool
air from the open window of a small conservatory,
which communicated with Clara's *chambre à coucher*.

They were soon as naked as Cupids, and Charlie,
making them lean back on the bed, sucked each cunt
in turn, till they writhed and spent on his active tongue,
as its ravishing touches then rolled round their
lascivious clitorises.

'This is Clara's house, so she is entitled to have the
first put-in,' said Lena, 'and you shall suck as much
honey as you can from my little buttercup fanny,
whilst you fuck her.'

'We'll show you a new position, Charlie dear,'
added Clara, as she extended herself on the bed. 'Get
between my legs and as soon as you are in — yes, that's
it; now throw your left leg up over my loins, and put
your right under my right leg, and then lay your body
away from me, fork fashion, and gamahuche Lena,
as she sits up and presents her fanny to your lips; isn't

it awfully nice? Your cock goes into the exact corner of my quim, and touches the very entrance to my womb! Ah, ah! Oh, oh! You do make me spend. I can't help it. Go on quicker, dear boy! Ah, Lena, it drives me mad. He seems to make me melt all over.'

Charlie, on his part, was in ecstasies, and his delighted prick was so sensitive to the clinging grip of Clara's lascivious fanny, that he was compelled to cry out he could not bear it any longer, as his hot spunk spurted into her cunt.

Lena was so randy that she took possession of Charlie's prick the instant he withdrew, and, doubling her knees up towards her face, threw her legs over his shoulder, as he rammed it into her longing gap, whilst Clara lovingly kissed, sucked, and tongued his balls, bottom, and buttocks from behind, her busy fingers doing their best by handling his impetuous shaft, as it worked in and out of that foaming cunt, which was literally overflowing with their thick creamy emissions.

He kept himself back for a final spend, and so drew out the length of that glorious fuck that Lena fixed her teeth in his shoulders, till her lips were crimsoned in his blood.

Clara, the while, frigged herself with one hand, and at the finish, they rolled over together in a perfect fury of amorous frenzy.

After this, Charlie dressed himself, placed two sovereigns on the dressing table, although the dear girls protested they would not take his money as he had pleased them so, then, taking leave of them as they still lay on the bed, rang the bell for the servant to show him out.

Emma, the servant, was a pretty little brunette, about eighteen and, as the saying is, 'fresh cunt, fresh courage', Charlie put half-a-crown in her hand, and he kissed her behind the door, and whispered, 'My dear, I should just like to fuck you. You shall have a half-a-sov if you run down and let me in at the area door, as I pretend to go out down the front steps.'

Without speaking she returned the kiss and shut the door sharply behind him, so, running down to the area, he was presently in the arms of another sweet randy girl.

His prick stood in a moment as he lifted her on to the kitchen table and put his hands up her clothes, their lips meeting in luscious kisses and tongueings.

Emma was quite as hot as her mistress, and fuck'd with all the abandon of a true little whore, till he gave her cunt a warm douche of the elixir of life.

Her eyes were shut, and her head rested on his shoulder, as she whispered, 'Oh, give me another before you go; it was such a beautiful fuck. I don't often get a treat like that. Oh, do, do! There's a dear!'

Luckily for him, just then the upstairs bell rang, and he was able to effect a hasty retreat up the area steps.

Taking a cab, he called on his cousins to arrange for the evening, after which he returned to his own rooms, and rested the remainder of the day.

About ten p.m. found our three chums, arm in arm, elbowing their way down Regent Street, where the crowd became denser every moment, and at places was quite impassable, where the illuminations were more splendid than ordinary.

The groping for cocks and cunts seemed the proper thing to do, everyone in the crowd seemed to understand that, and the three friends had immense fun with a modest old lady and her daughter who, although awfully indignant, were perfectly helpless, and were so teased and handled that they sighed and spent with desire, in spite of the shame that they felt.

Next a large closed furniture removal van which they were jammed against attracted their attention. It had portholes, like a ship, along the sides, and was lighted up inside.

Charlie mounted on one of the wheels, till he could peep inside, and found two old swells and several girls, nearly as naked as they could be, sporting their quims to amuse the old fellows, who had each got one of the nymphs of the pavement to frig him.

'Hullo!' shouted Charlie, forcing in the round glass, which acted as a pivot. 'Don't you want some real fucking in there? We've got three good stiff pricks out here, if you'll let us in.'

'Eh! Egad! It wouldn't be amiss,' said one of the old gents. 'Let's have them in for a lark.'

It was a matter of the greatest difficulty to effect an entrance by getting round to the rear of the van, and squeezing through the partially opened door.

'You look proper sharks,' said one of their entertainers, opening a bottle of fizz. 'Just a wet, by way of introduction, then the girls will soon take the stand out of you. Have you had some good gropes among the crowd?'

'Just what we wanted! They're three beauties,' exclaimed the girls, as they brought out the stiff pricks of Charlie, Harry, and Frank.

There were six girls in all, and the three chums had all their work to do to give a fuck to each girl in turn. This, however, they did, much to the delight of the two jolly old cockolorums, who handled their fine firm pegos with unbounded delight, postillioning their bottoms, and licking their fingers with the greatest of gusto, after they had thrust them into the reeking quims of the girls, to see how the fucking was going on.

One of their hosts in particular was ravenous to gamahuche and lick up all the spending from the swimming cunts after each go in.

Little notice was taken of the illuminations as the lumbering van slowly forged it way through the surging crowd, which little suspected the lascivious orgy being enacted inside the sober-looking van.

For three hours the game was kept up with spirit, till the three friends were so tired out and overcome by champagne they had taken that, when at length the van was driven into the grounds of a private house and stopped before the hall door, they were too stupid even to put on their clothes, and along with the girls were carried into the house by two or three flunkeys, who deposited the dissipated crew on some ottomans and sofas in a large and brilliantly lighted saloon.

Charlie was not quite so drunk but he had a dim

recollection of curious liberties which the old gents took with his naked person, and for a day or two afterwards Frank and Harry as well as himself confessed to feeling rather stretched and sore, as if their rear virginity had been ravished when they were helpless to prevent what they afterwards felt quite disgusted at.

But it is anticipating the course of events. At about five in the morning our hero quite recovered himself and, waking from the short deep drunken sleep, found the sun streaming in through a window so, drawing aside the light lace curtains he found it looked onto a beautiful croquet ground surrounded by parterres of splendid flowers and screened on every side by dense foliage of shrubs and trees.

Turning to the apartment, the two old gentlemen were fast asleep in armchairs, each with his trousers down and a naked girl resting her head on his thigh, side by side with the languid prick which she had been in the act of gamahuching when they were all overcome by sleep.

Frank and Harry were lying mixed up with the other four girls on a very large and splendid catskin rug, all naked, forming a charming tableau, as the golden rays of the sun glanced on the warm flesh tints.

Just then a lovely young lady wrapped in a dressing gown peeped into the room and Charlie, all naked as he was, bounded across from the window to meet her, but she, putting her finger to her lips, signalled him to follow her as she withdrew from the room. He crossed the vestibule close behind her into a magnificent boudoir, the door was locked, and she threw herself into his arms, exclaiming 'At least I am sure you are not one of the filthy unnatural fellows my uncles usually bring here, I have not the least doubt you three have been tricked, made tipsy and outraged by them! Oh pity me, for I am a prisoner in this house – they have cheated me out of my father's immense fortune – and made me their lady housekeeper. Just because I can't help myself and have the hope of some day succeeding to what they have cheated me out of, I have to shut my eyes and pretend not to see their horrible goings on, and even sometimes myself submit to their unnatural whims in my own person, without ever getting from them the satisfaction which a warm female nature requires. My case is like that of the lady you read of in the Arabian Nights who, although the jealous Genie kept her locked in a glass box, yet managed now and then to get a fresh lover, but very few suitable youths come to this house, they are mostly those debased men-women who prostitute themselves for money. Only four times in three years have I had the delight to welcome to my boudoir such a one as I could surrender myself to. Do you know why you awoke first? It is because, when I looked over the lustful group asleep after their beastly orgy, you charmed my eye. So, scattering some drops of a very somniferous essence over all the others, I applied reviving salts, &c., to your nostrils, and here you are my prize. We're safe for several hours!' she concluded, opening her dressing gown and throwing her lovely naked form upon his equally nude figure.

Receiving her in his arms, his prick as rampant as ever (how could it be otherwise when thus challenged by such a lovely creature), taking her in his embrace, he carried her a few steps till she fell back upon a soft, wide couch.

Her delicate hand had already taken possession of his throbbing staff and now at once applied its head to her burning notch, which was literally brimming over from a luscious anticipatory emission.

Drawing him upon her, her legs enlaced over his buttocks, she heaved up her bottom in enraptured delight as the shaft slowly entered the well-lubricated sheath.

Then they paused for a moment or two, billing and kissing, tongue to tongue, as both evidently thoroughly enjoyed the sense of possession that they imparted to each other by mutual throbs and contractions, till, giving a long-drawn deep sigh of desire, she challenged him by her motions to ride on and complete her happiness.

Charlie literally trembled from excess of emotion, and the rapidity with which this bewildering and luscious adventure had fallen upon him. Her first few moves made him spend before he wished to, and in spite of his unsatisfied desires, his pego at once lost its stiffness, to the great chagrin of the lovers.

'Ah, I understand,' she exclaimed; 'it is over-excitement, after the enervating debauch of last night. Wait a moment, my dear, and we will soon be happy enough!'

Saying which, she ran to a cabinet for some Eau de

Cologne, sprinkling a few drops over his excited face then, pouring the rest of the bottle in to a small china bowl with water, she sponged his limp prick with it. Then she dried it on a soft handkerchief and kissed, sucked, and caressed the manly jewel with such marvellous endearment that she soon had him standing again in all his glory of ruby head and ivory shaft. The sight seemed quite to ravish her senses, for she threw herself on the sofa and begged he would at once let her have the only thing that could possibly assuage her raging lasciviousness.

'Ah, I'm afraid you'll think me awfully lewd!' she sighed, blushing more crimson than ever.

This charming appeal was irresistible. He now charged her foaming fanny with such effect that she raved in ecstasies of delight, biting and kissing him by turns in her voluptuous frenzy, twisting and squirming her body, and then stiffening out straight in the dying ecstasies of spending. All the while his prick revelled in the warmth and extraordinary lubricity of the tight grasping sheath which held it so passionately that it stiffened more and more from excessive lust, so that when he came it was quite a painful acme of delight. The tip of his pego was so tender that he positively could not bear the loving, sucking contractions of her womb, as it drank up every drop.

After a while they renewed these delights, and kept it up till prudence dictated his return to the salon, where the sleepers were still unawakened; so Charlie, dressing himself, aroused Frank and Harry and assisted them to dress. Then, slipping away for a moment to his unknown inamorata, took a loving leave and by her advice they left the house.

It was almost five o'clock in the afternoon when our hero took leave of his cousins in Gower Street, sending them home to sleep off the effects of the long debauch. He also resolved to let this be the very last orgy for a long while to come, and content himself with the love of his little slavey and the occasional erotic osculations of Mrs Letsam, soliloquising to himself as, after a cup of tea, he lay on his own sofa; I mean to study and rise in my profession, so this of my sprees shall be . . . the end.

Suburban Souls

'Really true tales of sensuality are rare and I come forward to give you mine, where I have carefully endeavoured to keep my imagination within bounds and tell nothing but what did happen. It will hurt me and drag open smarting, half-healed wounds, but I mean to do it and go through it as an expiation . . .'

This is the voice of Jacky S., an Englishman who lives in Paris in the 1890s working at the French Stock Exchange, the 'very ordinary' hero of a rather extraordinary three-volume erotic epic – *Suburban Souls*. Jacky strikes up a friendship with a financial journalist, Eric Arvel, with whom he shares an interest in, among other things, scandalous literature. As will be seen, Jacky frequently procures naughty books for Eric and eventually he is invited to Eric's home in the suburbs of Paris where he meets Eric's mistress, Adele. More significantly, he meets Adele's daughter, Lily – a petite, brown-eyed brunette with an expressive face and a remarkable mouth in which 'all her emotions, all the secret inward movements of her mind betrayed themselves. Her sensual mouth resembled a brutal red wound across the dark olive tint of her face.' This is the woman, some twenty-four years his junior, who is destined to delight, infatuate, torment and utterly obsess him.

LILY TO JACKY

No date or place. (Received June 24th. 1898.)
It is five o'clock in the morning, but as I cannot sleep,
I get up softly so as not to wake the slumbering
household and quickly write a line to my well-beloved
master.

The most conflicting sentiments agitate me since
yesterday. I feel ashamed of my lewdness and yet I
regret having been so reserved.

I adore you, the thought of you alone drives me
absolutely mad. I am eager to see you again. I thirst
for you. I want to be yours, yours entirely; to be your
thing, your slave.

I have a prayer to offer up to you: Next time we
meet, if now and again, in spite of myself I refuse you
the least favour, I must beg of you only to repeat to
me this simple sentence: 'Do it to prove to me your
love!'

I know that I am very silly, but my dear and beloved
little Papa, I only ask to learn, and I often say to
myself that I am very foolish to reserve myself for
some creature I shall certainly never love, since you
alone possess my soul, my heart, my body.

How long the days will seem to me until the end of the month! And I fear already that I have wearied you by my ignorance and my timidity.

I remember your dear lips,

Your
LILY.

LILY TO JACKY

Sunday. (No date. Received June 27th. 1898.)
Adored master,

Your little girl is suffering to-day. Have no fear. It is nothing serious; in three or four days it will be all over.

How good and generous you are! You possess the patience of an angel, but your little daughter will really become your slave in every sense of the word.

One of the reasons which as well as my wretched shame prevents me from being as submissive as I should wish, is that I do not esteem myself handsome enough for you. I have an awful fear lest I should dispel all your illusions, you who have known so many women. If I was formed like a real woman and not like a silly, awkward young girl, it would be quite different.

I am well-built, I know, but really too thin. I should like to be marvellously beautiful for you; for your sole joy and pleasure.

I have a heap of questions to put to you the next time I see you. There are certain things that I do not understand at all, and that I should dearly like to know!

When you want to see me, make a sign, and I'll fly to you, my love, but not until the end of the month as arranged.

I adore you,

Your
LILY

ERIC ARVEL TO JACKY
Sonis-sur-Marne, 30th. June 1898.
My dear Jacky,
I am commissioned by Madame to tender you her very best thanks for the very handsome addition you have enabled her to make to her dressing-table. I cannot tell where you discovered such handsome cutglass bottles, such as they do not make nowadays, and which I can assure you are highly appreciated. We cannot help looking at them and since they arrived last night they have been in our hands time after time. You are really too good, and you embitter our minds when we think how handsomely you are always inclined to recognise a hospitality which in your case it is to us a true pleasure to exercise. Can you come down on Saturday and spend a long day with us so that we may thank you personally for all your kindness? We will have some fresh fruit and vegetables, and with a bit of luck we can give you some peas such as you have rarely eaten. Give my very best wishes to all your good folks at home, who I trust are well.

Yours very truly,
ERIC ARVEL

LILY TO JACKY

No date or place. (Received July 1st, 1898.)
My best beloved master,
Do come tomorrow, then we can settle about Monday
if you wish.

But I am longing to see your darling face.

Come as early as you can, and try to stay as late
as possible if you wish to please your slave and make
her very happy.

I should like to bite you,

LILY

JULY 2, 1898.
This day was a long and happy one. The best part of
the time I managed to be alone with my Lily. And she
was mine then, if ever a woman was. She was quite
changed, and I felt she was now entirely under my
influence. She was sweet, tender, and confiding.

As before, she asked me to help her to lay the table
for *déjeuner* and although Mamma kept coming in and
out of the dining-room, we managed to exchange many
a sly caress. Lily had pleasant touches of amiability
peculiarly her own. One spontaneous approach of hers
I shall never forget, as she never repeated it, and it
happens that I do not remember any other woman
having done the same thing to me. I was seated on a
little sofa at the end of the room and she was busy
at the table. I was supposed to assist her, but I never
did anything but kiss her. She dropped the plate she
held, and coming to me without a word, bent her head
and placed her cheek against mine. I did not speak,

neither did she. And there she remained for a moment. That is all.

I treated her with kindness, but I exacted obedience, and told her curtly to kiss me and touch me as my wayward fancy dictated, and being forced to be obedient to me pleased her greatly. She told me that she knew she had not a good temper, could not brook authority, and that neither her mother nor her father could get her to do what did not please her. And yet to me she willingly gave way.

What she wanted me to explain to her, according to her letter, was the entrancing mystery of manly erection. I told her briefly, and she said she thought that males were always stiff and hard. I asked her if she had never looked at her dogs. She replied that she did not like to, that she had never dared.

Papa had told me that Lilian hated reading books. He had tried to educate her mind a little by giving her a few healthy English novels to read. French romances, he would not have in his house. I thought of *Les Demi-Vierges*, but kept silent. I never spoke of the girl to him, never even mentioning her name; but we hardly ever conversed without he talked of her. I asked her if she cared for books and she confessed she adored reading. So I had brought with me *The Yellow Room*, which I gave her, and she ran and hid it away.

This story is thoroughly obscene and relates to flagellation and torture practised erotically on two young girls by the uncle of one of them.

During the day, in her impatience, she managed to slip away and peep into it, and in the evening told me that she thought she would like to read how the heroine suffered. I put her on her guard against the exaggerated cruelty therein described. I tried to make her understand the pleasure of subjecting a loved woman to one's most salacious desires, and that submission had its joys. I laid stress again on the enjoyment I should have in degrading and humiliating her when we were alone together, and she freely said that the efforts she would have to make, to curb her own disobedient nature for the sake of my despotic pleasure, would exercise a most extraordinary emotional effect on her sensuality.

I cannot tell how we kissed and fondled each other. I taught her to lick my face, neck, and ears, and I frequently made her feel my stiffened spear outside my trousers.

I would make her put her hand on it and note its softness. Then I joined her mouth to mine, and taking her fingers, placed them once more on the now hardened standard. This lesson of turgescent virility greatly delighted her.

I now come to the principal novel experience of the day. The last time I was at Sonis, I told her that when I came to visit at her house, I ordered her to tie a string or riband to the hair of her 'pussy', and let the end peep out of her frock. The colour was to be assorted to the hue of the dress fabric, so that I could pull at it now and then, unsuspected by anyone. By the slight smart the tug would give, I could thus feel that I was in intimate communication with the most secret part of her body, and could test her devotion to me by being able to inflict pain upon her whenever I chose.

She would prove her love by supporting this teasing inconvenience and therefore show that she loved me greatly by such humble submission to all my most weird and voluptuous caprices. She tried to laugh at the idea, but I could see she listened attentively and liked the originality of my strange whim. She found extraordinary delight in being the slave of a 'very dirty Papa', as she called me, and when I mentioned the word 'incest', as I did frequently, her eyes closed, her nostrils quivered, and her mouth literally watered, the moisture of her saliva bedewing her sensual and expressive lips.

Just before lunch, I said:

'You pretend you will obey me and yet you have not done what I told you on my last visit.'

She knew at once what I meant, gave me an arch look and said she would obey.

In the course of the afternoon, Mamma went up to Paris to fetch another new servant. Papa asked me to go out with him and give the dogs an airing, but I objected, complaining of pains in my ankles. It is true they did hurt me, but not as much as I made out. He begged me to remain on a bench in the garden, and called his daughter from the kiosque, where she was at work with her assistants, to keep me company, while he went out alone, and there was no one in the house, but Lily, her workgirls, and me. Lily showed me the end of a piece of tape which peeped out of the pocket-hole of her dress behind, she having fastened it to the hair on the left side of her mount, and brought it round her hip through the slit of her petticoat. She sat by my side and I pulled it frequently. She would wince, tell me I hurt her, and kiss me furtively, as she kept a sharp lookout, so that the girls should not see her. I told her that I did not believe she had really fastened it where I wanted, and putting my hand in this opening, I got it round to where it was tied, verifying her statement, and tickling the top of her furrow a little. I told her she had placed it badly, and another time it must come out over the top of her belt or waistband. She told me that could be done.

I informed her that my doctor was sending me away to Lamalou, to go through a treatment lasting twenty-one days, to get out of my system the remaining vestiges of the malady that still made me suffer. I could hardly walk or close my hands, but the protracted illness had not dulled my masculine energies.

She arranged to meet me on the 5th. of August, at two p.m. and as usual, I told her what I intended to do to her. I should have a small riding whip with me, and no doubt after she had received a few cuts with it, to avoid further punishment, she would be very docile, and not struggle against me, and thus in time I should succeed in breaking down the barriers of her shame, which I allowed without hesitation was excusable and natural.

I informed her that I meant to kiss every part of her frame, which she would have to lewdly expose to my bold gaze, and I would even thrust my tongue between the cheeks of her bottom and command her to do the same to me.

'Yes, darling! And what else – tell me?'

I taught her to take my fingers in her mouth and lick them, and suck them, and then I did the same to her.

'Gaston used to kiss my hands,' she said.

'But did he not kiss your lips?'

'Never!' she retorted, unblushingly. 'You are the first man who has put his mouth on mine.'

She forgot she had told me that 'Baby' was the man who had taught her pigeon kisses.

After this, we were not alone together, until she went off just before dinner to gather some herbs for the salad. I went strolling behind her and saw the fatal cord trailing round her feet. It had fallen from her hip to the ground. I told her of it in a whisper, as Pa and Ma were not far off, seated at table, for we dined in the open air. She got confused, and turning awkwardly round, trod on it herself and the sudden jerk made her jump with pain.

When dinner was over, her stepfather, accompanied by Lilian, saw me to the station by a round-about road, so as to walk the dogs a little, and we spoke of her business as a bonnet-builder.

'I suppose,' I said, 'when you make out the bills, you add a few francs here and there when the customer is one of the silly sort?'

'Never,' she answered, 'I wouldn't cheat one of my own weak sex. Robbing men, I understand, but not women.'

I never forgot this unguarded statement of hers.

Our conversation now turned upon marriage, and she once more said that she could not think of leaving her Papa and she nestled closely up to my host. I answered that I quite understood that and she was quite right to stop by his side, while he would be a fool to let her go. I added that he spoilt her, but a husband would exercise authority over her. I, for instance, believed in corporal punishment. Young women needed the whip, I should always have a small riding-whip handy and use it unsparingly. He agreed with me and I could see that he enjoyed my risky talk amazingly. His face grew serious, and then he laughed. A voluptuous feeling had crept over him, I am sure, by the peculiar look in his eyes and the general dullness of his physiognomy. Real sensual desire is a serious thing. Man is always serious and sulky-looking when his lechery is aroused, which is a sign of his dormant animality. Lilian laughed, with many a sly look at me. She knew what I meant. On nearing the station, she lagged behind, and signing to me that she had rectified her blunder, and got the end of the string above the waistband, in front of her dress. In the dark, I was able to approach her and pull it. I got a low, 'Ah! It hurts!' and then a squeeze of her hand, a hasty kiss, and a sigh of pleasure in return. I was off, and the mother and father thought I left on the 5th., but I had arranged to devote that afternoon to Lily and depart the next day.

The Horn Book was now ready and I promised Mr Arvel I would send it to him at once, as he was always pleased to read a smutty novelty. I despatched it to him a day or two afterwards. He said he would be careful to keep it out of Lily's way and would read it at his office. This remark struck me as quite unnecessary on his part, and during my little journey back to Paris I vaguely dreamt of Arvel and Adèle's daughter, reading *The Yellow Room* and *The Horn Book* together. I began to think that I could understand his talk in general much better if I believed the contrary of all he said, above all when he brought up Lilian's name.

I told her that Papa was going to have an obscene work from me, and that she should also read it on the sly when I returned to Paris. I told her I wanted him to have this naughty book so that he might be excited and perhaps violate her when I was away. In August, she would be alone at home with her Granny, as Pa and Ma were going to Germany for a short time.

With many cordial wishes for renewed good health by my baths at Lamalou, and a request that my first visit on my return should be for the Villa Lilian, I got into the train and shut my eyes to think of the delights in store for me before my departure.

JULY 2, 1898.
On my way to the Rue de Leipzig, where I was to meet Lily, I bought a light bamboo switch or riding-stick, preferring this to walking through the streets with a whip.

When she arrived, as she did punctually, and coquettishly dressed, showing that she had taken great trouble with her toilette, her first words were:

'Where is your whip?'

I showed her my switch:

'This is for you, Lily, and my dogs afterwards.'

She had in her hand *The Yellow Room*, which she had understood I wanted back at once. I told her she could keep it as long as she liked and not hurry through it. She had been reading it in the train. She said she liked it. It had made her *naughty*, and she had been obliged to finish herself with her finger. I replied that I thought she had told me she never did that.

'I do not as a rule, but now and again I can't help myself.'

I warned her to beware and not give way to the habit. When I went on to inform her that habitual masturbation deprives the sexual organs of women of their tone and elasticity, causing the secret slit to gape, and the inner lips to become elongated, she thanked me for the advice and told me she would resist the temptation, so as not to wither that pretty part of her body.

'I like my pussy,' she said, 'I like to look at the hair on it. I love to play with my hairs.'

I informed her that she had a very pretty one and it would be a pity to spoil it. The two large outer lips should close themselves naturally, but if Lily gives way to onanism they will do so no longer.

I asked her to show me the paragraph which had brought about this crisis. She did so:

'He inserted his enormous affair in her burning c. . ., etc.'

It was not exactly that sentence alone which so

unduly excited her, but what lead up to this termination. She did not understand certain words, but guessed them from the context. She thought that the extreme and bloodthirsty, long-drawn-out cruelty, described in the volume, was impossible, but thoroughly appreciated the idea of man's domination over a woman, and to bend her to his lewd will, a little brutality appealed to her imagination. She wanted more books later on, but not tales of Lesbianism. Anything, simple lust or cruelty, as long as it took place between men and women. She thought that everything and anything was possible and agreeable, if a male and a female were fond of each other. This was far from bad philosophy, springing naturally from a virgin of twenty-two. How changed she was now with me!

During our conversation, I had made her sit by my side on the sofa, with her clothes well up, as I wanted to see and feel her legs, calves, and knees. I made her open and close her thighs, and cross and recross her legs, as I chose to command.

I kissed her passionately. My lips wandered all over her face. I kissed her eyes, and licked and gently nibbled her ears. This last caress pleased her very much.

I made her stand up in front of me, and by threats of ill-usage and pinching the fat part of her arms, I got her, after a little resistance, to let me put my hands up her clothes, lift her chemise out of her drawers, and put my hand between her thighs, entirely grasping her centre of love. In this manner, my hand still gripping her plump, hairy lips, I walked her round the room, in spite of her blushes and protestations. It was an agreeable sensation for both of us. I had great enjoyment in feeling the movement of her soft thighs as she walked, my hand clasping her furry retreat. I halted in front of the looking-glass of the wardrobe, and forced her to look at the strange group we thus formed. She hid her face on my shoulder and I could feel she was now quite wet, heated, and ready for anything.

I asked her if she could take off her drawers without undressing. She replied in the affirmative.

'An English girl could not, but my drawers are fastened to my stays.'

I reclined on the sofa and told her to take them off slowly, without sitting down. She did so with docility, and I enjoyed the sight of seeing her get her legs out of her beribboned undergarments. I called her to me, and stood her up again in front of me and close to me, as I sat on the *chaise-longue*, while my hands, up her clothes, now for the first time roved without hindrance over her belly, bottom, thighs and nature's orifice. It was a delicious moment for me. I put the left index as far as possible up her crisp fundament, gradually forcing it up with a corkscrew motion, as I felt her pleasure in front increasing, for I was masturbating her scientifically the while, with the middle finger of the left hand. I had great difficulty in piercing her anus, but to my astonishment, she did not complain of pain. She afterwards told me that she liked the feeling of my finger in the posterior aperture. The crisis came quickly for her and she could no longer stand upright, but soon sank gradually to her knees, all in a heap, sighing with satisfied lust, her head pillowed on my breast. I kissed her sweet neck and finished her as quickly as my wrist would let me, until she tore herself from my grasp.

Now I tell her to disrobe before me, until she is entirely naked. She refuses indignantly. The moment has now arrived for me to take hold of my cane, and as she still refuses, I give her two or three stinging cuts over biceps and shoulders, and, smarting with pain, she consents to undress until she is in her shift. I kiss and lick again all the charms of the upper part of her frame, which is now quite bare, and I teach her how to suck my lips, and tickle my cheeks and forehead with the point of her tongue, not forgetting my neck and ears.

Sufficiently excited, I order the chemise to be taken off.

'Never!' she exclaims.

I get my stick again, and show her how silly she is to refuse, as it is already nearly down to her navel. But she still will not consent, and I cut her, not too severely, over her back, shoulders and arms. I love to see the dark stripes raised by the whistling bamboo. She hardly winces at each blow. I am certain she likes the chastisement of the male. Suddenly, I twist her round and tell her to remain quiet, and take three cuts on her naked bottom. I pull up her shift, fully exposing her plump posteriors and she is quiet on her knees, leaning over the sofa. I do not hurry, but count slowly: 'One, two, three!'

And the poor little bottom receives three severe cuts, stretching across both posteriors and equalling, although I do not tell her so, six stinging blows. I have tamed her, for she rises with a wry face, and drops the offending chemise to her feet. She is naked at last before me, in the full light of a sunny summer day. I kiss her, and caress her again, admiring her flat belly and her splendid bush, as black as night.

She seems uneasy, but I soon bring a smile to her face again, by telling her that I will never do anything to her by surprise.

'I will always let you know beforehand what I want, and if what I propose to do displeases you, tell me and I will then see if your master should give way or not.'

And now I make her plainly understand what I intend to do to her:

'I shall lick you all over and then suck you, and you shall suck me until I discharge boldly and without reserve in your mouth. But I want to tell you something which is very important. The first time I had you, you expectorated my elixir. That is an insult to the man who is loved by a woman. You must swallow all to the very last drop, and remain with your mouth on the instrument until told to go. If you cannot perform the operation as I describe, it shows you do not love me, as nothing, however seemingly dirty, can cause disgust in you coming from me.'

'But I can't. I shan't be able. I shall perhaps be sick?'

'You must try, and if you really love me, you will succeed.'

I now stripped quite naked, and took her in my arms, as if she was a baby. She was as light as a feather. I lifted her up, until her body was on a level with my chin, and threw her from me on the bed with all the strength I could muster. It was a pretty sight to see her naked body tumble down all in a heap.

We were soon entwined together, outside the bedclothes, and I cannot describe our mutual kisses, caresses and pressures. I licked her face all over and sucked her neck, her nipples, and waggled my tongue under her arms, while her belly, navel, and thighs came in for their share of the kisses of my eager mouth. She uttered little shrieks of pleasure, and anon cooed like a turtle-dove, or purred like the rutting kitten she was. I turned her round on to her belly, and the nape of her neck, her shoulders, spine, loins and bottom were soon wetted by my saliva. I wished to get my tongue between her round posteriors but she would not consent. I was now too feverish and unnerved to press the point. It was a very hot day. So I laid over her, and started pretending to copulate and the end of my dagger went in a little.

'Oh! You hurt down there. On the top it is nice.'

'Take hold of it yourself and put it where you like.'

She placed the head just on her sensitive button, and I moved gently, the swollen tip rubbing against her clitoris. This she approved of. I told her that a woman could be enjoyed in the hole of her bottom. Would she let me? She answered me affirmatively without hesitation. I warned her that it hurt the first time.

'What a pity it is that everything hurts the first time!'

She turned her posteriors to me, freely offering them with a loving look.

'I must lick you there to make it wet.'

'No! No!'

So I wetted my arrow with my saliva, and began to push between her rotund cheeks.

'You are not right!' she exclaimed.

'Guide it yourself, Lily.'

She did so, and I thrust home.

'Oh!' she shrieked, piteously. 'It hurts! You do hurt me so, Papa!'

At these words, a wave of pity broke over me. It would be a cowardly trick, I thought, to sodomize my confiding sweetheart. So I desisted, and my organ grew limp.

'Try again,' she said. And she seized my weapon.

'Oh! You are not excited enough now!'

I did not tell her what had crossed my mind. And I never did. I often thought since of warning her against ever yielding up her anus to a man, but the idea to speak of this escaped my memory. I am afraid it will be too late when she reads this book.

I was hot, tired, and perspiring, but still full of desire. I rested and gave her a little lesson in the art of manualisation, teaching her how to hold the manly staff, the way to move the wrist, slowly or quickly, and so on. She was an apt pupil.

Then she got up to arrange her hair and taking out the combs and pins, let her long black tresses escape in freedom. They fell below her tiny waist.

She seized my bamboo switch and began to tease

me as I laid on the bed, giving me slight blows with it. I jumped up to catch it, but the task was an impossible one. I chased her round the room and I must have looked a ridiculous sight with my semi-erection, and my testicles dangling as I ran. When I was about to seize her, she would spring on the bed, and landing on the other side, always get the couch between us. So, I, panting, lie down again and say coolly:

'It is disgusting to see a young lady jumping about a room stark naked. Lily, are you not ashamed?'

She took my words literally and rushed to huddle on her chemise.

'Of course, I'm naked! I forgot that!'

And she sat on the sofa trying to hide her pussy. I soon laughed her out of her chemise again and she was in my arms once more.

Then I gamahuched her seriously, reversed over her sideways, while she felt my spear, and stroked the appendages, masturbating me as I had just taught her. I did not ask her to touch me thus while I sucked her. She did it of her own accord. I opened the big lips of her little shaded slit, and looked well at it and inside it. It was small and pink, rather tight and thin inside, but seemingly little. The vagina was clearly closed up. She was a perfect virgin. She spent, and we rested awhile.

'Now *you*!' she said.

'How?'

'As you like!'

I opened my legs, and placed her on her knees

between my outstretched thighs. She bent her head and engulphed her play-fellow. After a few hints, she sucked me like a professional. Her large mouth and sensual thick lips proved that she was born to be a sucker of men's tools all her life. I took her cheeks in my two hands, and held her head still, as I moved slowly in and out of her mouth, telling her that I was having connection with her in a vile, unnatural manner. I then took it out of her mouth, and made her suck the balls alone, and tickle the erect member up and down the shaft, with the pointed end of her tongue. While she was busily engaged on the little olives in their purse, I rubbed my organ, all wet as it was, on her flushed cheeks, and informed her I should emit one day on her face, and in her hair, and in fact all over her, until every part of her body had been sullied by me. She got very excited by listening to this filthy talk, as she performed her task, and worked fast and furiously. I put my thigh between her legs and rubbed it against her furrow. At last, I felt I could bear the touch of her tongue no longer. I held her head, and pushed up and down myself, talking to her in a most disgusting manner, as the storm burst, and she tickled my member with her tongue until I was forced to push her away.

She looked up, and talked to me very gravely and seriously.

'You see it is all gone!'

I praised her, and she asked me timidly to be allowed to drink a little water. That I graciously permitted, and the voluptuous vestal begged me to let her suck again! She liked doing it!

It was five o'clock. We had been in the room since a quarter to three. I was dead beat, and I had not yet packed up my things for my departure the next day. We kissed and said goodbye effusively.

She showed great jealousy, and tried to get me to talk about other women, probably to hear about my mistress. She would not believe I was going alone to Lamalou. She told me that she would write to me every day to prevent me forgetting her. I was not to have any love affair with a woman, but she allowed me a night with a female now and again, as she was sure I needed it. She did not care how many different women I had, but would brook no rival. She could not receive any answers to her letters at her house, as the postmark would betray her. So I arranged to reply under initials to the post-office, Rue de Strasbourg, next to the Gare de l'Est. She was not allowed to go to Paris alone without valid reasons, but often unawares her people sent her up to fetch something, but she had to return by the next train. On those occasions she could go to the post office. She did not care much about the accommodation of the Rue de Leipzig. The little minx would have liked me to take a place of my own, where she could keep a *peignoir*, etc.

She was fully dressed again, and said that when she talked to me she got quite wet. I verified the fact. Inside the big lips, which were very large and hairy, there was an astonishing amount of moisture, but as they closed so perfectly, her cleft was dry outside.

I told her about French letters. She did not know what they were.

'Why don't you get some, and then you could have me entirely, without fear of getting me in the family way?'

'Why don't you . . . ' was a favourite expression of Lily's, but I knew I could not rely upon it.

I made her feel outside my trousers how the knowledge that she was so wet excited me, and she wanted to get on the bed again.

I asked her if her stepfather looked like a man who might be reading *The Horn Book* on the sly? I told her I was certain that he was in love with her.

'Why do you think that?' she asked me, assuming a very innocent air.

'Because you are a girl, who must fatally excite men's lust, and I cannot understand how he can live under the same roof with you, and not want you, especially as I know he is of a very voluptuous nature and don't care much for your mother.'

I watched her narrowly as I said this, but she did not turn a hair. There was no indignation, real or feigned, nor any disgust or astonishment.

'You should rub against him whenever you can, and let your cheek and hair touch his face while type-writing together, etc., and then look at his trousers and see if he is in erection. You will then know if he has the carnal desire for you that I suspect.'

'The other day,' she replied, 'he came into my bed-room without knocking. I was in my chemise, doing my hair in front of the glass. He turned very red and looked so silly. He scolded me for not locking my door and I answered that he ought to have knocked.'

But she forgot about the curtained opening between the two rooms.

She mentioned that her favourite Blackamoor had contracted the habit of getting on her chair behind her back, and sniffing under her armpits. I told her to wash that part frequently.

'I do, of course, every morning!'

'Then use a strongly perfumed toilet soap. Dogs hate perfumes of any kind.'

'Mother says I must never use soap under my arms. It is very bad.'

'If you want to catch the men by the odour of women; by all means do not use soap. But the advice of your mother is what might be given to a *cocotte*, not to a respectable girl, and surprises me very much. But I suppose she does not know.'

And then I slipped the promised fifty francs into her hand, and put her in a fly. With many protestations of affection, she left me, quite an altered girl; loving, and all her shame gradually going from her. I thought that after a few more meetings like this one, I should have no more to teach her.

The Yellow Room

So, what was it about *The Yellow Room* that so excited the lovers in *Suburban Souls*? This extract gives a flavour of that notorious narrative and an insight into the bizarre ways in which love sometimes manifests itself. As with Lily and Jacky, it seems pain and pleasure are on occasion close companions.

The Yellow Room is set in the Suffolk mansion of Sir Edward Bosmere, guardian to two attractive young ladies: Maud, and a newcomer, Alice Darvell. It is Sir Edward's delight to bend these young women to his command and the enactment of his whims takes place in an out-of-the-way wing of the house, in a room hung with yellow damask – the Yellow Room itself. It is there that Alice is first subjected to her 'Uncle's' perverse demands, in which agony, humiliation and rampant lust are commingled to the ultimate satisfaction of all parties.

It was a beautiful summer's night. The air was heavily laden with the sweet perfume of the flowers in the garden below the windows, which were thrown wide open. There were besides several china vases, or rather bowls, standing about the room, full of roses, of shades varying from the deepest crimson to the softest blush scarcely more than suggested upon the delicate petal. The only sounds were the gentle rustle of the summer zephyr amongst the trees and the weird hoot of the owls. The deeply shaded lamps gave animation to the rosy tints of the boudoir. They were emphasised by the yellow flame of the fire which, notwithstanding the season, crackled merrily in the grate. (A fire upon a summer's night is an agreeable thing.) Between it and Alice there at once appeared to be something in common. She and the fire were the only two black and gold things in the rosy apartment. The fierce flame struck Alice as being a very adequate expression of the love she felt seething in her veins. She felt intoxicated with passion and desire, and capable of the most immoral deeds, the more shocking the better.

This naughty lust was soon to have at least some

gratification. Maud had seated herself at the piano —
an exquisite instrument in a Louis Seize case — and
had played softly some snatches of Schubert's airs, and
Alice had been reclining some minutes on a rose-
coloured couch — a beautiful spot of black and
yellow, kept in countenance by the fire — showing two
long yellow legs, when Sir Edward noticed that every
time she altered her position she endeavoured, with
a slightly tinged cheek, to pull her frock down. Of
course he had been gazing at the shapely limbs and
trying to avail himself of every motion, which could
not fail to disclose more — the frock being very short
— to see above her knee. He thought once that he had
succeeded in catching a glimpse of the pink flesh above
the yellow stocking.

Alice, sensible of her uncle's steadfast observation,
was more and more overwhelmed with the most
bewitching confusion; her coy and timid glances, her
fruitless efforts to hide herself, only serving to make
her the more attractive.

Maud looked on with amusement from the music
stool, where she sat pouring liquid melody from her
pretty fingers, and mutely wondering whatever had
come over Alice, and whatever had become of the
healthy delight in displaying her charms of which she
had boasted before dinner. Maud felt very curious to
know how it would end.

'Alice,' at length said her uncle, with a movement
of impatience, 'have you begun to write out that
sentence I told you to write out fifty times?'

'Oh no, uncle! I have not.'

'Well, my dear, you had better set to work. It will suggest wholesome reflections.'

So Alice got up and got some ruled paper, an inkstand, and a quill pen; then, seating herself at a Chippendale table, began to fiddle with the pen and ink.

Her uncle continued to watch her intently. Maud had ceased to play, and had thrown herself carelessly on the couch which Alice had just left. Maud's dress, too, was quite low and very short; but in the most artless way she flung herself backwards upon the sofa and clasped her hands behind her head, thus showing her arms, neck, bust, and breast to the fullest advantage; and pulling her left foot up to her thigh, made a rest with the left knee for the right leg, which she placed across it, thus fully displaying her legs in their open-work stockings and her thighs encased in loose flesh-coloured silk drawers tied with crimson ribbons. Her attitude and abandon were not lost upon Sir Edward.

Alice's sensations were dreadful. How could she, there, under her uncle's eye, write that she had 'pea'd'? And not only 'pea'd', but with shame and anger she recollected the sentence ran, 'like a mare!' – like an animal; like a beast; as she had seen them in the street. And all 'before her uncle'. Whatever would become of her if she had to write this terrible sentence; to put so awful a confession into her own handwriting; to confide such a secret fifty times over with her own hand to paper? If it was ever found out she would be ruined – her reputation would be gone – no one would have anything to say to her — she would have to fly to the mountains and the caves. She had not realized until it came to actually writing it out how difficult, how terrible, how impossible it was for her to do it. If her uncle knew, surely he would not insist. He could not wish her to humiliate herself to such an extent; to ruin and destroy herself with her own handwriting; neither could he have realized what it would be for her to write such a thing. While these thoughts were passing through her mind, she kept unconsciously pulling and dragging at her frock. If only she could cover herself up. So much of her legs showed; and the long yellow stockings made them so conspicuous under her black frock. Although they were above her knee, unless she kept her legs close together she could not help showing her black garters. And her arms and her neck and her breast were all bare. She began to feel almost sulky.

'Well, Alice,' at length said her uncle, 'when are you going to begin?'

'Oh, uncle! it is dreadful to have to say such a thing in my own handwriting — I am sure you have never thought how dreadful.'

'You must chronicle in your own handwriting what you did, miss. Writing what you did is not so bad as doing it. And you will not only write it, but you shall sign it with your name, so that everyone may know what a naughty girl you were.'

'Oh, uncle! Oh, uncle! I can't. You will burn it when it is done; won't you?'

'No; certainly not. It shall be kept as a proof of how naughty you can be.'

And as she kept tugging at her frock and not writing, her uncle said:—

'Maud, will you fetch the dress-suspender? It will keep her dress out of her way.'

Maud discharged her errand with alacrity. In less than three minutes she had returned with a band of black silk, from which hung four long, black silk ribbons. Making Alice stand up, Maud slipped her arms under her petticoats and put the band round Alice's waist next her skin, buckling it behind, and edged it up as high as the corset, which Janet had not left loose, would allow. The four ribbons hung down far below the frock, two at the right and two at the left hip – one ribbon in front, the other at the back.

Maud then walked Alice over into the full blaze of the fire. Putting her arms round her and bending down, she took the ribbons at Alice's left side one in each hand, and then pulled them up and joined them on Alice's petticoats and dress up about her waist, disclosing her left leg from the end of the stocking naked. Maud, with little ceremony, then turned her round, and, taking the ribbons at her right side, tied them across her left shoulder, thus removing the other half of Alice's covering and displaying the right leg. She then carefully arranged the frock and petticoats, smoothing them out, tightening the ribbons, and settling the bows. And by the time she had finished, from the black band round her waist nearly to her garters, Alice was in front and behind perfectly naked

– her breast and arms and thighs and navel and buttocks. The lower petticoat was, it will be remembered, lined with yellow, and the inside was turned out. It and the stockings and the two black bands intensified her nakedness. She would sooner have been, she felt, stripped entirely of every shred of clothing than have had on those garments huddled about her waist, and those stockings, which, she instinctively knew, only heightened the exhibition of her form and directed the gaze to all she most wished to conceal.

'Now, miss,' said her uncle, 'this will save you the trouble of vain and silly efforts to conceal yourself.'

'Oh, uncle! Uncle! How can you disgrace me so?'

'Disgrace you, my dear? What nonsense! You are not deformed. You are perfectly exquisite. With,' he continued, passing his hand over her, 'a skin like satin'.

Feeling his hand, Alice experienced a delicious thrill, which her uncle noticing, recommended her to sit down and write out her imposition – a task which was now a hundred times more difficult. However could she, seated in a garb which only displayed her nakedness in the most glaring manner, write such words?

'Alice,' said he, 'you are again becoming refractory.'

Putting his arm round her, he sat down and put her face downwards across his left knee. 'You must have your bottom smacked. That will bring you to your senses.' (Smack – smack – smack – smack – snack – smack.)

'Oh, uncle! Don't! Oh!' – struggling – 'I will write anything!' – smack – 'Oh! How you sting!' – smack – smack – 'Oh! Oh! Oh! Your hand is so hard.'

Then, slipping his hand between her legs, he tickled her clitoris until she cooed and declared she would take a delight in saying and writing and doing the 'most shocking things'.

'Very well, miss! Then go and write out what I told you; sign it; and bring it to me when it is finished.'

So Alice seated herself – the straw seat of the chair pricking her bottom – resolved, however, to brazen out her nakedness, and wrote with a trembling hand. Before she had half completed her task, she was so excited and to such an extent under the influence of sensual and voluptuous feelings that she could not remain still; and she felt the delicate hair in front about her cunt grow moist. Before she had completed the fiftieth line she was almost beside herself.

At last, for the fiftieth time, she wrote the dreaded words and, with a shudder, signed it, 'Alice Darvell.'

During her task Maud had looked at what she was writing over her shoulder, and Alice glowed with shame. So had her uncle; but Alice was surprised to find she rather liked his seeing her disgrace, and felt inclined to nestle close up to him.

Now Maud had gone to bed, and she was to take her task to her uncle.

He was seated in a great chair near the fire, looking very wide awake indeed. He might have been expected to have been dozing. But there was too lovely a girl in the room for that. He looked wide awake, and there was a fierce sparkle in his eye as his beautiful ward, in her long yellow stockings and low dress, her petticoats turned up to her shoulders, and blushing deeply, approached him with her accomplished penance.

She handed it to him.

'So, Alice,' said he sitting bolt upright, 'here is, I see,' turning over a page or two, 'your own signature to the confession.'

'Oh, uncle, it is true; but do not let anyone know. I know I disgraced myself and behaved like a beast; but I am so sorry.'

'But you deserved your punishment.'

'Yes; I know I did. Only too well.'

He drew her down upon his knee, and placed his right arm round her waist, while he tickled her legs and her groin and her abdomen, and lastly her clitoris, with his hand and fingers.

He let her, when she was almost overcome by the violence of her sensations, slip down between his knees, and as she was seeking how most effectually to caress him, he directed her hands to his penis and his testicles. In a moment of frenzy she tore open his trousers, lifted his shirt, and saw the excited organ, the goal and Ultima Thule of feminine delight. He pressed down her head and, despite the resistance she at first made, the inflamed and distended virility was very quickly placed between the burning lips of her mouth. Its taste and the transport she was in induced her to suck it violently. On her knees before her uncle, tickling, sucking, licking his penis, then looking in his face and recommencing, the sweet girl's hands again very quickly found their way to his balls.

At last, excited beyond his self-control, gazing through his half-closed lids at the splendid form of his niece at his feet – her bare back and shoulders – the breast which, sloping downwards from her position, he yet could see – her bare arms – the hands twiddling and manipulating and kneading with affection and appreciation his balls; his legs far apart, himself thrown back gasping in his arm chair; his own most sensitive and highly excited organ in the dear girl's hot mouth, tickled with the tip of her dear tongue, and pinched with her dear, pretty, cruel ivory teeth – Sir Edward could contain himself no longer and, grasping Alice's head with both his hands, he pushed his weapon well into her mouth and spent down her throat. He lay back in a swoon of delight, and the girl, as wet as she could be, leant her head against his knee, almost choked by the violence of the delightful emission, and stunned by the mystery revealed to her. How she loved him! How she dandled that sweet fellow! How she fondled him! What surreptitious licks she gave him! She could have eaten her uncle.

In about twenty minutes he had recovered sufficiently to speak, and she sat with her head resting against the inside of his right leg, looking up into his face; her own legs stretched out underneath his left one – she was sitting on the floor.

'Alice, you bold, bad girl. I hope you feel punished now.'

'Oh no, uncle, it was delightful. Does it give you pleasure? I will suck you again,' taking his penis, to his great excitement, again in her warm little palm, 'if you wish.'

'My dear run along and go to bed.'

'Oh, I would rather stay with you.'

'Although I have whipped you and birched you and smacked you and made you disgrace yourself?'

'Yes, dear uncle. It has done me good. Don't send me away.'

'Go, Alice, to bed. I will come to you there.'

'Oh, you dear uncle, how nice. Oh, do let down my things for me before I go. Some of the servants may see me.'

'And,' she continued, after an instant's pause, with a blush, and looking down, 'I want to be for you alone.'

Touched by her devotion, her uncle loosed the ribbons; let fall, as far as they would, her frock and petticoats; and giving her a kiss, and not forgetting to use his hand under her clothes in a manner which caused her again to cry out with delight, allowed her to trip off to her bedroom. But not without the remark that she had induced him to do that which did not add to her appearance; for the rich, full, and well-developed girlish form had been simply resplendent with loveliness in the garments huddled about her waist; the petticoat lining of yellow silk relieved by the black bands from her waist to her shoulder crossing each other, and bits of her black frock, with its large yellow spots, appearing here and there. And as the eye

travelled downwards from the pink flesh of the
swelling breasts to the smooth pink thighs, it noted
with rapture that the clothes concealed only what
needed not concealment, and revealed with the greatest
effect what did; and, still descending, dwelt entranced
upon the well-turned limbs, whose outlines and curves
the tight stockings so clearly defined.

Sir Edward, who had made her stand facing him,
and also with her back to him, was much puzzled,
although so warm a devotee of the Venus Callipyge,
whether he preferred the back view of her lovely legs,
thighs, bottom, back, nuque, and queenly little head,
with its suggestion of fierce and cruel delight; or the
front, showing the mount and grotto of Venus, the
tender breasts, the dimpled chin and sparkling eyes,
with the imaginations of soft pleasures and melting
trances which the sloping and divided thighs suggested
and invited.

The first thing which Alice noticed upon reaching
her room was the little supper-table laid for two; and
the next that there were black silk sheets on her bed.
The sight of the supper − the chocolate, the tempting
cakes and biscuits, the rich wines in gold mounted jugs,
the Nuremburg glasses, the bonbons, the crystallised
fruit, the delicate omelette − delighted her; but the
black sheets had a somewhat funereal and depressing
effect.

'What can Maud have been thinking of, my dear,
to put *black* sheets on the bed; and tonight of all nights
in the year?' asked Sir Edward, angrily, the instant
he entered the apartment, and hastily returning to the

sitting-room, he rang and ordered Janet up. She was directed to send Miss Maud to 'my niece's room, and in a quarter of an hour to put *pink* silk sheets on the bed there.'

Then Sir Edward returned, and giving Alice some sparkling white wine, which with sweet biscuits she said she would like better than anything else, he helped himself to a bumper of red — standing — expecting Maud's appearance. Alice was seated in a cosy chair, toasting her toes.

Presently Maud arrived in a lovely déshabille, her rich dark hair tumbling about her shoulders, the dressing-gown not at all concealing the richly embroidered *robe de nuit* beneath it, and the two garments clinging closely to her form, setting off her lovely svelte figure to perfection. Her little feet were encased in low scarlet slippers embroidered with gold, so low cut as to show the whole of the white instep.

Her manner was hurried and startled, but this pretty dismay increased her attractions.

'Maud,' asked her uncle, 'what do you mean by having had black sheets put on this bed, when I distinctly said they were to be pink?'

'Indeed, indeed, uncle, you said black.'

'How dare you contradict me, miss, and so add to your offence? You have been of late very careless indeed. You shall be soundly punished. Go straight to the yellow room,' he went on to the trembling girl. 'I will follow you in a few moments and flog you in a way that you will recollect. Eighteen stripes with my riding-whip.'

'Oh, uncle,' she gasped.

'Go along, miss.'

Alice, to her surprise, although she had some little feeling of distress for Maud, felt quite naughty at the idea of her punishment; and, noticing her uncle's excitement, concluded instinctively that he also felt similar sensations. She was, consequently, bold enough, without rising, to stretch out her hand and to press outside his clothes the gentleman underneath with whom she had already formed so intimate an acquaintance, asking as she did so whether he was going to be very severe.

'Yes,' he replied, moving to and fro (notwithstanding which she kept her hand well pressed on him). 'I shall lash her bottom until she yells for mercy.'

'Oh, uncle!' said Alice, quivering with a strange thrill.

'Go to the room, Alice. I shall follow in a moment.'

Poor Maud was in tears, and Alice, much affected at this sight, attempting to condole with her.

'The riding-whip is terribly severe, however I shall bear it I can't tell.'

'Oh, Maud, I am so sorry.'

'And I made *no* mistake. He *said* black sheets. The fact is, your beauty has infuriated him, and he wants to tear me to pieces.'

Sir Edward returned without trousers, wearing a kilt.

'Now come over here, you careless hussy,' and indicating two rings in the floor quite three feet apart, he made her stretch her legs wide, so as to place her

feet near the rings, to which Alice was made to strap
them by the ankles. 'I will cure you of your carelessness
and inattention to orders. Your delicate flesh will feel
this rod's cuts for days. Off with your dressing-gown;
off with your nightdress.' Alice was dazzled by her
nakedness, the ripeness of her charms, the whiteness of
her skin, the plump, soft, round bottom, across which
Sir Edward laid a few playful cuts, making the girl call
out, for, fixed as she was, she could not struggle.

Alice then, by her uncle's direction, placed before
Maud a trestle, the top of which was stuffed and
covered with leather, and which reached just to her
middle. Across this she was made to lie, and two rings
on the other side were drawn down and fixed her
elbows, so that her head was almost on the floor, and
her bottom, with its skin tight, well up in the air. Her
legs, of course, were well apart. The cruelty of the
attitude inflamed Alice.

'Give me the whip,' said her uncle. As she handed
the heavy weapon to him, he added, 'stand close to
me while I flog her, and,' slipping his hand up her
petticoats on to her inflamed and moist organ, 'keep
your hand upon me while I do so.'

Alice gave a little spring as he touched her. her own
animal feelings told her what was required of her.

Maud was crying softly.

'Now, miss,' as the whip cut through the air, 'it is
your turn' – swish – a great red wale across the
bottom and a writhe of agony – 'you careless' –
swish – 'wicked' – swish – 'disobedient' – swish
– 'obstinate girl.'

'Oh, uncle! Oh! Oh! Oh! Oh! I am sorry, oh, forgive – ' – swish – 'no, miss' – swish – 'no forgiveness. Black sheets, indeed' – swish – swish – swish – 'I will cure you, my beauty.'

Maud did her best to stifle her groans, but it was clear that she was almost demented with the exquisite torture the whip caused her every time it cut with relentless vigour into her flesh. Sir Edward did not spare her. The rod fell each time with unmitigated energy.

'Spare the rod and spoil you, miss. Better spoil your bold, big bottom than that,' he observed, as he pursued the punishment. The more cruel it became the greater Alice found grew her uncle's and her own excitement, until at last she scarcely knew how to contain herself. At the ninth stripe, Sir Edward crossed over to Maud's right to give the remaining nine the other way across.

'A girl must have her bare bottom whipped' – swish – 'occasionally; there is nothing' – swish – 'so excellent for her' – swish – 'it teaches her to mind what is told her' – swish – 'it knocks all false shame' – swish – 'out of her; there is no mock modesty left about a young – lady after' – swish – 'she has had her bottom under the lash.'

Alice trembled but, when her uncle began to lecture Maud, Alice began to revive and she noticed that, while Sir Edward again approached boiling point, Maud gave as much lascivious movement as her tight bonds permitted.

'You will not forget again, I know,' said Sir

Edward, as he wielded the terrible instrument. 'You careless, naughty girl, how grateful you should be to me for taking the trouble to chastise you thus.'

The last three were given and Maud's roars and yells were redoubled; but in an ecstasy of delight she lost her senses at the last blow.

Alice, too, was mad with excitement. Rushing off, as directed, to her room, she, as her uncle had also bid her do, tore off all her clothing and dived into the pink sheets, rolling about with the passion the sight of the whipping had stimulated to an uncontrollable degree.

Sir Edward, having summoned Janet to attend Maud, hastened to follow Alice.

Divesting himself of all his clothing, he tore the bedclothes off the naked girl who lay on her back, inviting him to her arms, and to the embrace of which she was still ignorant, by the posture nature dictated to her, and looking against the pink sheet a perfect rose of loveliness. Sir Edward sprang upon her in a rush and surge of passion which bore him onwards with the irresistible force of a flowing sea. In a moment he, notwithstanding her cries, was between her already separated legs, clasping her to him, while he directed, with his one free hand, his inflamed and enormous penis to her virgin cunt. Already it had passed the lips and was forcing its way onwards, impelled, by the reiterated plunges of Sir Edward, before Alice could realize what was happening. At last she turns a little pale, and her eyes open wide and stare slightly in alarm, while, finding that her motion increases the assault and the slight stretching of her cunt, she remains still. But the next moment, remembering what had occurred when *it* was in her mouth, it struck her that the same throbbing and shooting and deliciously warm and wet emission might be repeated in the lower and more secret part of her body, and that if, as she hoped and prayed it might be, it was, she would expire of joy. These ideas caused a delightful tremor and a few movements of the buttocks, which increased Sir Edward's pleasure and enabled him to make some progress. But at length the swelling of his organ and his march into the interior began to hurt, and she became almost anxious to withdraw from the amorous encounter. His arms, however, held her tight. She could not get him from between her legs, and she was being pierced in the tenderest portion of her body by a man's great thing, like a horse's. Oh, how naughty she felt! And yet how it hurt! How dreadful it was that he should be able to probe her with it and detect all her sensations by means of it, while on the other hand, she was made sensible *there*, and by means of *it*, of all he felt.

'Oh! Uncle! Oh! Dear, dear uncle! Oh! Oh! Oh! Oh! Wait one minute! Oh! Not so hard! Oh, dear, don't push any further – oh, it is so nice; but it hurts! Oh, do stop! Don't press so hard! Oh! Oh! Oh! Oh! please don't! Oh! It hurts! Oh! I shall die! You are tearing me open! you are indeed! Oh! Oh! Oh!'

'If you don't' – push – push – 'hold me tight and push against me, Alice, I will – yes, that's better – flog your bottom until it bleeds, you bold girl. No, you shan't get away. I will get right into you. Don't,' said he, clawing her bottom with his hands and pinching its cheeks severely, 'slip back. Push forward.'

'Oh! I shall die! Oh! Oh! Oh!' as she felt she pinches, and jerked forward, enabling Sir Edward to make considerable advance, 'Oh! I shall faint; I shall die! Oh, stop! Oh!' as she continued her involuntary motion upwards and downwards, 'you hurt excruciatingly.'

He folded her more closely to him, and altogether disregarding her loud cries, proceeded to divest her of her maidenhead, telling her that if she did not fight bravely he would punish her and he slipped a hand down behind her, and got the middle finger well into her arse.

After this, victory was assured. A few more shrieks and spasms of mingled pleasure and pain, when Sir Edward, who had forced himself up to the hymen and had made two or three shrewd thrusts at it, evoking loud gasps and cries from his lovely ward, drew a long sigh, and with a final determined push sunk down on her bosom, while she, emitting one sharp cry, found her suffering changed into a transport of delight. She clasped her uncle with frenzy to her breast, and throbbed and shook in perfect unison with him, while giving little cries of rapture and panting — with half-closed lids, from under which rolled a diamond tear or two — for the breath of which her ecstasy had robbed her.

Several moments passed, the silence interrupted only inarticulate sounds of gratification. Sir Edward's mouth was glued to hers, and his tongue found its way between its ruby lips and sought hers. Overcoming her coyness, the lovely girl allowed him to find it, and no sooner had they touched than an electric thrill shot through her; Sir Edward's penis, which had never been removed, again began to swell; he recommenced his (and she her) upward and downward movements and again the delightful crisis occurred – this time without the intense pain Alice had at first experienced, and with very much greater appreciation of the shock, which thrilled her from head to foot and seemed to penetrate and permeate the innermost recesses of her being.

Never had she experienced, or even in her fondest moments conceived, the possibility of such transports. She had longed for the possession of her uncle; she had longed to eat him, to become absorbed in him; and she now found the appetite gratified to the fullest extent, in a manner incredibly sweet. To feel his weight upon the front of her thighs – to feel him between her legs, her legs making each of his a captive; the most secret and sensitive and essentially masculine organ of his body inside that part of hers of which she could not think without a blush; and the mutual excitement, the knowledge and consciousness each had of the other's most intimate sensations, threw her into an ecstasy. How delicious it was to be a girl; how she enjoyed the contemplation of her charms; how supremely, overpoweringly delightful it was to have a lover in her embrace to appreciate and enjoy them! How delicious was love!

Sir Edward, gratified at length, rose and

congratulated Alice upon her newborn womanhood; kissed her, and thanked her for the intense pleasure she had given him.

After some refreshment, as he bade her goodnight, the love-sick girl once more twined her arms about him, while slipping her legs on to the edge of the bed, she lay across it and managed to get him between them; then, drawing him down to her bosom, cried, 'Once more, dear uncle; once more before you go.'

'You naughty girl,' he answered, slightly excited; 'well, I will if you ask me.'

'Oh, please, do, uncle. Please do it again.'

'Do what again?'

'Oh! It. You know, What – what – what,' hiding her face sweetly, 'you have done to me twice already.'

'Don't you know what it is called?'

'No. I haven't the slightest idea.'

'It is called "fucking". Now, if you want it done again, you must ask to be fucked,' said he, his instrument assuming giant proportions.

'Oh, dear, I do want it ever so; but however can I ask for it? Please, uncle – will – will you, please – please – f – f – fu – fuck me once more before you go?' and she lay back and extended her legs before him in the divinest fashion.

In a moment he was between them; his prick inserted; his lips again upon hers; and in a few moments more they were again simultaneously overcome by that ecstasy of supernatural exquisiteness of which unbridled passion has alone attempted to fathom the depths, and that without reaching them.

Exhausted mentally and physically by her experiences and the exercises of the evening, Alice, as she felt the lessening throbs of her uncle's engine, found she was losing herself and consciousness in drowsiness. Her uncle placed her in a comfortable posture upon the great pillow, and throwing the sheet over her, heard her murmured words of thanks and love as she fell asleep with a smile upon her face. Janet came and tucked her up comfortably. And she slept profoundly.

French Skirt

In post-war England, many an ex-serviceman is scratching around trying to make a living, sometimes in the most dubious of ways. This is the fate of Roger Hartnell, a Cambridge Blue and former fighter pilot decorated for his exploits in the Battle of Britain, an accredited war hero still jobless six months after leaving the RAF. Is it any wonder he turns to crime?

A chance meeting in a Chelsea bar leads Hartnell into the arms of Dora, the former girlfriend of racketeer Francie who, though suspicious of Hartnell, recognises at once that the tough, well-spoken ex-pilot can be of use to his outfit. The complication is that the handsome Hartnell soon develops the hots for Francie's current girl, Gracie, who responds to his charms but lives in fear of Francie's wrath. Though no longer living under the threat of starvation, Hartnell is no happier. Occasionally, however, there are diversions − some of them very shapely indeed . . .

The lorry was black and the number plate had been altered. Nonetheless, Hartnell felt distinctly uneasy as he drove it east from London towards the coast.

It had been three days since he'd last seen Gracie and only a week since he'd first met her and taken her out to dinner. During that time Francie, it appeared, had spent quite a lot of time somewhere in the country and Gracie had not been bothered with him. But still she was not prepared to clear out. Hartnell had done his utmost to persuade her, but she was somehow numbed to the hope of success. And now she was afraid that he would cross Francie and that something terrible would happen to him.

So here they were hanging on, aimlessly, and here he was, with Johnny once more beside him, driving out on some unspecified job which he didn't want to do. It was as if some force outside himself had taken a hold on his life and was running it for him.

In front of them the Riley with Francie, Bill, Jake and Jim was nosing its way through the traffic, racing a long way ahead and then slowing down to wait for the lorry like an impatient terrier.

'What's the mystery about this one?' he asked

Johnny when they were out in open country, heading southeast.

'Didn't Francie tell you?'

'No.'

'I guess 'e doesn't trust you yet. Well, we're going to pick up some skirt!'

'Pick up some skirt?'

'That's right. Fresh from Gay Paree. 'Igh-class French skirt.'

'Don't talk in riddles, Johnny. What the hell do you mean?'

'Well, these girls are interested in the money what they can make in London, but they're all tabbed by the French authorities and they wouldn't be let out. So — trust Francie — we're going to pick them up from a fishing boat and they're going to join Francie's little business.'

'Francie's little business?'

'Yeah. I guess you an' Francie ain't bosom pals yet. 'E doesn't tell you very much.'

'What's Francie's little business?'

'Well, I don't suppose I'm breakin' any confidences. You'd know later on today anyway. 'E runs a call-girl outfit.'

Hartnell pursed his lips. Next, he'd be hearing that Francie ran an assassins agency. Whiskey and cigarettes! What a load of bull that had been.

'Course it hasn't been doing too well 'cos it needs fresh blood,' Johnny was continuing. 'But these Frenchies should revive interest in it quite a bit.'

The sooner I get out of this, Hartnell was thinking,

the better. Sooner or later there's going to be a crash somewhere and then it's going to be just too bad for everyone.

It was growing dusk when they drove through the little east coast village to the big house back from the beach which Francie had rented a month before for this special purpose. The Channel was calm, dotted with lights from boats way out on its sleek surface. A white foam rolled gently up the narrow stretch of beach.

'Not much around here,' Johnny said, as they drove over the dusty ground to the roughly fenced off grounds of the house. 'Trust the boss to find the best spot for the job.'

The Riley was already parked and lights flashed on in the house as they climbed down and walked towards the main door.

Inside, the other four were sitting smoking in the main ground-floor room. Francie was staring out to sea through the big windows which overlooked the beach. The house was sparsely furnished with enormous, old-fashioned furniture. There were heavy brocade curtains at the windows and covering the doors.

'Well, we've got quite a little while to wait,' Francie said. 'But, we'd better not show ourselves in the village just in case. We brought some food in the Riley.' He looked around the room. 'Hye, Jake,' he said. 'Go out and bring in the grub and the bottles — in the boot.'

Jake ambled out of the room and Francie stared back through the window. Still staring he said:—

'Well, Roger old chap, here we are and it's just as well you should know what we're up to.' He nodded out across the dim expanse of the Channel. 'Somewhere out there,' he went on 'is a little boat with half a dozen beauties on board. Not French racehorses, I mean, but French pros — high class mind you. They'll be pulling in here just down to our right about two in the morning. They're coming to make a bit of money for yours truly — and for the rest of us here.'

'Another nice little racket, Francie?'

'Not bad is it? Make us a mint of money they will. Nothing like a bit of ooh — la — la to make an Englishman's eyes light up.'

'How'd you get hold of them?'

'Oh, I got friends everywhere. 'Igh class friends. I'm going to make it worth somebody's while over there to bring 'em over here. Suppose you might speak French?'

'Yes, I do.'

'Thought you would. Well it's only the fishermen'll bringing them so you might have to talk some English to 'em. Les girls are supposed to speak English, but you can never count on that — and it's not very important from our point of view.

Jake came in with sandwiches and the whiskey and they all began to eat and drink.

'Bring the cards, Bill?' Francie asked. 'There, there boy. Don't look so bored, always worth the wait until they come, isn't it? Then you can 'ave one to yourself.' He chuckled and turned to Hartnell.

'We always try the goods out just to make sure we 'aven't been cheated,' he explained.

The lights in the house were put out at one o'clock and they sat for a while in darkness, smoking and looking out over the water. There was a crescent moon and no sound apart from the gentle breakers.

'A good night,' Francie commented. 'We'd better go down in a few minutes in case they come ashore further down.'

They left the house and walked over the rough ground past the vehicles. They jumped from the higher ground a few feet down to the sloping beach, their feet sinking deep into the silvery grains.

'You stay here, Jake,' Francie said, when they'd reached firmer sand quite near the water's edge. 'If they come in here and we don't see 'em, give a whistle.'

As he walked beside Francie along the shore, Hartnell wondered vaguely about coast guards and people like that. But, as was usual with Francie, he felt the man would have left nothing to chance, that everything would be known beforehand and taken care of. He felt like a child in comparison.

One by one at distances of a few hundred yards the others stopped and waited until only he and Francis were left striding along the beach with the salt breeze in their nostrils.

'We'll go along as far as those rocks,' Francie said, indicating a clump of boulders ahead. 'If they come up any further away than that they'll have to find their own way to the house.'

They sat in the shelter of the rock peering out to

sea. Lights were still winking far out. There were no lights coming from the village about a mile away.

'Hope they don't keep us waiting,' Francie said. 'Some of the boys haven't had a bit of skirt for a long time. It'd be a shame to have them getting frustrated.'

Hartnell was thinking of Gracie. He didn't dare look at Francie because every time he did he had to resist the temptation to sock him. How he wished he and Gracie could be out there now in the Channel, maybe heading for the French coast, or perhaps for Spain, anywhere away from this mess. He allowed his mind to dwell upon himself and he could hardly believe the reality of himself sitting here on this beach with this other man waiting for this strange, criminal arrival in this fantastic set-up.

For a long time he sat there, not saying a word, thinking — of Gracie, of Dora who'd been upset when he'd moved out, but had let him go without too much fuss, of Gracie again, always coming back to Gracie, the charm of her lovely face and voice and the beauty of her breasts, her slim woman's body, the desire with which the thought of her choking breath when he loved her, always filled him.

Francie was silent too, lost in his thoughts which were also of Gracie and that inner core which she had, which he couldn't get at, that something which she kept unattainable, the only woman he'd ever really wanted.

There was a low whistle from up the beach and they both scrambled to their feet and began to run along the surf's edge.

The dim shape of a large rowing boat met them, growing out of the dimness into phantom near-reality and then substance. Bill and Jim were already there, helping to pull it in.

'Ask them if everything went okay,' Francie said.

Hartnell addressed the nearest of the two French fishermen, asking what sort of trip they'd had.

The fisherman grinned and said it had been fine but the 'young ladies' had suffered a little from sea sickness.

Hartnell told Francie and then he noticed the women, huddled in the boat.

'That's all right,' Francie said. 'They'll be suffering more than a little from prick-sickness soon.'

Shivering slightly, in spite of the thick coats they were wearing, the girls began to climb from the boat, walking from seat to seat in their dainty high heels, helped by the fishermen as the boat swayed, and then jumping ashore.

'Well, well. Hello girls,' Francie said. '*Parlez vous anglais*?' It was one of his few expressions in the language.

'A leetle,' said the first girl. 'We all speak a leetle. We were seek, but it is better now.'

'I trust you all know how to *faire l'amour* a leetle,' Francie said with a coarse chuckle which was echoed by Bill and Jim and the others who had now arrived on the scene.

The girl giggled and rubbed her tongue along her lips at him.

As soon as they were all on dry land the fishermen

pushed off and rowed quietly and rapidly back towards their boat, leaving a strange little crowd of people behind them on the beach. It was just two o'clock.

They walked in a body up the beach. When they came to a high step to the road, the women were helped up by the men and there were so many playful shrieks as hands held buttocks and ran up between thighs that Francie called out for quiet.

As soon as they were in the house, Francie pulled the heavy curtains across the windows. He switched on the light and leaned against the door with a smile on his face.

'Well, well,' he murmured. 'It couldn't 'ave worked out better.'

Hartnell studied the women while Jake doled them out sandwiches and whisky. The colour began to come back to their pale cheeks as they ate and drank. They were certainly very attractive, he decided. Most of them had typical dark, French good looks, with a faint olive tint to the skin and prominent but delicate bone structure. They all looked astonishingly vivacious. When they began to remove their coats, the voluptuousness of their figures brought unrepressed whistles of appreciation from the men.

'Go and have a wash, dears,' Francie said, after they'd eaten, 'and then we'll see if you know your stuff.'

None of the girls seemed the slightest perturbed by his words and they all trouped out quite happily after Jake who was to show them to the bathroom. Impatient at having to wait, Jake seized the last one to enter and mauled her big breasts as he kissed her. She bit his ear and pinched his penis through his trousers.

Half an hour later they had all returned to the main room where the men were drinking fresh whisky. Eyes moved over them avidly as they came in.

Francie stood up and walked over to them. His sensual mouth was smiling, his eyes as hard as granite chips.

'I'm Francie,' he told them. 'And, I'm your boss. Tomorrow we'll all go up to London and start arranging for you to make a fortune. In the meantime, the boys here are anxious for a bit of continental screw an' I'm sure you must be a bit frustrated after that trip so tonight we're all going to get to know one another.' He paused, looked around the room and saw Hartnell. 'If there's anything you don't know how to say,' he added, 'then you can just ask the gentleman over there 'cos 'e's got class like me and he speaks your lingo like an onion boy.'

The girls looked at Hartnell with interest and several glances remained fixed on him even when Francie resumed speaking.

'Now girls,' he said. 'We'd all like to see how you look folies bergere style, you know, *nu* — so starting with you' — he pointed to a petite brunette — 'get those togs off and let's have a look at you.'

'Togs?' the girl queried.

Francie glanced at Hartnell and then grinned.

'Bit of Old Blighty,' he said. 'Clothes, my dear — skirts, brassieres, knickers — you know.'

The girl giggled, repeated the word 'togs' to herself and began to strip.

She took off her clothes with the tantalizing technique of a professional striptease and when at last she was standing naked in front of them the gang were breathing very heavily.

'Get a load of that,' Johnny muttered.

She had big breasts, almost too big for her size, with enormous, angry-looking nipples, her waist was slim and her hips were also broad for her size. They seemed to shine with an oily olive gloss and the tangle of dark hair at her thigh junction muffed out in glossy profusion.

'Yes, I think you'll do,' Francie said, with a leer. 'Let's 'ave a look at your behind.'

Unabashed the girl swivelled round like a mannequin and playfully jutted a pair of glossy, olive buttocks at him, arching her back inwards to accentuate them.

'I see you've been sunbathing without any togs,' Francie said and all the women giggled.

'All right,' Francie said, pleased with his own humour. 'Don't stop the show. Next buttocks please.'

The pantomime continued until all the girls had slowly peeled their clothes from their bodies and paraded before the watching, desire-filled eyes. They all had bodies well worth any man's money. Some, like the first, were plump in the right places to the point of being exaggerated, others were elegantly well developed with long, svelte lines.

'Anybody who can't wait for privacy?' Francie asked, hopefully.

And Jake, who still felt the pressure where the girl had pinched his organ, stood up with a deep flush. He took another swig of his whisky and then drained the glass with a grimace.

'Go on then, Jake. Give us a show,' Francie encouraged.

Jake's eyes were fixed on the girl who had first stripped — the one he had kissed outside the bathroom — while he unbuckled his belt. She came over towards him, seeing from his glance that she was the one he wanted.

'You wan' me to 'elp you?' she asked and began to unbutton his trousers.

'Go easy or he'll faint and then we'll all be sorry,' Francie said. Jake leered at them amidst the guffaws which followed.

With the help of the little brunette he got his clothes off. Towards the end she was taking them off for him alone, because he couldn't do anything with his hands except run them over every glossy portion of her body he could reach. The girl herself had begun to tremble and had jerked the last garments off him with some savagery.

'Go to it, Jake,' Francie cried.

Jake had a bit of a paunch, which wasn't too big, considering his size, and his penis jutted out from under it almost vertically. His big hands caught the girl, who squirmed up close to him and rubbed his penis between her soft, fleshy thighs. Jake uttered a couple of gasps which the laughs of the company did not affect. He kissed her and she clung to him passionately writhing, exploring his body with her fingers as he explored hers.

Suddenly, placing her arms up around his neck, she leapt up, twining her legs around his waist.

'She's a gymnast, as well,' Francie declared in a torrent of fresh guffaws, guffaws which held an edge of lewd violence.

Jake placed his hands under the girl's stretched behind, played with her anus for a moment, found his rod waving near her open vagina and wormed it in.

With a little gasp of 'Oh chéri!' the girl flopped down onto the fleshy mast and began to squirm on it, mouth open, murmuring in French and English.

With her jogging on him, Jake carried her to a rug, and flopped down on top of her. The company moved into a circle around them to watch, offering encouraging suggestions. One of the girls bent and gave Jake a couple of playful taps on his behind to a burst of fresh laughter.

The girl on the floor was squirming like a mad thing and Jake kept shuffling his knees further in between her widespread thighs, trying to stop himself from slipping on the rug. Panting, he leaned on her thighs, pushing them father apart and the spectators had a perfect view of his big, white organ ramming into the red gulf, surrounded by its forest of black hair between her legs.

'Oh chéri, oh chéri,' she kept murmuring as he split her apart.

Jake pushed her legs back now, pulling back the thighs against her big, trembling breasts, leaning forward on them so that she was bent almost double, holding out her nether portions to him as if she wanted only those parts to exist.

Jake leaned up off her and pushed forward his hips like a matador attracting the bull. His rod disappeared to the hilt with each thrust while the girl waggled her upturned bottom, whose gaping white roundness was there to further inflame those who watched.

Around the floor scene, some of the gang had caught hold of the naked girls as they watched, and, still watching, were fondling their breasts, running their hands over the svelte lines of bosom and belly, playing with buttocks. Without taking their dark eyes from the pantomime, the girls, too, were feeling for bulging organs, opening fly buttons, losing their relentless fingers inside protecting clothes.

With every stroke, now, Jake was belching forth a strangled gasp of breath, giving a final agonizing flick to his hips as his bulging, excited penis seared into the girl's moist vagina.

She had unwound her legs and wrapped them around his waist, squeezing them tight with every intrusion he made into her channel. Her grasping, clawing hands had made red weals across his back.

Jake held her buttocks, each in a cupped hand and lifted her slightly off the rug so that she rested on it only with her head and shoulders. The different position gave him even greater penetration and the girl gave a little shriek. Her eyes on the ceiling were unseeing.

'Fuck me, fuck me to death!' she pleaded.

'She certainly 'as a good grasp of the English language,' Johnny said as he sucked the ear of a slim, dark girl who, standing with her back towards him, had taken out his weapon and was rolling it between her legs.

Jake was straining into the girl whose head slid back on the rug every time he jerked into her. He had a finger in her behind and was seeing how far he could lose it, while the girl kept clamping her buttocks together tightly around it.

'Hurry, hurry cheri,' she spluttered. '*J'arrive*, I'm coming, hurry.'

Jake let her fall back onto the rug and lowered himself onto the soft ramp of her hips, still pistoning into her. He leaned onto her and bit her neck. She bit his ear in return and bit it again in passion.

'Uuuuuugh,' Jake bellowed as she bit him.

His mouth had opened, his eyes were wild, full of sweet pain, his strokes slowed, grinding in like a thick, slow screwdriver.

The girl's loins were almost turning circles, rotating furiously, her buttocks brushing the rug, screwing it up under them. They were both gasping as if their lungs would burst.

Jake's mouth moved, his hands held her shoulders as if he would pulverize them.

''Ere it comes,' he cried. ''Ere it comes, now . . . Uuuuugh!'

The girl gave a shudder. Her hips went into a paroxysm.

'Oh, oh, oh, oh, chéri, chéri, chéri – oooh!' she screamed.

As they both began to subside in dwindling activity, Francie turned to the other girls.

'She'll do,' he said. 'Now we'll see about the rest of you.'

The gang began to break up, each man leading a girl away into other rooms for a more private pleasure. Eventually Jake and his girl stood up and went off to find a bed for a fresh bout.

Only Hartnell was left, sitting on a table, his legs swinging nonchalantly to and fro. Across the room, the odd girl stood, undecided.

Hartnell, in spite of the show could not summon any great enthusiasm to make love to any of these professional women. He remembered his only-too-frequent nights with Gracie, the torment they left inside him, the feelings of love, passion and protection they left within him. All this was cheap in comparison and he could only think of her.

He looked at the girl who remained and realized she was waiting for him to do something. She was a slim, dark girl with big breasts and a rather sharp, attractive face. He noticed she was not wearing lipstick and that her lips were a gentle shade of pink, well shaped and soft-looking.

'Go to bed,' he said. 'I don't feel like it.'

She raised dark eyebrows in surprise and came across to him.

''Ow is that, darleeng?' she asked, putting her hand on his shoulder.

Hartnell grinned inwardly at the situation. He thought of earlier occasions when he would have loved to have had just such an attractive girl standing nude in front of him asking why he didn't want to make love to her. Things have come to a pretty pass, he thought.

'I guess I'm just tired,' he said.

'But I will make you wide awake again,' she insisted. 'Am I not beautiful enough?'

She made a little pirouette in front of him, displaying her curvaceous back view with the perkily protruding rounded buttocks, and giving a little laugh which brought out dimples in her smooth, brown cheeks.

Hartnell felt a sudden warmth down in his trousers.

'Oh, you're great,' he assured her. 'I just don't feel like it.'

'Perhaps you are un'appy in love?' she suggested, putting her finger unwittingly straight on the wound.

'Perhaps I am,' Hartnell agreed.

'Is true − this?' she asked.

'Is true,' he said.

She moved closer to him, throwing back her head a little so that her firm breasts stood out towards his face inviting.

'Then it is better that you make love − make you 'appier,' she assured him.

'I wish you were right,' Hartnell said.

She misunderstood his words a little and put her hand down on the bulge which had grown, without him being fully aware of it, in his trousers. She ran her fingers over it, feeling it, measuring it.

'You see – you want it really,' she said.

With her hand titivating his penis through a couple of thicknesses of material and her breasts so close under his face that he would only need to sway forward to kiss them, Hartnell felt a doubt in himself. He didn't really want her. But just for the few minutes of physical delight which would allow him to forget everything? Might it not be a good thing? But then he saw Gracie lying in the bed thinking of him, wanting him and the desire dissipated.

'Come. You come upstairs – or we stay here?' the girl asked. She was rubbing her thighs together, pressing against his legs, working herself into a state of excitement.

'No,' he said. 'No – not tonight.'

'No? Why is no?' she asked.

She began to undo his buttons and he realized his erection hadn't gone down. He couldn't make the effort to get up or push her away.

She undid them all the way down and searched for the opening in his pants, found it and worked his organ out into view. She held it gently in her hand looking at the blunt cudgel of a knob, the thick white staff.

'Is big,' she said appreciatively.

Her fingers on his penis had made a certain warmth of feeling gush into it and find an echo in his throat. He looked at her body, at the thin fingers stroking his flesh.

'You still not sure you want it?' the girl asked, but her eyes were twinkling with certainty.

She bent suddenly and took the knob in her mouth.

The movement took him by surprise, sending a sharp pain of sensation through him, making his penis swell in her mouth to even greater size.

She glanced up at him quickly.

'I eat it,' she said.

Her mouth went back to enclose him and he watched the top of her head with its short black curly hair jogging about.

She was using her tongue and he could feel it swiping around him, stimulating his rod to make little involuntary jerks in her mouth. Her lips were soft as they moved down the staff, taking all she could into her mouth, surrounding the flesh with the warmth of her breath, the moistness of her saliva.

Her tongue was like the suction end of a vacuum cleaner. As she licked his prick he felt as if this slender morsel of flesh, this tongue was drawing the very dregs of feeling out of him, electrifying his whole body.

She began to suck voraciously, rubbing her legs together all the time and he leaned back on the table, pushing his hips at her face, moving his penis farther towards her throat.

He wouldn't stop her now, he realized. It had gone too far now. He thought about Gracie and the thought quite apart from what was happening down there under her moving head. It was easier to recognize the difference when it was happening and it didn't matter so much.

She bit him gently and he squirmed. He leaned forward and ran his fingers through her hair and then reached down to stroke her breasts. She didn't look up, but continued with her sucking, continued rubbing her thighs together and breathing heavily over his rampant phallus.

His heart began to pound. He wanted to tense his legs together and strain his hips at her. His loins were growing hot. He was sweating between his legs.

Releasing her breasts, he let himself fall gently backwards until he was lying across the table. She moved back with him, keeping his penis in her mouth, burying her head in his loins.

Now he was on his back and could sense himself. He did so and felt an immediate crush of feeling at that stiff protuberance which her tongue was working on like a mad thing. His lips moved apart and his breath made the only noise in the room.

He felt her hand exploring in his trousers and then she pulled out his testicles so that his genitals were all exposed in a neat little triangle. She stroked the loose sacks of flesh while she sucked and he felt a fresh intoxication run through his body, finding its extreme point at the head of his cudgel.

His breath shot in little explosions into the still atmosphere of the big room. His hips were grinding against her face. He glanced down and saw her engrossed in her sucking, eyes closed, fluttering every so often, her breasts pressed against his knees, her legs still tight against him and rubbing. He bit his lip and tensed his hips watching her pretty, unrouged mouth eating sensually on his penis.

The stem of his penis, that part which wasn't

engulfed in her mouth, was dead white. In contrast, he knew, the knob would now be dark, flaming red.

It would be getting redder and redder, darker and darker, all the blood drawn into it just as the sperm was already tingling to move into it. He panted in a continuous stream, writhing his hips, gritting his teeth at the pinpoint of furious sensation lost in her mouth.

He wanted to grab her, twist her over and shove it in her with furious energy, but he couldn't move from his position. His passion had trapped him there, making him incapable of breaking the rhythm.

His fingers clawed at the polished tabletop, bringing out thin scratch lines on its smooth surface.

In his belly he could feel the imminence of the explosion, the boiling to great heat. He gasped, gasped loudly, so that the sound echoed in the big room and the girl renewed her tonguing with even greater energy.

Deep inside the boiling was under way. He could feel it growing and growing and the thought that he was going to flood into her mouth filled him with an overwhelming perversity of pleasure. He worked his hips, hurrying the climax for fear she would jerk away before it was reached.

He was lost now. It had to be finished. Not to finish now, for her to pull away now, was the equal of death, of torture and then death.

He gasped, uttering formless words. He looked down at her as he felt the flood start. Her face was flushed with passion, eyes still closed and fluttering, mouth working furiously. He forced his neck to stay in that position so that he could see her. His eyes screwed up with the effort. There were sharp spears running along the inside of his penis: an enormous flood of them hurtling along the tube with greater and greater velocity.

He cried out and her face didn't shift its position. She seemed to be entranced.

And as the sperm burst from his penis with agonizing gusts which were like the dragging of his entrails out into the light, he saw her swallowing gluttonously before he fell back, giving all his mind to the sensation and the effort of arching his hips at her face.

When he lay still, filled with lassitude, after it was over, she didn't let his deflated organ escape from her lips. She continued to suck it gently. She continued the gentle friction of her legs against each other. He lay back, letting her carry on, feeling momentarily exhausted, thinking that it had been one of the most acute feelings he'd experienced.

After a while his organ began to thicken again in her mouth. She licked it and bit it gently, revelling in her power to rejuvenate it after its collapse.

When it had stretched out, elongated to its full length once again, and he was starting to feel the desire rekindle in his loins, she took her lips off him for the first time.

'Are you going to make love to me now, darleeng?' she asked. 'I need it very bad.'

He slithered off the table and took off his trousers and shorts. She held his penis under his shirt and stroked his testicles.

'Let's have it here on thees table,' she said.

He caught hold of her. His prick was an enormous itch now, wanting to bury itself into soft flesh.

'I wan to be spleet in two,' she said.

She turned into his arms and stretched face-down across the table, so that its edge cut across the crease of her hips and her feet touched the floor. She spread her legs wide and reaching behind her caught his penis and dragged it at her open vagina.

With a grunt, Hartnell rammed it deep inside her. He leaned heavily on her while he shagged in and in and she clawed the table the way he had while her buttocks hollowed and filled under his eyes.

My Life and Loves

Frank Harris (1855–1931), the author of *My Life and Loves*, gets a bad press these days. The dynamic editor of the *Saturday Review*, biographer of Wilde, Shaw and Shakespeare, novelist, playwright and literary lion of *fin-de-siècle* London, is now distinctly out of fashion. Words such as 'braggart', 'scoundrel' and 'cheat' invariably accompany his name in literary reference works. Though much of the criticism that has been directed against him doubtless reflects the inevitable decline of an overblown reputation, the publication of his five-volume autobiography between 1922 and 1927 proved to be a turning point. Few men of any age, even in the sanctity of pub, club or analyst's couch discuss the intimate details of their love life at such length – and those that do are often earmarked as prone to exaggeration. Though Harris's purpose was serious – it is said he wanted to write the most honest autobiography every written – it provided his enemies with a convenient peg on which to skewer his legendary arrogance.

The following excerpt from Volume One of *My Life and Loves* places the young Irishman in America. Though not yet eighteen, he has already witnessed the great fire of Chicago, ridden as a cow-puncher throughout the Wild West, fought marauding Mexicans and Indians, earned a hatful of dollars – and developed a precociously forceful romantic style. Now he has joined his elder brother, Willie, in order to take up life as a student and it is here, in Kansas, that his life as a philanderer is to begin in earnest. In the dining room of his lodging he meets a man who, like many others in these memoirs, has a charming but as-yet-unsatisfied wife . . .

At the next table to me I had already remarked once
or twice a little, middle-aged, weary looking man who
often began his breakfast with a glass of boiling water
and followed it up with a baked apple drowned in rich
cream. Brains, too, or sweetbreads he would eat for
dinner, and rice, not potatoes: when I looked
surprised, he told me he had been up all night and had
a weak digestion. Mayhew, he said, was his name, and
explained that if I ever wanted a game of faro or
euchre or indeed anything else, he'd oblige me. I
smiled; I could ride and shoot, I replied, but I was no
good at cards.

The day after my talk with Smith, Mayhew and I
were both late for supper: I sat long over a good meal
and as he rose, he asked me if I would come across
the street and see his 'layout.' I went willingly enough,
having nothing to do. The gambling saloon was on the
first floor of a building nearly opposite the Eldridge
House: the place was well kept and neat, thanks to a
colored bartender and waiter and a boy for all work.
The long room, too, was comfortably furnished and
very brightly lit – altogether an attractive place.

As luck would have it, while he was showing me

around, a lady came in. Mayhew after a word or two
introduced me to her as his wife. Mrs Mayhew was
then a woman of perhaps twenty-eight or thirty, with
tall, lissome, slight figure and interesting rather than
a pretty face: her features were all good, her eyes even
were large and blue-grey; she would have been lovely
if her coloring had been more pronounced. Give her
golden hair or red or black and she would have been
a beauty; she was always tastefully dressed and had
appealing, ingratiating manners. I soon found that she
loved books and reading, and as Mayhew said he was
going to be busy, I asked if I might see her home. She
consented smiling and away we went. She lived in a
pretty frame house standing alone in a street that ran
parallel to Massachusetts Street, nearly opposite to a
large and ugly church.

As she went up the steps to the door, I noticed that
she had fine, neat ankles and I divined shapely limbs.
While she was taking off her light cloak and hat, the
lifting of her arms stretched her bodice and showed
small, round breasts: already my blood was lava and
my mouth parched with desire.

'You look at me strangely!' she said, swinging round
from the long mirror with a challenge on her parted
lips. I made some inane remark: I couldn't trust myself
to speak frankly; but natural sympathy drew us
together. I told her I was going to be a student, and
she wanted to know whether I could dance. I told her
I could not, and she promised to teach me: 'Lily
Robins, a neighbor's girl, will play for us any
afternoon. Do you know the steps?' She went on, and

when I said, 'No,' she got up from the sofa, held up her dress and showed me the three polka steps, which she said were waltz steps, too, only taken on a glide.

'What pretty ankles you have!' I ventured, but she appeared not to hear me. We sat on and on and I learned that she was very lonely: Mr Mayhew away every night and nearly all day and nothing to do in that little dead-and-alive place. 'Will you let me come in for a talk sometimes?' I asked.

'Whenever you wish,' was her answer. As I rose to go and we were standing opposite to each other by the door, I said: 'You know, Mrs Mayhew, in Europe when a man brings a pretty woman home, she rewards him with a kiss.'

'Really?' she scoffed, smiling; 'that's not a custom here.'

'Are you less generous than they are?' I asked, and the next moment I had taken her face in my hands and kissed her on the lips.

She put her hands on my shoulders and left her eyes on mine. 'We're going to be friends,' she said; 'I felt it when I saw you: don't stay away too long!'

'Will you see me tomorrow afternoon?' I asked. 'I want that dance lesson!'

'Surely,' she replied. 'I'll tell Lily in the morning.' And once more our hands met: I tried to draw her to me for another kiss; she held back with a smiling, 'Tomorrow afternoon!'

'Tell me your name,' I begged, 'so that I may think of it.'

'Lorna,' she replied, 'you funny boy!' I went my

way with pulses hammering, blood aflame and hope in my heart.

Next morning I called again upon Smith but the pretty servant ('Rose,' she said her name was), told me that he was nearly always at Judge Stephens', 'five or six miles out,' she added. So I said I'd write and make an appointment, and I did write and asked him to let me see him next morning.

That same morning Willie recommended to me a pension kept by a Mrs Gregory, an English woman, the wife of an old Baptist clergyman, who would take good care of me for four dollars a week. Immediately I went with him to see her and was delighted to find that she lived only about a hundred yards from Mrs Mayhew, on the opposite side of the street. Mrs Gregory was a large, motherly woman, evidently a lady, who had founded this boarding house to provide for a rather reckless husband and two children, a big pretty girl, Kate, and a lad a couple of years younger. Mrs Gregory was delighted with my English accent, I believe, and showed me special favour at once by giving me a large outside room with its own entrance and steps into the garden.

In an hour I had paid my bill at the Eldridge House and had moved in. I showed a shred of prudence by making Willie promise Mrs Gregory that he would turn up each Saturday with the five dollars for my board; the dollar extra was for the big room.

In due course I shall tell how he kept his promise and discharged his debt to me. For the moment everything was easily, happily settled. I went out and ordered a decent suit of ordinary tweeds and dressed myself up in my best blue suit to call upon Mrs Mayhew after lunch. The clock crawled, but on the stroke of three I was at her door: a colored maid admitted me.

'Mrs Mayhew,' she said in her pretty singing voice, 'will be down right soon: I'll go and call Miss Lily.'

In five minutes Miss Lily appeared, a dark slip of a girl with shining black hair, wide, laughing mouth, temperamental thick, red lips, and grey eyes fringed with black lashes; she had hardly time to speak to me when Mrs Mayhew came in. 'I hope you two'll be great friends,' she said prettily. 'You're both about the same age,' she added.

In a few minutes Miss Lily was playing a waltz on the Steinway and with my arm around the slight, flexible waist of my inamorata I was trying to waltz. But alas! After a turn or two I became giddy and in spite of all my resolutions had to admit that I should never be able to dance.

'You have got very pale,' Mrs Mayhew said, 'you must sit down on the sofa a little while.' Slowly the giddiness left me; before I had entirely recovered Miss Lily with kindly words of sympathy had gone home, and Mrs Mayhew brought me in a cup of excellent coffee; I drank it down and was well at once.

'You should go in and lie down,' said Mrs Mayhew, still full of pity. 'See,' and she opened a door, 'there's the guest bedroom all ready.' I saw my chance and went over to her. 'If you'd come too,' I whispered, and then, 'The coffee has made me quite well: won't you, Lorna, give me a kiss? You don't know how often I said you name last night, you dear!' And in a moment I had again taken her face and put my lips on hers.

She gave me her lips this time and my kiss became a caress; but in a little while she drew away and said, 'Let's sit and talk; I want to know all you are doing.' So I seated myself beside her on the sofa and told her all my news. She thought I would be comfortable with the Gregorys. 'Mrs Gregory is a good woman,' she added, 'and I hear the girl's engaged to a cousin: do you think her pretty?'

'I think no one pretty but you, Lorna,' I said, and I pressed her head down on the arm of the sofa and kissed her. Her lips grew hot: I was certain. At once I put my hand down on her sex; she struggled a little at first, which I took care should bring our bodies closer, and when she ceased struggling I put my hands up her dress and began caressing her sex: it was hot and wet, as I knew it would be, and opened readily.

But in another moment she took the lead. 'Someone might find us here,' she whispered. 'I've let the maid go: come up to my bedroom,' and she took me upstairs. I begged her to undress: I wanted to see her figure; but she only said, 'I have no corsets on; I don't often wear them in the house. Are you sure you love me, dear?'

'You know I do!' was my answer. The next moment I lifted her on to the bed, drew up her clothes, opened her legs and was in her. There was no difficulty and in a moment or two I came, but went right on poking passionately; in a few minutes her breath went and came quickly and her eyes fluttered and she met my thrusts with sighs and nippings of her sex. My second orgasm took some time and all the while Lorna became more and more responsive, till suddenly she put her hands on my bottom and drew me to her forcibly while she moved her sex up and down awkwardly to meet my thrusts with a passion I had hardly imagined. Again and again I came and the longer the play lasted the wilder was her excitement and delight. She kissed me hotly, foraging and thrusting her tongue into my mouth. Finally she pulled up her chemise to get me further into her and, at length, with little sobs, she suddenly got hysterical and, panting wildly, burst into a storm of tears.

That stopped me: I withdrew my sex and took her in my arms and kissed her; at first she clung to me with choking sighs and streaming eyes, but, as soon as she had won a little control, I went to the toilette and brought her a sponge of cold water and bathed her face and gave her some water to drink — that quieted her. But she would not let me leave her even to arrange my clothes.

'Oh, you great, strong dear,' she cried, with her arms clasping me. 'Oh, who would have believed such intense pleasure possible: I never felt anything like it before; how could you keep on so long? Oh, how I love you, you wonder and delight.

'I am all yours,' she added gravely. 'You shall do what you like with me: I am your mistress, your slave, your plaything, and you are my god and my love! Oh, darling! Oh!'

There was a pause while I smiled at her extravagant praise, then suddenly she sat up and got out of bed. 'You wanted to see my figure'; she exclaimed, 'here it is, I can deny you nothing; I only hope it may please you,' and in moment or two she showed herself nude from head to stocking.

As I had guessed, her figure was slight and lissome, with narrow hips, but she had a great bush of hair on her Mount of Venus and her breasts were not so round and firm as Jessie's: still she was very pretty and well-formed with the *fines attaches* (slender wrists and ankles), which the French are so apt to overestimate. They think that small bones indicate a small sex; but I have found the exceptions are very numerous, even if there is such a rule.

After I had kissed her breasts and navel and praised her figure, she disappeared in the bathroom, but was soon with me again on the sofa which we had left an hour or so before.

'Do you know,' she began, 'my husband assured me that only the strongest young man could go twice with a woman in one day? I believed him; aren't we women fools? You must have come a dozen times!'

'Not half that number,' I replied, smiling.

'Aren't you tired?' was her next question. 'Even I have a little headache,' she added. 'I never was so wrought up; at the end it was so intense; but you must be tired out.'

'No,' I replied, 'I feel no fatigue, indeed, I feel the better for our joy ride!'

'But surely you're an exception!' she went on. 'Most men have finished in one short spasm and leave the woman utterly unsatisfied, just excited and no more.'

'Youth,' I said, 'that, I believe, makes the chief difference.'

'Is there any danger of a child?' she went on. 'I ought to say "hope,"' she added bitterly, 'for I'd love to have a child, your child,' and she kissed me.

'Do you know you kiss wonderfully?' she went on reflectingly. 'With a lingering touch of the inside of the lips and then the thrust of the tongue: that's what excited me so the first time,' and she sighed, as if delighted with the memory.

'You didn't seem excited,' I said half reproachfully, 'for when I wanted another kiss, you drew away and said "Tomorrow"! Why are women so coquettish, so perverse?' I added, remembering Lucille and Jessie.

'I think it is that we wish to be sure of being desired,' she replied, 'and a little, too, that we want to prolong the joy of it, the delight of being wanted, really wanted! It is so easy for us to give and so exquisite to feel a man's desire pursuing us! Ah, how rare it is,' she sighed passionately, 'and how quickly lost! You'll soon tire of your mistress,' she added, 'now that I am all yours and thrill only for you,' and she took my head in her hands and kissed me passionately, regretfully.

'You kiss better than I do, Lorna! Where did you acquire the art, Madame?' I asked. 'I fear that you have been a naughty, naughty girl!'

'If you only knew the truth,' she exclaimed, 'if you only knew how girls long for a lover and burn and itch in vain and wonder why men are so stupid and cold and dull as not to see our desire.

'Don't we try all sorts of tricks? Aren't we haughty and withdrawn at one moment and affectionate, tender, loving at another? Don't we conceal the hook with every sort of bait, only to watch the fish sniff at it and turn away. Ah, if you knew − I feel a traitor to my sex even in telling you − if you guessed how we angle for you and how clever we are, how full of wiles. There's an expression I once heard my husband use which described us women exactly, or nine out of ten of us. I wanted to know how he kept the office warm all night: he said, we damp down the furnaces, and explained the process. That's it, I cried to myself, I'm a damped-down furnace: that's surely why I keep hot ever so long! Did you imagine,' she asked, turning her flower-face all pale with passion half aside, 'that I took off my hat that first day before the glass and turned slowly round with it held above my head, by chance? You dear innocent! I knew the movement would show my breasts and slim hips and did it deliberately, hoping it would excite you, and how I thrilled when I saw it did.

'Why did I show you the bed in that room,' she added, 'and leave the door ajar when I came back here to the sofa but to tempt you, and how heart-glad I was to feel your desire in your kiss. I was giving myself before you pushed my head back on the sofa-arm and disarranged all my hair!' she added, pouting and patting it with her hands to make sure it was in order.

'You were astonishingly masterful and quick,' she went on, 'how did you know that I wished you to touch me then? Most men would have gone on kissing and fooling, afraid to act decisively. You must have had a lot of experience? You naughty lad!'

'Shall I tell the truth?' I said. 'I will, just to encourage you to be frank with me. You are the first woman I have ever spent my seed in or had properly.'

'Call it improperly, for God's sake,' she cried laughing aloud with joy, 'you darling virgin, you! Oh! how I wish I was sixteen again and you were my first lover. You would have made me believe in God. Yet you are my first lover,' she added quickly. 'I have only learned the delight and ecstasy of love in your arms.'

Our love-talk lasted for hours till suddenly I guessed it was late and looked at my watch; it was nearly seven-thirty: I was late for supper, which started at half-past six!

'I must go,' I exclaimed, 'or I'll get nothing to eat.'

'I could give you supper,' she added, 'my lips, too, that long for you and – and – but you know.' She added regretfully, 'He might come in and I want to know you better first before seeing you together; a young god and a man! – and the man God's likeness, yet so poor an imitation!'

'Don't, don't,' I said, 'you'll make life harder for yourself – '

'Harder,' she repeated with a sniff of contempt. 'Kiss me, my love, and go if you must. Shall I see you tomorrow? There!' she cried as with a curse, 'I've given myself away: I can't help it; oh, how I want you always: how I shall long for you and count the dull dreary hours! Go, go or I'll never let you – ' and she kissed and clung to me to the door.

'Sweet – tomorrow!' I said, and tore off.

Of course it is manifest that my liaison with Mrs Mayhew had little or nothing to do with love. It was demoniac youthful sex-urge in me and much the same hunger in her, and as soon as the desire was satisfied my judgment of her was as impartial, cool as if she had always been indifferent to me. But with her I think there was a certain attachment and considerable tenderness. In intimate relations between the sexes it is rare indeed that the man gives as much to love as the woman.

Next day at three o'clock I knocked at Mrs Mayhew's: she opened the door herself. I cried, 'How kind of you!' and once in the room drew her to me and kissed her time and time again: she seemed cold and numb.

For some moments she didn't speak, then: 'I feel as if I had passed through fever,' she said, putting her hands through her hair, lifting it in a gesture I was to know well in the days to come. 'Never promise again if you don't come; I thought I should go mad: waiting is a horrible torture! Who kept you – some girl?' and her eyes searched mine.

I excused myself; but her intensity chilled me. At the risk of alienating my girl readers, I must confess this was the effect her passion had on me. When I kissed her, her lips were cold. But by the time we had got upstairs, she had thawed. She shut the door after us gravely and began: 'See how ready I am for you!' and in a moment she had thrown back her robe and stood before me naked. She tossed the garment on a chair; it fell on the floor. She stooped to pick it up with her bottom toward me: I kissed her soft bottom and caught her by it with my hand on her sex.

She turned her head over her shoulder: 'I've washed and scented myself for you, Sir: how do you like the perfume? and how do you like this bush of hair?' and she touched her mount with a grimace. 'I was so ashamed of it as a girl: I used to shave it off, that's what made it grow so thick, I believe. One day my mother saw it and made me stop shaving. Oh! how ashamed of it I was: it's animal, ugly, — don't you hate it? Oh, tell the truth!' she cried, 'Or rather, don't; tell me you love it.'

'I love it,' I exclaimed, 'because it's yours!'

'Oh, you dear lover,' she smiled, 'you always find the right word, the flattering salve for the sore!'

'Are you ready for me,' I asked, 'ripe-ready, or shall I kiss you first and caress pussy?'

'Whatever you do will be right,' she said. 'You know I am rotten-ripe, soft and wet for you always!'

All this while I was taking off my clothes; now I too was naked.

'I want you to draw up your knees,' I said: 'I want to see the Holy of Holies, the shrine of my idolatry.'

At once she did as I asked. Her legs and bottom were well-shaped without being statuesque: but her clitoris was much more than the average button: it stuck out fully half an inch and the inner lips of her vulva hung down a little below the outer lip. I knew I should see prettier pussies. Kate's was better shaped, I felt sure, and the heavy, madder-brown lips put me off a little.

The next moment I began caressing her red clitoris with my hot, stiff organ: Lorna sighed deeply once or twice and her eyes drew it out again to the lips, then in again, and I felt her warm love-juice gush as she drew up her knees even higher to let me further in. 'Oh, it's divine,' she sighed, 'better even than the first time,' and, when my thrusts grew quick and hard as the orgasm shook me, she writhed down on my prick as I withdrew, as if she would hold it, and as my seed spirted into her, she bit my shoulder and held her legs tight as if to keep my sex in her. We lay a few moments bathed in bliss. Then, as I began to move again to sharpen the sensation, she half rose on her arm. 'Do you know,' she said, 'I dreamed yesterday of getting on you and doing it to you, do you mind if I try?'

'No, indeed!' I cried. 'Go to it, I am your prey!' She got up smiling and straddled kneeling across me, and put my cock in her pussy and sank down on me with a deep sigh. She tried to move up and down on my organ and at once came up too high and had to use her hand to put my Tommy in again; then she sank down on it as far as possible. 'I can sink down all right,' she cried, smiling at the double meaning, 'but I cannot rise so well! What fools we women are, we can't master even the act of love; we are so awkward!'

'Your awkwardness, however, excites me,' I said.

'Does it?' she cried. 'Then I'll do my best,' and for

some time she rose and sank rhythmically, but, as her excitement grew, she just let herself lie on me and wiggled her bottom till we both came. She was flushed and hot and I couldn't help asking her a question.

'Does your excitement grow to a spasm of pleasure,' I asked, 'or do you go on getting more and more excited continually?'

'I get more and more excited,' she said, 'till the other day with you, for the first time in my iife, the pleasure became unbearably intense and I was hysterical, you wonder-lover!'

Since then I have read lascivious books in half a dozen languages and they all represent women coming to an orgasm in the act, as men do, followed by a period of content; which only shows that the books are all written by men, and ignorant, insensitive men at that. The truth is: hardly one married woman in a thousand is ever brought to her highest pitch of feeling; usually, just when she begins to feel, her husband goes to sleep. If the majority of husbands satisfied their wives occasionally, the woman's revolt would soon move to another purpose: women want above all a lover who lives to excite them to the top of their bent. As a rule, men through economic conditions marry so late that they have already half-exhausted their virile power before they marry. And when they marry young, they are so ignorant and self-centred that they imagine their wives must be satisfied when they are. Mrs Mayhew told me that her husband had never excited her, really. She denied that she had ever had any real acute pleasure from his embraces.

'Shall I make you hysterical again?' I asked, out of boyish vanity. 'I can, you know!'

'You mustn't tire yourself!' she warned. 'My husband taught me long ago that when a woman tires a man, he gets a distaste for her, and I want your love, your desire, dear, a thousand times more even than the delight you give me − '

'Don't be afraid,' I broke in. 'You are sweet; you couldn't tire me; turn sideways and put your left leg up, and I'll just let my sex caress your clitoris back and forth gently; every now and then I'll let it go right in until our hairs meet.' I kept on this game perhaps half an hour until she first sighed and sighed and then made awkward movements with her pussy which I sought to divine and meet as she wished, when suddenly she cried:

'Oh! Oh! Hurt me, please! hurt me, or I'll bite you! Oh God, oh, oh,' panting, breathless till again the tears poured down!

'You darling,' she sobbed. 'How you can love! Could you go on forever?'

For answer, I put her hand on my sex. 'Just as naughty as ever,' she exclaimed, 'and I am choking, breathless, exhausted! Oh, I'm sorry,' she went on, 'but we should get up, for I don't want my help to know or guess: servants talk − '

I got up and went to the windows; one gave on the porch, but the other directly on the garden. 'What are you looking at?' she asked, coming to me.

'I was just looking for the best way to get out if ever we were surprised,' I said. 'If we leave this window open I can always drop into the garden and get away quickly.'

'You would hurt yourself,' she cried.

'Not a bit of it,' I answered. 'I could drop half as far again without injury; the only thing is, I must have boots on and trousers, or those thorns of yours would gip!'

'You boy,' she exclaimed laughing. 'I think after your strength and passion, it is your boyishness I love best' — and she kissed me again and again.

'I must work,' I warned her; 'Smith has given me a lot to do.'

'Oh, my dear,' she said, her eyes filling with tears, 'that means you won't come tomorrow or,' she added hastily, 'even the day after?'

'I can't possibly,' I declared. 'I have a good week's work in front of me; but you know I'll come the first afternoon I can make myself free and I'll let you know the day before, sweet!'

She looked at me with tearful eyes and quivering lips. 'Love is its own torment!' she sighed, while I dressed and got away quickly.

The truth was I was already satiated. Her passion held nothing new in it: she had taught me all she could and had nothing more in her, I thought; while Kate was prettier and much younger and a virgin. Why shouldn't I confess it? It was Kate's virginity that attracted me irresistibly: I pictures her legs to myself, her hips and thighs . . .

The next few days passed in reading the books Smith had lent me, especially *Das Kapital*, the second book of which, with its frank exposure of the English factory system, was simply enthralling. I read some of Tacitus, too, and Xenophon with a crib, and learned a page of Greek every day by heart, and whenever I felt tired of work I laid siege to Kate. That is, I continued my plan of campaign. One day I called her brother into my room and told him true stories of buffalo hunting and of fighting with Indians; another day I talked theology with the father or drew the dear mother out to tell of her girlish days in Cornwall. 'I never thought I'd come to work like this in my old age, but then children take all and give little; I was no better as a girl, I remember,' – and I got a scene of her brief courtship!

I had won the whole household long before I said a word to Kate beyond the merest courtesies. A week or so passed like this till one day I held them all after dinner while I told the story of our raid into Mexico. I took care, of course, that Kate was out of the room. Towards the end of my tale, Kate came in: at once I hastened to end abruptly, and after excusing myself, went into the garden.

Half an hour later I saw she was in my room tidying up; I took thought and then went up the outside steps. As soon as I saw her I pretended surprise. 'I beg your pardon,' I said. 'I'll just get a book and go at once; please don't let me disturb you!' and I pretended to look for the book.

She turned sharply and looked at me fixedly. 'Why do you treat me like this!' she burst out, shaking with indignation.

'Like what?' I repeated, pretending surprise.

'You know quite well,' she went on angrily, hastily. 'At first I thought it was chance, unintentional; now I know you mean it. Whenever you are talking or telling a story, as soon as I come into the room you stop and hurry away as if you hated me. Why? Why?' she cried with quivering lips. 'What have I done to make you dislike me so?' and the tears gathered in her lovely eyes.

I felt the moment had come: I put my hands on her shoulders and looked with my whole soul into her eyes. 'Did you never guess, Kate, that it might be love, not hate?' I asked.

'No, no!' she cried, the tears falling. 'Love does not act like that!'

'Fear to miss love does, I can assure you,' I cried. 'I thought at first that you disliked me and already I had begun to care for you' (my arms went around her waist and I drew her to me), 'to love you and want you. Kiss me, dear,' and at once she gave me her lips, while my hand got busy on her breasts and then went down of itself to her sex.

Suddenly she looked at me gaily, brightly, while heaving a big sigh of relief. 'I'm glad, glad!' she said. 'If you only knew how hurt I was and how tortured myself; one moment I was angry, then I was sad. Yesterday I made up my mind to speak, but today I said to myself, I'll just be obstinate and cold as he is and now − ' and of her own accord she put her arms around my neck and kissed me − 'you are a dear, dear! Anyway, I love you.'

'You mustn't give me those bird-pecks!' I exclaimed. 'Those are not kisses: I want your lips to open and cling to mine,' and I kissed her while my tongue darted into her mouth and I stroked her sex gently. She flushed, but at first didn't understand; then suddenly she blushed rosy red as her lips grew hot and she fairly ran from the room.

I exulted: I knew I had won: I must be very quiet and reserved and the bird would come to the lure; I felt exultingly certain!

Meanwhile I spent nearly every morning with Smith: golden hours! Always, always before we parted, he showed me some new beauty or revealed some new truth: he seemed to me the most wonderful creature in this strange, sunlit world. I used to hang entranced on his eloquent lips! (Strange! I was sixty-five before I found such a hero-worshipper as I was to Smith, who was only four or five and twenty!) He made me know all the Greek dramatists: Aeschylus, Sophocles and Euripides and put them for me in a truer light than English or German scholars have set them yet. He knew that Sophocles was the greatest, and from his lips I learned every chorus in the *Oedipus Rex* and *Colonnus* before I had completely mastered the Greek grammar; indeed, it was the supreme beauty of the literature that forced me to learn the language. In teaching me the choruses, he was careful to point out that it was possible to keep the measure and yet mark the accent too: in fact, he made classic Greek a living language to me, as living as English. And he would not let me neglect Latin: in the first year with him I knew poems of Catullus by heart, almost as well as I knew Swinburne. Thanks to Professor Smith, I had no difficulty in entering the junior class at the university; in fact, after my first three or four months' work I was easily the first in the class, which included Ned Stephens, the brother of Smith's inamorata. I soon discovered that Smith was heels over head in love with Kate Stephens, shot through the heart, as Mercutio would say, with a fair girl's blue eye!

And small wonder, for Kate was lovely: a little above middle height with slight, rounded figure and most attractive face: the oval, a thought long, rather than round, with dainty, perfect features, lit up by a pair of superlative grey-blue eyes, eyes by turns delightful and reflective and appealing, that mirrored a really extraordinary intelligence. She was in the senior class and afterwards for years held the position of Professor of Greek in the university. I shall have something to say of her in a later volume of this history, for I met her again in New York nearly fifty years later. But in 1872 or '73, her brother Ned, a handsome lad of eighteen who was in my class, interested me more. The only other member of the senior class of this time was a fine fellow, Ned Bancroft, who later came to France with me to study.

At this time, curiously enough, Kate Stephens was by way of being engaged to Ned Bancroft; but already it was plain that she was in love with Smith, and my outspoken admiration of Smith helped her, I hope, as I am sure it helped him, to a better mutual understanding. Bancroft accepted the situation with extraordinary self-sacrifice, losing neither Smith's nor Kate's friendship: I have seldom seen nobler self-abnegation; indeed, his high-mindedness in this crisis was what first won my admiration and showed me his other fine qualities.

Almost in the beginning I had serious disquietude: every little while Smith was ill and had to keep to his bed for a day or two. There was no explanation of this illness, which puzzled me and caused me a certain anxiety.

One day in midwinter there was a new development. Smith was in doubt how to act and confided in me. He had found Professor Kellogg, in whose house he lived, trying to kiss the pretty help, Rose, entirely against her will. Smith was emphatic on this point: the girl was struggling angrily to free herself, when by chance he interrupted them.

I relieved Smith's solemn gravity a little by roaring with laughter. The idea of an old professor and clergyman trying to win a girl by force filled me with amusement: 'What a fool the man must be!' was my English judgment; Smith took the American high moral tone at first.

'Think of his disloyalty to his wife in the same house,' he cried, 'and then the scandal if the girl talked, and she is sure to talk!'

'Sure not to talk,' I corrected. 'Girls are afraid of the effect of such revelations; besides a word from you asking her to shield Mrs Kellogg will ensure her silence.'

'Oh, I cannot advise her,' cried Smith. 'I will not

be mixed up in it: I told Kellogg at the time, I must leave the house, yet I don't know where to go! It's too disgraceful of him! His wife is really a dear woman!'

For the first time I became conscious of a rooted difference between Smith and myself: his high moral condemnation on very insufficient data seemed to me childish, but no doubt many of my readers will think my tolerance a proof of my shameless libertinism! However, I jumped at the opportunity of talking to Rose on such a scabrous matter and at the same time solved Smith's difficulty by proposing that he should come and take room and board with the Gregorys — a great stroke of practical diplomacy on my part, or so it appeared to me, for thereby I did the Gregorys, Smith and myself an immense, an incalculable service. Smith jumped at the idea, asked me to see about it at once and let him know, and then rang for Rose.

She came half-scared, half-angry, on the defensive, I could see; so I spoke first, smiling. 'Oh Rose,' I said, 'Professor Smith has been telling me of your trouble; but you ought not to be angry: for you are so pretty that no wonder a man wants to kiss you; you must blame your lovely eyes and mouth.'

Rose laughed outright: she had come expecting reproof and found sweet flattery.

'There's only one thing, Rose,' I went on. 'The story would hurt Mrs Kellogg if it got out and she's not very strong, so you must say nothing about it, for her sake. That's what Professor Smith wanted to say to you,' I added.

'I'm not likely to tell,' cried Rose. 'I'll soon forget

all about it, but I guess I'd better get another job: he's liable to try again, though I gave him a good, hard slap,' and she laughed merrily.

'I'm so glad for Mrs Kellogg's sake,' said Smith gravely, 'and if I can help you get another place, please call upon me.'

'I guess I'll have no difficulty,' answered Rose flippantly, with a shade of dislike of the professor's solemnity. 'Mrs Kellogg will give me a good character,' and the healthy young minx grinned, 'besides I'm not sure but I'll go stay home a spell. I'm fed up with working and would like a holiday, and mother wants me . . .'

'Where do you live, Rose?' I asked with a keen eye for future opportunities.

'On the other side of the river,' she replied, 'next door to Elder Conklin's, where your brother boards,' she added smiling.

When Rose went I begged Smith to pack his boxes, for I would get him the best room at the Gregorys' and assured him it was really large and comfortable and would hold all his books, etc.; and off I went to make my promise good. On the way, I set myself to think how I could turn the kindness I was doing the Gregorys to the advantage of my love. I decided to make Kate a partner in the good deed, or at least a herald of the good news. So when I got home I rang the bell in my room, and as I had hoped Kate answered it. When I heard her footsteps I was shaking, hot with desire, and now I wish to describe a feeling I then began to notice in myself. I longed to take possession of the girl, so to speak, abruptly, ravish her in fact, or at least thrust both hands up her dress at once and feel her bottom and sex altogether; but already I knew enough to realize certainly that girls prefer gentle and courteous approaches. Why? Of the fact I am sure. So I said, 'Come in, Kate,' gravely. 'I want to ask you whether the best bedroom is still free, and if you'd like Professor Smith to have it, if I could get him to come here?'

'I'm sure Mother would be delighted,' she exclaimed.

'You see,' I went on, 'I'm trying to serve you all I can, yet you don't even kiss me of your own accord.' She smiled, and so I drew her to the bed and lifted her up on it. I saw her glance and answered it: 'The door is shut, dear,' and half lying on her, I began kissing her passionately, while my hands went up her clothes to her sex. To my delight she wore no drawers, but at first she kept her legs tight together frowning. 'Love denies nothing, Kate,' I said gravely; slowly she drew her legs apart, half-pouting, half-smiling, and let me caress her sex. When her love-juice came, I kissed her and stopped. 'It's dangerous here,' I said, 'that door you came in is open; but I must see your lovely limbs,' and I turned up her dress. I hadn't exaggerated; she had limbs like a Greek statue and her triangle of brown hair lay in little silky curls on her belly and then — the sweetest cunny in the world. I bent down and kissed it.

In a moment Kate was on her feet, smoothing her dress down. 'What a boy you are,' she exclaimed, 'but that's partly why I love you; oh, I hope you'll love me half as much. Say you will, Sir, and I'll do anything you wish!'

'I will,' I replied, 'but oh, I'm glad you want love; can you come to me tonight? I want a couple of hours with you uninterrupted.'

'This afternoon,' she said, 'I'll say I'm going for a walk and I'll come to you, dear! They are all resting then or out and I shan't be missed.'

I could only wait and think. One thing was fixed in me, I must have her, make her mine before Smith came: he was altogether too fascinating, I thought, to be trusted with such a pretty girl; but I was afraid she would bleed and I did not want to hurt her this first time, so I went out and bought a syringe and a pot of cold cream which I put beside my bed.

Oh, how that dinner lagged! Mrs Gregory thanked me warmly for my kindness to them all (which seemed to me pleasantly ironical!) and Mr Gregory followed her lead; but at length everyone had finished and I went to my room to prepare. First I locked the outside door and drew down the blinds: then I studied the bed and turned it back and arranged a towel along the edge; happily the bed was just about the right height! Then I loosened my trousers, unbuttoned the front and pulled up my shirt: a little later Kate put her lovely face in at the door and slipped inside. I shot the bolt and began kissing her; girls are strange mortals; she had taken off her corset, just as I had put a towel handy. I lifted up her clothes and touched her sex, caressing it gently while kissing her: in a moment or two her love-milk came.

I lifted her up on the bed, pushed down my trousers, anointed my prick with the cream and then, parting her legs and getting her to pull her knees up, I drew her bottom to the edge of the bed: she frowned at that, but I explained quickly: 'It may give a little pain, at first, dear: and I want to give you as little as possible,' and I slipped the head of my cock gently, slowly into her. Even greased, her pussy was tight and at the very entrance I felt the obstacle, her maidenhead, in the way; I lay on her and kissed her and let her or Mother Nature help me.

As soon as Kate found that I was leaving it to her, she pushed forward boldly and the obstacle yielded. 'O — O!' she cried, and then pushed forward again roughly and my organ went in her to the hilt and her clitoris must have felt my belly. Resolutely, I refrained from thrusting or withdrawing for a minute or two and then drew out slowly to her lips and, as I pushed Tommy gently in again, she leaned up and kissed me passionately. Slowly, with extremest care, I governed myself and pushed in and out with long slow thrusts, though I longed, longed to plunge it in hard and quicken the strokes as much as possible; but I knew from Mrs Mayhew that the long, gentle thrusts and slow withdrawals were the aptest to excite a woman's passion and I was determined to win Kate.

In two or three minutes, she had again let down a flow of love-juice, or so I believed, and I kept right on with the love-game, knowing that the first experience is never forgotten by a girl and resolved to keep on to dinner-time if necessary to make her first love-joust ever memorable to her. Kate lasted longer than Mrs Mayhew; I came ever so many times, passing ever more slowly from orgasm to orgasm before she began to move to me; but at length her breath began to get shorter and shorter and she held me to her violently, moving her pussy the while up and down harshly against my manroot. Suddenly she relaxed and fell back: there was no hysteria; but plainly I could feel the mouth of her womb fasten on my cock as if to suck it. That excited me fiercely and for the first time I indulged in quick, hard thrusts till a spasm of intensest pleasure shook me and my seed spirted or seemed to spirt for the sixth or seventh time.

When I had finished kissing and praising my lovely partner and drew away, I was horrified; the bed was a sheet of blood and some had gone on my pants: Kate's thighs and legs even were all incarnadined, making the lovely ivory white of her skin, one red. You may imagine how softly I used a towel on her legs and sex before I showed her the results of our love-passage. To my astonishment she was unaffected. 'You must take the sheet away and burn it,' she said. 'or drop it in the river: I guess it won't be the first.'

'Did it hurt much?' I asked.

'At first a good deal,' she replied, 'but soon the pleasure overpowered the smart and I would not even forget the pain. I love you so. I am not even afraid of consequences with you: I trust you absolutely and love to trust you and run whatever risks you wish.'

'You darling!' I cried, 'I don't believe there will be

any consequences; but I want you to go to the basin and use this syringe. I'll tell you why afterwards.'

At once she went over to the basin. 'I feel funny, weak,' she said, 'as if I were — I can't describe it — shaky on my legs. I'm glad now I don't wear drawers in summer, they'd get wet.' Her ablutions completed and the sheet withdrawn and done up in paper, I shot back the bolt and we began our talk. I found her intelligent and kindly but ignorant and ill-read: still she was not prejudiced and was eager to know all about babies and how they were made. I told her how my seed was composed of tens of thousands of tadpole-shaped animalculae. Already in her vagina and womb these infinitely little things had a race: they could move nearly an inch an hour and the strongest and quickest got up first to where her egg was waiting in the middle of her womb. My little tadpole, the first to arrive, thrust his head into her egg and thus having accomplished his work of impregnation, perished, love and death being twins.

The curious thing was that this indescribably small tadpole should be able to transmit all the qualities of all his progenitors in certain proportions; no such miracle was ever imagined by any religious teacher. More curious still, the living foetus in the womb passes in nine months through all the chief changes that the human race has gone through in countless aeons of time in its progress from the tadpole to the man. Till the fifth month the foetus is practically a four-legged animal.

I told her that it was accepted today that the weeks

occupied in the womb in any metamorphosis
correspond exactly to the ages it occupied in reality.
Thus it was upright, a two-legged animal, ape and then
man in the womb for the last three months, and this
corresponded nearly to one-third of man's whole
existence on this earth. Kate listened, enthraled, I
thought, till she asked me suddenly:

'But what makes one child a boy and another a girl?'

'The nearest we've come to a law on the matter,'
I said, 'is contained in the so-called law of contraries:
that is, if the man is stronger than the woman, the
children will be mostly girls; if the woman is greatly
younger or stronger, the progeny will be chiefly boys.
This bears out the old English proverb: 'Any weakling
can make a boy, but it takes a man to make a girl.'

Kate laughed and just then a knock came to the
door. 'Come in!' I cried, and then the colored maid
came in with a note. 'A lady's just been and left
it,' said Jenny. I saw it was from Mrs Mayhew, so
I crammed it into my pocket, saying regretfully: 'I
must answer it soon.' Kate excused herself and after
a long, long kiss went to prepare supper, while I read
Mrs Mayhew's note, which was short, if not exactly
sweet:

Eight days and no Frank, and no news; you cannot
want to kill me: come today if possible.

Lorna

I replied at once, saying I would come on the
morrow, that I was so busy I didn't know where to

turn, but would be with her sure on the morrow and I signed 'Your Frank.'

Of course, I went to Mrs Mayhew that next afternoon even before three. She met me without a word, so gravely that I did not even kiss her, but began explaining what Smith was to me and how I could not do enough for him who was everything to my mind, as she was (God help me!) to my heart and body; and I kissed her cold lips, while she shook her head sadly.

'We have a sixth sense, we women, when we are in love,' she began. 'I feel a new influence in you; I scent danger in the air you bring with you: don't ask me to explain: I can't; but my heart is heavy and cold as death. If you leave me, there'll be a catastrophe: the fall from such a height of happiness must be fatal. If you can feel pleasure away from me, you no longer love me. I feel none except in having you, seeing you, thinking of you – none! Oh, why can't you love like a woman loves! No! like I love: it would be heaven; for you and you alone satisfy the insatiable; you leave me bathed in bliss, sighing with satisfaction, happy as the Queen in Heaven!'

'I have much to tell you, new things to say,' I began in haste.

'Come upstairs,' I broke in, interrupting myself. 'I want to see you as you are now, with the color in your cheeks, the light in your eyes, the vibration in your voice, come!'

And she came like a sad sybil. 'Who gave you the

tact,' she began while we were undressing, 'the tact to praise always?'

I seized her and stood naked against her, body to body. 'What new things have you to tell me?' I asked, lifting her into the bed and getting in beside her, cuddling up to her warmer body.

'There's always something new in my love,' she cried, cupping my face with her slim hands and taking my lips with hers.

'Oh, how I desired you yesternoon, for I took the letter to your house myself and heard you talking in your room, perhaps with Smith,' she added, sounding my eyes with hers. 'I'm longing to believe it; but , when I heard your voice, or imagined I did, I felt the lips of my sex open and shut and then it began to burn and itch intolerably. I was on the point of going in to you, but, instead, turned and hurried away, raging at you and at myself — '

'I will not let you even talk such treason,' I cried, separating her soft thighs, as I spoke, and sliding between them. In a moment my sex was in her and we were one body, while I drew it out slowly and then pushed it in again, her naked body straining to mine.

'Oh,' she cried, 'as you draw out, my heart follows your sex in fear of losing it and as you push in again, it opens wide in ecstasy and wants you all, all — ' and she kissed me with hot lips.

'Here is something new,' she exclaimed, 'food for your vanity from my love! Mad as you make me with your love-thrusts, for at one moment I am hot and dry with desire, the next moment wet with passion, bathed in love, I could live with you all my life without having you, if you wished it, or if it would do you good. Do you believe me?'

'Yes,' I replied, continuing the love-game, but occasionally withdrawing to rub her clitoris with my sex and then slowly burying him in her cunt again to the hilt.

'We women have no souls but love,' she said faintly, her eyes dying as she spoke.

'I torture myself to think of some new pleasure for you, and yet you'll leave me, I feel you will, for some silly girl who can't feel a tithe of what I feel or give you what I give — ' She began here to breathe quickly. 'I've been thinking how to give you more pleasure; let me try. Your seed, darling, is dear to me: I don't want it in my sex; I want to feel you thrill and so I want your sex in my mouth, I want to drink your essence and I will — ' and suiting the action to the word, she slipped down in the bed and took my sex in her mouth and began rubbing it up and down till my seed spirted in long jets, filling her mouth while she swallowed it greedily.

'Now do I love you, Sir!' she exclaimed, drawing herself upon me again and nestling against me. 'Wait till some girl does that to you and you'll know she loves you to distraction or, better still, to self-destruction.'

'Why do you talk of any other girl?' I chided her. 'I don't imagine you going with another man; why should you torment yourself just as causelessly?'

She shook her head. 'My fears are prophetic,' she sighed. 'I'm willing to believe it hasn't happened yet, though — Ah, God, the torturing thought! The mere dread of you going with another drives me crazy; I could kill her, the bitch: why doesn't she get a man of her own? How dare she even look at you?' and she clasped me tightly to her. Nothing loath, I pushed my sex into her again and began the slow movement that excited her so quickly and me so gradually for, even while using my skill to give her the utmost pleasure, I could not help comparing and I realized surely enough that Kate's pussy was smaller and firmer and gave me infinitely more pleasure; still I kept on for her delight. And now again she began to pant and choke and, as I continued ploughing her body and touching her womb with every slow thrust, she began to cry inarticulately with little short cries growing higher in intensity till suddenly she squealed like a shot rabbit and then shrieked with laughter, breaking down in a storm of sighs and sobs and floods of tears.

As usual, her intensity chilled me a little; for her paroxysm aroused no corresponding heat in me, tending even to check my pleasure by the funny, irregular movements she made.

Suddenly, I heard steps going away from the door, light, stealing steps: who could it be? The servant? or — ?

Lorna had heard them, too, and though still panting and swallowing convulsively, she listened intently, while her great eyes wandered in thought. I knew I could leave the riddle to her: it was my task to reassure and caress her.

I got up and went over to the open window for

a breath of air and suddenly I saw Lily run quickly across the grass and disappear in the next house: so she was the listener! When I recalled Lorna's gasping cries, I smiled to myself. If Lily tried to explain them to herself, she would have an uneasy hour, I guessed.

When Lorna had dressed, and she dressed quickly and went downstairs hastily to convince herself, I think, that her maid had not spied on her, I waited in the sitting room. I must warn Lorna that my 'studies' would only allow me to give one day a week to our pleasures.

'Oh,' she cried, turning pale as I explained, 'didn't I know it!'

'But Lorna,' I pleaded, 'didn't you say you could do without me altogether if 'twas for my good?'

'No, no, no! a thousand times no!' she cried. 'I said if you were with me always, I could do without passion; but this starvation fare once a week! Go, go,' she cried, 'or I'll say something I'll regret. Go!' and she pushed me out of the door, and thinking it better in view of the future, I went.

The truth is, I was glad to get away; novelty is the soul of passion. There's an old English proverb: 'Fresh cunt, fresh courage.' On my way home I thought oftener of the slim, dark figure of Lily than of the woman, every hill and valley of whose body was not familiar to me, whereas Lily with her narrow hips and straight flanks must have a tiny sex. I thought, 'D . . . n Lily,' and I hastened to Smith.

* * *

I went downstairs to the dining room, hoping to find Kate alone. I was lucky: she had persuaded her mother, who was tired, to go to bed and was just finishing her tidying up.

'I want to see you, Kate,' I said, trying to kiss her. She drew her head aside: 'That's why you've kept away all afternoon, I suppose,' and she looked at me with a side-long glance. An inspiration came to me. 'Kate,' I exclaimed, 'I had to be fitted for my new clothes!'

'Forgive me,' she cried at once, that excuse being valid. 'I thought, I feared − oh, I'm suspicious without reason, I know − am jealous without cause. There! I confess!' and the great hazel eyes turned on me full of love.

I played with her breasts, whispering, 'When am I to see you naked, Kate? I want to; when?'

'You've seen most of me!' and she laughed joyously.

'All right,' I said, turning away, 'if you are resolved to make fun of me and be mean to me − '

'Mean to you!' she cried, catching me and swinging me round. 'I could easier be mean to myself. I'm glad you want to see me, glad and proud, and tonight, if you'll leave your door open, I'll come to you: mean, oh − ' and she gave me her soul in a kiss.

'Isn't it risky?' I asked.

'I tried the stairs this afternoon,' she glowed. 'They don't creak: no one will hear, so don't sleep or I'll surprise you.' By way of sealing the compact, I put my hand up her clothes and caressed her sex: it was hot and soon opened to me.

'There now, Sir, go,' she smiled, 'or you'll make me very naughty and I have a lot to do!'

'How do you mean "naughty",' I said, 'tell me what you feel, please!'

'I feel my heart beating,' she said, 'and, and — oh! wait till tonight and I'll try to tell you, dear,' and she pushed me out of the door.

For the first time in my life I notice here that the writer's art is not only inferior to reality in keenness of sensation and emotion, but also more same, monotonous even, because of showing the tiny, yet ineffable differences of the same feeling which difference of personality brings with it. I seem to be repeating to myself in describing Kate's love after Mrs Mayhew's, making the girl's feeling a fainter replica of the woman's. In reality the two were completely different. Mrs Mayhew's feelings, long repressed, flamed with the heat of an afternoon in July or August, while in Kate's one felt the freshness and cool of a summer morning, shot through with the suggestion of heat to come. And this comparison, even, is inept, because it leaves out the account the effect of Kate's beauty, the great hazel eyes, the rosied skin, the superb figure. Besides, there was a glamour of the spirit about Kate: Lorna Mayhew would never give me a note that didn't spring from passion; in Kate I felt a spiritual personality and the thrill of undeveloped possibilities. And still, using my utmost skill, I haven't shown my reader the enormous superiority of the girl and her more unselfish love. But I haven't finished yet.

Smith had given me *The Mill on the Floss* to read;
I had never tried George Eliot before and I found that
this book almost deserved Smith's praise. I had read
till about one o'clock when my heart heard her; or was
it some thrill of expectance? The next moment my door
opened and she came in with the mane of hair about
her shoulders and a long dressing gown reaching to
her stocking feet. I got up like a flash, but she had
already closed the door and bolted it. I drew her to
the bed and stopped her from throwing off the dressing
gown. 'Let me take off your stockings first,' I
whispered. 'I want you all imprinted on me!'

The next moment she stood there naked, the
flickering flame of the candle throwing quaint
arabesques of light on her ivory body. I gazed and
gazed: from the navel down she was perfect; I turned
her round and the back, too, the bottom, even, was
faultless, though large: but alas! the breasts were far
too big for beauty, too soft to excite! I must think only
of the bold curve of her hips, I reflected, the splendour
of the firm thighs, the flesh of which had the hard
outline of marble, and her − sex. I put her on the bed
and opened her thighs: her pussy was ideally perfect.

At once I wanted to get into her; but she pleaded:
'Please, dear, come into bed, I'm cold and want you.'
So in I got and began kissing her.

Soon she grew warm and I pulled off my night-shirt
and my middle finger was caressing her sex that opened
quickly. 'Ah,' she said, drawing in her breath quickly,
'it still hurts.' I put my sex gently against hers, moving
it up and down slowly till she drew up her knees to

let me in; but, as soon as the head entered, her face puckered a little with pain and, as I had had a long afternoon, I was the more inclined to forbear, and accordingly I drew away and took place beside her.

'I cannot bear to hurt you,' I said. 'Love's pleasure must be natural.'

'You're sweet!' she whispered. 'I'm glad you stopped, for it shows you really care for me and not just for the pleasure,' and she kissed me lovingly.

'Kate, reward me,' I said, 'by telling me just what you felt when I first had you,' and I put her hand on my hot stiff sex to encourage her.

'It's impossible,' she said, flushing a little. 'There was such a throng of new feelings; why, this evening, waiting in bed for the time to pass and thinking of you, I felt a strange prickling sensation in the inside of my thighs that I never felt before and now' — and she hid her glowing face against my neck, 'I feel it again!

'Love is funny, isn't it?' she whispered the next moment. 'Now the pricking sensation is gone and the front part of my sex burns and itches. Oh! I must touch it!'

'Let me,' I cried, and, in a moment, I was on her, working my organ up and down on her clitoris, the porch, so to speak, of Love's temple. A little later she herself sucked the head into her hot, dry pussy and then closed her legs as if in pain to stop me going further; but I began to rub my sex up and down on her tickler, letting it slide right in every now and then, till she panted and her love-juice came and my weapon sheathed itself in her naturally. I soon began the very slow and gentle in-and-out movements which increased her excitement steadily while giving her more and more pleasure, till I came and immediately she lifted my chest up from her breasts with both hands and showed me her glowing face. 'Stop, boy,' she gasped, 'please, my heart's fluttering so! I came too, you know, just with you,' and indeed I felt her trembling all over convulsively.

I drew out and for safety's sake got her to use the syringe, having already explained its efficacy to her: she was adorably awkward and, when she had finished, I took her to bed again and held her to me, kissing her. 'So you really love me, Kate!'

'Really,' she said, 'you don't know how much! I'll try never to suspect anything or to be jealous again.' She went on, 'It's a hateful thing, isn't it? But I want to see your classroom: would you take me up once to the university?'

'Why, of course,' I cried. 'I should be only too glad; I'll take you tomorrow afternoon. Or better still,' I added, 'come up the hill at four o'clock and I'll meet you at the entrance.'

And so it was settled and Kate went back to her room as noiselessly as she had come.

The next afternoon I found her waiting in the university hall ten minutes before the hour, for our lectures beginning at the hour always stopped after forty-five minutes to give us time to be punctual at any other classroom. After showing her everything of interest, we walked home together laughing and talking, when, a hundred yards from Mrs Mayhew's, we met that lady, face to face. I don't know how I looked, for being a little short-sighted, I hadn't recognized her till she was within ten yards of me; but her glance pierced me. She bowed with a look that took us both in. I lifted my hat and we passed on.

'Who's that?' exclaimed Kate. 'What a strange look she gave us!'

'She's the wife of a gambler,' I replied as indifferently as I could. 'He gives me work now and then,' I went on, strangely forecasting the future. Kate looked at me, probing, then, 'I don't mind. I'm glad she's quite old!'

'As old as both of us put together!' I retorted traitorously, and we went in.

These love-passages with Mrs Mayhew and Kate, plus my lessons and my talks with Smith, fairly represent my life's happenings for this whole year from seventeen to eighteen, with this solitary qualification, that my afternoons with Lorna became less and less agreeable to me.

As soon as I returned from the Eldridge House to lodge with the Gregorys again, Kate showed herself just as kind to me as ever. She would come to my bedroom twice or thrice a week and was always welcome, but again and again I felt that her mother was intent on keeping us apart as much as possible, and at length she arranged that Kate should pay a visit to some English friends who were settled in Kansas City. Kate postponed the visit several times, but at length she had to yield to her mother's entreaties and advice. By this time my boardings were bringing me in a good deal, and so I promised to accompany Kate and spend the whole night with her in some Kansas City hotel.

We got to the hotel about ten and bold as brass I registered as Mr and Mrs William Wallace and went up to our room with Kate's luggage, my heart beating in my throat. Kate, too, was 'all of a quiver,' as she confessed to me a little later, but what a night we had! Kate resolved to show me all her love and gave herself to me passionately, but she never took the initiative, I noticed, as Mrs Mayhew used to do.

At first I kissed her and talked a little, but as soon as she had arranged her things, I began to undress her. When her chemise fell, all glowing with my caressings, she asked, 'You really like that?' and she put her hand over her sex, standing there naked like a Greek Venus. 'Naturally,' I exclaimed, 'and these, too,' and I kissed and sucked her nipples until they grew rosy-red.

'Is it possible to do it — standing up?' she asked, in some confusion.

'Of course,' I replied. 'Let's try! But what put that into your head?'

'I saw a man and a girl behind the church near our house,' she whispered, 'and I wondered how — ' and she blushed rosily. As I got into her, I felt difficulty: her pussy was really small and this time seemed hot and dry: I felt her wince and, at once, withdrew. 'Does it still hurt, Kate?' I asked.

'A little at first,' she replied. 'But I don't mind,' she hastened to add, 'I like the pain!'

By way of answer, I slipped my arms around her, under her bottom, and carried her to the bed. 'I will not hurt you tonight,' I said, 'I'll make you give down your love-juice first and then there'll be no pain.'

A few kisses and she sighed: 'I'm wet now,' and I got into bed and put my sex against hers.

'I'm going to leave everything to you,' I said, 'but please don't hurt yourself.' She put her hand down to my sex and guided it in, sighing a little with satisfaction as bit by bit it slipped home.

After the first ecstasy, I got her to use the syringe while I watched her curiously. When she came back to bed, 'No danger now,' I cried, 'no danger; my love is queen!'

'You darling lover!' she cried, her eyes wide, as if in wonder. 'My sex throbs and itches and oh! I feel prickings on the inside of my thighs: I want you dreadfully, Frank,' and she stretched out as she spoke, drawing up her knees.

I got on top of her and softly, slowly let my sex slide into her and then began the love-play. When my second orgasm came, I indulged myself with quick, short strokes, though I knew that she preferred the long slow movement, for I was resolved to give her every sensation this golden night. When she felt me begin again the long slow movement she loved, she sighed two or three times and putting her hands on my buttocks, drew me close but otherwise made little sign of feeling for perhaps half an hour. I kept right on; the slow movement now gave me but little pleasure: It was rather a task than a joy; but I was resolved to give her a feast. I don't know how long the bout lasted, but once I withdrew and began rubbing her clitoris and the front of her sex, and panting she nodded her head and rubbed herself ecstatically against my sex, and after I had begun the slow movement again, 'Please, Frank!' she gasped, 'I can't stand more: I'm going crazy − choking!'

Strange to say, her words excited me more than the act: I felt my spasm coming and roughly, savagely I thrust in my sex at the same time, kneeling between her legs so as to be able to play back and forth on her tickler as well. 'I'll ravish you!' I cried and gave myself to the keen delight. As my seed spirted, she didn't speak, but lay there still and white; I jumped out of the bed, got a spongeful of cold water and used it on her forehead.

At once, to my joy, she opened her eyes. 'I'm sorry,' she gasped, and took a drink of water, 'but I was so tired, I must have slept. You dear heart!' When I had put down the sponge and glass, I slipped into her again and in a little while she became hysterical: 'I can't help crying, Frank, love,' she sighed. 'I'm so happy, dear. You'll always love me? Won't you? Sweet!' Naturally, I reassured her with promises of enduring affection and many kisses. Finally, I put my left arm round her neck and so fell asleep with my head on her soft breast.

In the morning we ran another course, though, sooth to say, Kate was more curious than passionate.

'I want to study you!' she said, and took my sex in her hands and then my balls. 'What are they for?' she asked, and I had to explain that that was where my seed was secreted. She made a face, so I added, 'You have a similar manufactory, my dear, but it's inside you, the ovaries they are called, and it takes them a month to make one egg, whereas my balls make millions in an hour. I often wonder why?'

After getting Kate an excellent breakfast, I put her in a cab and she reached her friend's house just at the proper time, but the girl friend could never understand how they had missed each other at the station.

I returned to Lawrence the same day, wondering what fortune had in store for me.

One evening I almost ran into Lily. Kate was still away in Kansas City, so I stopped eagerly enough to have a talk, for Lily had always interested me. After the first greetings she told me she was going home. 'They are all out, I believe,' she added. At once I offered to accompany her and she consented. It was early summer but already warm, and when we went into the parlor and Lily took a seat on the sofa, her thin white dress defined her slim figure seductively.

'What do you do,' she asked mischievously, 'now that dear Mrs Mayhew's gone? You must miss her!' she added suggestively.

'I do,' I confessed boldly. 'I wonder if you'd have pluck enough to tell me the truth,' I went on.

'Pluck?' She wrinkled her forehead and pursed her large mouth.

'Courage, I mean,' I said.

'Oh, I have courage,' she rejoined.

'Did you ever come upstairs to Mrs Mayhew's

bedroom,' I asked, 'when I had gone up for a book?'
The black eyes danced and she laughed knowingly.

'Mrs Mayhew said that she had taken you upstairs
to bathe your poor head after dancing,' she retorted
disdainfully, 'but I don't care: it's nothing to do with
me what you do!'

'It has too,' I went on, carrying the war into her
country.

'How?' she asked.

'Why the first day you went away and left me,
though I was really ill,' I said, 'so I naturally believed
that you disliked me, though I thought you were
lovely!'

'I'm not lovely,' she said. 'My mouth's too big and
I'm too slight.'

'Don't malign yourself,' I replied earnestly; 'that's
just why you are seductive and excite a man.'

'Really?' she cried, and so the talk went on, while
I cudgelled my brains for an opportunity but found
none, and all the while was in fear lest her father and
mother should return. At length, angry with myself,
I got up to go on some pretext and she accompanied
me to the stoop. I said goodbye on the top step and
then jumped down by the side with a prayer in my
heart that she'd come a step or two down, and she
did. There she stood, her hips on a level with my
mouth; in a moment my hands went up her dress,
the right to her sex, the left to her bottom behind
to hold her. The thrill as I touched her half-fledged
sex was almost painful in intensity. Her first
movement brought her sitting down on the step above

me and at once my finger was busy in her slit.

'How dare you!' she cried, but not angrily. 'Take your hand away!'

'Oh, how lovely your sex is!' I exclaimed, as if astounded. 'Oh, I must see it and have you, you miracle of beauty,' and my left hand drew down her head for a long kiss while my middle finger still continued its caress. Of a sudden her lips grew hot and at once I whispered, 'Won't you love me, dear? I want you so: I'm burning and itching with desire. (I knew she was!) Please; I won't hurt you and I'll take care. Please, love, no one will know,' and the end of it was that right there on the porch I drew her to me and put my sex against hers and began the rubbing of her tickler and front part of her sex that I knew would excite her. In a moment she came and her love-dew wet my sex and excited me terribly; but I kept on frigging her with my man-root while restraining myself from coming by thinking of other things, till she kissed me of her own accord and suddenly moving forward pushed my prick right into her pussy.

To my astonishment, there was no obstacle, no maidenhead to break through, though her sex itself was astonishingly small and tight. I didn't scruple then to let my seed come, only withdrawing to the lips and rubbing her clitoris the while, and, as soon as my spirting ceased, my root glided again into her and continued the slow in-and-out movement till she panted with her head on my shoulder and asked me to stop. I did as she wished, for I knew I had won another wonderful mistress.

We went into the house again, for she insisted I should meet her father and mother, and, while we were waiting, she showed me her lovely tiny breasts, scarcely larger than small apples, and I became aware of something childish in her mind which matched the childish outlines of her lovely, half-formed hips and pussy.

'I thought that you were in love with Mrs Mayhew,' she confessed, 'and I couldn't make out why she made such funny noises. But now I know,' she added, 'you naughty dear, for I felt my heart fluttering just now and I was nearly choking.'

I don't know why, but that ravishing of Lily made her dear to me. I resolved to see her naked and to make her thrill to ecstasy as soon as possible, and then and there we made a meeting place on the far side of the church, whence I knew I could bring her to my room at the Gregorys in a minute; and then I went home, for it was late and I didn't particularly want to meet her folks.

The next night I met Lily by the church and took her to my room. She laughed aloud with delight as we entered, for indeed she was almost like a boy of bold, adventurous spirit. She confessed to me that my challenge of her pluck had pleased her intimately.

'I never took a "dare"!' she cried in her American slang, tossing her head.

'I'll give you two,' I whispered, 'right now: the first is, I dare you to strip naked as I'm going to do, and I'll tell you the other when we're in bed.'

Again she tossed her little blue-black head. 'Pooh,'

she cried, 'I'll be undressed first,' and she was. Her beauty made my pulses hammer and parched my mouth. No one could help admiring her: she was very slight, with tiny breasts, as I have said, flat belly and straight flanks and hips: her triangle was only brushed in, so to speak, with fluffy soft hairs, and, as I held her naked body against mine, the look and feel of her exasperated my desire. I still admired Kate's riper, richer, more luscious outlines: her figure was nearer my boyish ideal; but Lily represented a type of adolescence destined to grow on me mightily. In fact, as my youthful virility decreased, my love of opulent feminine charms diminished and grew more and more to love slender, youthful outlines with the signs of sex rather indicated than pronounced. What an all-devouring appetite Rubens confesses with the great, hanging breasts and uncouth fat pink bottoms of his Venuses!

I lifted Lily on the bed and separated her legs to study her pussy. She made a face at me; but, as I rubbed my hot sex against her little button that I could hardly see, she smiled and lay back contentedly. In a minute or two, her love-juice came and I got into bed on her and slipped my root into her small cunt; even when the lips were wide open, it was closed to the eye and this and her slim nakedness excited me uncontrollably. I continued the slow movements for a few minutes; but once she moved her sex quickly down on mine as I drew out to the lips, and gave me an intense thrill. I felt my seed coming and I let myself go in short, quick thrusts that soon brought on my spasm of pleasure and I lifted her little body against mine and crushed my lips on hers: she was strangely tantalizing, exciting like strong drink.

I took her out of bed and used the syringe in her, explaining its purpose, and then went to bed again and gave her the time of her life! Lying between her legs but side by side an hour later, I dared her to tell me how she had lost her maidenhead. I had to tell her first what it was. She maintained stoutly that 'no feller' had ever touched her except me and I believed her, for she admitted having caressed herself ever since she was ten; at first she could not even get her forefinger into her pussy she told me.

About eleven o'clock she dressed and went home, after making another appointment with me.

The haste of this narrative has many unforeseen drawbacks: it makes it appear as if I had had conquest after conquest and little or no difficulty in my efforts to win love. In reality, my half-dozen victories were spread out over nearly as many years, and time and again I met rebuffs and refusals quite sufficient to keep even my conceit in decent bounds. But I want to emphasize the fact that success in love, like success in every department of life, falls usually to the tough man unwearied in pursuit. Chaucer was right when he makes his Old Wyfe of Bath confess,

And by a close attendance and attention
Are we caught, more or less the truth to mention.

It is not the handsomest man or the most virile who

has the most success with women, though both qualities smooth the way, but that man who pursues the most assiduously, flatters them most constantly, and always insists on taking the girl's 'no' for consent, her reproofs for endearments, and even a little crossness for a new charm.

Above all, it is necessary to push forward after every refusal, for as soon as a girl refused, she is apt to regret and may grant then what she expressly denied the moment before. Yet I could give dozens of instances where assiduity and flattery, love-books and words were all ineffective, so much so that I should never say with Shakespeare, 'He's not a man who cannot win a woman.' I have generally found, too, that the easiest to win were the best worth winning for me, for women have finer senses for suitability in love than any man.

Now for an example of one of my many failures, which took place when I was still a student and had a fair opportunity to succeed.

It was a custom in the university for every professor to lecture for forty-five minutes, thus leaving each student fifteen minutes at least free to go back to his private classroom to prepare for the next lecture. All the students took turns to use these classrooms for their private pleasure. For example, from eleven forty-five to noon each day I was supposed to be working in the junior classroom, and no student would interfere with me or molest me in any way.

One day, a girl Fresher, Grace Weldon by name, the daughter of the owner of the biggest department store in Lawrence, came to Smith when Miss Stephens and I were with him, about the translation of a phrase or two in Xenophon.

'Explain it to Miss Weldon, Frank!' said Smith, and in a few moments I had made the passage clear to her. She thanked me prettily, and I said, 'If you ever want anything I can do, I'll be happy to make it clear to you, Miss Weldon; I'm in the junior classroom from eleven forty-five to noon, always.'

She thanked me and a day or two later came to me in the classroom with another puzzle, and so our acquaintance ripened. Almost at once she let me kiss her, but as soon as I tried to put my hand up her clothes, she stopped me. We were friends for nearly a year, close friends, and I remember trying all I knew one Saturday, when I spent the whole day with her in our classroom till dusk came, and I could not get her to yield.

The curious thing was, I could not even soothe the smart to my vanity with the belief that she was physically cold. On the contrary, she was very passionate, but she had simply made up her mind and would not change.

That Saturday in the classroom she told me if she yielded she would hate me: I could see no sense in this, even though I was to find out later what a terrible weapon the confessional is as used by Irish Catholic priests. To commit a sin is easy; to confess it to your priest is for many women an absolute deterrent.

About this time, Kate wrote that she would not be back for some weeks: she declared she was feeling another woman. I felt tempted to write, 'So am I, stay as long as you please,' but instead I wrote an affectionate, tempting letter, for I had a real affection for her, I discovered.

When she returned a few weeks later, I felt as if she were new and unknown and I had to win her again; but as soon as my hand touched her sex, the strangeness disappeared and she gave herself to me with renewed zest.

I teased her to tell me just what she felt and at length she consented. 'Begin with the first time,' I begged, 'and then tell what you felt in Kansas City.'

'It will be very hard,' she said. 'I'd rather write it for you.'

'That'll do just as well,' I replied, and here is the story she sent me the next day.

'I think the first time you had me,' she began, 'I felt more curiosity than desire: I had so often tried to picture it all to myself. When I saw your sex I was astonished, for it looked very big to me and I wondered whether you could really get it into my sex, which I knew was just big enough for my finger to go in. Still I did want to feel your sex pushing into me, and your kisses and the touch of your hand on my sex made me even more eager. When you slipped the head of your sex into mine, it hurt dreadfully; it was almost like a knife cutting into me, but the pain for some reason seemed to excite me and I pushed forward so as to get you further in me; I think that's what broke my maidenhead. At first I was disappointed because I felt no thrill, only the pain; but, when my sex became all wet and open and yours could slip in and out easily, I began to feel real pleasure. I liked the slow movement best; it excited me to feel the head of your sex just touching the lips of mine and, when you pushed in slowly all the way, it gave me a gasp of breathless delight: when you drew your sex out, I wanted to hold it in me. And the longer you kept on, the more pleasure you gave me. For hours afterwards, my sex was sensitive; if I rubbed it every so gently, it would begin to itch and burn.

'But that night in the hotel at Kansas City I really wanted you and the pleasure you gave me then was much keener than the first time. You kissed and caressed me for a few minutes and I soon felt my love-dew coming and the button of my sex began to throb. As you thrust your shaft in and out of me, I felt a strange sort of pleasure: every little nerve on the inside of my thighs and belly seemed to thrill and quiver; it was almost a feeling of pain. At first the sensation was not so intense, but, when you stopped and made me wash, I was shaken by quick, short spasms in my thighs, and my sex was burning and throbbing; I wanted you more than ever.

'When you began the slow movement again, I felt the sensations in my thighs and belly, only more keenly, and, as you kept on, the pleasure became so intense that I could scarcely bear it. Suddenly you rubbed your sex against mine and my button began to throb; I could almost feel it move. Then you began to move your sex quickly in and out of me; in a moment I was breathless with emotion and I felt so faint and exhausted that I suppose I fell asleep for a few minutes, for I knew nothing more till I felt the cold water trickling down my face. When you began again, you made me cry, perhaps because I was all dissolved in feeling and too, too happy. Ah, love is divine: isn't it?'

Kate was really of the highest woman-type, mother and mistress in one. She used to come down and spend the night with me oftener than ever and on one of these occasions she found a new word for her passion. She declared she felt her womb move in yearning for me when I talked my best or recited poetry to her in what I had christened her holy week. Kate it was who taught me first that women could be even more moved and excited by words than by deeds. Once, I remember, when I had talked sentimentally, she embraced me of her own accord and we had each other with wet eyes.

My Secret Life

Frank Harris may have set out to compose the most sexually honest autobiography ever written but, compared to Walter, the pseudonymous author of *My Secret Life*, he stands firmly in the shade. Walter's endlessly fascinating, indeed endless — it runs to eleven volumes — account of his sexual life was privately published between 1885 and 1895. It is a labour of love in every sense, a diary of amorous encounters kept throughout the life of a man obsessed by sex and all matters sexual. Walter was a man with a mission, a Victorian male with the nerve and wherewithal to attempt the virtue of every woman who caught his fancy — and driven by a literary compulsion to set his exploits to paper. As such, he is not interested, like Harris, in creating his own myth; rather, he is compelled to explore exactly what it is that makes him tick.

In consequence the excerpts that follow are a far cry from the work of the average sex novelist (or self-aggrandising autobiographer, come to that) out to supply a fantasy of male prowess and willing female acquiescence. Here are three single-minded acts of fornication achieved by persistence, bribery and social intimidation. No writer bent on sexual titillation would, for example, allow his hero to trick a girl into bed by claiming she wore filthy knickers, as Walter does here. In these things, though at pains to obscure the clues which may identify him, *My Secret Life* is undoubtedly more honest and paints a more accurate picture of real life and the passions and peculiarities of human nature than any other sexual account yet published.

In late autumn this year I was at a Lancashire seaport town, and at about five o'clock one afternoon, wandering about looking at the shops, noticed a well made, well grown woman, with an absolutely lovely face and marvellously clear complexion — tho perhaps too white — who was sauntering along doing the same. I stood close to her whilst she looked at a bonnet shop, but she took no notice of me. Was she a harlot or not, wandering about alone? I'd had no sexual desire before, now in a minute it overwhelmed — desire for her.

She was dressed like a genteel, poorish, middle class woman excessively plainly, but the dress was worn with such an air of distinction, that for the moment I chased the idea of her accessibility. — I followed her a long distance noticing the swing of her haunches, and the way she placed her pretty feet which were visible — for her petticoats were short. — Her boots tho neat were common and thick. She took no notice of passers by, nor they of her. She cannot be a strumpet thought I, but a handsome offer may get her if she's poor. — But where to take her to? For I knew no place. Abandoning half formed intentions, yet with a voluptuous pego I stopped, and just then she turned round and retraced her steps, meeting me, looking casually at me just as any other woman might. I turned round and followed her, still with undefined intention.

Again she stopped at a shop. I stopped too and remarked that what she was looking at was pretty. She quietly looked at me and agreed that it was. Her manner made me now think she was to be had. She walked on and I did by her side. — 'How lovely you are, let me go home with you.' — 'Ah! No — impossible — good day Sir,' and she turned round. Yet there was something in her manner — I knew not what — which faintly bespoke the courtezan.

With hope I turned round also, and walked by her side repeating my wish, asking her to have a glass of wine, and so on. — She begged me to go, was waiting for a friend, it would do her harm if she were seen walking with a gentleman. — Yes, she expected him every minute. — 'I wish I were he, I'd give a couple of sovereigns to be half an hour with you.' She stopped short at once and looked at me. 'A couple of sovereigns! That *would* be a help to us just now.' — She said this as if reflecting, as if speaking to herself. — Then again she walked on, I keeping still by her side but keeping silence.

'Don't come with me, I'm expecting my lad.' Then she hesitated, then went on. 'If he doesn't come by this, he can't come for two hours — tell me the time.' — I did. 'An he come, we'll be off together at once, if not and ye'll give me two sovereigns, ye may, but I ain't got no lodgings, I've given them up, for I'm off tonight and for good.'

Then she said she must wait full ten minutes to make sure, she'd walk up and down, I was to wait at the corner of a street she pointed out, then if her lad hadn't arrived she be with me. – She spoke in broad Lancashire dialect, which I do not attempt to imitate, and which at times I could scarcely understand.

Never did ten minutes seem so long to me. – I counted every minute in a fever of impatience, pictured her secret charms to myself, wondered at split, motte, thighs, whether she'd fuck well, and if she wanted fucking. At times I furtively felt my pego which kept rising and falling with lust, and feared I should not have her, for full ten minutes had passed when she appeared. 'Where shall we go?' said I. – 'I've no lodgings now and only know a poor place about here.' – I would have gone to a pig sty with her, and in five minutes the poor place held us. It was a little obscure house in a court, almost a cottage, with but two rooms for hire, but the bed was comfortable with a good fire.

'My lad can't be here for two hours and a half now, there be'ant another train yet, and ye'll gie me *two*?' said she the instant the door was closed. – My reply was to produce the coins and put them into her hand. – 'It will do us a power of good just now, and ye'll be the last.' – 'Why?' – 'I'm going away to night to be married.' – I scarcely heeded what she said being so impatient for my pleasure, and put my hand up her petticoats. She repulsed them, and I thought for the instant she was going to bilk me.

Not the first time that idea has come over me when with a gay woman. 'Let's feel it.' – 'Wait a bit, you shall, don't fear.' Composed in manner and as unlike a harlot as possible, she took off bonnet and jacket most carefully and then sat down. 'Let's feel your cunt.' – 'I will.' Stooping I pushed my hand up her petticoats, and felt the silky fringed notch. – 'Ye're in a hurry' – laughing. 'Take your things off and let me see your cunt.' – 'You shall. – You shall, – never fear – wait a bit.' Slowly she took them off – I divested myself of clothing and showed my prick. – 'Ohooo,' she whispered, and stopped undressing. 'Take them off.' – 'What, all? – There' – and she stood naked.

A more beautifully made woman I never saw, and for a minute was speechless with admiration, then folded her in my arms, kissing, extolling her loveliness, pressing my stiff prick against her belly with mine. – Then, – still both standing – my fingers were titillating her love seat, when quietly her hand stole down and clasped my pego, and so we stood silent, I'd roused her passions. 'Let me see it.' Without reply, on to the bed she got and laid with thighs apart. A hurried look at the pretty groove, a sniff a kiss on the motte, a finger thrust rapidly up and down the moist avenue. – 'Let's fuck' – next minute we were embracing with voluptuous gentle sighs, my prick enclosed in her lubricious cunt and gliding up and down, our bodies one; and ah too soon, came tightening of her cunt around my prick, which throbbed and spent, and we lay quietly in each other's arms in soft repose. Then soon after. 'You enjoyed it?' a foolish question but I always put it. – She made no reply, but patted my arse cheeks in an affectionate, coaxing manner.

I uncunted at last and she 'It's cold. – Let me put on my chemise.' She did, we rose, pissed, washed – the usual routine – then sat by the fire – tho it wasn't very cold weather. – She asked me to give her 'a glass.' – 'What?' 'Whiskey.' – That was brought. I'd been wearing a cape which now I put over her, and put on my own frock coat over my shirt, then drinking we sat and talked side by side. The ecstatic sexual embrace cools desire, and for a time erotic curiosity is almost dead, but it soon revived in me, and I began twiddling her quim. 'I ain't in a hurry,' said she then, told me her history, partly before, partly after our second embrace, but it's told here continuously.

'Yes, a millhand, at a cotton mill,' – At seventeen the young master 'did me.' Her father was an engineer at the mill, found it out soon after, kicked up a row, and a hundred pounds was given *him* as damages, for the damage done to *her* virginity. – The money unsettled him, he drank a bit, she left the mill, worked then steadily at home for a while, and no one entered her preserve, and then, somehow she 'longed for a bit,' she supposed – and got fucked again. – 'Yes, for love only,' and then turned harlot. A young man in the mill also a mechanician, knew her history, knew her father, found her out, fucked her harlot wise, fell in love with her, then fucked her for love and she also with him. She saved money, and he saved a bit, her father approved and gave up what he'd not spent in liquor, her seducer had promised twenty pounds when

they were married, and they were going to marry and
open a little shop at **** where he'd found work. –
He was coming there now to meet her when I had, if
he could get away in time, but certainly he would get
away in time, but certainly he would come by the next
train. Her box was at the station, she'd given up the
key of her lodging – that baudy house was the only
place she could wait in 'till I meet my lad.'

'I didn't mean to let you – I've not done it for a
week and told him I wouldn't, but money will be so
useful to us at a start.' – 'Oh don't – you'll make
me queer.' – 'Oh, don't talk of *him* – come on and
do it then.' Lewed she was with my talk, with
titillation, and her feel of my shaft, and on the bed
again we fucked. She wanted it more than before, as
I guessed by her clasp, the way her tongue met mine,
her squeeze of my buttocks, her heaves, quivers and
love sighs.

She was only eighteen and a half, yet her form was
full and perfect as three and twenty. She'd the loveliest
thighs, the sweetest little silky fringed notch, scarcely
nymphae or clitoris – quite a young girl's cunt. –
She was proud of her shape and willingly let me see
all, delighted with my praise. Her manners were utterly
unlike those of a whore. The hair on head and tail was
light chestnut, no dark stain was on her bum furrow
which was nearly as white as her buttocks, and *they*
were ivory. It grew dark soon after I was there and
we had candles – for which they charged extra – and
I held one to the furrow to inspect her whilst she knelt
on the bed. Then after a time unable to tail her a third

time, I gave her pleasure with my tongue, and never licked a more delicate clitoris. She'd a face handsome in her bonnet, but it was far more beautiful without it. Her eyes were dark blue. – She hadn't the slightest look or allure of a strumpet.

The whiskey made her talk freely, and we had lots of time. Five shillings was her usual fee. – 'For I don't dress like swell ones.' – 'No, not often ten – I don't like speaking to gents. – I've only been three months at the business and don't like it – nor the gals.' 'Why did I go to millwork? Father made me so as to look after me, he, mother didn't want me to go. – You may wait and see me with him but don't come near me, I'm quite sure he'll come for me, – I shan't tell him what I've done tonight, I wouldn't ha' done it but we want money so.' I waited in the distance, saw her meet and go towards the station with a decent young man, her lad evidently. – I've met from time to time some interesting harlots and this was one of them, so retain the narrative about her.

Late on a dull, moist, dark night in November, I was passing along a quiet street in a poor neighbourhood, when two women approached me singing and loudly laughing. They held a short rope between them, and as they came near, thinking them a common frolicsome and half screwed couple, I moved to the edge of the footway to let them pass. They larking, lengthened the rope, and caught and entwined me with it just below my hips, laughing heartily at their trick. – 'We've caught you young man, what will you

stand?' — It was close to a gaslamp, and seeing it was
a handsome, bold faced woman who spoke. — 'Stand
my dear? — It won't stand any more, you've pulled
it off with the rope, look for it.' — I happened to have
a hottish ballocks that night, and baudy replies came
naturally — tho far from being young.

At that both laughed so heartily and I as well, and
we standing close together — the rope still round me,
— made such a noise, that some one on the other side
of the way stopped to look at us. — 'I can't see it,'
said the biggest and plump one, who looked about five
and twenty. The other a slim, poor-looking creature
of about eighteen, only giggled, and then became
silent. 'It's between your thighs perhaps.' — 'Ho, ho,
ho — it ain't, *you're* wearing it still.' — 'He, he, he,'
giggled the slim one. — 'No, between your thighs —
let me feel there. — It was stiff and if I find it there
I'll give you five shillings, and you shall put it back
if you can, I can't go home without it.' — 'Ho, ho,
ho — what?' — 'My peg,' — and I pushed at her
clothes in the region of her cunt. — 'Give me the five
bob then and you shall.' — 'Polly — Polly — yer dont
know what yer about,' said the other remonstrating.
— 'His peg — ho, ho, ho,' laughed the other.

They were game I saw, whores they didn't seem to
be, but workers of a poor class and who decidedly had
been drinking. That class doesn't mind baudy
language, they hear enough of it. — 'I call it a peg
to ladies, but there's another name.' — 'Tell us.' —
'Polly — come along.' — 'Feel if it's on yer yet. —
Ho, ho,' and Polly laughed still, as untwining the rope

she was putting her hands between the fold of my great coat, when the other pulled them away. 'Polly − yer don't know what yer about.' − 'Shut up,' − said Polly. 'Come along.' − 'I shan't.' 'Let's have a glass of wine and I'll feel if you've got it about *you* my dear,' said I. − '*You've* got it right enough.' − 'Lord, so I have, and it's still stiff.' − Then the other − named Sarah − again rebuked the elder, said she should go and was told she might, but, 'Don't be a fool, come and have a drink with the gent,' − which I'd offered. − 'Follow us, there's a nice pub around the next street,' said Polly, who seemed to know the locality.

I was going to the pub, knowing that Bacchus helps Venus, and thinking I might somehow get into the plump one who'd excited my desires, when it occurred to me as not desirable to be seen by a chance medley of poor people, at a public house in a poor neighbourhood with two common workwomen. I lusted for Polly now, and *because* she was so coarse and common − singular are my letches − and perhaps would have gone to the pub, sooner than lose the chance of seeing what I knew was a spanking bum. At the street corner was poor-looking coffee shop. 'Let's go in here, they'll fetch us all we want,' said I. − In we two went, the other loitered outside. − 'I'll wait for you.' − 'Come in, don't be a fool,' and in came Sarah.

They'd nothing but tea and coffee, but they fetched us liquor for which they charged highly. They sat at a table in a corner with me, the two drank gin and water, the eldest's tongue ran on incessantly, I chaffing baudily but without frank words, she delighted replying and looking in my eyes lustfully. Then under the table I grasped her large thigh outside her clothes, and nudged her belly. 'Now, don't.' — 'It's there.' — 'It ain't.' — 'It is.' — 'What?' — 'Don't, Polly,' said the thin one again. — Just then in came one looking like a cabman, who bought a roll and butter, and disappeared with it, but he'd eyed us so the whole time he was there that I felt uncomfortable, and so soon as he had gone, asked if they had a private room.

The mistress said 'No,' looked at the maid, and they held a conversation in a low tone. Then she said they had no private rooms, but there was one I might have till the house was closed. I accepted it, and we went up a narrow staircase to a bedroom. There the servant, 'We don't let rooms, but this is it, five shillings — will you please pay first, Sir?' — I gave it her, the liquor was brought up, but Sarah wouldn't stop when she saw the bed. — 'I shan't then — your agoin' on too far — yer don't know what yer adoing.' — Down stairs she went, and I was alone with the plump one. — 'I'll take her some gin,' said she, and pouring out half a tumbler, down she went returning alone, Sarah wouldn't come. 'We'd best perhaps go down agin,' said Polly thoughtfully.

After seemingly a minute's reflexion, again she said, 'Perhaps I'd better go.' — 'Nonsense, what did you come up here for?' — saying that I locked the door, closed on Polly, pushed her against the bed, and assaulted her privates. She'd so egged me on to baudy chaff and smutty suggestions, that I'd felt sure of having her, but as my hand touched her thighs she resisted, pushed down her clothes, pushed me away stoutly, laughing as if half pleased tho refusing, and squalling loudly. — 'You shan't — don't now — a joke's a joke — I won't — I'm married.' — 'You're not — where's your ring?' — 'Pawned.' — 'I *will* fuck you. 'You shan't' and she scuffled as much as virtuous servants have done whom I've assailed similarly. I was so annoyed at my hindrance, felt so spiteful, that leaving off I angrily said, 'You're not married, your linen's dirty, that's why you won't let me.' I didn't mean it, but savagely wanted to offend her, to say something to annoy, and *that* came impromptu. I said much of the same sort, but all in the same strain.

'Dirty? Me dirty? Cleaner than you I'll swear. Dirty! I'd wash my shift to rags rather than be dirty. — You *have* cheek. — Show me *your* shirt — look.' — Saying that she turned up her petticoats to her garters, and I saw that stockings and all she had on was as white as could be, tho her ankle jackboots were muddy. — 'Your cunt's dirty then.' — 'You lie, it ain't.' 'Let's put this up it,' — pulling out my prick. — 'Shan't.' — But she looked at my cunt-prodder which was in splendid force. She was lewed before, now leweder still and she laughed. I closed on her again, got my fingers on the soft slit with but trifling hindrance, and frigged away at it. — 'Now don't — oh don't.' Voluptuous sensations were conquering for me. — What woman can refuse a prick when the man's fingers have been in full possession of her cunt a minute? 'Feel my prick.' – She slid her hand down to it after twice saying, 'Shan't' and in another minute it was up her cunt, as she lay at the bedside on to which I pushed and lifted her. Quiet, absorbed in carnal pleasure, the delicious crisis came on, and dissolved us, spending into immobility and silence.

Quietly she lay as holding up her thighs, nestling my pego into her, we looked into each other's eyes in silence, enjoying the carnal junction. Fucking is in its essential always the same, the idealities are everything, therein lays the charm of variety. I felt singular delight in fucking this common woman whom I'd only seen half an hour. – It takes longer to tell than to act. – Who might be married or single, or of any occupation, and whose cunt I'd not even seen. Relinquishing one thigh I pushed her petticoats up, and looking down saw a dark fully haired motte, the hair mingling with mine, and put a finger on to the clitoris – 'Isn't fucking lovely?' – 'Isn't it?' replied she.

Catching hold of her thigh again, I squeezed my belly well against hers, feeling my pego to be dwindling. 'Has your friend been fucked?' 'Dunno, but she had got a lover.' – 'Where's your husband?' – 'God knows, on the tramp I suppose.' – 'You *are* married.' – She nodded. 'Who fucks you now?' – 'No one.' – 'What a story.' – She laughed, and it squeezed my cock out of her. Then we washed in the same basin, there was no towel, so shirt and chemise did duty.

Afterwards – 'Show me your cunt.' – 'All right, I'm clean, – look,' – pulling her clothes up to her

motte, she let me see, saying how clean her linen was.
I saw a cunt fat-lipped, and full-fledged. 'No, I ain't
had a child,' said she, noticing my investigations. –
Another letch came on. 'I'd give *you* ten shillings to
see your friend's cunt, and *she* ten to show it.' – She
seemed surprized. – 'Will you? Don't think she will.'
– 'Try to get her upstairs.' – 'I will, but she's a
stupid, don't say you've done it to me.' – Saying that,
she put on her bonnet and went downstairs.

The two had as said 'had a drop' before I'd met
them. They'd had gin since, Sarah had had a tumbler
more than half full to drink whilst down stairs.
Opening the door I heard much laughing, and Sarah
appeared, pushed upstairs by Polly into the room. No
sooner there than I told her I wanted to see her little
quim and would give her ten shillings – I'd got their
names pat. 'Polly says then she'll show me hers.'

Tho slightly screwed she refused and there was much
talk. – 'We ain't whores,' said she. – Polly pulled
her petticoats up to her garters, and then she pulled
out my prick, again fairly stiff. – Both laughed at it.
– Polly said, 'It's getting late – will yer or won't yer?
– I'll show him mine if you'll show him yours.' –
'Suppose Jack hears on it.' – 'Jack be blowed, how
can he know unless you tells him.' – I put on the table
the two half sovereigns and they eyed them. – 'Will
you now? If not we'll go.' – 'It's agoin' too far,' said
Sarah – I put the money in my pocket. – 'You show
him first.' – 'There, then,' said Polly, putting her
bum on the bed and exposing her charms. – The other
chuckled. – 'He, he, he, look at you.' – 'You've seen

it before, come on, show it him.' – She went to Sarah and pushed her up chuckling. 'he, he, he' but she was yielding, and next minute was laying on the bed, petticoats up to her navel, legs hanging down, her crack just visible, whilst Polly in a similar position but with thighs well apart, lay laughing by her side.

I investigated the cunts of both, but the young one didn't like that. – 'You've been fucked,' said I. – 'I ain't.' – 'She has,' said Polly. – 'I ain't been.' – 'I'll fuck you then.' – 'No, you shan't.' – She roused herself and half got off the bed, I promised not to attempt it and got her to lay down again with cunt showing. 'I'll fuck *you* then,.' – 'All right,' said Polly. Next second my balls were banging against her buttocks. – 'Oh! If Jack ever heard,' giggled the slim one. – 'Jack be buggered,' said Polly, heaving her rump responsively to my thrusts. Silent were all three now as I fucked, feeling Sarah's thin thighs and quim. – 'Aha – fuck – cunt,' I cried. – 'Ahrr – Ahrr,' sobbed Polly. – 'Oho, you hurt,' cried out the slim one. In the paroxysms of pleasure I'd hurt her cunt with my fingers.

'We'd better get home or there'll be a jolly kick-up,' said the slim one whilst still my prick was in the other's quim. – I was in a hurry also, uncunted, and in five minutes was out of the house, after giving the two half sovereigns. – They were not sisters they said, which was all I could learn, excepting that they'd carried something home between them tied up with the rope, and had had a drop with the money they'd got. I think they were laundresses.

I enjoyed this chance amour immensely, it was so different from the business-like fucking with a harlot, price agreed beforehand. But how strange! As we met as strangers in the street, who could have imagined that they'd show me their cunts, and that one would be fucked twice within an hour. These impromptu amours are delicious.

About six one warm evening in autumn I was near a market at ***. The great traffic of the day was over as I sauntered out of curiosity thro a street I'd never seen before, one of much trade, but where every shop was closed for the night, and but few pedestrians in it. − Near a public house stood two porters talking. At the corner of a narrow street, three common girls were lolling against the wall, talking and larking with a couple of lads looking scarcely sixteen years old, the girls seeming of about the same age.

Sturdy, thick-built wenches, looking like market or coster girls (they were) and clad in good tho coarse work-soiled clothing and with short petticoats and boots suitable for their work and class. They had dirty hands and looked sweaty, dusty, and work-worn. Two had hats, the other none, she was a superbly handsome creature with a very light-coloured hair of bright hue, which evidently crimped naturally, a florid face, retroussé nose, and big mouth with white teeth, she'd light blue eyes, a fine bust and large hips, and the very picture of coarse health she looked. As I took her points in at a glance and thought her beautiful, then I also thought of her secret charms, wondered if she'd been fucked, and thought how well she'd look if washed and well dressed, those accessories of beauty.

I stood looking up now and then seemingly at the houses to hide my object, which was to see *her* and the group, and to watch their horse play. The lads were chaffing the girls, one snatched a kiss and got a slap on his head, tho the wench was evidently pleased. — The other lad suddenly made a dig at the fair-haired one's clothes outside her grummit, making some remark which I couldn't hear, but at which all laughed. He ran off up the short narrow street, pursued by the girl who seemed really angry, and in a second they had turned a corner and were out of sight. The girls with hats and the lad remaining looked round the corner laughing, and resumed their position against the wall. The lad loudly said. 'Tom wants it bad don't he, Loo?' — 'I dunno, ask him,' said the girl. He on that put his hand round her and snatched another kiss, disarranging her bonnet in doing so, got another hard slap and a push, and 'I'll kick your bloody arse if yer does that again.' All this occurred almost simultaneously, and far quicker than this account of it is written. The street was quite quiet, and every word easily heard.

The group took no notice of me, neither did the very few passers-by. The sight gave me a spasmodic, voluptuous throb in my pego, for I was very fit that evening, and with sexual instinct — I suppose — slowly I walked up the narrow street, as any other pedestrian might, and turning the corner saw the couple struggling together, he snatching at her petticoats as before, she hitting him. 'Let's feel it, Jenny.' 'Get away you blackguard.' – 'I've felt it.' 'You ain't, yer liar,' came clearly to my ears as I turned the corner. – My appearance immediately stopped the fun, and with a parting slap from her the lad ran off, leaving her alone with me, no other person was in the passage – a footway only – indeed excepting at market hours few passed that way.

Quickly as thought and to begin a conversation with her, – almost anything does for that, – I asked her the way to a place and she began to tell me. – 'Show me the way, you are so lovely and I'll pay you.' – The opportunity had come so suddenly that I'd not time to think about a course of action. Civilly she began to explain the road, then thanking her I said, 'How lovely you are, I've been watching you and longing to be him.' – 'Whart?' – and she laughed. 'Yes – come with me and I'll give you two sovereigns.'

'Whart?' – said she again standing amazed with staring eyes. – Just then some one approached. 'Is it that way?' said I as a blind. – Amazed as she had seemed by my offer, she took the hint, and began explaining the way, pointing to it. – In a few seconds the pedestrian had vanished and again I said 'I'll give you two sovereigns to come with me.' Again she repeated, 'Whart?'

Then reflecting she added, – 'Ain't you just a cheeky one.' – 'I will by God, and more, you are so lovely.' – She laughed, then in a strangely confused and half-ashamed manner, looked at me hard and shook her head. – 'Do.' – 'No thankee, Sir, I can't.'

— 'Do, I'll be back here to meet you in a quarter of
an hour and I'll give you two bright sovereigns.' —
'No.' Again she shook her head, again I pressed and
repeated my offer. At length — 'I'm so dirty.' —
'Never mind, you're lovely, and it will be dark.' —
Twilight was already coming on. 'Mind two
sovereigns?' 'What for? And I've got no bonnet.'
'Never mind, in a quarter of an hour be here, will you?
We'll go in a cab.' — 'Yer ain't alying?'

Another pedestrian passed whilst these few words
were being exchanged, and as she — a woman now
— appeared, I pointed again as if seeking direction,
and the girl did the same. None are so cunning as those
in lust, and I think *she* was a little so now.

Just then the lad reappeared at the corner and I
began pointing as before as a blind. She saw the lad
might suspect, and not wishing to be caught by him
talking to a gentleman, bawled out, 'The gent wants
to know the way to . . . .' He approached and told me
— pointing in another direction. — 'Show me and I'll
give you twopence.' He went ahead. 'In twenty
minutes here,' — said I in a low voice, and followed
the lad cursing him in my heart for interrupting us,
and wondering if the two sovereigns would bring back
the wench to the meeting place. I saw that the offer
of two sovereigns had quite staggered her, she who
perhaps had never been paid five shillings for her
pleasures — if paid at all — for she evidently was no
strumpet. But all women are paid for their favours
either in meal or malt.

As soon as I was well away from the place I gave

the lad threepence, and off he went. A few minutes after, I got into a four-wheeled cab, and setting myself well back told the driver, to go at walking pace along the street where the group had been standing. There stood the same lot seemingly about to separate as the cab passed them, they didn't see me. In three or four minutes I went back again at a trot. The lads were gone, the girls going in another direction. I was delighted. I've many times been helped in my amours by cabmen, and through the window said, 'Follow those girls — don't lose sight of them, I don't want to be seen.' 'All right, Sir.' — At the end of the street where it joins a large thoroughfare, he drove past but never lost sight of them, and stopped as they did.

I could then see the three girls standing together and talking for ten minutes. Then to my delight two went off leaving my wench alone, who retraced her steps very slowly, stopping from time to time and looking back, then turned towards the place of rendezvous at the corner of the narrow street. She stopped there for a second as if considering, wiped her face with a dirty handkerchief, arranged her hair with her hand, then quickly went up it and round the corner — I got out of the cab, paid him, told him to wait and went after her. It was now quite dusk. There she stood and when I'd joined her, said she was afraid to come, she thought she'd tell me to prevent my waiting uselessly. After a few words of persuasion and the two sovereigns offered again, she was in the cab with me and off we drove.

After we had been in the cab a minute I kissed her,

she returned it saying, 'You're a cheeky one.' Soon after. − 'If you'll stop here two or three minutes I'll get me a bonnet. − Where are you ataking me? I really can't stop out late. − What are you agoin to do?' − 'Never mind your bonnet − I want to feel your little cunt and you to feel my prick.' − 'Oho − no you shan't − you *have* bloomin' cheek. − I'm sorry I've comed.' − 'Don't be a fool, you'll have two sovereigns.' − She chuckled and on went the cab. − 'I'm hungry. − It's near my time to grub, and they'll wonder where I am.' − 'I'll get you something,' and at a public, getting out but keeping her in the cab, I took her ginger beer with gin in it and two big buns. − On we drove, and then, but with much resistance, and dropping her bun in preventing me, I got my fingers well on a moist cunt. − After a further struggle my finger remained there which seemed to quiet her much, but she seemed offended and remarked. 'I ain't that as yer thinks, I works for my living and pretty hard too.' − 'You've been fucked and you live with a man.' − 'No I don't, I lives with the old people.' − She didn't deny the fucking. By the time we reached the house I was hugging her closely and had felt her lubricious orifice both inside and out, as far as the position enabled me, and had satisfied myself she wasn't virgin. She got again silent, seemingly thinking whilst enjoying the play of my digits on her quim. Such are lovely moments for any couple, and it was I'm sure for her, tho she seemed frightened at what she was doing.

The mistress who knew me was astounded to see a

common wench without a bonnet, and in a whisper hoped all was right. She feared consequences, suspecting I'd brought a chance virgin and had made her screwed. In the bedroom the girl curious — as all such as — looked everywhere. — 'It's a baudy shop, ain't it?' — 'Yes, take off your things.' — 'No.' She resisted that earnestly as a half-modest girl would, but longing to see her notch, I pushed her on the bed and then her clothes up. 'Oh now, I won't.' A more dingy sight of petticoats and chemise I don't recollect, but her fat backside, plump thighs, and smooth belly were white and clean, and the prettiest little notch lay between them. Crisp, curly, short hair surrounded a delicate coral stripe, not much was on the motte, and it looked most enticing, was the charming cunt of sixteen. She was a little over sixteen. A cunt is in its highest beauty at about that age, I now think, tho in my youth I loved them larger and very hairy.

I produced my pego which she quietly admired long — and I felt sure from her looks she hadn't seen many — in delicious silence. Soon after she handled it whilst my finger titillated her. — 'Do you want it?' — 'No,' said she wriggling. 'Let me fuck you.' — 'No,' said she squirming about — then quickly after. — 'Oh! — Don't — aha — shove it in,' — murmured she very vulgarly. In a second we were fucking at the bedside, she was full and randy, and soon we spent in unison. She was young, artless, hot-blooded, sighed much, and gave way freely to her pleasure. — My prick lingered in her long whilst I looked down at her white belly and thighs, and anon at her dirty linen. But the lovely conjunction ceased, the evidences of our pleasure rolled out, and I pushed up her thighs, holding them apart to admire the pearly issue. Then she washed her cunt giving a mere outside sluice, and in spite of her struggles, I washed her cunt outside again myself and much to her astonishment. − Had she been a strumpet she'd have washed it up enough. *Her* washing in fact showed she was not habitually gay, and her pleasure in seeing my pego, and a shyness of manner, made me sure she was no harlot.

'Has no one washed your cunt but yourself?' 'Lord no − what do you think − what did *you* want to do it for?' − 'For pleasure.' − 'Ho − ho − I must go.' − 'You shan't yet, get naked and so will I.' − 'Oho, no − there then, I won't do *that*.' − 'Have you never been naked to a man?' − 'Never, but only to my own chap.' − He'd first had her when sixteen, she said. He had a cart, was getting on, but drank much.

I insisted, she stripped, I did the same, and in nudity, stockings excepted, we played with each other's sexual organs. Persuading her was delicious, for she was modest and no sham, and she was evidently voluptuously delighted as in silence she pulled my prepuce up and down, and handled my balls as if she'd never seen a full grown ballocks before. Not a bit was it like the experienced manipulation of a harlot. I questioned her, and she answered straight, I felt sure, tho no doubt suppressing many things. − 'You've been fucked.' − 'Why, in course, *you* knows that.' − 'How did I?' − '*You* knows it.' − 'How many men have fucked you?' − 'Only one.' − 'That's a fib.' — 'It's true, so help me God. — You's the only other chap. — Why I ain't had it two months, and lives at home at ***** I ran away once with him, the night I was done — but they got me back. — So help me God, it's true. — Yes I lets him when he gets the chance, but they says he's taking on with another gal. — I'll serve her out if I gets hold on her.' — Then my prick being stiff and her cunt ready with our handlings again, they joined. — Then our sexual ecstasies over — and didn't she enjoy the fuck? — I had a cab got and put her into it with two sovereigns in her hand. — She'd never in her life had a sovereign before of her own, she said. — Many a girl has had her first bit of gold from me, has found out the ready money-value of her cunt.

'No, it's no good your awritin' me and I reads badly, and praps they'll get hold on it, tho they can't read.' But she agreed to meet me again and I wrote down time and place. — 'I'll put on a bonnet next time, but I can't put on my best things, they'll want to know why and I'd like to come earlier.' So it all came about, I met her that day week and she was cleaner, had better boots and white stockings. She was a fine model from head to foot, such solidity of flesh, so satiny, and tho she said she never took a bath in her life, she was as sweet as a nut. I fucked, then gamahuched her, giving her her first pleasure that way. 'No,' no tongue had touched her clitoris before, she said. Then I fucked her again and she went off with two sovereigns again, all I'd promised. She earned at work sometimes eighteen pence a day, sometimes not that sum. When with her father he gave her nothing of her earnings. 'But he keeps me.'

She told me much more about herself, but evidently not all, how she sometimes went out with a barrow, and after work was done into the streets to talk with friends. Her 'young man' had said, 'that if he caught me with another chap he'd smash both our bloody noses, and now *he's* after another gal.' — 'What if he knew I'd fucked you?' — 'Dunno — but he can't know. — Shiners ain't got at barrows are they?' — She said that the two shiners promised had made her come with me. — 'You'd make plenty if you liked.' — She knew what I meant — looked long at me and shook her head. — 'I ain't agoin' at that game — no thankee — not if I knows it. He'll marry me I think now if father lets him — if he won't I'll run away agin. — Yes, I'll come here with you agin if you like, but I can't have a letter if you knowed where I lives even.'

A splendid strapping, healthy creature she was, many rich would give anything for such an offspring. — A bit fit for a Prince's prick, and what a lovely cunt! Yet a coster spent in it first, and will yet take his pleasure in it.

I had her once more. She quickly got at my tool and played with it as if lewed to her bum hole. — It was deliciously exciting to see her at my prick. — She grinned and admitted her young man had had her in the interval. — 'No, only once — shan't tell you where. — Give me? — nothing he didn't — he never gived me nothing — never he didn't, but he says he'll marry me' — her very words. — My letch was over, her coarseness annoyed me, and I saw her no more.

Will she marry? her sexual enjoyment was immense, her delight in handling my pego and even in showing me her naked beauties at our third meeting was delicious. Lasciviousness had set in, the delight of the secret meetings with a gentleman gave her undisguised pleasure and she'd have let me fuck her to any extent. When I told her I could name no time to meet her again, but would some day be at the market where she talked with friends when the day's work was done, her countenance fell, and she became dull. − Did the sovereigns make her turn harlot? Or fucking and sovereigns together − or did she become a virtuous coster's wife? − And she also was fucked when sixteen, all her class are, they *will* be fucked. − Ladies must only frig themselves till they are married, − until five and twenty often. What a loss of pleasure!

FOLLIES OF THE FLESH

ANONYMOUS

FOLLIES OF THE FLESH -

drunk on carnal pleasure and inspired by the foolish excitement
of their lust, the crazed lovers in these four delightful, naughty,
bawdy tales flaunt their passion shamelessly!

Randiana: the scandalous exploits of a witty young rogue whose
wanton behaviour is matched only by his barefaced cheek...

The Autobiography of a Flea: the notorious misadventures of
sweet young Bella, as chronicled by one who enjoys full
knowledge of her most intimate desires...

The Lustful Turk: imprisoned in an Oriental harem, a passionate
Victorian miss discovers a world of limitless sensual joy...

Parisian Frolics: in which the men and women of Parisian
society cast off propriety and abandon themselves in an orgy of
forbidden pleasure ...

FICTION/EROTICA   0 7472 3652 6